I0672511

Lord of the Seas

The Viking Lords Series by Sabrina Jarema

Lord of the Runes

Lord of the Mountains

Lord of the Seas

Lord of the Seas

Sabrina Jarema

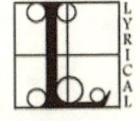

LYRICAL PRESS
Kensington Publishing Corp.
www.kensingtonbooks.com

To the extent that the image or images on the cover of this book depict a person or persons, such person or persons are merely models, and are not intended to portray any character or characters featured in the book.

LYRICAL PRESS BOOKS are published by

Kensington Publishing Corp.
119 West 40th Street
New York, NY 10018

Copyright © 2017 by Sabrina Jarema

All rights reserved. No part of this book may be reproduced in any form or by any means without the prior written consent of the Publisher, excepting brief quotes used in reviews.

All Kensington titles, imprints, and distributed lines are available at special quantity discounts for bulk purchases for sales promotion, premiums, fund-raising, educational, or institutional use.

Special book excerpts or customized printings can also be created to fit specific needs. For details, write or phone the office of the Kensington Sales Manager: Kensington Publishing Corp., 119 West 40th Street, New York, NY 10018. Attn. Sales Department. Phone: 1-800-221-2647.

Lyrical Press and Lyrical Press logo Reg. U.S. Pat. & TM Off.

First Electronic Edition: August 2017
eISBN-13: 978-1-60183-882-7
eISBN-10: 1-60183-882-4

First Print Edition: August 2017
ISBN-13: 978-1-60183-885-8
ISBN-10: 1-60183-885-9

Printed in the United States of America

ACKNOWLEDGMENTS

Even though writing is solitary, many people stand beside an author and help make each novel much better than a sum of its words. This happens every step of the way . . .

First, I want to thank my wonderful agent, Nalini Akolekar, who found a home for my Viking Lords. Every ship needs a port—even Viking longships.

Then I have a huge thanks for my lovely and talented critique partners, Karen Fleming and Carol Post. Our plotting sessions help me flesh out my ideas and you give me the encouragement to bring my stories to fruition. And after I've written that final sentence, you take my diamond in the rough and help me polish it until it sparkles.

Next, the manuscript goes to my editor, Martin Biro, who cuts and carves my words until they're the best they can possibly be. My deepest gratitude for all your fine work.

I want to thank the production, marketing, and social media whizzes at Kensington for everything they do to get the word out about my books. It is greatly appreciated.

And, most importantly, I want to thank the readers who have enjoyed my stories. You're the reason I do this and I hope I have brought these fascinating and sophisticated people to life for you.

Glossary

Arrha—A down payment on the bride-price of a woman, made to show good faith during marriage negotiations.

Bailey—A large open space, or courtyard, inside a fortress in Anglo-Saxon England.

Blótgythiur—Priestesses who made blood sacrifices in the temples.

Draugr—A spirit of the dead.

Einvigi—An unregulated duel of honor, fought with any weapons and no rules or judges.

Ell—A unit of measurement, about 20 inches, often calculated as the length of a grown man's forearm from elbow to fingertips.

Færing—A small, four-oared boat.

Fjells—Mountains.

Fólkvangr —The realm where the goddess Freya's hall, Sessrumnir, was located. Half the warriors who fell in battle came here.

Fylgjur—Personal guardian spirits in the form of an animal. Seeing one indicates death is near, but not always that of the person being guarded.

Handsal—A ceremony sealing the marriage contract. It must be witnessed by at least six men and the agreement is in effect as long as any of them are alive.

Heiman Fylgia—The bride's "accompaniment from home" or dowry. It remains hers as a sort of life insurance policy in case she is widowed or divorced.

Hólmgang—A duel of honor with specific rules and customs, overseen by judges.

Hólmgangustadr—A bounded dueling area.

Hóvgythiur—A temple priestess.

Kasa—A drinking vessel with two handles often used at weddings.

Keep—The main building, usually made of stone, inside a fortress in Anglo-Saxon England.

Kennings—Highly complex poetry of ancient Scandinavia using circumlocution in the Old Norse, Old English, and Icelandic languages.

Knörr—A merchant vessel, partially enclosed with a lower deck for carrying cargo.

Landvaettir—Land spirits.

Miklagard—Viking name for Istanbul. The "Great City."

Mjölnir—Thor's hammer.

Mundr—The bride-price paid to the family of the woman to compensate them for the loss of her labor.

Nithingr—A coward, without honor.

Saydalani—Highly skilled pharmacists in the ancient Middle East.

Seax—A long knife, worn horizontally below the belt.

Seith-kona—A practitioner of shamanistic magic.

Sjaund—The "Funeral Ale." Seven days after a person died, the heirs gathered at a feast, drank ale, and settled his affairs. After this, the deceased was considered truly gone.

Tafl—An ancient Scandinavian board game played by both men and women. The full name is *Hnefatafl*.

Thing—A regional assembly of free men who met to consult on important matters and to administer justice.

Varp—The warp strings on a loom, weighted with stones.

Vefkona—A weaver.

Vefr—Also *vefstathr.* A standing, or warp-weighted loom. Common throughout the world.

Vipta—The woof strings on a loom, attached to the shuttle and worked horizontally.

Völur—Plural of völva.

Völva—A practitioner of indigenous magic and prophecy, normally an elderly woman who had released herself from family bonds.

Wergeld—Amount of money each person's life was worth according to rank.

Wyrd—Fate, destiny.

Prologue

The village of Haardvik
Hardangerfjorden, Hordaland, Norway
Summer, 851 A.D.

Even after all these days, the anger still seared him. Consuming.
Bloody.

Familiar.

Rorik of Vargfjell set his jaw. He would not lash out in rage. This time. His aunt, the rune mistress Lifa, had shown him how to control his fury when he was a child.

Only, he had never truly been a child.

He stood on the cliff, glaring down at the shoreline and the three damaged ships he'd managed to save from the bastard Northumbrian earl's treachery. The fourth was gone. His favorite, his flagship, *The Sword of the Waves*. He'd sailed away as it writhed in flames on the banks of a foreign river. Closing his eyes, he clenched his fists when the sight flared into his mind.

The wood screamed as the fire licked at the dragon's head. The striped sail billowed up from the heat like the wings of a dragon struggling to take flight and escape. Then it, too, was engulfed. Blackened and crumbling, the great ribs heaved as though the vessel breathed its last. The crimson reflection of the flames spread like blood on the dark waters.

The earl had taken what Rorik held most dear to him. Now he'd return the favor.

Chapter One

Redbank, The keep of Earl Edward
Along the Humber River, Kingdom of Northumbria

The dragon's head snapped off. It hit the water and sank as the men pulled it further out into the river. Little by little, the remains of the burned ship were dismantled to lie in the depths of the Humber where they belonged. The ribs of the vessel still rose above the water like the skeleton of the beast, but soon they, too, would be gone.

Elfwynn, daughter of Earl Edward, shuddered. It had lain on their shoreline for several weeks, like some ugly, dead monster from the north. And yet, wasn't it true? The Northmen were monsters, coming here to rape and pillage. Her father had driven them off, proving his strength to the foreigners who infested Northumbria each summer. He would keep them safe.

"Father wanted me to see if the men are nearly finished."

Elfwynn looked up at her half brother. He'd come from the keep so quietly, she hadn't heard him. "They're working hard, Wulf, but that thing won't be gone too quickly for my taste. I'd like to forget I ever saw it."

"We may see more of them. The Northman who stopped here with his ships, Rorik, wasn't alone. A larger fleet continued up the river, no doubt to attack other holdings near York. Father wants to make certain there's no evidence of what happened when they return, on their way out to sea. We don't want to give them a reason to stop here." He rubbed the back of his neck under his long hair. "We're still trying to figure out who gave the order to burn the ships. No one knows. Father wanted to pay the Northmen and let them leave. With so many of them in this area now, we can't afford to antagonize them."

"What does it matter who gave the order? It worked. We defeated them. They won't try that again."

"Wessex defeated the Northmen in a large naval battle last year near London. It didn't stop them from wintering on the isle of Thaley near the Thames. Now they threaten the south." With a slight smile, he ruffled her hair. "It's nothing to concern yourself about anyhow. Father and I have agreed if the Northmen attack, my first duty is to get you and your mother to safety. Even if you were so foolish as to leave the keep to look at them when they were here. As beautiful as you are, it would serve you right if one of them fell in love with you and carried you off."

"Rowena wanted to see them. She heard their leader, the one with the long black hair, was nice to look at. At times, she and I are friendly. I try, at least. Except when your mother is poisoning her against me, like she does so many here."

"My sister has no sense. If she did, she'd see what our mother is. Even Father avoids her as much as he can. You can't give in to Rowena in the hopes she'll like you. Not if it puts you in danger from the Northmen or anyone. If that ever happened, I'd give my life to go after you."

"And I'd sell my soul to stop you. In that, we're much alike."

"Except I'm better with a sword than you are."

"That wouldn't be difficult since I know nothing of warfare. Only weaving. And music."

"Let's hope it stays that way. Besides, you're too fine to waste your soul on battles."

"To save you, Father, my mother, and the people here, it would be a small price to pay."

"Even those who turn their backs on you for your birth?"

"They only seek to ingratiate themselves to your mother. Not everyone holds it against me that I'm baseborn. They conveniently forget about that detail when they want to buy the cloth I weave." She looked at the ship as the men rowed another piece of it out to the middle of the river. "Wulf, do you think they'll come back? For revenge?"

"If they do, we'll be ready. I'm leaving soon to gather more of our forces in case we have to fight."

Her muscles knotted as she met his gaze. "I already lost my older brother to war. We both lost a cousin on Father's side. I couldn't stand to lose you, as well."

"I felt their loss, too, Elfwynn. Randal was my half brother. He, our cousin, and I were more like full brothers. I'll never forget the sight of him falling before me in battle with the Picts."

"Ever since then, whenever you or Father have gone to fight, such fear comes over me, I can't breathe right the entire time you're gone. My heart races and I shake so hard I can barely weave, even though it's the only thing that calms me. Nothing seems real until you return safe."

"It just means you love us." He squeezed her shoulder. "God will protect us against the pagans."

That was true. So far.

"Let me walk you back to your house. There's nothing more to see here and I'll feel better knowing you're closer to the keep. Both Father and I would be more at ease if you and your mother would consent to live within the keep itself."

"We're so close, we're well protected. Father makes certain of that. If we moved in with you, your mother would start a war to rival even that of our people and the Picts. I don't understand why she's so resentful that Father loves us when she hates him anyway."

"Pride. She's bitter that you stand to inherit along with Rowena and me. That Father should love a village woman more than he does his highborn wife enrages her."

"And my mother wastes away, pining for a man she can never marry. Sometimes I wish . . ." She didn't finish the sentence. It would not be Christian to want Mildburg's death or divorce so her parents could marry.

"I know." He took her hand as they walked. "Sometimes I wish, as well. She's been no mother to me, except to bear me into this world. Father can't divorce her without cause. It would bring her family down on us. She would have to commit adultery or treason, then none could gainsay him. She's too careful to get caught."

That was why she and her mother couldn't stay there, waiting for Edward to be free. Elfwynn wasn't certain how much longer her mother could live for a day that would never happen.

As they walked up to the house, her mother was tending herbs in the front.

Wulf strode ahead of Elfwynn. "Rohesia, it's good to see you out on this fine day." He gave her a quick embrace.

"And it's always good to see you, Wulf. You come here far too seldom. How much like your father you look with your curling brown hair and blue eyes." She smiled at Elfwynn, but it held a sadness, as always. "Both of you. So similar to each other. Will you stay for a time and have some ale? I brewed it fresh."

"Thank you, Rohesia, but I'm going on patrol with my men. With the burning of the longship, we must be vigilant. I'll send some of Father's men to watch over you in the days ahead. I wanted to make certain Elfwynn came back safely. She shouldn't have been down by the river to begin with." He gave her a quick frown.

"I've been walking to the farms to get wool for years, Wulf. The Northmen being in this area is nothing new. I've always been fine. But I promise, if I go any place, I'll take some of the men with me."

"I'd feel better knowing that. I'm leaving soon to find our forces who are patrolling against Mercia and bring them here." He took Elfwynn by the shoulders. "Be careful. We've lived in an uneasy peace with the Danes since they arrived here, but that could change. We burned the ship of the most powerful of the Northmen. They won't care that we don't know how it happened. They only understand revenge. If anything happens, promise me you'll go to the keep as fast as you can. I don't care what my mother thinks. Father will be there. You'll have a place."

"I promise, Wulf. We'll be fine."

He gave her a dubious look before letting her go. "Keep her out of trouble, Rohesia. I'll be gone a couple of weeks at most."

"She'll be too busy weaving with all the orders she has. I doubt she'll leave her loom, even to eat."

He shook his head. "Why you insist on making your own money, Elfwynn, is something neither Father nor I understand. He gives you everything you need."

"People value what they pay for," she said. "My weavings are the finest in the region. Should I not get recompense for my hours?"

"Of course." He kissed the top of her head. "Just remember to sleep once in a while. I'll see you when I return."

She watched him walk in the direction of the keep until he was lost in the trees. Father gave them all they needed, yes. For their lives here. But he would never fund a journey to Rohesia's people in Strathclyde. Elfwynn had to work to save for that. It might be the only thing that would spare her mother's life. If they remained here, the memories of her dead son and the unrequited love she bore for Edward would cause her to fade away until she died. If she were among her own relations, she could start anew. She was not so old that her life needed to be over.

She was still beautiful. Elfwynn looked at her as she tended to her herbs. Over time, her beauty had become more translucent, like a fine glass. Each day it thinned, as though she were being worn out from within. One day, she would fade away.

Only a few more pieces of cloth, a little more silver, and Elfwynn would have enough. She wanted to leave as soon as possible, even before the fall.

Elfwynn breathed in the air scented with the herbs and flowers growing nearby. The aromas of home. This place was all she'd ever known. Still, many of the people she'd grown up with had never truly accepted her. It wasn't because of her baseborn status. That wouldn't matter so much in their land, as long as she was freeborn. Because Rohesia was free, Elfwynn was as well.

No, it was because of Mildburg. Many of her father's people didn't want to make an enemy of the lady of the keep, so they shunned both her and her mother. While there were some who remained friendly, it still made for a lonely life. They needed to go where they would be accepted and welcomed. Among her mother's people, they would be.

She had a single regret—leaving Wulf and their father. Edward loved her. It was the one unaltered fact of her existence. It gave her strength, even in the face of the losses she'd endured. Her brother. Her cousin. So many others who had died in the never-ending wars. Her father was always there for her and there were many times his arms were her sole support. If only he could see her mother's pain the same way. His mind was always elsewhere, protecting his people who were foremost in his life. And yet, he was blind to so much of what lay before him at home.

Elfwynn picked up a shawl lying on a bench against the house and spread it over her mother's thin shoulders. Rohesia smiled her thanks, then continued weeding.

She walked to the house, but before entering, she glanced back at her mother's bent frame. If the earl had made a clean break with them years ago, it would have been better for all of them, especially her mother. But he hadn't.

Now, it was up to her.

Chapter Two

"Daughter, stop frowning when you embroider. You'll get wrinkles and be so ugly no man will want you."

Rowena glanced at her mother and pasted on a pleasant expression. As though that was all she was—a face. It was all men saw. That and her dowry. Sometimes, she wished she could live as Elfwynn did, in a little house away from the keep and all its intrigue. Away from her mother. Her brother, at least, could escape by fighting battles. Wulf was gone, even now, and would have blessed peace for a couple of weeks. And Father had gone also. It had been a last-minute decision, so they could find as many of their forces as possible.

"Go see if the midday meal is ready. Not that you need to eat. You can't afford to lose your waistline. Those lazy cooks will probably be late with it while the earl is gone. As though we don't matter. I suppose in his eyes, we don't. His indifference spreads to the staff. Go on now. Let me know when it's ready."

Rowena set aside her embroidery and stood. "Yes, Mother."

"And change your gown. You look dowdy, like a village woman."

"Yes, Mother." She'd worn the older dress because it was comfortable. It wasn't as though they were expecting anyone at the keep with her father gone. None of that mattered to her mother. As lady of the keep, she dressed well with the fine gowns and jewels befitting her rank. Rowena preferred less formality, but her mother would have none of it. Rather than cross her, Rowena gave in. Always. It was safer that way.

She slipped out of the room before her mother could think of another cut and breathed a sigh of relief. As she hurried along the hallway, Wigberht ran into her. The nasty man her mother had brought along as part of her dowry years ago didn't even acknowledge her. He continued toward the sewing room and entered without knocking.

"Lady Mildburg, I have grave news."

The tone of his voice caught Rowena's attention. She stepped back to the door. He hadn't closed it all the way, so she leaned in to listen.

"I was riding along the river road to the east when I heard foreign voices in the woods. With all the Northmen in the area, I thought I should see who they were. Five of their longships are beached on the shore. There must be over two hundred warriors there."

"The ships of the Northmen come and go all the time, Wigberht. They infest this part of Northumbria like fleas."

"Yes, my lady. But three of the ships bore signs of burn marks. The Northman Rorik has returned. I saw him there among the men."

"Do they plan to attack?"

"I got as close to them as was safe. Their language and ours are similar enough that I understood much of what they said. He spoke of seeing the earl's daughters when they were here before. He described both Elfwynn and Rowena to his men. They plan to take one and hold her for ransom. Rorik wants the value of his ship and of the men we killed."

A piece of furniture scraped and crashed against the floor. "He will not have Rowena. You know what happens to women they take."

"Then I fear they'll attack. I'll alert the keep, call the men."

"Wait. You said one of the earl's daughters. They know he has two of them. What if we were to give them Elfwynn?"

"They want a ransom, not the girl. The earl is gone and we don't have access to the treasury. What will happen when we don't pay them?"

"They'll take Edward's bastard daughter with them to sell as a slave to get their money. Or they'll rape and kill her. Either way, it gets rid of her. Wulfric and Rowena won't have to share their inheritance with her. Her whore of a mother is ailing, I hear. Pining away from the death of her son and the love she has for my husband. The loss of her precious daughter will surely send her to her grave." She sighed. "Such a pity."

"How will we get Elfwynn to the Northmen, my lady?"

Rowena trembled with—fear? Anger? Shock? Her mother had

been bitter since she'd learned of Elfwynn's existence years ago, but not even she could be so heartless. She peeked through the partly open door. The chair her mother had been sitting in was overturned on the floor. She was pacing, her head down, then spun and faced Wigberht.

"I need the pure white wool from Hunfrith's farm. Immediately. Elfwynn is the only one who can make certain of its quality. If you tell her I want her to get it for me, she'll suspect you. There are men among Edward's warriors who are loyal to me. I have shown them my appreciation for all they've done over the years with a great deal of gold. She'll trust them. They'll accompany her, of course, to guard her. She'll have to travel right past where you said the ships were beached. The Northmen will be spreading out by that time and her guards will happen to lose sight of her. They might even make noise and lead those barbarians to her. If this Rorik saw her earlier, he'll know who she is.

"Follow behind to make certain this happens. When they send the ransom demand, intercept it. Wait a suitable amount of time, as though you've brought it to the earl. He left so suddenly, I doubt Elfwynn knows of it. Then, go back and tell them he says a bastard isn't worth the price. They may keep her as their payment. The last thing she'll know is that the father she thought doted on her doesn't love her after all. She'll die with that thought.

"We can't risk the two guards talking, so you'll take care of them for me before they return here." The corners of her mouth turned down in an exaggerated frown. "How tragic they'll die trying to save Elfwynn from the evil barbarians."

"Yes, my lady."

"Afterward, report back to me. I'll be waiting, to reward you quite handsomely, as I have all through the years."

Wigburht dropped to his knees in front of her, gazing up at her as though he worshipped her. "I'll do this for you, my lady. I was your man before you came here to marry the earl, and I always will be."

Rowena's blood ran cold. The rumors about her mother's infidelity were true. She gasped before she could stop it and Wigberht looked around Mildburg toward the doorway. His eyes widened. She spun and ran, but he caught up to her and dragged her back to her mother.

"What have you heard, Rowena?" Mildburg advanced on her.

"I don't know what you mean." She jerked away from Wigberht and rubbed her stinging arm. "I was coming back to tell you—"

"Don't lie to me." She shook her. "You've been listening. If you say one word to anyone about this, you'll wish you were the one the Northmen took. I'll sell you to the old, fat earl in East Anglia who wants you. He's been married four times and every wife has died. Most say he murders them. Now he's asked the earl for your hand. Do you want that, Rowena?"

"N-No." Her legs shook as she stumbled back, and her eyes filled.

"I do this for you." Mildburg's voice softened as she touched her on the cheek. "Because your father acknowledged Elfwynn as his, she's entitled to a third of his estate, stealing what is rightfully yours and Wulfric's. This way, it will be divided into just two portions. I'm only thinking of you, my daughter."

Only thinking of herself. If Elfwynn disappeared, Rohesia would grieve to death and that would give her mother revenge against Edward. Rowena eyed her. She couldn't take the chance that she'd be given to the East Anglian earl. She'd heard of him, how all his wives died under mysterious circumstances. No doubt her mother could bring this about.

"I've never liked Elfwynn anyhow. I won't say anything." At least not until she could find someone she could trust. Who knew how far her mother's reach went? But Elfwynn's time was short.

"Wigberht, take her to her room and make certain she stays there. Post a man you can trust outside. She'll remain there alone, contemplating her disobedience. My own maid will bring her food, but no one else is to enter there."

"As you wish, my lady."

He took her arm but she wrenched it away when they walked into the hallway. "You'll not touch me."

He said nothing while they walked to her room. As he opened the door, he sneered at her. "Don't think to try to escape. The Lady Mildburg might not want to harm you, but if you get in the way of what I have here, I won't be so squeamish. And that goes for when the earl returns as well. Remember that. If I fall, you fall with me."

After he closed the door, she sank onto the bed. While she had always been ambivalent about Elfwynn, no one deserved the fate her mother had planned for her. But what could she do? Father and Wulf might be gone for weeks and by the time she was freed, it would be far too late to do anything. The earl was a great warrior and a fine tactician, but it was obvious he knew nothing about what went on in his own home. Neither had she. They'd all been so blind.

She clenched her fists, her nails biting into the palms. She loved her father. He'd always been good to her, even if he didn't like her mother. That shrew had betrayed him all these years. Now, she endangered them all by not telling the guards about the Northmen. If they were attacked, they'd be unprepared. Treason and adultery. Both were reasons for her father to finally divorce his wife.

When the earl came home, she *would* have her revenge. If she was quick about it, Wigberht and her mother wouldn't be able to act on their threats. Then, she would be free of the insults, the abuse, and never being good enough.

Looking around her tiny room, she hugged her knees to her chest. For now, she was at her mother's mercy.

And, as she knew all too well, Mildburg had none.

"Elfwynn, two of the earl's men are here to see you." Rohesia carried a basket of vegetables from their garden into their small house. "They said the Lady Mildburg needs you to go to Hunfrith's farm for more of their white wool."

She sighed. Anyone could do that. Mildburg always said it was so Elfwynn could be certain she was getting the best wool, but all of Hunfrith's was of very high quality. Still, it wasn't an unusual request. Or rather, demand. At least she wouldn't have to see the woman. She'd give the wool to the two guards and they'd take it to the keep.

It might be good to stop for a time, anyhow. She'd been weaving continuously for several days. Her arms were cramping at night. Time away from her loom would be beneficial. Patting her belt pouch, she made certain she had her silver and gold coins with her. She never went anywhere without it, to be certain nothing happened to it. Her mother wouldn't be able to prevent anyone from taking it and they couldn't risk that. She'd worked too hard for it.

"I won't be long." Her mother's body felt so thin as she hugged her. "You'll eat a good dinner tonight if I must feed you myself."

Rohesia set the basket on the table. "I'll try. Take your time. It's early yet and you've been closed in this house for days. You work too hard."

"I'll be fine. I love you."

She grabbed her shawl, for the breeze along the river road might be chill. It was unique, with many different colors, the only one she'd ever woven like that. It was so beautiful, she'd never been able to part with it, her one indulgence.

Walking outside, she swirled the shawl over her shoulders and pinned it closed with her brooch. Two of her father's men stood outside, waiting with their horses. They were new, having joined the army only a year ago. She knew them though, so Wulf would be pleased she was under their protection.

"Litwin, Oshern, did you draw the short straws to have to come with me? At least it's a pleasant day."

Neither of them would meet her gaze, each looking in a different direction. "It's no trouble, Elfwynn," Oshern said. "And, as you said, the weather is fine."

They seemed uneasy. She gave them a questioning look, but they still wouldn't glance at her. Then again, they must have just come from speaking with Mildburg. Who knew what abuse she'd threatened them with? Encounters with her would make anyone nervous.

Oshern mounted his horse. Litwin helped her up behind him, then climbed on his own. They rode into the forest and onto the river road. Though deep woods stood between it and the water, the road followed the Humber east to the outlying farms. The forest hid the keep from ships, so most of the time the Northmen passed them by. The one who came here weeks ago must have known of them from some other source.

They were halfway to Hunfrith's farm when Litwin held up his hand. They reined in their horses.

"I thought I heard voices." He studied the woods toward the river. "We'd better make certain who it is."

Oshern reached behind him and took her arm. "It's better if you remain here, Elfwynn. If we have to fight, we couldn't protect you." He let her down from the horse.

She gathered her shawl around her as she glanced around them. "What if it's Northmen? You can't just leave me here."

He pointed. "Stay in the trees. They'll keep you hidden until we come back for you."

They rode off, leaving her standing in the road. Her heart pounded. Why didn't one of them stay with her? Surely it didn't take both of them to see what the noise was. She hadn't heard anything, and her hearing was better than most.

She darted into the shadows and leaned against a tree, her heart racing. Straining to listen, she heard nothing. Not voices, nor the men's horses. Not even birds. The forest was too silent. Her rapid breathing was the only sound. She tried to calm herself. If anything were to happen, she had to think. She couldn't do that if she were frightened.

Long moments passed. Then the sound of hoofbeats came, growing louder. The men were returning. She leaned around the trunk to look, not wanting to give herself away if it wasn't them.

It was. She recognized their horses as they trotted through the trees. But when she stepped out to greet them, they veered away and urged their horses faster. She ran after them, shouting. They gained the road and galloped away.

Standing in the sun, she stared after them. Why did they leave her? They had to have heard her, knew where she was. Even if they were running from other men, they should have stopped for her.

Other men? She jumped as something crashed through the forest toward her. She ran for the woods in the opposite direction as a horse broke out from the trees. The man mounted on it looked to the west, where the two guards had gone. He started to turn in that direction as she tried to run into the shadows before he saw her. But he reined the horse around and their eyes met.

"Now I have the real prize." He rode toward her.

She ran. Then the horse was at her side and the rider grabbed her shawl. She pulled away from him. The thin wool tore where it was fastened with the brooch, freeing her. He dropped it.

She scrambled away again, heading for the thick brush just ahead. If only she could disappear into it . . .

A strong arm reached down and wrapped around her waist. The rider hauled her in front of him, laying her across his thighs. She reared up, trying to slither off head first, but he took her wrists in one hand and held them behind her, pressing on her back. She couldn't move. Her hair cascaded around her, blocking her ability to see anything but the ground.

"Let me go." She kicked, but hit only air.

"All in good time." He walked the horse back into the trees, toward the river.

The river? Where the Northmen were? He had an accent, one she'd never heard before. Was he one of them? Her heart stuttered. "My guards will be looking for me. You must have seen them."

"Ah yes. The brave men who ran at the first sight of us. And if they're yours, then they're cowards for leaving an earl's daughter alone in the woods. They led me right to you."

He knew who she was? How could that be? "I don't know what you mean."

"I saw you and your sister when I was here negotiating with your treacherous father a few weeks ago. You both came to the keep gateway. I recognize you. Which is convenient, since I need one of you."

That didn't sound good. She tried to break free, but his hand tightened around her wrists. Jerking hard, she twisted one of her hands free and swung at his head. He blocked it.

"I didn't want to do this." He caught her free hand and brought her arms back behind her as she bucked. A soft rope wrapped around her wrists and she screamed in frustration as he tied her. She had no chance against him. Even if she broke free and fell from the horse, she couldn't catch herself. She tried to calm her breathing. Think. She had to think.

Taking her by the waist, he lifted her up as though she weighed nothing, until she sat in front of him. To her shock, he was very gentle as he did so. He brushed back the hair that had fallen in her face. She truly looked at him for the first time.

Silver-green eyes froze her. His hair was black, falling straight to his belt, and he was much larger than any of the men of Northumbria. Except, perhaps, her brother. Then she knew.

"You're the Northman who came to our holding and spoke with my father. You wanted gold in exchange for leaving us in peace."

He inclined his head. "I'm Rorik of Vargfjell. I won't harm you. That, I promise. I only want the value of the ship he burned and *wergeld* for the loss of two of my men. Once your father pays me, I'll free you." He studied her. "What is your name?"

She hesitated. He didn't seem inclined to let her go, so at this point telling him her name wouldn't matter. "Elfwynn."

"Very pretty." His voice softened. "You and your sister look nothing alike. She's dark, while you're the image of your father. Your light brown hair is the same as his, and your brother's. All three of you are very similar, even to your blue eyes. I would know you by that, if nothing else."

There was no sense denying it. "Then send the message to him. I would be away from you as quickly as possible."

Rorik grinned as he tightened his arms around her and urged the horse forward. "Yes, my lady. Whatever she demands."

Rowena had said he was reputed to be handsome, but that didn't begin to tell the tale up close. When his smile washed over her, she had to look away. He was like no man she had ever seen. He had the face of a fallen angel. His body was as solid as a brick wall behind her, his arms like iron bands. His scent was that of the wind and waves, mixed with leather. But no matter what he looked like, he was a pagan, barbaric and crude. Still, something in his words rang true. He wouldn't hurt her.

Her breathing slowed. Father would lose no time sending the ransom. He had intended to pay the Northman anyhow until the ship had burned. He would surely do so now.

She faced forward. "You can untie me now. I won't go anywhere. I can't outrun you on the horse you obviously stole. If not for that, you might not have caught me."

"Don't be so certain. Whatever I want, I get." His breath moved her hair as he spoke very close to her.

A shiver ran along her arms. He didn't move to untie her and she didn't ask again. She was too vulnerable, too helpless, and she couldn't risk antagonizing him. His large arm was wrapped just below her breasts. If he wanted to take advantage of the situation, he had only to lift his hand and touch her. She could do nothing to stop him. But he kept his arm where it was, pressing her back closer to him as he signaled the horse to move faster.

Men stood to greet him when he rode into the clearing. The longships were visible through the trees. The five vessels rested on the shore, their great dragonheads rising into the sky.

He slid off the horse, then lifted her down into his arms. As he carried her through the gathering crowd, she kicked.

"Set me down. I'm not a babe to be carried."

"Be quiet. I'm taking you to where you can sit down."

Around them, the men talked. She could grasp some of what they said, which surprised her. "How is it I can understand some of your language? And why do you speak mine?"

"Our languages are very similar. Our peoples must have come from the same place in the past. I speak many tongues, including yours, as does my sister, Kaia. And I imagine I'll be hearing her curse me in both languages very soon."

As he set her on a fallen tree trunk, a tall, very beautiful woman strode toward them. She was dressed the same as many of the men, with a long tunic and leggings. Her black hair was braided back from her face and she looked much like the Northman. She was frowning. She was also wearing a sword.

Gripping the hilt, she spoke to him in their language, and Elfwynn could understand enough to know she wasn't pleased. Kaia gestured toward her bound arms and Rorik shook his head.

Kaia crossed her arms, scowling at her brother as she spoke in Northumbrian. "Rorik said you're to remain tied. He's an idiot."

Elfwynn shifted on the tree trunk. All the men in the camp were staring at her. There must have been over two hundred of them. They were large, their hair long, or shaved in odd ways. Many of them had designs on their bodies, and their beards were braided with beads and gold. Some of them had dark pigment painted around their eyes, giving them an exotic appearance. They were hard, cold-looking men.

Kaia moved in front of her, head up, feet apart. She spoke in a sharp voice to them and they moved off. Rorik stood to the side, watching. Elfwynn glanced at him. His expression was inscrutable.

He nodded to her. "I'll send a man with the ransom demand to your father." He walked away.

Elfwynn studied Kaia. Her arms were well-muscled, yet slender. Her body was tight and hard. She not only wore a sword but a long knife suspended horizontally below her belt. The slight scars on her skin attested to the fact that she fought.

"You go into battle alongside the men?" She couldn't help her curiosity.

"I'm a *skjaldmœr*. What you would call a shieldmaiden in your language. I fight. There are not so many of us among the Norse, but the Danes have had hundreds. I lead five others for my brother. They are there, around the fire." She pointed with her chin. Five tall, elegant women laughed with several other warriors.

They were so magnificent, it took her breath away. Like something from the old tales.

Kaia said, "My cousin just married one this past spring. Do you not have any here?"

"No. Our histories tell us that women once fought. Long ago. I never thought to see such a thing."

Kaia smiled. She was quite striking. Like her brother. Elfwynn looked away, her cheeks heating. What was she thinking? He was a barbarian. The last she saw of him couldn't come soon enough.

It appeared she'd have to see him a bit more. He walked across the camp toward her. Men gave way before him. Others stopped him to speak with him, then rushed off. He commanded the attention of all near him and she couldn't keep from watching.

Another man joined Rorik and they spoke as they walked. His shoulder-length hair was dark, the sun picking up gold streaks in it. As they stopped in front of her, he narrowed his eyes at her, then spoke to Rorik. Kaia tossed out a sharp word at her brother. Rorik shrugged.

Moving behind her, he said, "Kaia and Leif both feel it's safe to untie you. And they don't agree on much, so it must be true."

The ropes fell away from her wrists and he walked around in front of her. She rubbed her skin while glaring at him. "As though I could go anywhere with hundreds of your men surrounding me."

"Keep that in mind. Would you like to eat? Are you thirsty?"

"I'm fine. I don't intend to be here long. I'll eat when I get home." She crossed her arms and looked away from him. "You needn't concern yourself with me."

He leaned forward, his hands gripping the tree trunk on either side of her. She tried to back away from him, but she couldn't escape. His silver-green eyes caught hers and held them. "You are my concern while you're here. I brought you here and it's my responsibility to make certain you're cared for. I told you that you would come to no harm and that includes going hungry or thirsty. Now, are you hungry?"

"No." Not with his face so close to hers, his gaze boring into her. Her stomach was twisting. "But I am a bit thirsty."

"Would ale suit my lady?"

"Fine."

As he pushed away from her, his hair slid over his shoulder and brushed her arm. She swallowed. He spun away from her and shouted an order to a servant who ran off as though the gates of Hell were opening behind him. No wonder the poor man was so thin.

"Don't let my brother daunt you." Kaia frowned at Rorik. "He's too accustomed to women falling all over themselves for him."

"You're probably the first one he's actually had to chase, though." Leif shrugged as Rorik and Kaia stared at him. "You're not the only one of our people who can speak Northumbrian. I'm a trader and it comes in handy. Especially when talking to beautiful foreign ladies."

He grinned at her and his smile was infectious. Elfwynn couldn't help but return it. This would be over soon. They were treating her well. Litwin and Oshern were, no doubt, already back at the keep and her father was amassing his forces. Word of the ransom would come. He'd either pay it or rescue her. Her shawl was still near the road and it would help guide them to her. By nightfall, she'd be home.

But why had the two men left her to begin with? It wasn't as though all the heathens chased them. Only the Northman. Why had they run from one man and not stopped for her?

She looked at the massive warships lining the shore, remembering what he had told her. *They led me right to you.* Bile rose into her throat as her certainty faded. Something was very, very wrong.

Chapter Three

Elfwynn swallowed the last of the ale as she watched the Northman and one of his warriors speaking. The man shook his head, making a slashing motion with his hand. They spoke together for another moment, then Rorik yelled out to his men. They all shouted and rushed toward the tents, drawing their swords. Many of them grabbed spears, axes and shields.

He strode to her, Kaia and Leif following. She would not meet him sitting down, so she stood.

Stopping in front of her, he bit out his words between clenched teeth. "Your father has refused to pay the ransom. He says because you're illegitimate, you're not worth that much."

Her legs gave out and she sank to the ground. It could not be. Her father loved her, no matter what her birth.

There had to be a mistake. "Your warrior must have heard him incorrectly." Her voice hardly worked. "He didn't understand my language well enough."

"He speaks it as well as I do. I made certain of that. Turns out I picked the wrong flower. The one that doesn't belong in the garden."

All through the camp, men gathered weapons, sharpened blades, and put on mail. Rorik pivoted and called out orders to waiting men.

"Northman." She whispered the word, but he heard and turned back to her.

"What is it?" His hard eyes pressed her into the tree trunk behind her.

"What's happening? What are you going to do?"

"I told you I wouldn't harm you and so I won't. I'm raiding your keep. I'll get the gold one way or the other. It was your father's choice and now people will die because of his foolish decision." He turned back to his men.

People would die? Her mother. Her father. All the people she knew. Her head spun and she wanted to be sick. The Northman wanted gold. She had a small amount, but not enough to pay for one of those ships. She could weave for the rest of her life and never make enough for that. Think. How could she get the ransom?

Ransom. That was it. "Northman."

He rounded on her so fast, she almost forgot what she was going to say. "What?"

"I know how you can get the money."

He held his hand up and all the preparations stopped. He came to her and sat on his heels in front of her. "I'm listening."

Even crouching down, he overshadowed her. She buried her hands in her skirt so he wouldn't see them shaking. "The Church. It will pay for hostages of the pag—the Northmen. You could take me to a church. They'll give you gold."

"No church close to here would have that much."

She grasped at anything she could. "London. Canterbury. They have large churches. Wealthy churches. They would pay."

He barked out a laugh. "Can you see me sailing down the Thames into London, getting off the ship, walking you to a church and asking them kindly for gold? I'm not suicidal. Second, a massive force of our longships has recently attacked London and Canterbury, sacking them and destroying everything. I assure you, there isn't any gold left anywhere in those cities. And probably not much else. I can't take you to a church in your lands. I'd be slaughtered before I could even go ashore with you."

He stood and shouted at his men and they continued preparing. There had to be something else she could use. She'd told Wulf she'd sell her soul to protect the keep and all within. Offering herself would do no good. He could have taken her already if he wanted, but all he desired was gold.

If only he were a Christian, she could speak with him on that level. Then she'd use the risk to his soul to get him to listen to reason. But he had no soul. He came from a place where God didn't exist. And yet, there was a monk, Anskar, who traveled through the northern lands converting the pagans, and it was said that even the Danish king, Horik, had found God. He'd allowed Anskar to build a church . . .

She tried to stand, but she was shaking too hard. "Northman."

He whipped around and sat on his heels again, face to face with her. "What now?"

Fisting her hands in her skirt, she gathered her courage. "There's a church in Hedeby where the Danes live. It was built last year. Those are your allies, are they not? Don't your people trade there? You could take me to that church. I'd go with you willingly. Just don't attack my home. Please."

Her vision blurred with tears. If the Northman agreed to take her to Hedeby, then Redbank would be safe. Her mother, and all the people there, would live.

And her father. She fought down a sob. In spite of his betrayal, she couldn't let anything happen to him. He'd at least take care of her mother if she were gone. No one else would.

Until that day, she'd felt safe and secure in her father's love for her. He had always carried her above the waves of a cold, empty ocean. Now he'd left her out in that turbulent sea, without a sail, without oars, without even a star to guide her back home. She could never face him again. If the Northman agreed to take her to Hedeby, she didn't know how she'd get home again, but it didn't matter.

Because, after this, she had no home.

Rorik stood and spun toward Kaia. "What do you know of this church? Do they truly pay for Christian hostages?"

How could this have gone so wrong? It was all supposed to be simple. Those fools even led him right to one of the earl's daughters. He'd thought he'd have to be here for days, weeks, spying and hoping to catch a glimpse of one of them. Then Elfwynn was delivered right into his hands. Except she was the wrong daughter. He hadn't heard that one of them was baseborn. It shouldn't have mattered. What father would abandon his own flesh and blood this way?

Kaia nodded. "I know of it. You haven't been to Hedeby in the past few years. There's talk that Horik has, indeed, turned from the old gods. At least, on the face of it. It's likely so the Christian merchants will do business with him. Still, his rule is becoming tenuous because of that. He did allow a monk to build a church there. And I have heard of the ransoms they pay. They don't want us to poison their flock's beliefs, so they'll pay to get them back."

"I don't have time for this. I have to get back to Vargfjell to meet with Jarl Thorir. If I don't, he'll act without me against the southern jarls who encroach on our lands, and that would upset the balance of power."

"I didn't tell you to come here and start this mess." She stepped closer and lowered her voice. "If you back down and let her go, all these men will see it and say you're weak. Word will spread that you gave in to the earl, exactly what you didn't want to happen. You might as well throw blood into the water and jump in after it. Both your enemies and those who seek your favor would become as sharks, ready to rip you apart."

"I've never harmed a woman. I promised her that I'd let her go."

"I know. But that was before her father did the unthinkable and refused to pay. I don't like it any more than you do, but you know I'm right. You can't go into negotiations with Thorir with this on your back. You have to go in from a position of strength. He has to know you don't back down. If you let her go, you'll be sliding down the slope so fast, you'll never see the top again. And right now, even with my two ships and the three you had with you, you don't have enough strength to assure yourself of a victory."

Kaia had a point. He needed more ships, more warriors. As for Elfwynn, it wouldn't be as though he was taking her to sell as a slave. He was giving her—well, ransoming her—to her own people. Christians.

He took a deep breath. "I don't suppose it's so different from what I wanted to do with her father. Except she'll be going to a church instead of her home. Just not right now. I have to return to Vargfjell. I had to strike the earl immediately, but I've already spent too long on this. She'll have to come home with us. Later this summer, I can take her to Hedeby. Until then, she'll be our guest. I'll wager Vargfjell is far grander than anything she's ever seen. It won't be too much of a hardship."

Kaia was grim. "If her father's this much of a bastard, she's probably better off not returning. Who knows how he treated her? It strikes too close to home for my taste."

"Mine as well." They shared a long look. Then he regarded

Elfwynn. Her eyes were watery and she gazed at him with such hope and pleading, he almost changed his mind about the entire thing. This wasn't her fault, yet she was paying the price. He glanced at the men waiting on his signal to attack. They watched his every move, every decision. His fortune, reputation, and the welfare of his people rested on this moment. He couldn't afford to exhibit any weakness.

She'd shown remarkable strength. As upset and terrified as she was, she'd had the fortitude to think of a solution and present it to him. Not many Christian women would. Perhaps it was because her father was heartless, she was baseborn, and no one wanted her. She'd had to remain strong to survive. She'd be all right in the end. He'd make certain of it.

"Do you get the sea sickness?"

She paled, but gathered herself with a visible effort. "I've never been in a boat before."

He chuckled and clapped his hand on Kaia's shoulder. "Good luck, Sister. She goes with you."

He went to the center of the camp and his men gathered around him. "The earl has refused to pay the ransom, and we don't have the numbers to attack him. So I'm taking his daughter." The men banged their weapons on their shields in approval. "He won't be able to make allies through her marriage, so his position is weakened. That gives us a better chance to defeat him when I can come here with all my ships and the two thousand warriors I command." A great shout went up around him. "We will not fight and raid this day, but I swear to you that before this summer is ended, your sea chests will be filled with silver. I will regain what I have lost when I sell the woman in the slave market at Staraya Ladoga later this season. Understand this. She is mine. No one is to touch her or speak to her. Her maidenhead is her value to me and I keep what is mine. For now, we sail for Vargfjell. Prepare the ships."

The roar that went up probably reached the earl in his distant keep. Rorik smiled as his men dispersed to load the vessels. His reputation was safe.

Leif stayed behind after the men had gone. His usually light-hearted manner was absent as he bent his head to keep his words hidden from the others. "I trust you don't mean what you said to them about the woman."

"Of course not." He kept his voice low, as well. "I've never sold a woman in my life. I've bought a few to save them from the slavers, then set them free, but that's all. I'll keep my word to her. A few raiding trips, silver in their pouches, and the men will forget about all this."

"When will you tell her about the change of plans?"

"Not until after we've made the crossing, if even then. I'm certain she doesn't know where Hedeby is, or the Danes' land for that matter. She won't have any idea where we're going. I can better handle any problems with her if we're on dry land. Also, she'll be on Kaia's ship and I don't want to saddle my sister with a distraught passenger. She'll have her hands full with her as it is. I can take Elfwynn to Hedeby before the fall. I'll still get what I want, she'll be free, and this will all blow over. What could go wrong?"

Leif rolled his eyes. "The gods laugh when we ask questions like that. Now, I came along with you on this trip on a whim. But I need to decide what to do with the rest of my summer. Will you stop at Eirik's village on the way back?"

"Only if I need provisions after the crossing. And if that, I'll stay as short a time as I can to reload the ships. I have to get back to Trøndelag. I'm afraid I can't spare the time to take you home to Thorsfjell. It's a day's journey to the end of the Sognefjorden where it is, then another day's voyage back to the sea. It will take too long."

"Then you're stuck with me." He glanced at Kaia. "I can think of worse places to spend the warm months than drinking your ale and eating your food."

"And I can think of worse company. You're welcome to stay as long as you like. You're family, twice over, after all, with your brother and sister marrying my cousins." Rorik hit his shoulder. "We could make it three times over."

"I don't have another sister for you. At least, not one I know of."

Rorik shook his head. "The gods spare me. I wasn't referring to me. Being at Vargfjell will give you more time to be around Kaia."

"She *is* beautiful. But her tongue is as sharp as her sword. I don't want to lose any part of me to either of them." Leif looked at Kaia as she brought a bowl of stew to the little Christian.

Elfwynn set it in her lap, but didn't eat. She stared out over the river, her shoulders slumped, her eyes reddened. She seemed defeated, resigned to a horrible fate, but there was a determined set to her jaw as she straightened, picked up the bowl, and sniffed at it.

"I think I will stay with you for the summer." Leif glanced between him and Elfwynn, a mischievous glint in his eyes. "It could be interesting."

"What do you mean by that?"

"Nothing. Nothing at all. I have to load my things on the ship." Leif sauntered off.

Now Rorik understood why Magnus always looked as if he wanted to pound Leif into the ground. Still, he had a feeling Leif saw more than he let on. That could be useful. Or not.

The camp was simple. In an emergency, they could leave everything and board the ships. The vessels could move in either direction. They'd be out on the river in moments, beyond arrow shot, without having to turn around. With so many warriors working, the ships were ready to sail quickly.

As the men waded out to board the vessels, he walked to the woman. She'd finished her stew and had settled on the tree trunk, waiting.

"We need to get you on Kaia's ship."

She stood, not looking at him. Her eyes still glistened.

She squeaked as he scooped her into his arms. "You wouldn't be able to go through the water or climb on board with your long skirt."

As he headed to the ship with her, she trembled. But she hung on to him, her arms around his neck. Her scent was sweet, like the roses he'd smelled in other lands. Her hair was a cloud of curls around him as the breeze blew it. She was so light, he had no trouble lifting her over the side of the ship.

One of the shieldmaidens reached to steady her, but she held up a hand. "I can do this." She walked over to a sea chest and sat down.

"My sister will take care of you." He hesitated as her chin quivered. She stared beyond the other side of the ship, her eyes dull. He almost jumped up there to reassure her that she would be unharmed, but his men were watching, waiting on him. If he put too much importance on a foreign captive, they'd see it as a vulnerability. She'd probably be more comfortable with the women around her anyhow. Even shieldmaidens.

He left and climbed aboard his ship. Not his flagship, the *Sword of the Waves*. That lay burned and blackened on the shore farther up the river. Or probably in it. The earl wouldn't want other Norsemen to know what he did, so he'd most likely sunk the evidence. That suited Rorik.

He didn't want them to know, either.

Standing at the stern, he glared down the river as the men lowered the oars and turned the ship to the east. The loss of his daughter obviously hadn't bothered Edward, so he still hadn't paid for his treachery. But he would.

Rorik gripped the afterstem rising at the back of the vessel until his nails bit into the wood. No, if his beautiful ship was at the bottom of the river, it would keep the other Norsemen from seeing it and destroying Edward in revenge.

That was a pleasure he wanted for himself.

The banks of the Humber slid past them. Elfwynn had known them all her life, but had never seen them from this angle in the middle of the river. She couldn't enjoy the sight. Huddled under a fur cloak Kaia had given her, she was numb to everything, which was a blessing. In the boat ahead, the Northman stared behind them. He was so strong and arrogant, he could crush her like he'd crushed her life. At least she'd be away from him soon. Away from all of them.

She had to admit they'd treated her well. And they'd released the horses they'd no doubt stolen from a nearby farm instead of killing them. Perhaps there was some humanity in them after all. But she'd thought her father was a good man and look how wrong she'd been about him.

How had she so misjudged him throughout her life? She'd have given her loom rather than believe he could betray her like this. But a few weeks ago, she'd have denied he could behave so dishonorably toward the Northmen by burning their ship while negotiating with them. He had to have known it would have repercussions.

Perhaps he felt he got off light with them taking only her. It was obvious he didn't care about her. Why had he always acted as though he loved her? Was it to find favor with her mother so he could continue to have her whenever he wanted? Rohesia might have been nothing more than a convenience, but her daughter wasn't. Had he suspected she was planning on taking Rohesia to her people in Strathclyde and this was a way to stop that?

What would her mother go through when she found out she was

taken? The loss of her son had almost killed her. If Edward thought he could have her to himself now, he might lose her anyhow. Her mother was so weak already.

Oh Lord, grant her the strength to live with her shock and sorrow. And grant me the strength to survive the Northman.

Once the church in Hedeby paid the ransom, she couldn't remain there. It was a major trading center. There must be ships from all over the world coming and going. The silver and gold she had hidden in her pouch might buy passage back to Northumbria. Redbank wasn't home any longer, but she had to get back to her mother before she faded away from even more grief. Then she'd take her mother to Strathclyde, even if she had to sell her beloved loom and harp to raise the money to do so.

Her muscles quivered and it was all she could do to sit still. She wanted to hurl the chest she sat on as hatred, hot and painful, rose in her. For her father. For the Northman. If it weren't for both of them, she'd be back at her loom, with her mother embroidering by the fire.

"Elfwynn?"

She shook her thoughts away and looked up at Kaia. She sat down on a chest nearby.

"Once we leave the river, we'll be making a crossing through the North Sea. I've ordered a shelter put up for you at the front of the ship so you can have privacy and protection. Now, I thought you should meet my warriors. Perhaps they won't be so frightening to you then."

She nodded behind them and Elfwynn turned around. The five shieldmaidens and several men who weren't rowing stood in front of the mast, watching her. They were dressed in leather and were all fully armed. Frightening indeed.

"Not that I expect you to remember their names, but this is Visna, my second-in-command." The chestnut-haired woman inclined her head. "The next is Aldis, then Svala, Valka, and Hafthora. The overly handsome man who is staring at you, and shouldn't be, is Galinn."

Visna slapped the back of his head. He muttered something to her, then grinned with a good-natured shrug.

"Shieldmaidens are all so beautiful," Elfwynn said. "Men would give you every comfort. Why risk yourselves in war?"

Kaia's silver-green eyes hardened as she raised her chin. "Any woman can spill her blood giving birth. We spill ours protecting our land. Both carry our people into the future. Besides, have you done so much less for your own people? You may not have accomplished it with a sword, but you saved them just the same by giving, not your blood, but yourself for them. You show the heart of one of us." A tint of admiration colored her voice.

Elfwynn shook her head. Kaia and the others would never be afraid of anything, or anyone. It showed in their pride of bearing, their confidence, and their strength. She was shaking, frightened half to death, a thought away from flinging herself overboard. But then, Rorik would lose his precious ransom, turn back, and attack the keep. He didn't have to tie her to make certain she didn't escape. Her own conscience chained her here.

Two men walked between them, carrying a large piece of cloth similar to the sails. They went to the front where there was a small deck and tossed the material over the front rigging so it formed a tent of sorts. They tied the two ends to the sides of the ships.

Kaia watched them. "It's not much, but it's raised and we have furs we'll put in there for you. We don't have luxuries here. Everyone is the same on a longship, and sleeping under the stars is good enough for us. We weren't expecting to bring along a—" She paused.

"A prisoner?"

"You're not a prisoner. Rorik said you were a guest."

"Is that what you call holding someone for ransom?" Her shoe was wet and she looked down. There was water in the bottom of the boat and she brought her legs up with a gasp. "God spare me. We haven't even left the river and already the boat is sinking."

Kaia laughed. "We're not sinking. There's always some leakage, especially with the damage because of the fires. The planks forming the ship overlap and we seal the spaces with tarred animal hair. It's not entirely watertight and the heat from the fires probably melted it. But with this large a crew, no one has to bail for very long. Sometimes we measure distances by how often we take turns."

Was she serious?

"Wait until we get to the sea. We build the ships so they bend in the waves and then they leak even more."

They were insane. "You go to sea in ships that aren't solid and leak like a broken bucket. Don't you fear death?"

"No, we don't. These ships have carried us all over the known world and beyond. There's nothing else like them. They'll get us where we're going."

"It's a good thing no other ships are like this. The sea floor would be piled high with sunken wrecks. And don't expect me to bail."

"Of course not. You're a *guest*, after all." Kaia chuckled and stood. "Keep your feet up and you'll be fine." She strode to the back of the boat, calling out orders.

Elfwynn picked up the dripping hem of her skirt and wrung it out. She closed her eyes and took a deep, calming breath. Just how far was Hedeby? Or the land of the Danes, for that matter? Days? Weeks? She had no idea.

Wulf had told her of faraway places from the time she was young, but she had no idea where they were. Their priest had mentioned the ransom, and at least she'd remembered it. With all the Northmen camping in the region, he'd warned them to be careful lest they be taken. It would cost the Church precious money to free them from the heathens' terrible influence.

She just never thought his exhortation would apply to her.

Redbank, the keep of Earl Edward of Northumbria

Wulfric breathed a sigh of relief as he, his father, and their men rode into the bailey. All seemed normal. He'd been afraid the Northmen had attacked while he and his father were both gone. They had argued about it. He'd believed it was better for one of them to remain, but his father wanted them to head to different places in order to bring back as many of their men as possible, then meet again to head back home.

They were spread too thin. Between providing men to King Osbert for the constant conflicts with Mercia to the south, and having to ward off attacks by King Kenneth MacAlpin of the Picts to the north, they had few enough forces to guard their own lands from the northern invaders. That was why he'd followed an unorthodox path his father didn't know about in regards to the Northmen.

Everything appeared peaceful, so perhaps it was working. The people came out of the keep to greet them as they rode through the gates. A long line of warriors followed them and soon the bailey was filled with horses and crowds of villagers.

As Edward swung down off his horse, Wigberht ran to them. Wulf had never liked the man. He was one of the men Mildburg had brought with her from Wessex as part of her dowry. He had always been too close to his mother for Wulf's liking. More of a personal bodyguard, as though that was needed in the keep. He'd never been able to catch them at anything improper, and his father, as usual, was oblivious to all except warfare.

He leaped off his horse as Wigberht reached them and addressed the earl. "My lord, there is grave news. Vikings took Elfwynn. We believe it was Rorik, the Northman whose ships were burned. He must have taken her in revenge."

The earl froze as Wulf dropped his horse's reins and took the smaller man by the shoulders. "When did this happen?"

"About a week ago, my lord. A couple of men and I searched, but we never found anything. Only the remains of their camp on the shore to the east. Although a farmer thought he saw a body— a woman's body—in the river not long afterward."

Wulf shoved him away, heat flaring through him, his muscles tightening in rage. "Three men? There were only three men searching for her?"

"It—it was all we dared, my lord. Who knew if that was only the beginning and they'd attack full force? We had to defend Redbank, the Lady Mildburg, and your sister."

"Rowena. Where is she?" Edward was pale, the side of his neck twitching.

"She is safe, my lord. She was disobedient and so the Lady Mildburg locked her in her room. Thank the Lord, or she might have been taken as well."

"How did it happen?" Edward's voice shook. The people in the courtyard were silent, listening.

"She wanted to go to a farm to get a certain type of wool, my lord. She was taken then."

"She promised me she would take guards if she went anywhere." Wulf clenched his fists.

"Two men did go with her. Litwin and Oshern, my lord. But they disappeared as well and we fear the Northmen killed them to take Elfwynn."

"How could this happen? My girl. My precious, beautiful girl." Edward's eyes glistened. "I knew I should have made her live in the keep. She was my heart, everything to me. So precious." He looked at Wulf, his color high. "What of Rohesia?"

"I'll go see to her." He jumped on his horse and rode out of the bailey at a gallop, people scattering in front of him. He didn't care. How had this happened, indeed? This was because of the burned ship. If they had negotiated with Rorik, he wouldn't have come back for revenge. Instead, someone had instigated the burning and subsequent battle. And this was the result.

There was no doubt Rorik was the Northman who took her. Earl Edward was a very good man, but all he knew was warfare. Wulf had contacts with the northerners in the area his father didn't know about. He'd kept a peace of sorts with them. Because of this, they'd left the population alone, for the most part. Elfwynn had always been able to go to the neighboring farms in safety.

Until now. Whoever took her could not have been operating from this area. In other words, Rorik. He had the reason and the anger to avenge the loss of his ship and his men.

Wulf pulled his horse up in front of Rohesia's small house, jumped off, and burst inside. She was sitting by the cold fireplace, staring into space and shaking. He found a shawl and wrapped it around her.

"Rohesia?" He turned her face to him. Her eyes were red and watery. "Look at me. Tell me what happened."

She remained silent for a moment, then sobbed as though she couldn't hold it in any longer. "Oh Wulf. My baby is gone. It's not enough that God took my son. Now He's taken her, as well."

"We don't know that. Only that a Northman kidnapped her. She might still be alive. Tell me what occurred on that day."

When he said she might still live, Rohesia's gaze found his. "Two of the earl's men came here. They said the Lady Mildburg wanted the pure white wool from Henfrith's farm, and only Elfwynn would know which was the highest quality. They left here on their horses." She bowed her head, tears falling. "The last thing she said to me was that she loved me."

"And she still does." He embraced her, then rose and put wood in the fireplace. As he started a blaze, he said, "I'm going to ride toward Henfrith's farm and take a look for myself."

When the fire burned well, he knelt before her. "I'll come back and take you to the keep. You can't stay here by yourself. This may cause a rift between the Northmen and us and you'll be too vulnerable."

She shook her head. "I can't live there, Wulf. Mildburg would never tolerate it."

"I don't care what my mother wants. I'll find a place for you. One of the smaller houses in the village where the people like Elfwynn. There are many of them. You'll be welcome with them. Stay warm. I won't be long."

He mounted his horse and cantered to the river road. A week had passed. He might not find anything, but he had to try. The warriors had probably dispatched the guards, but many times, they took women for wives or concubines. Or slaves. They didn't often kill them. A woman as beautiful as his sister was worth more alive. So why didn't they try to ransom her? If Rorik had slain her in revenge, he'd have left her body where it would be found. Where it would leave a message. Why simply dump it in the river where it would float out to sea? He'd never sent any word gloating about it either.

A flash of color in the dirt at the side of the road caught his eye. He slid off the horse and knelt to examine it. Elfwynn's shawl. His breath caught. He'd know it anywhere. Shaking it out, he studied the forest around him. If men had looked for her, as Wigberht claimed, they would have seen this and picked it up. It was too obvious.

The bushes at the south side of the forest were broken and bent, as though a horse had crashed through them. He grabbed his horse's reins, mounted, and followed the damaged underbrush into the woods.

It led him to the river and the remains of a camp. There had been a large force here. Trash, cold fire sites, and discarded food that animals had disturbed were scattered everywhere. Faint marks from five beached longships scarred the shoreline.

Five ships? Rorik had had only four including the one that had been burned. He must have found reinforcements, but still not enough to attack outright. Taking one of the earl's daughters may have been the only way Rorik had to get revenge. For now.

He needed more information. Riding along the river, he kept an eye out for a body. Each time he saw something in the water, his heart stopped. The objects were only tree limbs and other debris, and that raised his hopes. With the way the currents ran, a body should wash up. A man thought he saw one, but wasn't certain. Wulf needed solid proof of her death before he gave up.

As he neared the camp of the Danes, several Northmen stepped in front of his horse, blocking his way. He kept his hand from his sword hilt, but he didn't back down. He spoke in the Norse he'd learned over the years from his contacts. "I'm Wulfric, son of Edward. I come to speak with Brandr. He will know me."

One of the men moved forward and Wulf tensed. "Come with us."

He remained on his horse, following them to the campsite. Men rose, eyeing him as he passed them. He made no sudden moves, but met their scrutiny. He'd been there before and could show no weakness.

A large, dark-haired man came out from one of the tents and put his hands on his hips. "Wulfric. You do not cling to life today?"

He laughed as he dismounted, affecting more ease than he felt. "What kind of life would it be if I stayed home, safe from the likes of you?"

The man roared with laughter. "That is true. Better to die in glory. And if you are not careful and keep riding into our camps like this, you'll know more glory than you planned on."

"Ah, but if we fought, Brandr, we'd finally see which is real, Odin or God."

"Very true. But let us not find out today."

"That suits me well."

"Come and share some ale with me. I don't imagine you came here just to see my pretty face."

"It's a bit too hairy for my taste."

"I should hope so." Chuckling, they walked inside the tent.

Brandr poured ale into two soapstone cups and handed him one as they sat. "Skoal."

"Skoal." They drank.

He almost toyed with his cup, but it wouldn't do to reveal any hesitancy. "I need information about a Northman. He goes by the name Rorik of Vargfjell."

Brandr's eyes widened. "What of him? He sailed with Ragnar Lothbrok toward York earlier this summer. They put in here for a day or so, then went on."

"He returned a bit over a week ago. He and my father had a falling out the first time he was here and this time he took my half sister. I just returned to find out about it." He leaned forward. "I need to know if you've heard anything. One of our people thought he saw a woman's body in the river."

Brandr stroked his beard. "Come to think of it, I did see him sailing to the west not long ago, then back toward the sea. But I saw no women except shieldmaidens on his ships. I will tell you this, though. If Rorik of Vargfjell took her, she's in no danger from him."

"Why is this?" Hope flared in him.

"Rorik's love for women is well-known. As well-known as he is. He's the richest and most powerful of the Norse. He rules a huge village, and most of the farmland in the Trøndelag area is his. His fleet of ships is vast, his men are the best warriors, and he commands respect in all of the known world. Almost every woman who sets eyes on him falls in love with him. And he loves them back. He's notorious for it. He will never harm a woman and if any of his men had done so, it would be his body you'd find in the river. I can't see him even taking a woman. It's not like him. Either there's a mistake, or something extraordinary happened to cause it. But one thing I can guarantee you is if Rorik did so, he'll see she's not harmed."

His heart could beat again. Perhaps. "Is there any way to get a message to him?"

"Who knows where he is? Could be any place from here to the sea that has no tides, to his home. If he's gone to Vargfjell, he's across the North Sea by now." He took a drink of ale. "I can keep an eye out for one of his ships to pass by and signal them to come in if they do, but that's all."

"It's more than I had when I rode in here." If only there were some way to go to Rorik's lands to find Elfwynn. But his people didn't have the ships to do that. They could mount a naval defense and sail shorter distances. However, a journey that far was impossible.

He eyed Brandr. "Do you ever sail to this Vargfjell?"

"I'm a Dane, not Norse. Still, I have gone there to trade since it's so lucrative, but not often. It's very far to the north. Just to get from here to Kaupang in the south of their land takes about four days and it's another five or so to Vargfjell. Depending on the winds and the currents, of course, and whether I stop for the nights. If I do decide to go, I'll send word. Who knows, we might make you one of us yet."

Wulf returned his grin, but his pulse was racing. There was hope. Hope that Elfwynn was still alive, and hope that he could find her. Hope might be the one thing that would keep Rohesia alive until Elfwynn returned.

This entire incident reeked of something very wrong. Someone had given the order to burn the Northman's ship while they were negotiating with him. Then Elfwynn disappeared and a number of their men had died under suspicious circumstances since the battle with Rorik. He might have to hold off looking for Elfwynn for the time being, but it didn't mean he wouldn't continue to search for answers.

If one day that meant sailing to the ends of the world, and even Vargfjell itself, he would do it. He'd told Elfwynn if anything ever happened to her, he'd give his life to bring her back. And so, he would. His hand tightened on the cup as cold knifed through him. She'd said she'd sell her soul to stop him and to save their people.

What if she had?

Chapter Four

Trøndheimsfjorden, Trøndelag
Western Norway

Elfwynn peered over the edge of the boat as they turned toward the coastline. Rorik had mentioned something about sickness in the sea. So far, nothing had flown out of the waters to make her ill, though the food on the ship might.

For the past nine days, they'd eaten little but dried fish and vegetables they'd made into a stew and eaten with dry, hard bread. To be fair, some of the men caught fish and cooked them over a tiny grill for her. They had nuts, as well as apples and other fruits preserved in honey, so it wasn't all bad. But she would have killed for a slice of rare beef, or even soft, fresh bread. And clean, pure water. The water in the barrels was stale, and though it was fortunate they hadn't had any storms on their journeys, Kaia had said the rain would have given them a chance to replenish their supply. At least they'd brought plenty of ale, which was safer to drink than the water. By the time they landed, however, she'd never want to see it again.

Kaia had wanted to stop at a place called Haardvik for new provisions. But when she'd yelled to Rorik about it, he'd shouted back that they were sailing straight on. The shieldmaiden hadn't been happy about it.

At least they'd get to Hedeby sooner and she could buy a new dress and shoes. She'd long since given up on the latter. The water in the boat had ruined them and she'd taken to keeping her skirt tucked up in her belt to try to keep the hem dry. It was hopeless. She'd almost cut it off at her knees. But she still had to wear it when she disembarked. It would be unseemly to walk through the town that way.

She got up from the chest she'd been sitting on and went to the front. Hanging on to the dragonhead ornament, she looked at the coastline they approached. Mountains rose in the distance while islands guarded the land. Throughout the journey, she'd been able to tell by the sun's rising and setting that they were headed northward. Now they turned to the east.

The ship just ahead of them on the left was the largest of them all. Rorik stood at the right rear, holding the rudder. His black hair whipped in the wind and his confident bearing spoke of absolute mastery of the sea. Each day, they'd guided their ships close together to report to him. Even across the expanse of water, his gaze had burned into her. She'd met it with a pride she didn't feel.

These were a strong people. They respected strength, even in women. At home, she'd held her own against those who disliked her for her birth. Even Mildburg, whom everyone feared, hadn't cowed her. If she could stand up to her father's wife, she could stand up to anyone. She had to be as assertive and forceful as the shieldmaidens were.

At least she wouldn't be around the Northman for long. Just until they went to the church and he got his gold. Then she'd be rid of him forever.

He glanced back, as though he'd felt her eyes on him. She looked away toward the land, then brought her gaze back to him. She'd give him no reason to think she feared him. Even though she did. He watched her for a moment longer and she lifted her chin. His teeth flashed in a grin before he faced front again.

They passed several islands, then wound their way through turns within the great fjord. Green hills rose around them. The narrower waterway widened into a vast open channel. The longships sailed straight across, heading for the land jutting out into the expanse.

As they drew closer, Elfwynn studied their destination. A massive building rose on a hill. It was made of wood, with gables and staves, and was far larger than any building at home. Smaller structures surrounded it. She hadn't expected such sophistication among people she'd always considered barbarians.

At least ten longships were docked or beached at the shoreline. Of course, if this was a major trading center, that would make sense. But shouldn't there be more crowds and movement? People were gathering at the docks as they glided in. They were happy, calling out greetings. Why would that happen in a market center? Rorik was very well known and so perhaps that was their way here.

She wouldn't know. On the voyage, Kaia had urged her to learn their language. Everyone on the ship had offered to teach her. It helped pass the time. She'd complied, for she couldn't know how long she'd stay at Hedeby before she returned home. Their words were close enough to her own that she comprehended many of them. But that didn't mean she understood their customs.

When the men on the ships disembarked, women hugged them. Two women walked away, crying while others consoled them. It was difficult to believe this was the way between people who didn't know each other.

Something wasn't right. She caught Kaia's arm before she stepped off the ship onto the dock. "Where are we? This isn't a marketplace."

The shieldmaiden paused. "Rorik will speak with you about it. He's coming now."

Elfwynn looked down the dock. He walked toward them, stopping every few steps as people spoke with him. Kaia disembarked and said something to him. He nodded and came to her. She ignored the hand he held out to her, and climbed onto the dock unaided. The ground swayed under her and she almost fell.

With a chuckle, he caught her arm, and steadied her. "You have to find your land legs again."

Was this the illness he had spoken of? She had no choice but to grip his arm as the land moved. While they stood there, people came up to speak to him. A blonde woman threw herself at him, breaking his hold on Elfwynn. She grabbed one of the dock posts.

The woman wrapped her arms and legs around Rorik and kissed him. He laughed, returning the kiss. She moaned, then whispered in his ear. He nodded and she slid off, giving him a sultry look as she sauntered away.

He watched her for a moment longer, then regarded Elfwynn. "Come with me. We must talk."

She didn't move. "This isn't Hedeby, is it?" The ground had stopped shifting as though it was trying to tip her over. She let go of the post.

"That's what I have to talk to you about." He held out his hand. "We can speak more privately elsewhere."

"Just answer my question." She crossed her arms. She was not going off with him alone. Not after having seen the kiss he'd given the blonde woman and not with the inviting looks others were giving him. It was clear he was popular with the women and was no doubt used to getting his way with them. He had a surprise coming if he thought the same about her.

He drew closer. The trace of wind and salt spray, mixed with his scent wafted over her. "We will speak alone if I have to haul you over my shoulder and carry you there. My people would enjoy a laugh."

"Your people? Then I was right. You lied to me."

His eyes hardened. "I don't lie. Are you coming willingly?"

"Rather than have you touch me again, I'll come." She followed him through the crowd.

"Where are we going?"

"To the docks over there." He tilted his head. "We can speak without the interruptions."

"Most likely so you can throw me into the fjord and drown me."

He smiled. "It's too shallow here, more's the pity. Besides, if I had wanted to do that, I'd have ordered it while we were at sea, not when you could walk back to the shore."

"You escaped from me in a different boat, then."

"Are you such a threat to me that I need to escape?"

"It depends on what you have to say." They reached the other dock and she stopped herself from leaning against one of the posts. She had to remain strong. "This isn't Hedeby."

"No. It's Vargfjell. My village and lands. I rule here."

Her head swam with dread and she fought to regain her composure. She didn't need the fear taking her over now. She clung to her resolve to meet him head on. Then he'd understand he couldn't walk all over her. "Why doesn't that surprise me? As I said, you lied. You were to bring me to the church in the land of the Danes." She looked around. "What land is this?"

"The land of the Norse. And I will bring you to Hedeby. Just not right now. To get there I must go through the Skagerrak and the Kattegat waterways. I don't make that difficult voyage unless I have a full ship of goods to sell and trade to make the risk worthwhile. Besides, I have urgent business here requiring my attention. I couldn't take the time to sail so far off my course."

"But you had the time to go all the way back to Northumbria and kidnap me."

"Revenge does not wait. Your father betrayed our negotiations. He set all this in motion."

She straightened her spine, rising to her full height. "You were the one who threatened us, wanting money for nothing. I know how my father thinks. He never would have burned your ships. He wanted peace between your people and his."

"You say you know his mind, but you also thought he would pay the ransom for you."

At that, her bravado wilted. In spite of her determination to stand firm before him, tears welled up. No wonder he was so feared. He knew just where to strike. She turned away from him lest he see her despair, and looked out at the waters.

"I shouldn't have said that. I'm sorry for hurting you. It was not my intent." His voice was soft as he touched the back of her shoulder.

She jerked away from him, his perfidy tightening her stomach. She didn't need his apologies. "So when do you plan on sailing to Hedeby? Preferably before I'm old and gray?"

"A few years before that."

She spun back to face him. "Years?"

He shook his head. "Later this summer. I have to meet with a neighboring jarl first. We have much planning to do. Once our business is concluded and the situation is settled, I can take the time to go there."

"You have many other ships. On our journey, Kaia said you have twenty-three of them. Won't any of them go there sooner?"

"You're my responsibility. I don't trust anyone else to take you. Besides, my ships have other places to go."

"Other places to plunder, you mean."

"That, as well." One side of his mouth curved up.

"And to take slaves, I suppose." She glared at him in disgust.

"They're more trouble than they're worth, always wailing and crying. I'd have to feed and clothe them. That bites into the profits."

She studied the distant hills. "Then I should have wailed and cried. Perhaps you would have left me alone. You'll still have to clothe me since this gown is ruined." She lifted her stained skirt. "And I hope you serve better food than I had on the boat. It was terrible."

"I think you'll approve. I've ordered a feast to celebrate our return." He stepped around her so she would see him. His eyes were solemn. "I give you my word that I'll take you to Hedeby before the fall."

"Why should I trust the word of a heathen?"

"We don't hold with good and evil, as you Christians do. We have only our word and our honor to live on after us. If I say it is so, then it is so." He smiled at her and the full power of his masculine beauty broke over her. He, no doubt, used it to get what he wanted. She couldn't forget he'd threatened her people, took her from her ill mother, and destroyed her life.

Her anger flared anew. "You say you don't take slaves, but apparently you do take hostages. Which am I?"

His eyes glinted with humor as he reached out and caught a lock of her hair. He ran it through his fingers. "If I made you my slave, I'd have to shear off your glorious hair and put an iron collar around your neck. I couldn't give you beautiful dresses to wear while you're here, but then, you would be mine. All of you." He leaned toward her, his voice husky, rich, deep. "Perhaps you wouldn't need dresses at all."

She narrowed her eyes at him as she jerked her hair away. Carried on the warm timbre of his voice, his words drove deep into her, and she suppressed a shudder. He thought to melt her to his will, as he likely did all other women. It was not going to work. She hoped. "I thought you said slaves weren't worth it. I can weep and wail quite loudly when I want to. Keep you up all night. Make your life into a hell. My father's wife gives us all a good example of how to do that. I learned from the best." She gave him her sweetest smile.

He burst out laughing, causing many of the people on the far dock to look their way.

She blushed and lowered her head at the unwanted attention. "Then I suppose that leaves me a hostage."

"If you want to see it that way, you can. As far as I'm concerned, you're a guest. I think you'll find life here is very good. You can stay in Oslafa's house in the village. She came from your land long ago when she was captured as a slave. She speaks your language and can help you make your way here."

If she was a slave, then he probably bought her. Slept with her. Used her for his own pleasure. So much for not dealing in them. Could she trust anything he said? "That would be acceptable."

"With your gracious approval, my heart can beat again. I have to go to the longhouse. I'll have new dresses brought to you." He glanced down at her bare feet. "And shoes."

"Can I help it if your boats have more leaks than an old barrel?"

A muscle in his jaw jumped as he cleared his throat. "My *ships* are the finest in the world. But your father damaged the one you were on and so it wasn't quite as seaworthy. My shipwrights will repair them, though no vessel is entirely watertight. The next time you're on one, it may meet your approval."

"Only if it's taking me to Hedeby. It can sink after it hits the docks there and I'll bid it a fond farewell."

He shook his head. "The slave idea is sounding better. I could gag you and no one would gainsay me. Though if you're like this to everyone here, they'd cheer me on, slave or no slave."

"The rest of the village isn't responsible for my being here. I reserve that honor just for you."

"A slave. Looking better and better." He peered toward the other dock. "I see Oslafa, thank the gods. I'll introduce you and we can be rid of each other."

"That suits me very well."

"At least we can agree on something."

"Don't get your hopes up too much."

He eyed her as though she were some strange object he was trying to figure out. She probably was. She didn't soften into a puddle of desire like other women must. Why did he bring out the worst in her? Mildburg had never cowed her. It was part of the reason the woman hated her so.

Rorik was in another realm altogether. Big, powerful, and arrogant, he was lord of everything and everyone here. His air of self-importance goaded her into saying things she shouldn't. She needed to take care. He could kill her and no one would blink. It was fortunate she was going to live under a different roof. She could avoid him. If she did come across him, she'd need to control her emotions to keep smooth waters between them. He could so easily change his mind about her status here.

He had gone ahead of her and by the time she caught up to him, he was speaking to a plain-looking woman about the same age as her mother.

He barely glanced at her. "Oslafa, this is Elfwynn. Since Turold isn't at the house much, would you have room for her? It's just for a short time. As short as I can make it." He shot her an irritated look.

"Of course. You're more than welcome, Elfwynn. It will be good to see someone from home again. You'll have to tell me who is attacking whom these days."

"Everyone." She held her hands up and shrugged. "Everyone is attacking everyone. The same as always."

Oslafa laughed. "We'll get along fine, Rorik. She'll need some clothes, though. And a few other things, I'm certain."

"I've already sent for a dress for her. See to whatever else she needs. And don't forget to come to the feast this evening." He strode away as though he couldn't leave Elfwynn behind fast enough.

"Come with me, Elfwynn. After so long in the ship, you'll want the sauna. I have wine and fruit. This will be enjoyable."

What slave called her master by his name? And she had a house of her own? Elfwynn walked beside her up the path toward the village, gazing at the buildings. They were beautiful, intricate and majestic. In the midst of them all stood the building that she'd seen from the ship. It rose high, its peaked roof sharply angled, overlooking the fjord.

"Is that Rorik's longhouse?" She nodded at the building.

"Yes. It's quite beautiful inside. Of course he has the best of everything here. Where are you from in Northumbria?"

It was good to hear her language spoken without a foreign accent. "On the north shore of the Humber. My village is called Redbank from a battle fought near the river many years ago. Where did you come from?"

"Farther north, near the Tyne."

They reached the top of the path and Elfwynn stopped. The longhouse rose before her and she could only stare. Intricate carvings decorated the doorframes and the entire structure was built with the same care as the ships. There were glass panes in the windows to let in the light but keep out the cold. A rarity, even in her own country, and a great expense. Smaller buildings lined the road, while others were nestled in the hills beyond.

She glanced behind her, toward the water. Ships lined the shore, both at the docks and pulled up onto the beach. All this belonged to Rorik? He stood amidst a crowd of people, a woman under each arm.

"You'll see it all later. We'll get you cleaned up, fed, and dressed, and you'll feel like new." Oslafa led her toward a tidy little house down the road. "I used to live here with several other women and our children. They all remarried, but I never did. My son and I remained here. He's gone most of the time, working on Rorik's farmlands. Even when he's here, he'd rather spend his time with the men instead of with me. Though he does come to visit. I don't blame him. What young man wants to live with his aging mother when a world of adventure awaits him?"

"You don't seem to be aging, Oslafa." It was true. She was a plain woman, but her skin was clear, her brown hair shiny and her figure was trim. Warmth shone from her and Elfwynn was drawn to her immediately.

They walked into the house. It was clean and simple with a central fireplace, a table with chairs and several beds. "I'm afraid there's not much privacy. They don't have it here, like we do at home. But since it's just the two of us, I hope you don't mind."

"Not at all. I live with my mother in a one room house, so this is what I'm accustomed to."

"Sit. I'll get you some milk and fresh bread. I have butter and honey also. I know I promised you wine, but I think this will do you more good for now." She went to a sideboard and gathered plates, a loaf of bread and a pitcher.

"It sounds delicious. Especially after all the dried food in the boat. I could eat anything, then sleep for a year."

When they had settled into their meal, Oslafa said, "This is simple fare. I usually don't keep much here and take my meals at the longhouse with the others. Everything is the finest there and the serving girls do all the cooking."

"The men don't cook here?"

"It's not like Northumbria, where we did much of the baking, and they made the meats and most of the food. Here, all the cooking is women's work."

How odd. While men of her father's rank wouldn't cook, all the other men hunted, brought home the meat, and either roasted it or made soups and stews. Just what did these men do besides raid?

"It seems to me many things are different here," she said as she spread honey on her bread. "If you don't mind my saying so, Rorik said you were a slave. They certainly eat and live well here."

Oslafa laughed. "It's like him to leave out the details, especially when it comes to his concern for others. I was a slave, but he saved me."

"I don't understand. Everyone knows the Northmen take people from all the isles and sell them as slaves in the East."

"And that is what happened to me. Ten winters ago—they judge years here by winters—Northmen came from the sea and attacked my village. They destroyed everything and killed all the men and many of the women. Those they didn't slay, they took to sell, including my son and me. He was eleven winters then, but short for his age. When we got to the great market in the East, they tried to separate us." Her voice shook.

"I'm sorry. I shouldn't have pried. You needn't tell me if it's too difficult."

"I have a feeling we'll be good friends and you should know. Besides, it's a tale I have told many times, though it gets no easier. In any event, when I realized what they intended, I screamed and pled with them to let us remain together. I didn't care at that point what happened to me. My husband was dead, my people slaughtered, and I would never see my home again. To lose Turold and never know what had happened to him was more than I could bear. He, too, begged and cried, but to no avail. They said if I wasn't quiet, they'd kill him in front of me.

"Rorik heard us and came to see what was happening. We'd attracted quite a crowd by that time. He had to push to the front, followed by his men. He was so young, just over twenty winters. But he had already made a name for himself. He looked at my son and me clinging to each other, then threw the men a small bag of gold. He said if it wasn't sufficient, he'd offer the point of his blade to make up the difference. They said it was enough. Everyone in the crowd stepped aside for him, then, as we left.

"He took us aboard his ship and assured us we wouldn't be separated. All through the journey here, I didn't know what would happen to us, but at least we would be together. Not long after we arrived, Rorik said we were free. I had the choice of whether to stay here at Vargfjell or return home."

Elfwynn stared at her. "And you chose here? Why?"

"Everyone I knew had been killed or taken. There was nothing left to call home, no reason to return. He and everyone else here treated us decently. Nothing is too good for his people. They are well fed, well housed, and want for nothing. He took me in and has never asked anything of me. I'm an excellent seamstress, though. So I make clothing for the people here in return for my keep. He doesn't like it, but allows it because he knows it makes me happy. Though Rorik is having clothing sent for you now, I'll make dresses for you, as well."

Warmth swelled her heart. Not only for what this woman had endured and survived, but for the contentment and joy coming from her. She had found her place, even though it lay in a foreign land with the very people who had taken everything from her. And yet, Rorik wasn't the one who had done so. He had saved her.

Elfwynn tightened her jaw. That wasn't the case with her. There'd be no rescue. He'd swept into her life and taken her away from everything she knew. Even though she had offered to go with him, she had done it to save her people from exactly what had happened to Oslafa's village. The good woman's story had a happy ending, where most didn't.

It remained to be seen how her own tale would be told.

"I scarcely recognize you, Elfwynn. Neither will Rorik."

She frowned at Oslafa. She didn't care what he'd recognize. She smoothed the skirt of the dress he'd sent over. It was blue, with a colorful ribbon around the hem. Oslafa had shown her how to fasten the two bronze brooches at the shoulders. The dress had no pockets. None of the northerners' clothing did, so she'd had to hide her small bag of silver under the mattress of the bed she'd chosen. It was the best she could do until she fashioned a hidden pocket in the skirt.

Oslafa had arranged the front of her hair into intricate braids, letting the rest of it curl down her back. At least she was clean, for Oslafa had taken her to the sauna. Since there were other women there, she'd kept a towel around herself while she sat in the steam. They weren't so modest. But by the end, when they'd poured buckets of warm water over her, she'd let the cloth drop because it felt so good. Weeks' worth of sea and salt were washed away, leaving her renewed.

With a new gown and shoes, clean hair, and a brief rest, she was ready to face the people of Vargfjell. And Rorik. Now that she wasn't a half-drenched, salt-encrusted, hungry waif, she could better control her words and her temper. But she still wouldn't allow him to step on her. She just needed to keep the peace between them until she left.

As they walked toward the longhouse, Oslafa nodded toward it. "Normally, longhouses are low and narrow, with thatched roofs instead of wood. Inside, they have three sections down the length of them. But Rorik saw buildings in other lands and wanted something grander. He brought builders here and they constructed this. It's far taller and has more room inside. It's unique in all of the north."

They entered the longhouse and Elfwynn stopped. Grander, indeed. The walls and tall ceiling were made of wood. Intertwined animals and plants were carved into the posts and on panels set into the walls. Fine weavings of all colors hung between them. The open glass-covered windows let in air and light, as did the smoke holes in the high ceilings. The floors were of smooth wood and the furnishings were well crafted. Polished tables filled the center of the hall, and doorways led to other rooms she couldn't see. Silver plates and goblets shone on the tables, with food piled high in their midst.

"We'd best sit down before the men devour everything in sight." Oslafa showed her to a table near the back of the room. "Not that Rorik is close-fisted by any means. But with so many warriors here, it's difficult for the servants to keep up with their appetites. Things will ease up when many of them leave to raid or trade."

"Rorik does both?" She stabbed a piece of beef with her knife as the plate passed her.

"Of course. He has to sell what he raids to make gold. As most of the people in the north do, he trades, buys, sells, and barters. He's just better at it than most."

She feasted on goose, venison, shrimp, carrots, peas, and onions. Passing on the fish, she slathered butter on wheat bread and devoured that. She'd never eaten so well, not even at her father's table.

She didn't see Rorik, nor did she look for him. If she could eat and then leave, it would lessen the chance of a confrontation. In a room filled with his people, a clash with him wouldn't be wise. Something uncontrollable sparked between them that left her uncomfortable. She would rather it didn't burn her.

As she ate, people looked at her, whispering and craning to see her. She kept her eyes down, not wanting to attract any more attention.

"You came here on one of Rorik's ships and they saw you talking with him after you landed," Oslafa said. "They're wondering who you are. We have many visitors here, but few who sail with him. Whether they want to or not."

While they'd finished their small meal at Oslafa's house, Elfwynn had told her of how she'd come to be here. If word got out that she was little more than a hostage, there was no telling how they would treat her. Several beautiful women eyed her, the same ones who had hung on Rorik at the docks. Including the very tall, haughty one. They had no reason to worry about her where Rorik was concerned. They were welcome to him.

As she met their stares, they changed their demeanor. They sat up and preened, moistening their lips and stroking their braided hair. They'd apparently seen Rorik somewhere behind her. She didn't turn around. Perhaps he wouldn't notice her.

"Have you enjoyed your meal?" His words slipped over her as he laid a hand on her shoulder.

"It was very good." She kept her voice level and her eyes lowered. With any luck, he'd go on his way.

"Come with me for a moment." He held out his hand.

So much for avoiding him. Oslafa nudged her. She had no choice with everyone in the hall watching them. Placing her hand in his, she stood. His eyes widened as he swept her with his gaze. A surge of female satisfaction cascaded through her and she lifted her head, giving him a slight smile. All her life, those around her had told her she was beautiful. She hadn't believed them until now when she saw it in his eyes.

He'd bathed as well. His long black hair was combed smooth and sleek over his wide shoulders, his clothing was of the finest leather, silk, and wool, and he wore thick twisted wire neck and arm rings made of gold. A sense of wealth and power surrounded him, more so than any man she'd encountered. As important as her father was, she'd seen many of them. They were pale pretenders next to him.

He didn't say anything, only stared at her while all the people watched. It was enough to make her blush and she had to break the moment.

"I thank you for the dress, Northman. And the food was excellent, as you promised."

He blinked, then inclined his head. "I'm glad you approve. Come with me to the front of the room. I want to introduce you to my people so there is no mistake about you."

Introduce her as what? He kept hold of her hand as they made their way between the tables.

He bent to speak in her ear. "Try to be nice."

"I will, if you will." She spoke through her clenched teeth.

"I think I can manage that. The gods forefend I should forget the sharp tongue behind that beautiful face."

Heat burned her cheeks as he turned her toward his people. He spoke in Norse, so she couldn't understand everything he said, but she did grasp quite a few words. When he finished, the people spoke among themselves, still casting glances her way.

She took her hand from his. "What did you tell them?"

"That you're my bed slave and that I'm going to chain you to my headboard and do all manner of perverse things to you." He grinned.

She wanted to hit him. "You did not. I heard the word for guest."

"I see Kaia taught you some of our language on the voyage." He sighed. "Where's the fun in that? You're right. I told them you're an honored guest here and that they're to welcome you in all ways. They are to make your stay a pleasant one."

It was her turn to blink. His kindness was unexpected and it made her uncomfortable. She didn't want to be beholden to him for anything. It was his fault she was here to begin with. She was more at ease feeling angry with him. If he smiled at her, and said kind things, it might soften her resolve. That mustn't happen. He was the enemy.

She had to get away from him before she said something she shouldn't. Again. "I'd like to leave now. I rested a little bit after the sauna, but I need to sleep in a bed that doesn't rock and isn't wet."

"I can think of many reasons why a bed would move and be damp. And they don't involve rest."

She gasped, her cheeks flaming again. "Heathen."

His laughter followed her as she headed for the door. Then she skidded to a stop. In the corner, where she couldn't have seen it before, a harp leaned against the wall. It was carved with leaves and flowers, its strings glistening in the soft light. All her embarrassment forgotten, she went to it and touched the top.

Her father had given her harp to her when she was very young. They'd had their own harpist at the keep then, and he had taught her. She often played for her mother because it soothed her pain and sorrow. Her father's gift to her was something they both shared. Now it would stand quiet and Rohesia's anguish would go uncomforted.

She stroked the strings and they trembled under her fingertips. How could she ever play again without thinking of her father's betrayal and lies? The sound, the notes, would drive it all home to her again. Her throat closed with sorrow and unshed tears.

"No one here knows how to play it. Do you?" Rorik stood beside her.

She blinked the moisture away so he wouldn't see her weakness, and splayed her hand on the strings to stop their vibrations. "I used to. Not any longer."

Leaving the harp and him behind, she stepped outside. Night had fallen and a soft breeze came from the fjord. On the water, the ships floated in the moonlight. She breathed in the night, seeking its calm. Her music brought peace to those who listened, but no one here needed it. Except her.

Though from now on music would never bring her comfort, only sorrow. She could never play again. Both harps, at home and here, would remain forever silent.

Chapter Five

Rorik watched her leave, the sound of her fingers on the strings still playing in his mind. Gods, she was beautiful. In Northumbria, she'd fallen in the dirt, her hair was messed, and she was angry and tearful. He'd been too frustrated to care what she looked like. After the long voyage with no bath, none of them had looked attractive. When she'd stood in front of him, the full impact of her beauty hit him. He'd stared like an untried youth. She'd looked up at him with her large, blue eyes, her honey-colored hair braided in the front. The curls poured down her back to her waist and he could only imagine them covering him as he drew her naked body over his.

He would not think of that. She was too caustic, too foreign. He liked his women blonde, Norse, and willing. None of those criteria applied to her. She'd be worth more as a hostage if she remained a virgin. Which was one reason he'd warned the men away from her. Even if she became interested in someone here, he couldn't allow it and would have to make certain she remained untouched. She had to go to the church in Hedeby. Christians were obsessed with a woman's purity. With her beauty, it might not be easy to keep the men from her. He might have to stake a claim to her himself. As a ruse, of course. His other women would love that.

Grimacing, he went back to his seat. Leif was pouring another draft of beer for himself and he filled Rorik's goblet without asking if he wanted any. He did.

"She cleans up well." Leif raised his cup then took a drink.

"I suppose so. I didn't notice."

"Of course not." He smiled as he studied the beer in his cup. "You both were too busy staring into each other's eyes to notice much of anything else."

"I don't know what you're talking about."

"Now you sound like my brother. You shouldn't be so concerned about what I saw. They saw it as well, and there may be some repercussions." Leif nodded to the table where several of Rorik's women sat.

He winked at them. They smiled back, but there was a hint of uncertainty in a couple of them, and wariness in the others. Gunnhild, who imagined herself his main lover, was the proudest of them all. If any of them gave Elfwynn trouble, it would be her. Still, she wouldn't press, or she would lose him entirely. "They know better than to be jealous. I won't tolerate it and there's no need. There's more than enough of me to go around."

Leif gave him a narrow-eyed look as he popped a honeyed nut into his mouth.

"What?"

"Nothing." He ate another.

"You have that expression you get when you see something in someone. I've seen you do it before. Your twin always takes note of it and asks your opinion. Now you're looking at me."

"I've always had a gift for seeing into people. Magnus, in his wisdom, uses it to his advantage. Perhaps it's kept him from killing me. I do have my uses."

"And what do you see now?"

Leif took a deep breath. "I see a man who lacks what he needs most. He scatters himself among many, never feeling, always searching, not finding. Always skating on the ice, never looking for what lies beneath. So he moves on, afraid to peer too deeply into the depths."

Rorik raised his head. "First, I do not fear. Anything, or anyone. Second, I do not lack. Look at everything here. I have all I could ever want. Wealth, women, power. Every day, I see my gold increase and every evening, I have all my people and women to celebrate with me."

"All very true. If we surround ourselves with enough lamps and the glitter of gold, we needn't see the darkness. In the night, when we are alone, though, is when the shadows come."

Rorik stiffened. "But I'm never alone in the dark at night." He drained his cup and rose. "I like you better when you're cracking jokes."

Leif gave a soft chuckle. "So do I. But you did ask."

"And I'll know not to do that again. A good night to you." He walked by the table where his women sat, brushing Gunnhild on the shoulder. She followed him into his room and shut the door behind her. Servants had lit all the oil lamps so the chamber was bright. He didn't turn to her yet. She would wait.

Leif had hit too close to home with his words. Damn him. The shadows were always there within him. Of the past, his own failures, and the fear of madness. His cursed father's blood still roared in his veins, and it would go no further. He did not seek comfort, for he could never find that in this lifetime. He only sought to exhaust himself every night with his women so he could fall asleep and not dream. Not see his past replayed over and over, and not see the blood that spattered it. In the day, his people surrounded him, keeping him busy. At the great markets, there were the sounds, the colors, and the mind games of commerce. In his ships, the wind and the seas cleansed him. In warfare, he focused on survival and his next opponent.

But at night, that was when the shadows threatened. He turned to Gunnhild. She was already naked, her eyes hooded with desire. He'd bury his face in her fragrant hair until all he saw was its golden radiance, and lose himself in her pale body until he knew of nothing else. The fulfillment he gave her and all the other women lifted his sense of failure. The light they brought him and the pleasure he gave to them drove back the horror of the past, allowing him to make up for some of it. At least, for that brief time.

That was why he was never alone in the dark.

"I need an emissary to meet with Jarl Thorir and invite him here for a talk."

Rorik sat at a table in the longhouse with his best warriors. He shouldn't have stayed away for so many weeks. He had a mountain of work to do in handling the problems and business that had piled up in his absence. All that time spent away, and he had nothing to show for it except the memory of a burned ship and the tears of the women whose men had been slain in the battle with the earl. And one caustic little Christian woman.

Several of the men were still feeling the effects of last night's feast, but it never bothered him no matter how much he drank. They were bleary-eyed, wincing as the servant set the platters out for the morning meal.

"I'll go to Holtvik and speak with Thorir." Galinn, the warrior who had sailed with Kaia, yawned. "As soon as I find my head. I know it's here somewhere." He peered into his cup.

"Trust me. You don't want to find it," Leif said. "I know where mine is and I'm ready to cut it off to ease the pain. You're better off without it."

"Whenever your head makes a reappearance, Galinn, you can leave. Take at least six men with you. We know Oddr and Kolbienn have forces coming into my lands. So far, they're in the southern areas, but it pays to be careful."

"Those are the two jarls you're having problems with?" Leif dragged a plate of cheese toward him, considered it, then pushed it away with a wince.

It might be wise to tell him the situation. Leif could be useful. At the meeting with Thorir, he could study him without the jarl knowing. He had been a bit too close for comfort in his assessment last night, but Rorik would never admit it. Leif had some skill with seeing into people and if need be, he was a good fighter.

Two of his men were snoring with their heads on the table, and the others didn't seem much better off. It would be a while before he could continue any kind of business with them. Leif, at least, was coherent.

"Very little of our homeland is farmable. Just here and the area around Haardvik and farther south into Rogaland. I own most of it near the Trøndheimsfjorden. A jarl named Thorir owns a large area of fertile land to my east. We've always had a truce between us, along with Grjotgard Herlaugsson Lade to my west. If we fought each other, it would destroy many of the villages here, unbalance the political power, and cause instability to trade and commerce. We're all too powerful. Our people would suffer the most and none of us want that.

"In the last year, two jarls to the south have eyed Thorir's lands and mine. Perhaps they feel that since the two of us aren't allies, if they joined forces, they could encroach on our lands and we wouldn't have the strength to stop them."

Leif frowned. "Are they insane? You're more powerful than most kings. You could be one yourself, if you wanted."

"I'm like you. You don't want the responsibility of being a jarl, and neither do I. I don't even call myself one. Then I'd have to perform rituals and all those bothersome duties I have no interest in. I took over this village when I came of age because I owed it to the people here. But I'd just as soon live on my ships, raiding and traveling the world. No cares. Just fighting, drinking, and making the ladies very, very happy."

Leif gave him a weak smile. "When do we leave?"

"Perhaps one day, I'll do that. Unfortunately, this situation with those jarls means I'll have to remain here for a month or two. I have my people to look after."

"Gods, you do sound like my brother." He lowered his head to the table with a thunk and groaned.

"From what I know of Magnus, I'm honored. King, jarl—whatever I am, I have to stop this before it goes any further. I'm asking Thorir to meet with me to discuss an alliance. We have to make a good show of force to dissuade Oddr and Kolbienn. If we present a united front, it should drive them back. I don't want to wait until their people move onto my land. Families would be caught in the middle. I have to head this off now."

"And this is a warning shot, like an arrow fired across the bow of a ship."

"Exactly. Just the rumor that Thorir and I have joined together might be enough to send them scurrying back to their own lands. I hope."

"It would encourage me to do so. But then, I wouldn't cross you to begin with. If you need another sword, I'd look forward to a good fight. With Hakon, Toke, and the outcasts all slain, I was beginning to fear it would be a boring summer."

"I'd also like you to sit in on the meetings and let me know what you think of him."

Leif crooked a brow at him. "And yet, I was completely wrong with what I told you last night."

"There's always a first time."

"Of course. Anything I can do to help, let me know."

"My thanks." He looked at his men. "I don't think I'll get any work out of them today. I have to go down to the ships and see to the loading of cargo and provisions."

"I'll go with you," Leif said. "It's better than sitting here watching them drool on the tables."

Rorik nodded in agreement. "Several of my ships will leave in the next few days for raiding forays into Francia. The kings there tend to hand over gold and silver for us to go away, so it pays to return each year. Their king, Charles, started it all with Ragnar Lothbrok six years ago. In many ways, Francia is the easiest target with its long coastline and many rivers. We've had a number of defeats in the western islands, including last year near the mouth of the Thames and in Ireland. I think I'll avoid them for a while." He stood.

"Ireland." Leif rose as well and walked with him outside. "It's such a mess there, we're even attacking our own people who hold the camps, like Dublin."

"That's the Danes for you. They attack everyone, including us. There are so many kings among the Irish, they can't coordinate any resistance to us. Makes it a little easier."

"Remember, only four years ago, they defeated us four times."

"Still, the island's been raided so much that the entire situation is a disaster and I avoid it altogether. I'll take an easier target any time."

Leif regarded him. "My mother was from Ireland. My father took her as a hostage there, fell in love with her, and when her ransom arrived, it became her dowry." He stopped and smiled as he looked up the road. "Sometimes, the easiest target becomes the most complicated, wouldn't you say?"

Rorik paused. Elfwynn and Oslafa walked toward them, talking. The sun hit Elfwynn's hair and it shone like dark gold. She wore the same blue dress she'd had on last night. It set off her coloring and her slender body, the skirt outlining her legs.

His women were all icy Nordic beauties, tall, cool, and certain of their studied allure. They rimmed their eyes with dark pigment, bringing out the blue color. Their clothing was rich, their jewelry heavy. They understood their power over men and used it to get what they wanted. Including him.

Elfwynn's beauty was earthy, like the forests and deep, growing things. Last night, when he'd stared at her like a shield-struck youth, a gleam of feminine knowledge had flashed in her eyes. Just for a moment. She knew her own beauty, but didn't use it as a weapon. It was simply a part of her. Was it because, unlike his women, she had so much more to offer?

She replied to something Oslafa said. Three bondsmen who were working on one of the houses stopped their labors and watched her, nudging each other and whispering. That was going to stop.

As he walked to the women, he cast a hard stare at the men and they turned back to their work. He smiled. "If you're going into the longhouse to find something to eat, Oslafa, I fear there are many half-dead bodies still in there. That's fortunate for you, since most of them either couldn't stomach food, or haven't woken up yet to get sick. There's plenty of breakfast there."

She glanced between Elfwynn and him, a spark of mischief in her eyes. "I'll check to be certain there aren't any indecent sights in there. One never knows after a feast."

"But Oslafa, every night is a feast."

"So true, Rorik. That's how I know." She hurried into the building.

Gunnhild sauntered from the longhouse, her hair mussed, a contented, sleepy look on her face. She sidled up to him and slipped her hands up his chest, then down the front of his body and cupped him. "Good morning, Rorik. I was surprised to wake alone."

With a glance at Leif and then Elfwynn, he removed Gunnhild's wandering hand. He kissed it. "Anyplace but in the street, love. Too much company."

"The next time you leave the street, I'll hold you to that. And that's not all I'll hold." With a smile, she walked off toward her house, her hips swaying.

No doubt she'd been so forward for Elfwynn's benefit. Staking her claim. Clearing his throat, he turned to the blushing little Christian. "Good morning to you, Elfwynn. I trust you slept well, and your bed was solid and dry last night."

She pursed her lips. "And I trust you didn't, and yours wasn't."

He deepened his voice, which had brought women all over the known world to their knees. "You have no idea."

She crossed her arms. "A point I am very glad of, I assure you. If you'll excuse me, I find I'm quite hungry. For food. And more pleasant company."

"Everyone in there is still stinking of beer, passed out in their own drool on the floors and tables, or wishing they were."

"As I said, more pleasant company."

He barked out a laugh as she spun and headed for the longhouse. He watched her, bemused. Words didn't come out of her mouth, icicles did. Very sharp ones. He should reprimand her for her lack of deference. It was so unexpected, he found it amusing and, worse, interesting. Women simpered and cooed around him. Like Gunnhild.

They couldn't jump to do his bidding and please him fast enough. It had always been that way and became all the same after a while. As long as she didn't deride him in public, he might let this play out. A verbal battle with a beautiful woman would be intriguing and novel.

His little Christian was a force unto herself. *His?* When he had made love to Gunnhild last night, for the first time he'd seen another woman beneath him. Elfwynn. It had startled him, for when he was with a lover, he focused solely on her. Her pleasure, her desires. Why had that changed? And why had he envisioned *her*?

Shaking his head, he looked up to see Leif leaning against a post, grinning. "The easiest target, indeed."

He strode past him. "Shut up, Leif. You don't know what you're talking about."

Leif burst out laughing and kept it up all the way down to the ships. To kill a family member was one of their few offenses punishable by death. Leif, damn him, was family now. If he kept this up, though, it just might be worth it.

She'd done it again. Let the Northman incite her. He was a heathen, letting his lover feel him all over, right in the street for anyone to see. It was no business of hers what he did, but to allow it in public bothered her. That, and his teasing eyes that made her constant, simmering anger toward him burst into flames. One presumptuous look, one goading word from him, and she wanted to strike out. She needed to avoid him. Hide. Run away if she saw him. It was going to cause trouble for her if he became angry. But it never irritated him. He seemed to enjoy it. Maybe that was what these Northmen wanted in their women.

She entered the longhouse. Oslafa picked her way between the inert bodies strewn about the hall, heading toward the tables of food. Didn't any of the men go to bed? Or did they just drink until they fell over where they'd sat?

Most likely the latter. She found the sideboards and filled her plate with eggs, cheese and fruit. As she poured a cup of buttermilk, Oslafa came to her.

"This is pathetic. Let's not eat here. I know a better place and you can meet some of the women."

Rorik's women? After the stares they'd given her last night, she didn't need that. As she followed Oslafa through a doorway, a familiar sound came to her and she relaxed. Rorik's women certainly wouldn't be here. Maybe this would feel more like home now.

She stepped into the weaving room. Six large warp-weighted looms stood against the far wall, women at two of them. Rolls of yarns and threads lay stacked on shelves, and bolts of cloth were folded on tables. Bags of wool waited to be carded and then spun on the distaffs lying on chairs.

Elfwynn set her food aside and went to the looms. Four of them had cloth in them. She leaned closer to see if the weave was familiar to her. It was. The first she examined was a plain tabby weave with single weft threads passed over and under the warp threads. The cloth in the second loom was a twill pattern. The weft threads passed over one thread, then under two others, forming a diagonal pattern. They were well-known weaves and seeing them brought a sense of comfort to her. This was not so foreign.

"Elfwynn, I'd like you to meet Finna and her mother, Kolla." Oslafa placed her hand on the younger woman's shoulder. "They are the two most skilled weavers we have. They speak only Norse, though."

"I've learned a little." She smiled at them, trying to remember what Kaia had taught her during the journey. "Good morning to you. It's nice to meet you. I'm Elfwynn."

They laughed and nodded their encouragement. Oslafa gave Finna a kiss on the top of the head. She was a cute, blonde girl, with large blue eyes and a round face.

Oslafa brought her plate to a table and pushed aside a pile of wool to clear a spot. Elywynn did the same and they settled into their meal. She buttered her bread. "You and Finna are close?"

"My son is sweet on her, and she on him. We all hope they'll marry one day."

"What's stopping it? Surely she's old enough."

"Oh yes. But her father sets his sights higher than Turold and has raised her bride-price to an impossible level. He wants her to marry Rorik, but that will never happen. You've seen the type of woman Rorik is attracted to. As pretty as Finna is, she'd never catch his eye. I doubt Rorik will ever marry unless it's to produce an heir, and he seems in no hurry to do so. Besides, she returns Turold's affection. He's a hard-working young man, but he doesn't earn much doing farm labor. That's not good enough for Finna's father. I make money for my dresses and I save it for Turold since Rorik gives me all I need to live, but it will never be enough for the bride-price. I don't hold much hope for the two of them." She sighed and ate her eggs.

Elfwynn took a bite of the fresh wheat bread. Oslafa had been so kind to her, giving her a place to stay, being a friend she so desperately needed in this strange land. If it weren't for her, she'd be more lost than she was now. If only there were something she could do to help.

There was the silver and gold coins she'd brought with her. But they might be her only way to buy passage back home once she got to Hedeby. She couldn't imagine the grief her mother was going through, not even knowing if her daughter was alive. The thought of it ate at her. Would the sorrow sap more of her strength away? Would she fade even more? No doubt Wulf would take care of her, but could he encourage Rohesia to live until Elfwynn found her way home?

This wasn't just about her. It was her mother's very survival. She had to put that first and keep the money in case she had the chance to buy a way home. However, she'd made money before by weaving, and she could do so again.

She set down her slice of bread. "I'm known for my weaving skills at home, and my cloth brings a great deal of silver. Could I use one of these looms to weave cloth for you to sell or make into clothing? I've created unique patterns no one here will have seen before. I think you could fetch a good price for it. It would help you raise money toward Finna's bride-price, and give me something to do while I'm here. It'll bring a bit of home to me. I won't feel so lost."

Oslafa frowned. "I would never ask recompense for my hospitality. But needing to do something, I can understand. If it would make you feel more at home, I'm certain you can use one of the looms. I have thread of my own you can work with. I won't take any payment, though."

"Then consider it my way of thanking you for the dresses you said you'd make for me. An even exchange." She took her hand.

"That, I can do."

"Then we have an agreement."

A warm touch of lightness spread in Elfwynn for the first time since Rorik had taken her. She couldn't tolerate being idle, and at least she had a goal now, a purpose. It might help the numbing pain of missing her mother, giving her something else to concentrate on. She would have to weave quickly, though, to make a full length of cloth. She didn't intend to be here long.

The only problem was that she was determined to avoid Rorik as much as she could. In Oslafa's house, it wouldn't have been difficult. But here in the longhouse? He lived here. Still, it wasn't likely he'd risk entering into this woman's domain. If she could come and go undetected, she should be safe. With the unpleasant fire sparking between them, he had no reason to seek her out.

In time, he'd probably forget she existed. As long as he remembered his promise when it came time to leave for his trading voyage to Hedeby, that was fine with her.

Elfwynn blinked as she stepped out into the sunlight. She'd spent all morning setting up the loom and once she returned to Oslafa's house, she could pick out the thread she wanted to use to start her cloth with.

She stretched as she looked at the fjord. Rorik's men were preparing for their voyages. At the shoreline, they loaded ships, made last minute repairs, and checked the rigging. Were they going to trade? Or were they heading out to raid and plunder? How could Oslafa see this every summer and not remember what the Northmen had done to her village? Just watching the activity made her think of Rorik's ships pulled onto her shore at home when he was talking with her father. It sent a chill up her spine. What misery would come of the journeys they were preparing for?

Troubled, she started up the road to Oslafa's house. She froze. The three men who had stared at her earlier had left their work and stood in the road, blocking it. Their smiles were not comforting.

At times, new warriors at Redbank had harassed her, thinking that, as a single woman of the village, she would be an easy target. They'd learned differently. She'd held her own with her wit and sharp tongue and had emerged unscathed. Plus she'd had the protection of her father's name. Here, she couldn't even speak to these men, tell them she was Rorik's guest.

She raised her head, looking directly at them. "Oslafa's house." She pointed behind them.

Their unpleasant grins became wider as they moved toward her. They said things she couldn't understand, then laughed. She looked around for help, but the road was empty. Oslafa had gone back to her house early. If she tried to run for the longhouse, they'd catch her before she could reach it. There were men near the ships, though. They would hear her if she screamed loudly enough.

She drew a deep breath. One of the men went down with a yell, clutching his leg. Kaia strode from the doorway of a house behind them, drawing her sword. The injured man tried to rise but his leg gave out. A long dagger was embedded deep into the back of his thigh, and his blood poured onto the dirt. Kaia must have thrown it. The two other men backed away from her, their hands up.

After kicking the wounded man back down, Kaia bent and withdrew her knife from his leg. She stood over him, and shouted at them in Norse. They spoke fast, looking at Elfwynn and shaking their heads. The shieldmaiden regarded them with narrowed, hard eyes, her shoulders back, her hand gripping her gleaming sword. She was magnificent.

From behind, Rorik stormed past Elfwynn, stopping just in front of her. Leif and several other men followed him, their swords unsheathed, and stood between her and the men who had threatened her. All of them spoke at once until Rorik held up his hand. His voice, usually so deep, was even lower, harsh, as though he spoke through clenched teeth. He advanced on the men, his fists tight. They knelt, cowering in front of him.

She couldn't understand much of what they said. She was trembling too hard in fear and shock to concentrate. But she caught enough words to know the men lied, saying she had encouraged them to join her in a tryst. When she heard that, it was too much. She snapped. Surging forward, she tried to rush past Rorik to scream at them, but he grabbed her. He pulled her against his body, his arm around her waist.

"They lie." She twisted to get away from him. With everything she'd been through in the past few days, she had reached her limit. It was bad enough she had to live here, among these pagans. But for them to threaten her, then lie about her, was too much to bear. "I didn't live all those years, dodging my father's men, avoiding the Northmen, and now selling my soul to you to keep the women in my village from getting raped, only to have it happen here."

"No one is getting raped. You're safe now." He spoke into her ear. His breath was warm against her skin, his words deep. They spiraled into her, making her feel protected and secure. She quieted. He caressed her waist for a moment. "Kaia heard the entire exchange. Thank the gods she can throw a knife."

Still holding her, he spoke to his warriors and they hauled the protesting men away, the injured one still clasping his bleeding leg.

"Are you injured? Can you stand?" He loosened her just enough to turn her to face him.

"I'm fine. What will happen to them?" She tried to push away from him, but he didn't let her go.

Kaia spoke Northumbrian as she walked to them. "Since they didn't actually rape you, we can't execute them. Unfortunately. Rorik, you got here too soon. I was just getting warmed up." She sheathed her sword, then cleaned her knife on the ground.

"I'll decide what to do with them later. All men here know my stance on taking an unwilling woman. They have no excuse. I let everyone know Elfwynn is under my protection."

"It appears she still is." Leif looked at Rorik's arm.

Rorik let her go and she stumbled back, a bit unsteady. He'd been so strong and solid beside her. He was like a great shield against anything that might harm her. But that was insane. He was the one who had caused the greatest harm to her. Or was it her father? She wasn't thinking straight.

"Kaia, I want you to teach Elfwynn how to handle a knife," Rorik said. "Nothing fancy. She's not a shieldmaiden."

"Thank the gods for that, or you'd have been dead back in Northumbria." Leif chuckled.

"True. Kaia, show her how to keep a man from her so she can protect herself, if need be."

Kaia gave him an innocent smile. "Are you quite certain, Rorik? You might regret that one day."

"Just teach her. And find her a knife she can carry starting now."

"Don't I have a say in any of this?" She crossed her arms.

"No." Rorik, Kaia, and Leif spoke at once.

She rolled her eyes. "Well, at least I know I don't have a choice." Then again, learning to defend herself might make her feel better. She never wanted to feel so vulnerable again.

"Come." Rorik took her arm. "I'll walk you to Oslafa's house."

She tried to pull away from him, but couldn't. "I think I can walk down the road by myself." When he ignored her, she said, "I always thought the women here had many rights and laws protecting them."

"They do. But they apply to Norse women, not foreigners. The story has spread of how you came to be here and some still aren't certain of your status. Hostage, captive, slave, guest."

"The last, or so I've heard. If that's true, you need to enlighten them more than you already have. Then let me know, since even I'm not certain."

"Guest, I assure you. And we have a long tradition of hospitality. Therefore, I'm walking you home. Call it my responsibility."

"You're known as the lord of the seas, but not even you could walk across them to take me home to Northumbria."

He laughed, his fingers sliding along her arm. He didn't appear to realize he'd caressed her, but the sensation shot through her like an arrow and she edged away from him as far as she could. So much for trying to stay out of his sight.

When they entered Oslafa's house, she was sitting at the table with a young man. She rose, giving a pointed look to Rorik's hand still holding Elfwynn's arm. Clearing his throat, Rorik released her.

Oslafa gave a rap on the shoulder to the young man who stared at Elfwynn, his eyes wide. "Stand up, Turold, when Rorik comes in."

"Sorry." He rose. He was tall and slender, with the promise of great width in his shoulders, a fine-looking youth about her own age.

The older woman sighed. "Elfwynn, please meet my son, Turold of the bad manners. He's not usually so wooden-headed. He speaks our language, of course, so feel free to berate him as you need to."

"It's good to see you here visiting your mother, Turold," Rorik said. "How are your repairs coming on the barns?"

"Quite well, Rorik. There wasn't as much winter damage as we feared. We'll have them finished soon."

"Excellent. You do fine woodworking."

"Sit and have something to drink, Elfwynn." Oslafa hurried to the sideboard. "May I offer you some wine, Rorik?"

He hesitated, then shook his head. "Thank you, Oslafa, but I have to go. I have business to discuss with my men. Perhaps they've recovered enough from the feast last night to form words now."

"They'll only start drinking all over again once they can walk straight enough to get to the ale."

"Then I'd best hurry." He inclined his head. "I'll see all of you at the evening meal."

When he left the house, it seemed like the air had gone with him. Elfwynn sank down at the table, light-headed.

"Are you well, child? Can I get you anything to eat?" Oslafa patted her on the back.

"I'm all right. I just had a bit of a fright." Over wine, she told them what had happened.

Osalfa set down her cup. "Rorik's warriors would never do that. But those were bondsmen, working off debts they've incurred. I can't imagine why they felt they could try for you, unless they thought they could force you to say it was consensual. With the three of them against one foreign woman, another man might believe them. Not Rorik. He'll always listen to the woman first. They didn't realize that. Here, Rorik's word is law. He'll decide what is to happen to them."

Turold's face hardened and he didn't look as young anymore. "I have some time off. I'll stay here and keep an eye out for you. Rorik is too busy. I promise you, Elfwynn, it won't happen again."

She smiled her thanks. No, it wouldn't. At home, her father's name was her protection. But here, in spite of what Rorik had said, she had no one else to depend on except herself. She'd learn how to handle a knife and wouldn't be so complacent about her safety. Just because she wasn't a shieldmaiden didn't mean she was weak. She'd survived vicious threats from Mildburg, villagers looking down on her because of her birth, and living in a region infested by Northmen all her life. This was only a few distasteful weeks, at most.

Then, she would return to Northumbria where she belonged, even if *she* had to walk across the sea.

Chapter Six

Elfwynn ran her hand over the area of cloth she'd just finished weaving. In the two weeks she'd been working on the piece, she'd completed twenty *ells* of the complex pattern, which equaled six of her own height. Not as much as she might have done with a more basic pattern, but she wanted it to be unique so as to bring the greatest amount of silver for Oslafa.

The other weavers were determined to teach her Norse, so they interrupted her often with lessons about what their equipment and household objects were called.

She touched the warp strings. *Varp*. And the weft threads. *Vipta*. And the loom itself was called *vefr*. The other weavers and she were known as *vefkona*.

Sitting down on a chair near the loom for a moment, she arched her back. At home she also walked back and forth at the loom as she wove, but she seldom worked for such long periods at a time. There was always something else she needed to do. Here, that wasn't the case.

As the women had chatted among themselves, she could understand more of their words each day. She had Turold to thank for much of that. He'd spent part of each morning walking with her through the village, showing her objects, telling her their names, and speaking to her in Norse. With how similar it was to her own language, she grew to understand it fast.

But she learned it even more quickly with Kaia. Rorik's sister had taught her how to handle a knife. As first, she was leery of it. Kaia insisted, though, and once Elfwynn lost some of her trepidation, the shieldmaiden pressed her harder and harder. A man, she'd said, wouldn't give her any quarter, and neither would she. When they'd started the lessons, Kaia had used Northumbrian to instruct her. Little by little, she'd increased her use of Norse, and now she spoke it completely. Elfwynn had to understand her, or pay the consequences. She had.

She rubbed the three healing nicks on her arm. Kaia was lethal coordination perfected. Her body was a weapon and she wielded her blade with cool efficiency. The Norse prized strength of body and mind, even among the women. Kaia had both.

Elfwynn sighed. She didn't have the strength of body. Or grace. Or speed. She had to use her wits and intelligence in her lessons with Kaia. The warrior didn't compliment her as they trained, but her nod at the end gratified her more than effusive praise from anyone else.

Rorik had watched one of their sessions. He'd walked by with several of his men and they'd all stopped, distracting her. Kaia had seen it, and that was where one of the nicks had come from. He didn't say anything, but continued on with his men, and Elfwynn never made that mistake again.

She hadn't seen him after that. The women said he'd ridden out to check on his lands and wouldn't return until he met up with Jarl Thorir and they came back here together. With him gone, the evening meals were simpler and quieter, and his women deserted the hall for their own homes. Which suited her. She didn't have to worry about avoiding him, and one could take only so much feasting. And unpleasant stares from Rorik's lovers. What they didn't understand was that they had nothing on Mildburg's venomous glares, so their haughty regard didn't bother her.

The wives and women of the village, however, welcomed her, especially when they learned of her skill with the loom and the needle. They asked her to teach them the more complex methods of embroidery known in her land. So in the evenings, they gathered in various homes. Some carded wool and spun with their distaffs while others, including Oslafa, made clothing. Elfwynn showed them the various stitches she knew to create beautiful patterns in wool and silk.

She didn't want any of them to know how Rorik had brought her there. But Oslafa told them and they rallied around her, comforting and supporting her. Such total acceptance was a new feeling for her. The people, and the land, weren't as cold and soulless as she'd been led to believe.

She stood, stretched, and walked to her loom. Only two were in use, the others standing empty. That was unusual. To make clothing for people in a village of this size and the material Rorik would need to trade with, all the women should have been working. With the long days, they'd have the light to weave well into the evening. Yet production had slowed quite a bit. She didn't want to ask them about it. They might think she was criticizing them. Perhaps it was their custom to ease up on work in the warm summer and pick up again when it was too cold to go outside in spite of the expense of the oil needed for the lamps.

The great doors in the hall banged open. At the sound of men's voices, she rushed to the door of the weaving room and peered out.

Rorik walked in. The man who entered beside him was tall and imposing, like Rorik. His hair was golden brown, hanging in waves below his shoulders, and he wore wide gold neck and arm rings. His sword and clothes were as rich and well made as Rorik's.

This must be Jarl Thorir. He was a fine yet hard-looking man, perhaps a few years older than Rorik. As the servants rushed to bring them mead and food, the two men sat at the head table. The other warriors who had entered with them settled around the hall, talking and laughing. Elfwynn recognized only some of them. The rest must be the jarl's.

She withdrew and leaned against the wall, fingering the knife hanging from her belt. Just what she needed. Strange men at Vargf-jell. She'd become familiar to the men here and they all treated her with respect and politeness, especially since the incident with the bondsmen. She hadn't seen those men again and never asked what happened to them. She didn't want to know and she didn't want more men disappearing on her account.

If she remained in the weaving room until Rorik and Thorir had eaten and left, she'd be all right. Her loom was situated in the corner, out of sight of the hall. They'd never know she was there.

Her features were unlike those of the Norse. The visiting men would see she was a foreigner and that might make her a target. Couple that with wanting to stay away from Rorik, and she had little choice but to remain out of sight.

Or did she? She'd never hidden from Mildburg or the men of Redbank, even though she knew they would try to bring trouble for her. One of the things she admired about Kaia was her courage. She'd told Elfwynn that a confident attitude was a better defense than any shield and as long as she didn't doubt she could face a situation, no one else would either. Never step one foot from battle, but always advance, she'd said. It was the Norse way.

She wasn't alone here. The weaving women, Kaia, Oslafa, Turold, and many of the other villagers were her friends. She carried her knife with her all the time. Vargfjell was her home for now and she had as much right to be here as anyone. Thorir's warriors were men, like the rest.

Shoving away from the wall, she took a deep breath. When she entered the hall, the conversation muted, making her legs shake, but she walked toward the door with her head high. As she passed the harp, she ran her hand along the strings to soothe herself.

When she reached the doorway, she glanced at Rorik. He and the jarl watched her. Rorik looked at the men in the room, then nodded to someone at another table as she walked outside.

She hadn't taken more than a few steps when Galinn, Kaia's warrior, came out behind her. He smiled as he caught up with her.

"Rorik wanted me to go with you to Oslafa's house." He spoke clearly, as though he wasn't certain she could understand him.

"I can speak quite a bit of Norse now," she said. "Thank you."

Her muscles relaxed. In spite of all Kaia had taught her, it was good to have a warrior beside her. Her show of courage had worked, even if it was false. Still, acting certain of herself had made her feel that way, if only a little bit. Kaia was right. If confidence was the face she needed to show the world, then confidence was what the world would see.

The feast that night was larger and grander than any she'd seen at Vargfjell so far. And that was saying quite a bit.

Elfwynn followed Oslafa through the crowd, Turold at her side. Servants had brought extra tables into the hall so it was difficult to move between them. People milled about, trying to find a place to sit, but the weaving women had saved Oslafa and her a place.

When Elfwynn sat down, she caught her breath. All the plates were either gold or silver and the cups were made of glass, an unimaginable expense.

"Rorik is out to impress Thorir," Oslafa said as a servant poured wine into their cups. "Don't drink yet. Kaia must first serve Rorik, Thorir, and their men in order of their rank."

"Kaia? Serving?"

"It's considered the greatest honor. Women have been known to fight over it." She laughed. "Though no one would dream of fighting Kaia. Besides, she's the highest-ranking woman here and the prestige belongs to her. According to their beliefs, the Valkyries serve the gods in this manner, and if they can do it, so can a shieldmaiden."

Kaia, dressed in a beautiful wrap-around dress of the expensive russet color, approached Rorik with a horn cup. It was polished and decorated on the rim and tip with gold and gems. She held it high so all could see it, her gold bracelets gleaming.

"Drink of this, Rorik, my brother, my lord, breaker of rings, giver of treasure. Your hall is strong with warriors, your ships filled with silver, and bright is your fame in all the world." She handed him the horn, then presented one to Thorir. A servant followed her with a silver bucket of mead and she dipped it out with a long-handled ladle. One by one, she served wine to all the men with them.

Oslafa nodded to them. "Only men of the highest rank may drink from the horns. They are for ceremonies and since they can't be set down once they're filled, the men must drain them. They'll switch to cups after that."

"What is the breaker of rings? Did I understand that correctly?"

"You did. It means that Rorik breaks rings made of gold and silver, and passes the pieces out as gifts. He is generous with his wealth."

Rorik stood. He wore a blue silk shirt under a tunic of deeper blue wool that was fitted and closed in the front with gold clasps. His narrow, tailored trousers were dark wool. His black hair was braided in the front with gold beads and gleamed in the firelight. They matched the gold torc around his neck and wrists. He raised the horn to everyone in the hall and his eyes met hers even though she sat near the back. As she looked at him, warmth spread down her thighs. The edge of his mouth curled up.

To Elfwynn's shock, he made the sign of the cross over the horn. She leaned toward Oslafa. "Why did he do that? He's no Christian."

"That's how they make the sign of Thor's hammer. It shows that Rorik believes in his own strength and might. Now they'll drink to the gods. Odin is toasted first for victory and power, and Rorik will dip his fingers into the wine and flick drops into the fire. This is to commemorate that Odin swore he would drink nothing until his blood brother, Loki, had been served as well. Then they'll drink to

Njord and Freyr for good harvests and peace between Rorik and Thorir."

Shouts erupted throughout the hall as the people raised their cups to the gods. As a Christian, Elfwynn couldn't bring herself to drink with them. One thing she had learned about the Norse was their tolerance of other religions. These people had the same loves, joys, and sorrows, and their lives weren't so different from hers. Their kindness to her proved they must have souls of some kind. They did not look down on her for her beliefs, which was more than she could say for the people of her land with their predilection for damning anyone who believed differently than they did. What else had the priests been wrong about?

Rorik sat down as the servants filed in with platters of food. They placed them on the center of each table and Elfwynn could only stare. There were several kinds of fish, as well as oysters, shrimp, seal meat, beef, mutton, lamb, chicken, goose, venison, and pork. Carrots, spinach, peas, beets, and mushrooms were served, along with dried apples, cherries, and prunes. Hazelnuts and very rare, expensive walnuts were piled high in bowls. She'd never seen such a feast. Not even in her father's hall. This would beggar any man, yet it must have been prepared since this morning when Rorik had returned home.

The extent of his wealth staggered her. So why did he need the ransom money for her? A ship must cost a great deal of gold, but with the riches he commanded and the shipwrights he employed, it would not hurt him at all to rebuild the burned ship. He wouldn't even notice the expense.

But it had cost her everything.

Her stomach turned and she couldn't eat. If Rorik was struggling financially, just able to afford the ship for his trading, she could understand his need for her ransom to replace it. She looked at him as he sat at his leisure, laughing with Thorir. He raised his gold-covered drinking horn as a servant placed a filled plate before him.

He had everything—wealth, respect, and power, as well as twenty-three ships and the warriors to crew them and fight for him. Yet that wasn't enough. He demanded more. He couldn't have just let it go, and let *her* go.

"I'm not hungry after all." She pushed her chair back. "I think I'll return to the house and lie down for a time."

"I'll walk you home." Turold rose as she did and looked with longing at his loaded plate. "Save this for me, Mother, if I don't return."

Why wouldn't he come right back? But as they passed Finna, the pretty girl glanced at him. He gave her a quick nod. She blushed, and returned it.

Elfwynn stepped into the night. "Is she going to meet you?"

"She's going to try. With all the people coming and going from the hall, she might be able to slip out without her father noticing. We'll spend a little time together before she has to return."

"I wondered why you'd volunteer to see me home, then not go back." She sent him a teasing smile.

"I would see you safely home anyhow. I have said it." He paused in the road and she stopped with him. "I would ask you not to say anything to anyone about my meeting with her. That's all the excuse Orri, her father, needs to marry her off quickly to anyone else wealthier than I am. And that's just about everyone. I save all I make for her bride-price, but it's nowhere near what I'll need. He doesn't want her to marry a mere farm worker. The only good thing is that her father wants to save her for Rorik, who has no interest in her. Still, Orri hopes and that gives us time."

He took her hand and leaned close to her, lowering his voice. "My mother says you're weaving a cloth of great beauty for her to sell for the bride-price. I cannot express my thanks enough, but I cannot take your money. I want to earn it."

She smiled up at him. "Then consider it payment for being my bodyguard. After all, look at everything you have to give up to take me home. A fine meal, song, revelry, drinking with the warriors."

"I'm walking a very beautiful woman home, then afterward I'll be with the woman I love. Not so great a hardship. I'll be the most overpaid guard in the north."

"It's well worth it. You've given up money by remaining in town for my sake, so this will help balance the difference. I can also help you and Finna. I can ask her to go with me someplace, or you and I can be seen going down the road. Then you can be together for a time and no one will be the wiser."

"You would do that for us?"

"Of course. Think nothing of it."

He squeezed her hand in thanks, then dropped it. They continued toward Oslafa's house. Elfwynn had seen what happened to those whose love was denied. Her mother had grieved over the earl all her life and it was destroying her.

After Turold left her at Oslafa's house, she got a cup of ale, then sat down on the bench outside near the front wall. It was too beautiful a night to remain indoors and she'd be safe enough there.

She looked up at the stars. Perhaps it was cruel to encourage Turold and Finna when they might be torn apart in the end. But let them have joy in each other while they could. Love was rare enough in this world. To know someone loved you, held you above all others, and was willing to give up anything to be with you would be worth any sacrifice.

She had always given of herself to others—her mother, her people, her father—and this had been her ultimate sacrifice. It was unlikely they knew what she had done for them, but that didn't matter. God willing, they were safe.

But perhaps, just once, it would be nice to have someone give up something for her sake, to be worth the sacrifice. To be loved.

Rorik nodded his thanks to Galinn. As the tall warrior went back to his seat, Rorik smiled at something Thorir said, though he was seething. Turold and Elfwynn had left together, when the feast had barely begun, and he had sent Galinn after them to see where they went. He'd reported that they'd stopped in the road and Turold had taken her hand as they'd spoken, their heads close together. Galinn hadn't heard what they'd said, but they'd smiled at each other, then continued on to Oslafa's house. There, the young man had left her.

A good thing, too. Otherwise he'd have to go there and break them up, no matter what stage of undress they were in. If the whelp thought he was going to take her virginity, he was in for a rude awakening. If he hadn't already. Much could have happened while he was away.

Rorik took a long drink and slammed down his cup. A servant rushed to refill it. Perhaps he should go there anyhow, make certain her value to him wasn't being compromised. But he couldn't leave yet. The feast had just begun.

"I see your little captive left with a young man. Such beauty shouldn't be wasted like that. Instead it should be enjoyed by someone with the years to appreciate the experience." Thorir watched him, humor in his eyes.

"Who says she's a captive?" He speared a hunk of rare beef with his knife.

"I noticed her this afternoon when she walked through here. She's not Norse, so I had my men ask around. Is she for sale?"

The jarl was a bit too interested in Elfwynn. Every sense came alive, as though he faced an enemy in battle. It wouldn't be wise to kill a neighboring jarl. Especially not with most of his men in the hall. It would be a blood bath. Rorik smiled as he chewed the beef, though it had turned to leather in his mouth. He had to handle this without causing a diplomatic incident. Or death. Thorir's death, preferably.

He would be angry over such disrespectful talk about any woman. It wasn't only because it was about Elfwynn. Of course.

"It's well known I don't deal in women. I love them too well. Her father owes me money, so she remains here until he pays me." Not entirely true, but his mind was turning red at the thought of Thorir with her. That was never good. Why he felt this way was not important right now. He had to calm down.

"So you take her against her will and make her stay here. I'd say that's a captive. Or a slave."

"I'm not selling her to just anyone with the money. I'm returning her to her people eventually. Once I get paid what's owed me." That wasn't a lie. Christians were her people. And if they continued this feasting in the coming days, he'd have to go to Hedeby sooner than he thought to replenish his wine stores. It was imported from the Rhineland and he could only get it in Hedeby or from Dorestad in Frisia. He always insisted on sampling the wine first, trusting no one else to buy it for him. Dorestad was near the Rhineland, so the prices would be lower, but he had a shipload of cargo to take to Hedeby. It was closer and the trading there would make the trip worthwhile financially. He'd promised Elfwynn that when he went there, he would take her.

The stab of longing startled him. As though he missed her already, which was ridiculous. He never missed a woman. If a certain one was not available, he asked another to join him. Each one brought his body different pleasures.

Elfwynn might not bring pleasure to his body, but she pleased him with her mind. Their verbal sparring was as exhilarating as any sword training. Her quick wit and sharp word jabs were exercise for his thoughts and he'd found himself missing that while he'd been gone. It was interesting, but no doubt her sharp attitude would become tiresome eventually.

He smiled to himself at that thought. "Besides, Thorir, I wouldn't foist her on anyone I counted as a friend. She's beautiful, yes, but acerbic. Her tongue is sharper than any sword and she'll slice you to ribbons with it. I don't gag her because I'll be rid of her soon enough, though it has crossed my mind more than once. I put her in a house down the road and that's still too close for me. I value our alliance and friendship too well to risk selling her to you. In revenge, you'd attack me and decimate my lands in very short order."

"I'll take your warning to heart, then." He raised his cup to Rorik. "Besides, I'm not looking for a slave or concubine. I'm searching for a wife, a sweet one. Mine died of the fever two years ago. I loved her well, though she never gave me children. But now I must think of my legacy and find a woman I can get on well with. I hear you have two sisters."

At least Thorir was backing off of his interest in Elfwynn. He was an honorable man and would make a fine husband, but neither of his sisters would make good wives. "I doubt that would be wise and for much the same reasons. You saw my sister, Kaia, when she served us the horns of wine. She's a shieldmaiden and won't surrender to any man willingly, for she's chosen not the couch but the kill. The only man she'll consider is the one who can best her in a fight. So far, no one has. Kaia would be far from the sweet wife you want."

"I can see that. She's very beautiful, but a shieldmaiden? They're said to be quite vicious."

"They are. Five others fight for me along with Kaia and I can attest to that. Of all the women I've been with, I've been with none of *them*. I'd want them beside me in battle, but not in bed."

"What of your other sister?"

"Ellisif. She's a wise woman of the forest."

Thorir turned to him. "I've heard of them, but have never seen one. Does she truly run with wolves?"

He grimaced. "She has two of them. Freki and Geri, named after Odin's wolves. Raised them from pups after the Wanderer she knows found the mother dead. She has a stunning, brilliant mind, but lives alone in the woods. I built her a house there under the condition she lives in it, not in a cave with the animals, and that she comes back to Vargfjell during the winters. I don't want her out there during the snows. She's an excellent hunter. When she encounters my huntsmen in the mountains to replenish our meat, she joins in. You may meet her yet, but she's very reclusive. Again, not what you're looking for."

"You have an interesting family." He took a drink.

Thorir didn't know the half of it. Rorik sighed as he toyed with the remains of his dinner. Few people knew why he and his sisters were . . . interesting. He couldn't press either of them into marriage for the same reason he couldn't wed. They understood each other all too well, the darkness of their shared past forming a shield wall around them few others ever breached.

He waited as long as was polite, then, with a grin, excused himself to go outside. Thorir was listening to Leif, the gods help him, and seemed to be enjoying the tall—and probably untrue—tale he was telling.

He headed down the road toward Oslafa's house. Perhaps he could find out if he had anything to worry about between Elfwynn and Turold. Though it was midevening, there was still enough light for him to see she was alone, sitting on a bench with her eyes closed. At first it appeared she was sleeping, but as he drew nearer, she opened them and watched him.

He sat beside her. Neither of them spoke. The quiet of the night was calming and he relaxed back against the wall in the same way she did. As he breathed in her scent of flowers and warm breezes, all the tension drained out of him. Did she do this to him? Or was he simply tired at the end of a very long day?

Whenever he was around others, he was required to be the lord, the hardened raider, or the cunning merchant. With his women, he had to be the consummate lover, tireless and uninhibited. He couldn't let down his shield for a moment, lest others see it as weakness and take advantage of him. But now, here with her, he could simply be. And again, it was a new experience.

If only he could bring her a smile, something to make her happy as he did all other women, it would please him even more. For her, there was only one way to do that.

"I'll have to go to Hedeby sooner than I thought. Within a few weeks."

"Oh?" She didn't move.

Though the words stuck in his throat, he spoke them. "I haven't forgotten our agreement. I'll take you with me. First I have to make certain the situation here is stable, then I can leave for a short time. As I told you, I always honor my word."

She sighed. "So you did. Thank you."

The question burned in him, to see what she would answer. It shouldn't matter, but it did.

"I saw Turold escort you out. The feast had hardly begun and yet you left with him. Why?"

She hesitated, twisting the ends of the tablet-worked belt she wore. "I didn't feel well. He offered to walk me here since there were so many other warriors about. I don't know where he went after that."

She wasn't telling the truth. Christians believed they would burn after death if they lied. Because of that, many of them were terrible at it. Including her.

Why was he pursuing this? It was only going to anger her. It was as though, deep inside, he didn't feel he deserved the peace she'd just brought him. The questions continued to come, like prodding an aching tooth.

"Are you interested in him?"

She straightened and glared at him. "I don't believe that's any of your business."

"I believe it is. Your purity is important, according to your church, which means you're worth more to me if you're untouched."

"How do you know I'm untouched?"

"There's always a way to find out." At the look of panic she gave him, he softened and brushed her arm with his fingers. "I only meant there are women who can find out these things. But I don't need them. You're a virgin. With as much experience as I have with women, I know."

"I would think the only experience you have is with those who aren't pure."

"And how better to tell the ones who are? You needn't worry. I avoid virgins. Why ride an unbroken mare who doesn't know what you want, when you can enjoy one who knows how to respond to your slightest command?"

She stood, blushing. "And you have quite the stable of them. So I suggest you go back to the barn and choose the one you want to ride for the night." She rushed into the house, slamming the door behind her.

He leaned forward, his elbows on his knees, his face in his hands. As stimulating as his verbal wars with her were, the brief moment of peace before was even more enticing. And yet, he'd sabotaged it, goading her into a confrontation. Didn't he deserve to rest? He had lights and laughter, feasts and riches. It was all fleeting, so very fleeting. Didn't he deserve the moments of deeper joy others took for granted? Apparently, not even he believed so.

He'd had it for only a few breaths. And now he had promised to send her, and the strange peace surrounding her, far from him forever. He'd send her into her chance for happiness, and away from his.

Chapter Seven

Thorir threw the spear at Rorik as their men shouted.

It came, straight and true, directly at him. Rorik shifted to the side, spinning at the same time, and caught it as it passed him. He continued the movement and hurled it back at the jarl. Thorir stepped back, knocking it aside with his shield. It skittered away, harmless.

Thorir laughed as he struck his shield with his hand. "That's a good trick. The old tales tell of such tactics, but I never knew a man who could do them. I'll have to learn it."

"I can teach you sometime. Now you'll have to show me how you fight with two swords." He'd suggested they train for part of the morning. It would let him see what Thorir and his men were made of, what kind of support he could expect from them. Now that his blood was up, showing a few tricks wasn't going to wear off the edge.

"I'll have one of my men spar with me."

Rorik unsheathed his sword. "No, I'd like to try facing you. It'll be interesting."

"It'll be a risk."

"I've fought from the western isles to the desert lands and I've encountered many types of fighting. I'm still alive. Unlike them, you're not trying to kill me."

Thorir grinned and drew his sword as one of his men brought a second one to him. He dropped his shield and hefted them. Rorik smiled back. A good warrior used his shield as well as his sword or axe to attack, and a man had to watch both. This would be little different. Except both weapons had a sharp edge.

He met Thorir and raised his shield, but not too high. That would leave his legs unprotected. It was a mistake men made when they were uncertain of themselves. He wasn't.

Thorir brought his right sword around toward Rorik. He didn't need to see the weapon, only where the jarl's upper arm moved. He blocked it with his shield while arcing his blade to meet Thorir's. They met in a hail of sparks. Rorik shoved both swords away from him. Moving slower than he would in true battle, he cut at Thorir's legs while sweeping his own shield to the side. The jarl leaped back, crossing his swords between them. He pulled them apart. Rorik had to step back or risk his sword hand being caught between them.

Thorir sliced both weapons toward him. Rorik dropped as they passed over him, then rolled into the jarl, bringing him down as well. They lay on the ground for a moment, panting, then Rorik chuckled. With two blades whirling over him, it was the surest way to knock the jarl off his feet. Thorir laughed with him and their men joined in.

"What was that move?" Thorir sat up. "I've never seen it before."

"I've never done it before." Rorik rested back on his elbows. "I couldn't think of anything better at the moment. I'll teach you to catch a spear if you teach me to fight with two swords like that."

"Done." He got up and offered his hand to Rorik. He took his wrist and Thorir pulled him to his feet. "That was a good session, but we need to discuss our alliance and plans."

"After we clean up, I'll meet you in the hall. We can talk then."

Most of the men stayed to continue their sparring. Kaia and her shieldmaidens were there, as well, though they practiced on their own. Thorir's men had challenged them earlier. They had learned why none of Rorik's men were doing so and were nursing their cuts and bruises off to the side.

He might have just enough time for a steaming, if his servants had warm water ready for him to rinse off with in his private sauna. When he walked into the outer room, clean clothes were waiting. A silver cup of ale, chilled in a nearby stream, sat on a small table. He drained it. All that was missing was one of his women to help him bathe. But there was no time. His meeting with Thorir was too important.

A good fire was burning in the sauna chamber, several buckets of water beside it. The other men wouldn't be washed and ready for a short time yet. He tossed water on himself to rinse the dirt off, then poured more on the fire. Steam billowed up. He sank down on the wood bench and leaned back against the wall, as he had last night when he'd sat beside Elfwynn. If she were in here, naked, awaiting him, then Halfdan the Black, King of the Vestfold, could be in his hall and he'd not care.

He closed his eyes. To have her here, laid out on the bench, her skin slick under his hands as he ran them over her breasts, down her flat belly . . .

He'd come here to relax before the meeting, but these thoughts weren't helping. It would never happen anyhow. Not with her. She was a Christian, for one thing, and their god frowned on such pastimes. For another, she was worth more to him as a virgin.

Unless I keep her for myself. He opened his eyes and stared into the fire. No one would fault him for possessing her as a slave since her father had refused to pay her ransom. Then he would have all the time he needed to persuade her, entice her, seduce her into wanting him. He'd awaken her slowly, so slowly she wouldn't be aware of what was happening until she wanted him just as much. Then she would be his. His reputation would be secure, and so would she. He could have the best of all worlds.

Except. He leaned forward, his elbows on his knees, hands clasped together. Except he had given her his word that he would take her to Hedeby. But what did that matter? She could say nothing, do nothing if he refused. She was not one of them. The only rights she had were the ones he chose to give her.

But the sorrow, the betrayal in her eyes would be the same as what he'd seen in them when she'd learned her father had abandoned her. This time, he would have caused it. She'd hate him more than she already did. It also went against everything his aunt and uncle, Lifa and Ivar, had taught him so long ago. Keep your word, hold to your honor and, because of the love and gratitude he had for Lifa and his cousin Silvi, respect all women. Always.

He stood, lifted a bucket of water, and poured it over his head, rinsing the sweat from his body. If he broke his word to her, he would be throwing away all the beliefs Lifa had raised him to follow. He didn't have any good options. He could take her to Hedeby, keep his word, and lose the fascination and strange peace she brought him. Or he could force her to remain here for his pleasure, retain his hard-edged reputation and the approval of others, yet tear her apart.

Either way, he lost. He grimaced. Lost what? This was insane. She was but a means to an end. He'd do what he had to in order to get his money, come back to his village, his people, and his women, and move on. It was what he always did and it had suited him well enough. Until now.

Gathering his hair in front of him, he wrung it out, the water hissing onto the fire. He tossed it behind his shoulder and grabbed a towel. After drying himself, he combed his hair, dressed in his fine clothes, then went into the hall.

The servants had set the table that stood in the center of the room with shining platters of bread, butter, fruit, nuts and cheese along with pitchers of chilled ale and beer. He and Thorir would sit opposite each other, neither being at the head of the table. Their men would sit to either side of them. He'd wanted Kaia to be there as well, as commander of the shieldmaidens. If it came to war, they'd fight also.

As he passed the door to the weaving room, he glanced in. Only one woman stood at the looms. Elfwynn. He couldn't imagine what she was weaving, but the cloth was very long. It was rolled up on the top bar, so he couldn't see what its length was, but there was a great deal of material there.

The rest of the looms stood idle. Odd. He'd noticed it the other day, but with the jarl here, he had forgotten to ask Kolla why they'd stopped their work. After the meeting, he'd have to attend to village matters.

He paused. He could go in and speak with Elfwynn, but it would only end in a fight, as always. Of course, then it would show Thorir he was telling the truth about her temper.

Thorir strode into the hall, his men following him, and the chance was past. Rorik sat at the table with them while the servants poured the ale and beer. Kaia settled beside him, eyeing Leif as though daring him to crack a joke. Leif met her stare, his eyes crinkling at the corners, his lips twitching. What was that all about?

"The situation with Oddr and Kolbienn has become troublesome." Thorir took a hunk of cheese from one of the platters as the other men grabbed for the food and drink. "They've skirted the edge of my land for the past year, but they've never encroached onto yours until this summer."

"Have you faced off against them?" Rorik waited as a servant set full plates in front of Thorir and him. "Do you know yet how strong their forces are?"

"Strong enough to think they can come up against both of us. That may be recent."

"They're getting help from somewhere else."

"Agreed."

A nasty feeling twisted Rorik's gut. "Halfdan. As king, he controls the Vestfold in the south, but has spread his interest to Sogn and now he's eyeing the wealth of the north. It has furs, sea ivory, hides, down, and timber. Perhaps we've become too strong and he fears we'll control the routes along the coast in this region and block his access. My own ancestors, and those of Lade, came together from the Malangenfjorden for this very reason. They needed to control the sea routes from Troms, north of Hålogaland, to the markets in the south. So they settled here." He shook his head. "To challenge Halfdan would take more strength than even I have."

"But not more than both of us. I don't think he'd be concerned by one of us, but he may have heard we've started an alliance and he fears our combined power."

"Then he's going about it the wrong way. It's only driving us together to make a stand."

"He can't be certain of that." Leif took a hunk of bread from a platter. "He might be using Oddr and Kolbienn to test you. Give them enough men to poke at you and see what comes of it. Have there been any actual settlers on your lands?"

"Not as yet." Rorik pried open a walnut shell with his knife. "We've found evidence that they've started building. Foundations, fencing, and such. No people as yet."

Leif smeared honey on the bread. "And were these places along your borders?"

"Most, yes." Thorir straightened, his eyes narrowing. "They're trying to make it appear as though we're each moving in on the other."

"They want to see whether we'll fight among ourselves or not," Rorik said. "They don't realize how skilled my patrols are. They've seen the jarls' men. If we were so foolish as to attack each other, the destruction would be complete."

"And the king could move in." Kaia stabbed the table with her eating knife. "Control this region and its farmlands and wealth. He's seeking to expand out of the south."

"I'm no king," Rorik said. "But I'll face one any day to protect what is mine."

Leif snorted. "You may as well be one. I've never seen such wealth as you have here and Halfdan may want some of it eventually. That includes your farmlands, ships, and power. What about Lade? They're your neighbor also and a rising power here."

"They have their lands and we have ours. We've always lived in peace with them since the early days. As long as they don't interfere with our access to the sea, it will stay that way."

"There are times I'm grateful to my ancestors for settling as far into the interior as they did," Leif said. "It kept us out of the eye of kings and other jarls, as they intended. We had enough trouble with our own neighbors."

"I say we strike Oddr and Kolbienn. Now. With all force." Thorir's golden eyes were hard. "That will give the king his answer. Then we can take their lands and people and become even stronger."

The men sitting to either side of them shouted, banging their knives and cups on the table, but Rorik held up his hand.

"We can take the jarls. The problem is the men Halfdan will send to back them up. We should consider stopping them before they get to this region. They'll come by sea and that's where we can block them and defeat them. To do this would take every ship we both have and then some. Many of my warriors are off raiding, but they'll be back soon. Once they return with their cargos, I'll keep them here to add to our strength. But right now, my numbers are down."

"And if you strike with all your forces," Leif said, "the king may find out just how strong you are. That's likely what he wants. Never show all your pieces on the board."

"So what do we do in the meantime?" Thorir frowned. "Let them encroach on us? Make us look weak?"

"Let them think that for now. And they're not truly encroaching, are they?" Rorik tore off a chunk of bread and reached for the butter. "They just want us to think they are. I say we let them continue. Not provoke a battle. Not until *we're* ready. Let my ships and men return in the coming weeks and build our strength. I'd wager you have ships out also and we'll wait on them. In the meantime, we won't sit idle. I'll send some men south to study Oddr, where his strengths and weaknesses are, how many men he has. Thorir, you'll do the same with Kolbienn to the south of your lands. I'll also send a couple of my smaller ships to scout along the coast, asking fishermen and farmers what they've seen. We'll call on our allies, then meet again when all our forces are at their strongest. What say you?"

Thorir studied him, his fingers drumming on the table. "Agreed. But this needs to be done by the end of the warm season."

Rorik nodded. "Our attack on the king's ships will be, but his eye may not turn from us even then. There's too much wealth here. We can hold off the inevitable for a time, perhaps even years. But one day, I think that, even if we manage to turn him away, our sons or their sons may not. And those in Lade may grow into a major power. Eventually, they may seek an agreement with Halfdan to keep the peace."

"I'm only concerned with the now," Kaia said. "And I say we contact Eirik, ask for his help. He'll give it."

"He also gave three of his ships and a large number of his men to my brother as Silvi's dowry." Leif grinned. "It looks as though I'll have to send a message to Magnus as well, asking for help. He can find out what people have seen along the Sognefjorden where Halfdan is said to be settling in. They'll have no reason to love him and Magnus is well respected there, especially after the *thing* when he acquitted himself so well. We'll all be together again, only this time it's a war, not a wedding. Much the same thing, only the war is more fun."

"For once, I agree with you." Kaia took a deep drink, then bared her teeth in a grimace. "That's depressing."

They all laughed and Rorik relaxed a bit. The difficult part was out of the way now. At least they'd agreed and not tried to kill each other over the table, though with the glare Kaia was giving Leif, he might be premature with that.

A movement near the door drew Rorik's attention. Turold came in and skirted into the weaving room. A moment later, he left—with Elfwynn. She was laughing very softly at something he said to her. Rorik nearly growled. She never did that with him. In fact, he'd never heard her laugh at all. They walked outside, heads bowed together.

"It looks as though your lands aren't the only things being encroached upon." Thorir smiled as he lifted his cup. Leif choked out a laugh. Even Kaia grinned and nudged him.

Rorik ground his teeth together as he looked at the empty doorway. Turold, Kaia, Leif, Thorir, it didn't matter. Perhaps it wasn't too late to spill some blood after all.

The knock on the door startled Elfwynn as she sorted threads. She was going to give another demonstration of embroidery to the women that evening and needed to gather her supplies.

She didn't have a chance to answer. The door opened and Rorik strode in. He appeared so much bigger in the small house than he did in the vast hall. He glanced around, as though searching for something. Or someone.

No doubt he'd seen Turold and her leaving the longhouse together, which was just what they wanted. It would throw anyone off his trail with Finna.

She gave him a sweet smile. "If you're looking for Oslafa, she's not here. Can I help you?"

"Are you alone?"

She raised her brows and made a show of looking around the single room, even checking under the table. "I would say so. Unless there's someone stuffed inside the thatch on the roof."

He chewed the inside of his cheek for a moment. "I came to tell you that I have to get more wine, and I have other goods to take to Hedeby. We're leaving in a week."

She nodded. It should make her happy to get away from this place and back with other Christians, if not her family. But with the unexpected kindness and generosity of the people and the beauty of the land, she'd found a certain contentment here. And yet, this wasn't about her. Her mother would be pining for her, perhaps getting even weaker. Wulf had said he'd never give up on her if anything happened. She had to go back for their sakes, even if it meant facing her father.

She swallowed the lump in her throat. "I'll be ready whenever you are."

He stepped toward her until she had to look up at him. He towered over her, but she stood her ground, not giving him the satisfaction of stepping back. "I don't want Turold taking liberties where you're concerned."

"He's making certain I get home safely after I weave for the day. With what happened with those bondsmen and all the unfamiliar warriors here now, he's watching over me."

"I'll assign a man of my own to guard you."

"And, no doubt keep an eye on me, as well."

"Is there a reason I need to keep you out of trouble?"

"The only one here who causes me trouble, Northman, is you."

He took a step closer and his gaze dropped to her mouth. "Little Christian, I can show you just what kind of trouble I could be."

She wavered. What would it be like to let him kiss her? His clean scent of the sea and the wind would wrap around her like his arms. His strength would fill her as she opened to him. But he'd used the sea and the wind to take her away from all she loved. His strength gave him the ability. Everything he was had taken away everything she loved.

Glaring up at him, she spoke low. "I've seen you with your women in the hall. I don't need any more of a demonstration than that."

"There's seeing, and then there's doing."

"Whatever I do, it won't be with you."

"It had better not be with Turold either. Until I have my money, you're mine in trade for my burned ship. Don't forget it." He pivoted toward the door, but she followed him a few steps.

"I thought I was a guest. You speak as if I'm a slave."

He turned back to her. "Right now, you're a means to an end. Your only value to me lies in your purity." He hesitated, as though he was uncertain of himself. Then he walked to her and lifted a hand to her cheek. His thumb brushed her skin. "But you make it harder and harder to remember that."

His touch was so gentle, she barely felt it on her skin, but it hit her inside like a bolt of lightning. She opened her mouth to retort that he'd best improve his memory, but the words never came. As he leaned toward her, she remained where she was, gazing up at him. He looked again at her mouth, then lower, and his hand cupped her face more firmly, as though he wanted to hold her still.

A sensation built in her, but what was it? She trembled, and it wasn't from fear. As she shuddered, something flickered in his eyes. Doubt? He took a breath and the spell was broken.

She backed away and his hand fell to his side.

"One week." Her voice shook. "Only one more week. Then you won't have to remember me any longer."

He inclined his head. "Yes. But then there are the days, and nights, on the ship. Why do I feel that, of all the voyages I've taken, this is the one I won't soon forget?"

As he left, she sank down on the bench at the table. There was a tone to his voice, a poignancy, that had pierced her. Did he truly speak of journeys across the sea, or did he speak of something else? He'd been with so many women. Was he talking about them? She shook her head. With all his conquests, he had no reason to remember her. She was a ransom to be paid. That was all.

She continued to sort the pile of threads on the table, then stopped and touched her lips. She should have let him kiss her, just this once. To see what it was like. Where else could she know the touch of such a wild, powerful, beautiful man? But then, she'd have to leave him behind forever and never know such a moment again.

With everything she'd been through since her father's betrayal, that would hurt her most of all.

The longhouse was quiet, a rarity even this late at night. Oslafa had told her that unlike most other longhouses, no one slept in Rorik's. It was the village's center for gatherings, meals, socializing, and meetings. The people had their own houses scattered along the shoreline and farther inland. Only Rorik, Kaia, and several other high-ranking people had small rooms to themselves off the hall.

Still, there were usually men drinking well into the night. Thorir and his men had returned home, so things were much quieter now and the peace enveloped her as she walked inside. She wove every chance she had, to finish as much of the cloth as she could before she left. Sleep had eluded her this night, so she had come here to work.

As she passed the harp leaning against the wall, she paused. Could she ever play again? It had always brought her such joy and was one of the few things that made her mother smile. Even Wulf often sat in their house and listened to her in the evenings.

She made the music. It wasn't born of her father. True, he had given her the harp, but her fingers created the notes and the melodies. They were hers alone. Would it bring her restfulness?

She sat down on the small chair, picked up the instrument and set it on her thigh. The harp was similar to the one she had at home, except this one had intertwined leaves and vines woven across its front in a beautiful, intricate pattern. No doubt, Rorik or one of his forebears had stolen this in a raid someplace and no one here knew how to play. Supporting it with her left hand, she placed her fingers on the strings to mute the ones she didn't want to sound. She strummed with her right hand. It was out of tune, so she plucked the strings very gently, adjusting them.

Bowing her head, she played. The music flowed out around her, soft and lilting. She didn't want to wake anyone, so she barely touched the strings. With her eyes closed, she could almost imagine she was back home, her mother with her, Wulf smiling as she brought dreams to both of them.

She played the song over again, letting the vibrations enter her, resonate through her. The music became a part of her. When she was finished, she rested her palm against all the strings and the sound faded.

"You said you didn't play."

She snapped up her head. Rorik stood just outside the door to his chamber, dressed only in a pair of well-fitting linen trousers. His ebony hair was tousled, cascading down his muscular bare chest, his eyes sleepy. He must have been with one of his women.

Straightening, she took the harp off her lap to set it aside.

"Don't." He walked toward her. "I heard you play in a dream. I woke, but still the music continued."

She wanted to say she was surprised he found time to dream at all during the night. Instead, she watched him as he pulled up a small bench and sat down.

"Play something else. Like the song you just did."

She'd heard that note of poignancy in his voice a few days ago when he'd come to tell her they'd be leaving soon. A tint of longing. The hall was still, the only sound and illumination coming from the central hearth. The glow lingered on the planes of his beautiful face, like that of a fallen angel. Why did she have the feeling that, like the angel, there was something he wanted that he could never have again? Something sublime, of the light. It sparked in her soul.

She placed the harp back on her leg and played, choosing a song her mother loved for its beauty and tranquility. Before, she'd just brushed the strings, wanting to be quiet. Now, she gave the harp its full voice. Moving with the music, she became one with it. Her heart swelled with the notes and a tear slipped from her eye for the memory of the last time she'd played this song. It connected her to that moment, when she could never have dreamed of the next time she'd hear these notes.

She ended the song, the link with her past breaking, her head still lowered to the harp. He was silent. She didn't want to look at him, couldn't look at him. Yet, lifting only her eyes, she did.

"So beautiful." He was gazing, not at the harp, but at her. He seemed lost in a trance, but then blinked and sat up. "Thank you. I wish I'd known you played before this. I'd have asked you to do so at the feasts. Will you play tomorrow night for everyone? It will be your last evening here."

"I don't think so." She leaned the harp against the wall and stood.

He rose and came to her. "You've managed to charm everyone here. Do you know what Kolla said when I asked her yesterday why the women haven't been weaving as much lately?"

"No." She'd wondered that, herself.

"She said the women of Vargfjell don't approve of how I took you away from your home. And until I keep my word to you, they're slowing down on their work."

She looked up at him, speechless.

"You've made my own village upset with me."

"I didn't do anything on purpose. I didn't even know. I swear—"

He placed a gentle finger against her lips. "I know. It wasn't anything you did, but how you are. It was because of your kindness, generosity, and sweetness. It won them over. Tomorrow night, give them another piece of you to remember once you're gone. Play for them."

It was as though he wasn't speaking of them so much as he was speaking of himself. And yet, she hadn't been sweet to him, or kind. He *was* keeping his word to her, and it wasn't only because the women of Vargfjell were upset. He had said she was coming with him to Hedeby even before he knew about that.

She gave a soft smile. "I imagine you or one of your crazy ancestors took the harp from some hapless minstrel in my land."

"No, we didn't. It's always been here. Tomorrow, will you play at the evening meal?"

To say goodbye and thank them for all they'd done for her in making this bearable. To leave a piece of herself in a place that would always be a part of her. And to leave a memory with a man she'd never forget. She drew in a breath and looked at the harp. "I'll play."

* * *

The last notes of the song died away. There was a pause and then, throughout the hall, shouts erupted, the men slamming their sloshing cups on the tables, the women clapping. Elfwynn stood, her face heating as she listened to their cheers. It had been the same with each song she'd played for the people of the village.

Rorik's musicians had even joined in on one of her pieces. She hadn't been too certain, but they'd followed her lead with their flutes, drums, and a strange stringed instrument. To her surprise, it had worked. This song, the one she'd played for Rorik, was her last. She set the harp where it had always been.

From somewhere in the back, a man yelled, "Rorik, you better keep her. If you don't, I'll pay her ransom myself."

Another man said, "You and your sons and their sons' sons. It would take that long to make enough money."

A warrior she recognized in the front said, "If she leaves, who'll play the harp? No one has since—" A woman sitting next to him smacked him and he fell silent.

Everyone looked at Rorik as he stood. If he wanted to, he could keep her here. He smiled. "My word is my bond. All of you know that. I have made a promise, and so it will be. She leaves with us tomorrow."

Groans echoed through the hall, but it was good-natured. She held up her hand.

"Thank for your good wishes. I have already said my farewells to most of you. And the rest I'll see tomorrow before I leave." To her shock, tears welled up. Rather than embarrass herself in front of them, she inclined her head and left.

She hurried down the road, but a strong hand caught her arm. She reached for her knife, but Rorik grabbed her hand.

"You haven't killed me thus far. It's a bit late to try now."

She relaxed and he let go of her. "I didn't know it was you. You might have said something."

"If I had known Kaia had done so well teaching you, I would have." He looked down at her, his face grim. "You know, you could stay here. You have the entire village wrapped around your finger. I could use another weaver of your skill. I saw what you were working on and I've never seen the like. There are several grades of quality in the cloth at the markets and the length you have on the loom would fetch the highest prices."

"That's for Oslafa in thanks for making me dresses." She smoothed her skirt, but her heart pounded. He wouldn't take it for himself, would he?

"I know it's hers. But if you stayed, you could make more, teach my weavers how you do it."

"I already have. They've watched me design the pattern."

"And, no doubt, you know even more. I'd give you your own house, even your own loom if you want. You'd be held in very high esteem here."

It was tempting. To be someone accepted, welcomed. The people here had become friends. But there was someone who needed her. Her mother. Every day she was away, Rohesia might be fading even more. She couldn't tell him of her. He'd wonder how she'd get home from Hedeby. Then she'd have to tell him of her silver and gold, and that was a secret she'd kept from everyone there.

"I thank you for your offer, but I can't. I hope to return to Northumbria one day."

He speared his hand through his hair. "I can't understand why you'd want to go back to a father who doesn't want you. What did you have there?"

The pain of his words struck her hard and she jabbed a finger in his chest. "No matter what my life was like, it was *my* life. At least until you came along. Who are you to judge whether it was good or bad? I may not have had servants anticipating my every whim and lovers lying at my feet every night like you do, but I was happy. Who were you to take me from it against my will?"

"You offered. Don't forget that."

"So you wouldn't destroy it all. What choice did I have? I may not be there, but at least everything I love still is."

"Then that's all, isn't it? I'll see you home. But, I forgot, it's not your home." He looked at her, his jaw hard. Then he pivoted and headed up the road. She caught up to him and they walked to the house, silence stretching between them.

When they arrived, he opened the door for her. "We leave after the morning meal. I'll send someone for your things then."

She nodded and went past him into the house. She lifted her hand to the door to shut it. Before she realized his was there, she placed hers on top of it. She moved her hand, but he took hold of it and held it. Breathing hard, she looked up at him.

If she stayed, she'd see him each day, his smile, his confidence. Perhaps she might even taste his kiss. And risk falling in love with him. In spite of how angry he made her at times, it would be so easy, as so many other women had learned. And she would never be one of the many. It would kill her, the way her mother's unrequited love for her father had leeched the life from her.

With a slight smile, he turned her hand and placed a kiss on the palm. Then he closed her fingers over it as though to keep it there always. "I'll see you tomorrow."

After he left, she shut the door. She opened her hand, looking at the place where his lips had been. One of the many. Her pride would never allow her to accept that.

Besides, to remain here would be to leave her mother to her fate, as her father had left her to this fate. At least she could take with her the memories of these good people, the cool beauty of the land, and a tiny, gentle kiss given in the night.

She closed her hand.

Chapter Eight

Off the village of Haardvik
Hardangerfjorden, Norway

As Rorik guided his ship toward the shore, Eirik, Asa, and Lifa waited for him on the cliff above. He didn't see Magnus or Silvi, so they must have returned to Thorsfjell. It was a good thing, then, he'd sent one of his smallest ships there. The two vessels had traveled together from Vargsfjell until they'd reached the Sognefjorden. Then the other ship had peeled off for the one day journey to the end of the fjord where Thorsfjell was. There, his men would ask for Magnus's help in the coming battle.

Rorik lifted his hand in greeting as they drew closer. He'd ask Eirik for aid. His cousin might not have all his ships and men for the time being, but he had the largest, most impressive longship in the north, *The Wind of Njord*. When it pulled into the Trøndheimsfjorden, word would spread, eventually reaching Halfdan himself. That word would be a powerful message.

His ship slid up onto the beach, next to the massive warship. Elfwynn stood in the bow. She'd kept to herself most of the voyage, doing needlework and watching the land pass them by as they'd sailed down the coast. She'd given the pieces she'd worked on to his men to give to their wives and lovers. Or to women they wanted to become their wives and lovers. They'd gone out of their way to make her comfortable, rigging a tent for her, filling it with furs and blankets.

On the way to Vargfjell, he hadn't stopped here, even though they could have used the fresh provisions for the remainder of the trip. Lifa would have had his head for what he'd done to Elfwynn. He couldn't face her then. But now, he was returning her to her church.

His aunt would still have something to say about it, but wouldn't try to interfere. After all, he was doing what Elfwynn had agreed to, and her god was getting her back.

He walked forward through the sea chests, ropes, and oars until he reached her. "I'll help you off. It's only knee deep here, but it's a ways down."

She peered over the side. "How do you know how deep it is?"

"The keels are a standard depth. We know if the ships are beached, we can jump off the bows safely and not be over our heads in water while an enemy is coming."

"You mean, while you're raiding?" She gave him a wry smile.

He chuckled. "Something like that."

She looked up the cliff as Eirik walked down the narrow path to meet them. "Are these your relatives you told me about?"

"Yes, this is Haardvik. We'll be here only a day or so while I speak to my cousin Eirik about the situation with the southern jarls. He's the jarl here and is married to Leif's sister, Asa. She's the woman on the cliff with the red hair. Asa's a shieldmaiden, like Kaia. Let's get you on the beach." He picked her up without warning so she couldn't try to escape, then swung his legs over the side and jumped off. She gave a yelp and wrapped her arms around his neck while he waded to shore. He set her on the beach as Eirik strode up to them.

They clasped wrists. "Rorik, welcome. We saw your ship on the fjord and I ordered food and drink prepared." Eirik gave Elfwynn a questioning look.

"My thanks, Eirik. I'm having trouble with jarls to the south of me, but it may be bigger than that. I need your help."

"You have it."

Rorik nodded his thanks. "This is Elfwynn of Northumbria. I'm taking her to Hedeby and wanted to stop here first to speak to you."

She smiled. "I've heard much of Haardvik. It's good to be here." She was getting very proficient with Norse.

"My mother and wife are above, no doubt bursting to find out who you are. Come, have something to eat and drink, and we'll take your things to your rooms."

"We must leave tomorrow, so we won't unload much." They started up the steep path. He walked behind Elfwynn to steady her if necessary. "I have to get to Hedeby and back as soon as possible."

"Then we'll grab some food and meet right now. Leif isn't with you?"

"He remained behind at Vargfjell. I sent a ship to Magnus to ask for his aid. Leif could have gone home with them, but he said if there was going to be a war, he didn't want to risk missing the fun."

"That sounds like Leif." Eirik chuckled.

When they reached the top of the cliff, Lifa and Asa were waiting for them.

"Rorik." His dark-haired aunt embraced him. All his anxieties melted away as her sweet scent came to him. She'd been his green, sheltered valley when all else had been bleak, frozen storms in his mind. If only he could have that all the time. But he only found it here.

Except those few moments at Vargfjell, when that same peace had enfolded him. When he'd been with Elfwynn. Soon she'd be gone and it would never come again.

He stepped back. "Lifa, Asa, this is Elfwynn. Since I'll be leaving her in your tender care, I'm certain she'll tell you why she's with me. But I'm remedying that now." They were going to throw him in the longhearth for this anyhow. Might as well own up to it.

Lifa raised her brows and Asa narrowed her eyes at him. Already, they were plotting his demise if they didn't like what they heard from Elfwynn. And they wouldn't.

He looked at Elfwynn. "Do you mind going with them? They'll see to making you comfortable. I have to confer with my cousin."

Her eyes glittered as though she was about to make some retort. But then she smiled. "Of course, Rorik. I'm certain I'll be fine."

He gave her a lingering look. She didn't need to offer him one of her verbal stabbings. She'd have plenty of time to seek her revenge when she spoke with the two women. His stomach dipped as he went into the longhouse with Eirik. Perhaps he could leave her here, sail away, and never return. What had he been thinking, coming here first? He should have waited until his return trip, when she wasn't with him.

He ignored the emptiness that thought gave him. Eirik needed to know about the jarls as soon as possible so he could gather his men and make the voyage to Vargfjell. By the time Rorik got back from Hedeby, everyone should be there, or well on their way.

They settled in Eirik's meeting room with their plates of food, cups, and a pitcher of beer. He told him about Thorir and their alliance, and about the situation with the southern jarls.

"I know Halfdan has a presence in Sogn," Eirik said. "I can practically hear him breathing as he passes us while heading up the coast. Do you think he's after your lands?"

"I think, right now, he's afraid of this alliance between Thorir and me. That we'll block the routes to the north and all the walrus ivory, hides, and furs there. He might be trying to bring us down or divide us."

"Then why wouldn't he have Herlaugsson of Lade do it? They're powerful, like you."

"My family has been on good terms with them for generations. We have a long history together. Even when my father fell and they could have taken everything, they didn't."

"That's because my father held Vargfjell for you, until you came of age."

Shadows of that time moved over him, but he shook them off. "Still, they could have tried for it, but didn't. I think Halfdan knows better than to try to divide us."

"So he bought himself two dogs who want to impress him by doing his bidding."

"Yes."

"You might make an enemy of the king."

"Only if he wants to admit what he's doing. I don't think he will. That's why he's not coming at us himself. It would make all the smaller kings throughout our land restless and wary. He doesn't want that."

"No, he wouldn't." He sat back. "I don't know how much help I can be. I have the *Wind*, of course, but I gave my three other ships to Magnus as Silvi's dowry, and I'm still building replacements. The warriors to crew them went with them until he attracts more of his own."

"And they'll be there, just through Magnus instead of you. I'm certain Halfdan will send men to one of the smaller fjords along the coast and they'll travel overland to the south of me. We'll attack before that. We'll use the *Wind* as our flagship since it's the largest. You need a lot of men to sail her, so they'll add to the numbers." He took a sip of his beer.

"True. Of course, I'll come. And I'm certain Asa won't want to miss a good fight, either."

At Eirik's mention of his shieldmaiden wife, Rorik grimaced. She'd be talking to Elfwynn, finding out why she was with him. He should have worn his sword. Then he'd at least stand a chance when he next saw Asa.

"Either you don't like the beer, or something else."

"The beer's fine, as always. It's Elfwynn."

"When you left here, you said you were going to ransom a daughter of the earl who burned your ship. I take it Elfwynn is the daughter and things didn't go quite as you planned."

"That's putting it mildly." Eirik would find out soon enough. Rorik wanted to tell his side of the story. While he still could.

Over another couple of cups of beer, he told him everything from the start. He hadn't intended to tell him of the feelings Elfwynn gave him, but he had come here long ago when all in his life was darkness and rage. Haardvik was his haven. He'd always been able to talk to Eirik, both while they were young, and even later while they were raiding throughout the world together for three years. Fighting beside him had infused a deep trust in him. And Eirik wouldn't judge him, any more than Lifa would. Asa, on the other hand . . .

He shouldn't have left his sword on the ship.

Eirik was grinning at him when he'd finished. "You've put your foot in a big pile of it this time."

"I spill my guts to you and that's all you have to say?"

"I don't have to say anything else. You're troubled enough by what you've done. If you weren't, you wouldn't be so conflicted about it."

He clenched his fist on the table. "I did what I had to. Our reputation is everything we are. How could I maintain my power if men saw me as weak? They follow the strongest leader, the one who can pass along his wealth and prestige to them. If I get nothing from the loss of my ship, everyone will say I'm slipping, afraid to take revenge however I can get it. I rule the seas by fear and respect, Eirik. Not by how nice I am."

"Leadership is a balance. If it weren't, my father would have let you remain as you were when you came here—like your father. You could have ruled with terror and brutality as he did. My parents tempered that. They showed you the other side of leading and ruling, and look where it's brought you. You have to walk both sides of the blade."

"I'm giving her back to her own people, aren't I? Yes, it's for money. But at least she'll be safe and I'll have my ransom. We both win."

"Or you both lose."

"Even if I were to forego the ransom and take her to Northumbria, there's her bastard of a father to contend with. He didn't want her back. With everything my sisters and I went through, how can I return her to that? Who knows what atrocities she lived with? She's safer with her church."

"Why don't you tell her how you feel?"

"First, she'd kill me with her derision. Second, what *do* I feel, Eirik? I'm attracted to her, but I'm attracted to many, many women. She's a Christian. They expect monogamy, the gods forefend." He rose and paced away from the table toward the far wall.

Eirik laughed. "So do we, if we know what's good for us. Asa keeps her sword by the bed."

Rorik turned back to him and leaned against the wall, his arms crossed. "She has no worries where you're concerned. Even I can see it, as depressing as that is. We had some good times with a lot of women while we were raiding."

"Yes, we did. But there comes a time when you find the one who's different from all the rest. The one who changes everything. Then you know."

"What if I don't want to change anything? My women please me and I please them."

"You spoke of how Elfwynn gives you peace, even though she fights with you. The other women bring you pleasure, yes. But they do nothing for you deep inside. If they did, Elfwynn wouldn't intrigue you as she does, and you wouldn't still be unsatisfied. Can you truly say you bring your women happiness? I'm certain you bring your bevy of women passion, but each one knows she's one of many. How happy can they be? They say nothing to you, though, but do you blame them? If one of them mentioned it, you'd drop her because you don't tolerate jealousy. That doesn't stop them from feeling it. Just as they do little for your mind, you may be doing little for theirs."

He stared at Eirik. He'd never looked at it that way. Every night was a feast, a celebration. His women laughed with him, preened, and acted as though they were enjoying themselves. Then he picked one, or more, and the enjoyment continued through the night. On the outside. What if, all this time, he'd been cruel to them without even realizing it?

"Any one of them can leave me if she wants. And some have. They've found men who will marry them and I wish them well."

"And do you think that makes them feel better, to know you felt so little for them that it didn't bother you when they left?"

He wiped his hand over his face. The last thing he ever wanted to do was hurt a woman. Any woman. Had he been doing that all along? He pushed away from the wall and walked toward the table.

"Rorik, why don't you speak to Elfwynn? Test the depths of the waters, so to speak."

"I'm not looking for a wife. You know why." He sat across from Eirik.

"So you'll not risk passing on your father's blood. But you're not your father. If you were, it would have shown up by now."

"You don't know that."

"I know if you don't see to your legacy, Vargfjell and its people will fall into another's hand. The jarls of Lade, any number of petty kings, Halfdan, or someone worse." Eirik poured more beer into their cups.

"Then I need someone who will be strong enough to stand at my side. And strong enough to deal with me."

"You're right. Not someone who is intelligent, beautiful, talented, and can be an asset to Vargfjell. Whom its people have already fallen in love with, and who can stand toe to toe with a feared Northman who has faced off against kings and pirates all over the world. A woman of strength, conviction, and pride. If everything you've told me about her is correct, that is. No, Rorik, you don't need a woman like that. Like everything Elfwynn is." He raised his cup to Rorik and took a drink.

"She despises me and I don't blame her. All she wants from me is to take her to Hedeby."

"So you're not even going to speak to her about it? Just let her slip through your fingers? This is a first. I've never seen you give up something you wanted."

"And you've never seen me go back on my word. It's part of what earns me the respect I have. You're right. There are two sides of leadership. It's as hard as the iron grip, and as soft as the spoken word. To my people, my family, my warriors, I've always kept my promises. Just words. But they are as binding as chains and in this, I have no choice.

"For her sake, and for my own, I'm letting her go."

"I'm going to kill him."

Asa stood caressing her seax, a glint in her eye.

"Now, Asa." Lifa took hold of her wrist and pulled her hand from the hilt. "Elfwynn's a Christian and that's not what they do. At least, not the women. Usually. She might not understand it if you slay the man she—" Lifa smiled. "The man she might be a bit fond of."

Heat rose in Elwynn's cheeks. Lifa projected a calmness around her. She listened, not just with her ears, but with her soul. She was a pagan priestess, and the Church would say she was damned and in league with the devil. But surely that could not be right. No one who was evil could be so kind, so understanding. Elfwynn bit her lip. She'd blurted out far more than she'd meant to when Lifa had asked her about why she was with Rorik.

"I don't want to cause a family rift. Even if I were fond of him, as you say, I won't be one of many."

Asa beamed at her as she sat back down at the table. "Now you're talking like a shieldmaiden."

"I don't mean to." She ducked her head, then looked up at Asa with a slight smile. "But Kaia did show me how to use a knife to defend myself."

"I knew I liked her," Asa said. "She should have also taught you that if you want something, you must take it."

She shook her head. "I can't. Not with Rorik. I'm a Christian, and he's . . . not."

Asa snorted. "My mother was a Christian from Ireland and my father was a raider. He took her for ransom, as Rorik did you, but fell in love with her. Her ransom became her dowry. They lived very well together until he died while on a trading voyage, and then she returned to her homeland."

Lifa gave her a beautiful, gentle smile. "So you see, it can happen. And it does. More often than people think."

"Perhaps. If both of them want it. Even if I did, and I'm not saying I do, he doesn't. All I want is to put this behind me."

Lifa and Asa looked at each other. Lifa sighed. "You must find your own way, Elfwynn. If it is meant to be, then events will align that way."

Asa frowned. "Lifa—"

"No, Asa. It is the way of the *wyrd*, the fate. Or, in Elfwynn's case, the will of her god. Either way, it is not ours to interfere with."

"I'd like to interfere. With a shield cracked across his foolish head." Asa slumped back in her chair, arms crossed, her dark brown eyes flashing.

"Asa, not everything can be solved with violence." Lifa gave her a hard look.

"No, but it helps. Fine. I won't interfere." She sat up. "But if we can pay the ransom—"

"No." Elfwynn shook her head. "I don't know how much a longship is, but it must be a great deal of gold. I won't be beholden to you. You have a village and people to support here and I won't have all that money wasted on me. The Church is large, wealthy. I'm one of its children. It cares for its own."

But if she could find a way, the Church wouldn't have to spend its money on her either.

"I hope, Elfwynn, you'll understand him one day." Lifa looked down, but her pain was evident. "Even with all I tried to do for them, Rorik and his sisters have much darkness still within them. Their tale is one they each must tell if they wish to. It is not for me to do so." She rose. "Eirik and Rorik must be finished with their talk by now, and the meal we ordered prepared will be served soon. Elfwynn, I'm certain, would like some time in the sauna. There's still a long journey ahead of her."

Something in the way Lifa said the words made Elfwynn study the rune mistress. Was she speaking of the coming voyage to Hedeby? Or did she mean something else altogether? Lifa only held out her hand and she took it. Together, they walked out into the main hall. Eirik and Rorik were standing by the hearth, speaking with other men. They were both so fine looking, tall and powerful. There could be no doubt they were warriors.

Rorik glanced at the knife hanging below Asa's belt and appeared uncertain. Did he suspect they'd spoken about him? Eirik and he certainly had other things to speak of besides her. She was of little importance to him except as a means to an end, as he had said.

Asa went to Eirik and drew him aside. They spoke together so low she couldn't hear them, but Asa wasn't happy. For some reason, Eirik didn't appear pleased either.

Probably the talk of war had them concerned. He and Rorik, and quite likely Asa, would go to battle, and in battle people died. If Rorik fell in the coming war, she would never know it. Although the Northmen lived to fight, they still had to be concerned about those they loved.

She glanced at Rorik. In that, her people and his were very much alike.

The trading town of Hedeby
Schlei Fjord, Denmark

As they passed through the narrow strait from the fjord into the Haddeby Nor inlet, Elfwynn leaned over the side of the bow to better see the town. Rows of narrow streets ran from the shoreline into the buildings. Wooden houses lined the roads, so close their thatched roofs almost touched. It was the largest place she'd ever seen. Galinn had told her there were nearly a thousand people living there and it was one of the biggest markets in the northern lands. She couldn't imagine so great a population.

The men had furled the sail to steer into the bay, using only the oars to bring them into the piers. They pulled them in when they glided close, and men on the dock threw them lines.

"Rorik of Vargfjell." One of the men on the docks greeted him when Rorik jumped off. "What brings you here? Trading and not raiding, I hope."

Rorik laughed. "With only one ship? Just honest trading, I promise you, Rothmarr. Have to stay on Horik's good side."

"That lover of the White Christ." Rothmarr bared his teeth and lowered his voice. "They say he converted. If that's the case, his days might be numbered."

"Even if it's so, he might have done it to better deal with the Christian merchants and kings. They don't like to do business with those who have different gods than they do. His lands are very exposed to other countries and it might have been expedient, for the Christians sometimes hesitate to attack one of their own. Besides, if he does fall, his family will tear itself apart. I'm not certain that's a good thing."

Elfwynn listened as she stood on the bow. If the king of the Danes was a Christian, he might help her. If she could find him. Was he even here in Hedeby? She'd have to get off the ship to ask someone. Perhaps when Rorik went to the church, she could slip away.

In spite of what she'd said to Lifa about the Church paying her ransom, she didn't want to be the cause of such an outlay of gold. If she could get away, hide, and go to a sanctuary where she'd find help, the Church wouldn't have to pay. Then she could use her silver and the tiny bit of gold she had to buy passage back home.

As his men tied the ship to the dock, he jumped back on and came to her. "I want you to stay here. I'm going to find the church and speak to them." He searched her eyes. "If this is what you want."

She looked away from him, focusing on the water. "It is. You want your money and I want my freedom. This gives us both what we desire."

He lingered for a moment. Would he ask her to stay with him? To reconsider and go back with him to Vargfjell? Instead, he left the ship, striding toward the town. She watched him until he disappeared between two buildings.

He was so much taller than the other men, so much more powerful, beautiful . . . Everything. Life blazed from him as though his gods had poured their own spirits into him. It made him desirable and completely beyond her reach. She would never be enough for him, so this was for the best. She'd not waste her life weeping for a man as her mother had.

It took some time, but eventually all the crew had gone ashore, carrying the cargo they were going to trade. Some of them stood on the beach, speaking with merchants. Others went farther into the town, no doubt to look for items they wanted. This might be her only chance.

She'd brought all the beautiful dresses and gifts Oslafa and the people of Vargfjell gave her, but such things would only weigh her down. The Church would see to her needs. After checking to see if she had her money and the knife Kaia had given her, she wrapped a blanket around her shoulders. It hid the dress she wore so she could remain less conspicuous if anyone saw her from a distance.

Lord, protect me. Keep me hidden from those who will seek me. Guide me to where I may rest in your light once again.

She climbed onto the pier. No one called out to her, so she raised the blanket over her head like a scarf, letting it drape around her. There were other ships tied to the pier, so she might have come from any of them. If she ran, it would only call attention to her, so she walked at a steady pace until she got to the shore. A raised wooden walkway ran most of its length, and beyond that stood the buildings. She made it to the walkway and turned from where Rorik's men bartered some distance away.

Planks formed the streets and she picked the closest one. Breathing a bit easier once she got into the shelter of the buildings, she merged with a crowd of people who were moving into the town. She couldn't speak to just anyone. Rorik was too well known and people might remember her if he asked about a foreign woman alone, looking for the church.

She wandered down more streets than she could remember, looking behind her each time she made a turn. A small waterway ran through the town, and as she crossed the bridge over it, she saw the robes of a priest. He was headed away from her. Her heart pounding, she ran the rest of the way across, then skirted merchant booths and animal pens until she caught up to him.

"Father." She touched his shoulder and he turned. He was a portly, tonsured man, with a kind, round face. "The Northmen took me." She panted, speaking in her own language. "They want to ransom me to the Church here, but I got away. I seek sanctuary."

His eyes widened. "Of course, my child. Come with me. Quickly. We're not far."

She followed him through the streets, glancing over her shoulder, expecting to see Rorik striding after her. But the streets were clear. Perhaps God had heard her prayer.

The church stood just ahead of them. A cross rose above the staved roof and she'd never seen anything so beautiful. Sanctuary. While Northmen might pillage the churches of other lands, surely they wouldn't invade this one, where even the king was Christian.

The priest slid to a halt and she nearly careened into him. She peered around him, her pulse pounding in her throat.

Rorik blocked the way, his sword unsheathed, six of his men flanking him. She glanced behind her. More of them blocked her escape in the narrow street. There was no place for her to go.

"Is this the Northman who took you, my child?" The priest kept his eyes on Rorik.

"Yes, Father. He's the one."

The priest drew himself up. "Stand aside. You'll not have this precious lamb of God. She seeks sanctuary."

"But she's not at the church yet, priest. And no building will keep me from taking what is mine, no matter what symbol you put on top of it."

"You risk the fires of hell. Let us pass."

"Then your god will have to grapple with Odin for me when I die and ascend to Valhalla. Give the woman to me. I have no wish to harm you."

"I cannot allow a child of God to fall into the hands of pagans." He stood firm as Rorik advanced and placed the tip of his sword at his throat. The priest trembled, but didn't waver. A crowd had gathered around them, murmuring and staring.

How had Rorik known she was gone so soon? She looked at him and he locked her in his gaze. His eyes were the steel of his sword blade's edge, his color high, and he clenched his jaw. He was livid.

"What will it be, Elfwynn?" His voice was rough and deep. "Come with me, or have the death of this priest on your soul?"

The priest swallowed. "My death will be on your soul, Rorik of Vargfjell. Along with a multitude of others. So many, I think God Himself has lost count. Yes, I know who you are. And so will your King Horik."

"He's not my king and your God is not mine." He pressed the tip of the blade closer.

"Father, don't." She grabbed his sleeve. She couldn't let this brave man of God die for her.

Rorik backed off a step, lowering his sword, and the priest turned to her, a drop of blood at his throat. "I would give my life to see you out of their filthy hands."

She shook her head, her eyes filling. "If he kills you, they'll still take me. I can't allow it. I'll go with him. Please, Father. I couldn't live with knowing you died for me."

He gave her a tremulous smile. "It is no less than our Savior did. Still, I'll honor your wishes. You are truly a child of God. I'll go to our bishop. He'll know what to do."

"Thank you, Father."

"I'll pray for you every day."

She tried to smile as she glanced toward the seething Northman. "I'll need it, I fear."

He blessed her, then faced Rorik. "May God curse you, Rorik of Vargfjell, if you harm this woman. The prayers of all of us here will follow her to your land."

Rorik inclined his head and stepped aside to let him pass. He hurried through the crowd, toward the church. She looked at it with longing. So close. But then, nothing would have stopped Rorik. He would have destroyed the building to get what he wanted. Always, what *he* wanted.

He pinned her in his glare. "I had just left the church when one of my men met me and told me you were gone. Imagine my delight. I waited here, knowing it was where you would go. You're too predictable."

"What did the Church say?" He'd been there, spoken to them. There was still hope.

That died as he shook his head. "They don't have the kind of money I need. There is no ransom."

Chapter Nine

Dearest *Lord, no.* Her legs gave out and she crumbled as her world reeled. He caught her around the waist with his free arm, but she shoved away from him, shaking. "Then lower your price. Damn you, Rorik, you don't need this money! You're so wealthy, you could build an entire fleet and never feel the expense. Why are you so obsessed with this?"

"I'm not going to discuss this with you for everyone to hear while we stand in the street." He sheathed his sword and grabbed her wrist. "We're going back to the ship."

Hatred, fear, and rage, red and searing, burst in her mind like a glass of boiling water shattering. Her muscles coiled and she swung, hitting him in the side of the head. He cursed and took both her wrists, hauling her to his chest. He didn't hurt her, but she couldn't wrench free.

He spoke through his clenched jaw. "All I have to show for my loss is you. You're mine now. Accept it. I can do as I please with you and no one will stop me."

She'd never known him like this. He didn't even seem to see her but looked through her, as though he saw another place, another time. This was what men, and even kings, feared—his legendary temper. The women of the village had whispered to her about it, warning her to never provoke it. And she just had.

"If I can't sell you to the Church, then I'll sell you as a slave. And likely get even more for you because of your virginity." He put both her wrists in one hand and pulled her after him. His men split apart to let them pass, then followed him, their swords still unsheathed. She couldn't look at them.

A sob tore from her. This wasn't happening. Everyone swore he would never hurt a woman. Ever. But he wasn't thinking any longer. Some said he could lose himself for days in the rage. He'd sink so deep, no one could find him until he came out of it on his own. Like a berserker. Except it came on him when something slammed into his emotions, something he cared about.

Certainly not her. This involved his burned ship and his wealth. It was all that meant anything to him.

He led her toward the outskirts of the town. She tried to resist, but he was too strong. In front of a house ahead of them, a man in long robes stood watching them approach. He looked foreign, with a hooked nose, curling dark hair, and a long beard.

"Ah, Rorik, friend of friends. What do you bring to me?" He grinned as he studied her.

Rorik took hold of her upper arms and turned her to face the man. "A beautiful treasure from the western isles, Ibrahim."

"I can see that. Is she untouched?"

"As the snows on the tops of the mountains in my land."

She couldn't speak, couldn't even move. Her breath came short and she wanted to be sick. She looked at Rorik's men. They kept the crowd back, their swords held in front of them. They appeared displeased, giving Rorik sour looks. If she could appeal to them, they might intervene.

Rorik pulled her around to face him so that the man could see her hair. She looked up at him, her eyes filling, but he focused on the merchant. She had to reach him somehow.

He still held her upper arms. She couldn't touch his face, so she grasped his forearms. "Remember the night I played the harp for you? If you bring me back to Vargfjell, I can play every night for you. I touched something then, something sweet and deep within you." She placed her hand on his chest. "I know it's still there. This isn't you. Don't do this to me. Don't stop the music only I can play for you. *Please,* Rorik."

The blankness in his eyes changed. They became sharper, clearer. He blinked and looked down at her. A tear fled down her cheek as she gazed up at him. Glancing around them, he took a deep breath as though he were just awakening.

"She is exquisite," the merchant said. "Perhaps I need to take her into my house and, ah, make certain of her purity. Not that I mistrust you, Rorik, but women can fake such things. They are ever deceitful."

Rorik's head snapped around as he took in the crowd who was watching, waiting to see what would happen. His men stood still, their faces grim.

He lowered his gaze to hers, his voice very low. "I'll make this right. Trust me."

"Never again." She tried to free herself, but couldn't. "You lied. You promised to take me to Hedeby so I could return to my people."

"I promised to bring you here, yes. But not what I would do with you once we got here. Perhaps I betrayed you. Like your father did." He had the gall to smile at her and his hands loosened just a bit.

She did yank free of him then. Backing away, she drew the knife Kaia had given her and held it out between them. "Don't, Rorik. Don't come near me. Just let me go." He might as well take the knife and cut out her heart. It would be kinder.

He stalked her, a feral look in his eyes. "Do you think you can do more than scratch me with that? The people here will convict you of trying to kill me. With all these witnesses, it would be easy. You'll be sold into slavery anyhow."

"I don't care. I don't—"

She sliced at him, but he was on her in an instant. She didn't have time to react before he took the knife from her and put it under his belt. Wrapping one arm around her, he hauled her to him, her back to his chest. She tried to swing at him, but he pinned her arms to her sides.

"Damn you to Hell for all eternity, Northman! I hate you."

He cut off her words with a hand over her mouth and turned them both to face the merchant. "My most humble apologies, Ibrahim. I thought I had her well-trained and submissive, but I can see I have more work to do. I would throw myself off the edge of the world if I were to sell such a termagant to you. I could never expect you to accept such poor-quality merchandise."

"It would be a pleasure to tame her myself." He rubbed his hands together. "Of course I would have to cut out her tongue first, but she would learn very quickly if she were rendered silent."

Oh God. She bit Rorik's hand. Hard. He let go of her mouth just long enough for her to scream. He put his hand over her mouth again and she kicked him in the shin. He cursed under his breath as he backed away with her. As she twisted, he picked her up against his chest, her feet dangling off the ground. She still tried to kick him. With both heels.

"I would ask my gods to let a thousand horses run over me every night rather than curse you with such a burden as she has been to me. I would sink all my ships so I could never see another market again rather than disgrace myself by selling her to you in this condition. I know you only purchase the finest of women, not one such as this. May the scorpions of all the deserts of your homeland infest my bed were I to insult you so."

She shifted her hips to one side, as Kaia had taught her, and slammed her fist between his legs. It wasn't as hard as she would have liked since he still pinned her arms to her sides. But it was enough that he groaned. He continued to back up, carrying her with him.

"Allow me the honor of teaching her what her place is and I'll return with her when she is subdued. Only then will she be worthy of your esteemed consideration. And to compensate you for your valuable time, I'll send some of the best wine I've just purchased."

"Very well, Rorik. I'll expect it. And her. Soon." He frowned as he bowed, still eyeing her.

They backed around the corner of a house, his men following, watching the crowd. Rorik let her down, his arm loosening. She broke free and tried to slap him. He caught her hand, then her, and slung her over his shoulder.

"To the ship. Fast." He ran with his men through the streets as people jumped out of their way. She reared up and he tightened his grip on her thighs. With his shoulder cutting into her stomach, she couldn't keep up the position and flopped back down. His long black hair flowed past her and she gathered up a handful and yanked on it.

"Damn you, Northman, let me down."

"Not until we're on the ship. Now be quiet. You've done enough for one day."

"*I've* done enough?" She gave his hair another good tug.

"Stop that." He smacked her rear as he ran onto the walkway along the shore. His warriors caught up to him as he slowed to a fast walk. "Get the men here. We're leaving now."

"But the cargo."

"Never mind that now. We have the wine. Whatever hasn't been traded will have to wait for another time. We're going to have the Christians breathing down our necks, and the Arabs, then most likely Horik. I don't plan to be around for that."

They hurried onto the dock where the ship was tied. He leaped over the water with her still on his shoulder and their landing knocked whatever breath she had left out of her. He strode to her tent in the front and set her on her feet. With a hand on her arm, he made certain she was steady but she jerked away from him.

She couldn't go back with him. Not after this. Who knew what she would be now? A slave? A bondservant working off this debt? He said she was his to do with as he pleased, and she knew what pleased him the most. She leaped for the side of the ship, but he caught her. Tears coursing down her face, she collapsed in his arms. He picked her up, took her into the makeshift tent, and laid her down on the furs.

She scrambled away from him. "Don't come near me. You betrayed me. You said so. Like my father."

"I had to say something to get you angry. If you'll let me explain." He reached out to touch her arm.

She smacked his hand away. "You explained everything to that— that slave merchant. That's what he is, isn't it? And you took me to him. To sell me." She couldn't say anything else. Her soul was so badly torn, it would never heal.

"I get angry." He gazed out of the tent toward his men who were loading crates and chests onboard. "I only know the rage. Nothing else. When you hit me in front of everyone, after having been turned down by your Church, I saw red. Half of Hedeby must have been there and witnessed it. My reputation was sinking to the bottom of the fjord and I couldn't stop it. I snapped."

"Just once, why don't you think of your reputation with *me*? Oh, that's right. I'm a means to an end. Nothing more. Now I'm not even that." She kneaded the blanket beneath her. "No matter what it takes, Northman, I'll be free of you. Even if I have to swim the sea that has no tides to get home."

He bowed his head and his hair fell around him. She caught the start of a smile he was trying to hide. "That's not how you get to Northumbria. You might try the North Sea instead."

"North Sea, Valhalla, or Hell itself. I don't care how I do it, I'll get away from you."

"It doesn't have to be this way, Elfwynn. If you'd just listen to me." He tried to take her hands, but she pushed him backwards.

As he landed on his back on the deck, she bolted over him and headed for the side of the ship again. It didn't matter if she drowned. Perhaps she would, and then she'd escape him forever.

He grabbed her ankle. She fell and kicked at him but it didn't stop him from grabbing her leg. "Galinn, get me some rope." He picked her up, deposited her on her back in the tent again and held her wrists until Galinn returned. Sitting on her thighs, he reached back for the rope Galinn handed him. "I won't hurt you, but I have to do this to be certain you don't hurt yourself."

"Too late." She quieted as he bound her wrists in front of her. There was no point in fighting any longer. Kaia taught her that if one had to give in for the time being, it wasn't defeat. It was only victory delayed. He got off of her, then tied her ankles as well. After he placed her on the furs again, he pulled a blanket up to her shoulders.

Putting his hands on either side of her head, he stared down at her. "Now you will listen to me. You will not say a word. If you do, I'll gag for you the rest of the way home. Then you'll have no choice. Do you understand?"

His glossy soft hair fell down over her, brushing her skin. She was beneath him, helpless, She had to do as he said. She started to answer, but at his warning look, she only nodded.

He sat beside her. "That's better. Outside Ibrahim's house, I don't remember anything until I heard you say 'Rorik'." He looked down at her. "You've never called me anything but 'Northman' before. Yet when I heard you say my name, the bloody haze that fills my mind disappeared and the anger faded. We were standing there at Ibrahim's house. I was talking to him about selling you. I was horrified. I've visited slave markets before, but only to try to save women and children, not sell them.

"Everyone was watching me to see what I would do. I had to save face, come up with some way to get out of it without offending him too badly. I remembered Thorir being interested in you and I told him of your temper and sharp words in order to dissuade him. It worked then. I hoped it might this time as well. But it wouldn't be enough to tell Ibrahim of it. He had to see it to know I spoke the truth. So I tried to make you angry. Fortunately, it doesn't take much." He rubbed his temple where she'd hit him.

"I didn't want to hurt you, but I had to in order to keep you from greater harm. I know your father is a tender place for you. I had to strike there."

"And you drew blood. The wound will never heal." At that point, she didn't care if he gagged her. She had to speak her mind, even if it meant being silenced the rest of the journey.

But he only brushed back her hair. "My temper is why I can't tie any woman to me. Although at the moment, it seems I have." He gave her a tentative smile.

She looked away. "So what now? Where do we go from here? To the slave markets across the Baltic to get rid of me?"

"Heard about them, did you? Not this trip. Maybe next time. But for now, it's back to Vargfjell. If we can get out of the harbor without half of Hedeby coming after us." He checked outside. "I have to go." Taking her cheek in his hand, he pressed until she had to look at him. He was very gentle, but she couldn't resist it. "I told you. I'll make this right between us."

"There is no 'us'. And how can you make it right, when you're what's wrong?" She turned over, burying her face in the furs.

With a sigh, he caressed her shoulder, then went onto the deck.

"We have company, Rorik." Galinn sounded alarmed.

"I see them. Is everyone here?"

"We're all here, along with the wine and cargo."

"Cast off."

She sat up and peered out as best as she could. The men hurried to untie the ship and shove away from the pier. As the ship drifted into the bay and the men set out the oars, a group gathered on the dock. The priest who had helped her was among them, along with other members of the clergy and well-dressed warriors. Were they the king's men? The priest hurried to the end of the dock and shook his fist at them. He had tried to come for her, to save her from the Northmen. But it was too late.

She lay back down and dried her tears on the furs. Everything was too late.

The Kattegat, between Denmark and Norway

When they'd passed the islands separating the Baltic and the Kattegat, Rorik came into the tent and untied her. On their way to

Hedeby, Galinn had pointed out the landmarks and bodies of water to her. At least now, she knew where they were. Coming here, they'd skirted the North Sea, then sailed into the Skagerrak, then the Kattegat. Now they'd head back through them. And they likely weren't on their way to Northumbria.

"I'll see that you have something to eat," he said as he inspected her wrists. There were no marks.

She pulled them away. "Don't bother. I'm not hungry."

"I'll send Galinn in later with something. At least you won't try to kill him. I think." He backed out and left her alone. Thank God. She stayed in the tent. The ship wasn't that big, so she heard him speaking with Galinn.

"Those were Horik's men on the pier." Rorik sounded frustrated.

"I know. So now Horik is mad, the Christians are mad, and the Arabs are mad. At you." Galinn chuckled. "We sent the wine you promised Ibrahim, but that won't go far in assuaging his disappointment at losing Elfwynn. If you don't return with her by winter, he won't be amused. I suppose this counts out trading at Hedeby for the time being."

"And Kaupang. Don't forget the Danes rule there as well, though it's across the water. They hold all the southern parts of our land. That leaves Birka and Dorestad, both much farther away. At least I'll still have a place to get good wine since Dorestad is in Frisia next to the Rhineland."

"The markets at Gotland and Öland are closer than Birka, though," Galinn said. "And there is always Halikko in the land of the Finns. Still far, but not so far as Staraya Ladoga, and they have access to the eastern markets."

"True, but I've seen enough Arabs for now." Rorik looked toward the stern. "I have things to do. Watch Elfwynn for me. I don't trust her not to hurl herself into the sea. Don't leave her out of your sight, even if you're taking a piss off the side of the ship."

"I'm certain she'd appreciate that view. You should have left her tied."

"I can't do that. Not all the way home. That's days."

"All right. I'll—Wait, Rorik. Look. There's another ship on the horizon, just ahead to the west."

"I see it. The sail is full on to us. It's coming this way. It might be another trader heading east toward land, but we can't take any chances." He raised his voice. "Take the shields from the sides of the ship and get out your weapons."

The men dropped what they were doing and followed Rorik's orders. Elfwynn backed further into the tent. What if they were attacked? Rorik's warriors were said to be the best, but then, few ever challenged him on the seas. If the crew of the unknown ship did, they must be very powerful.

Rorik climbed past the tent, heading for the front of the ship. Curious, she went outside to see what was happening. He leaped up behind the dragonhead on the forestem and hung on to it. Shielding his eyes with his hand, he studied the approaching ship. His long hair streamed out behind him as he braced his legs apart, straddling the bow. The ship dove into the waves, sending prismatic spray around him. He was as untamed as the wind, surely the lord of the seas.

"Odin's eye." He spoke over his shoulder. "It's Alvida. And she's seen us. If she wants to fight us, let's turn the ship and oblige her."

He laughed as the men cheered, banging their weapons on their shields. The ship changed course and the sails snapped taut. Unsheathing his sword, he faced the approaching vessel. He brandished it high and his men let out a great shout.

Were they insane? They wanted to fight? She watched the ship coming closer. Of course they did. There was a brawl at Vargfjell nearly every night, late, when the men were well into their cups.

But this was war. Her chest tightened as she gripped the side of the ship. *Oh Lord, not now.* Ever since she'd lost her brother in war, the fear came on her when someone she loved was going into battle. Wulf. Her father. The world tilted and it wasn't because of the waves. It was the gripping terror. It shouldn't happen now, for there was no one here she loved, no reason to feel this.

She broke out in a sweat and yet her blood ran cold. Galinn came to her side.

"You need to go back inside. We can't let them see you. They shouldn't harm you, but we can't know for certain." He took her arm and guided her into the tent.

Rorik jumped down off the side. "Here, take this." He removed the knife he'd taken from her from his belt and handed it to her, hilt first. His eyes met hers as she took it. "Don't do anything foolish. We'll all watch out for you, but there's always a chance you may have to defend yourself. Remember what Kaia taught you."

With the knife in her hand, the terror receded slightly. She nodded. "Who's Alvida?"

He chuckled. "A Geatish princess turned pirate. We're ... old friends." Grinning, he backed out, letting the flap fall closed behind him.

"A what?" She stared after him. Had the world gone insane? Princesses turning pirate and sailing the seas? It didn't surprise her that he was friends not only with a pirate, but with a woman pirate. She could just imagine what kind of "friendship" that entailed.

In spite of Galinn's warning, she had to see what was happening, so she parted the flap enough to peer out. Rorik and his men lined the right side of the ship, grinning. But they had no swords, or axes, or spears. They'd set their shields aside. They were being attacked, and yet, they had no weapons in hand? The world *had* gone mad.

The ship glided close to them and Rorik shouted across the distance. "Alvida, what are you doing in the Kattegat? Aren't you a little too close to the Danes? You know they're still looking for you."

"I thought that was you on the bow, Rorik." A beautiful voice floated across the waves. "I didn't recognize this longship. It's not your usual one. If I'd known it was you, I might not have bothered. Then again, perhaps I would have. Anything to see your beautiful face again, besides in my dreams." Her tone dropped to a sensual purr.

"You should speak of beautiful faces, Alvida. And that ship met with an accident in Northumbria. You're usually on the seas, not in these waters."

"I thought I'd lie in wait for merchants returning from Birka, Gotland, and Staraya Lagoda. Nice, rich merchants. No place for them to run, here. I'll wager you're returning from Hedeby. Have a profitable trip?"

He laughed. "I've had better. I won't be welcome there for a while."

"Now why doesn't that surprise me? Whose wife did you swive this time?"

"No wives. Why fight with a husband when there are so many unmarried women to be enjoyed?"

"True. And it's not like you have to chase any of them. If anything, they chase you. So, Rorik, what do you have for me to take from you today?"

"Come aboard and find out."

"I thought you'd never ask."

The ship shuddered as the other vessel scraped against it. Men and women surged on board and Rorik's crew met them, some jumping onto the other ship. She stared. It wasn't a war. It was a brawl. With fists, not weapons. And the warriors were grinning and laughing. They were enjoying this.

Some of Alvida's crew tried to take chests and crates, but Rorik's men knocked them flat. They rose, swinging. Rorik was in the thick of it, his white teeth flashing as he pounded a man into the deck. Men leaped back and forth with stolen cargo, only to have it taken back again.

She lifted the flap a bit more so she could see the other ship. On the bow, hanging on to the forestem, stood a stunning woman. Her flowing hair was white-blonde, her eyes a startling shade of blue. She was dressed as the men, in leather and mail with a gold-hilted sword at her side. Elfwynn had never seen a more beautiful woman.

Laughing, Alvida watched the melee. People landed in the water, only to climb out and rejoin the fight. Blood flew, but it was from punches, not blades. Rorik lifted a pirate and tossed him overboard. Another attacked him from behind, but he threw back his head, smashing the man's nose. Blood sprayed everywhere.

One of the pirates looked toward the tent. She ducked, but not before he grinned at her. She scrambled back, gripping the small knife as though her life depended on it. The tent was tied down to the sides of the ship and there was no way out.

Kaia's words came to her. *Step not one foot from battle, but meet it head on. That is the Norse way.* She wasn't Norse, but this was a Norse ship and it would appear she'd be living with them for a time. Not that she had a choice, in both cases.

She braced herself. As the flap opened, she sprang forward into him, as she had when she'd bowled over Rorik. The pirate crashed backward, onto the deck, and she sliced him across the arm. He yelled. She straddled him, aiming at him again.

Rorik pulled her off and took the knife from her, then picked the pirate up and threw him overboard. The man surfaced, shouting in anger. Men helped him aboard Alvida's ship. She jumped down off the bow and looked at his wound. Everyone stopped fighting.

She spun toward them. "We've always agreed no blades, Rorik. Do you go back on your word?"

"And no rape, Alvida. He went after this woman." He drew her to his side. "She's mine. She cut him defending herself."

Alvida kicked the man in the rear. He flailed and fell over the other side of the ship, into the water. He came up sputtering.

"Enough," she said. "We've traded punches and cargo. Shall we call it a draw, Rorik?"

"As always, Alvida."

She considered Elfwynn as the men and women sought their own ships. "I see you already have a valuable bit of cargo there. If you didn't, I'd invite you to pirate with me. We could be so good together. In many ways."

He bowed to her. "Ah, beautiful princess, I'd welcome you into my bed, but never into my boat. There's no telling what would come up missing. Besides, I know your heart lies elsewhere."

"Perhaps. But so, I think, might yours." She inclined her head to Elfwynn, then smiled at him. "May we meet again soon, Rorik of Vargfjell."

"We will. But not, I hope, before we heal." He held up his bloody knuckles.

She laughed and called out to her crew. They cast off and the two longships moved apart. Rorik leaned over the side of the ship and rinsed his hands clean of the blood. Then he walked toward the stern, checking with his men as they put the deck to rights.

"I don't believe what just happened." Elfwynn shook her head as Galinn stood beside her to watch Alvida sail away. "How does a princess become a pirate?"

"Her father, the king of the Geats, decreed that any man who wanted to marry her had to get past two guardian snakes. Many tried, and many died. But one man, a raider who was also a prince, killed the snakes. Her father turned her against him, saying the prince had rejected her. She did not want to continue the secluded life her father forced on her, so in despair, she gathered other men and women who were like-minded, and went pirating. She found another ship and crew who had lost their captain and they accepted her leadership. And so she sails the seas, pillaging and plundering. The Danes have tried to stop her, but to no avail. They say the prince still chases her, but so far, he hasn't caught her either."

He sucked on an injured knuckle, then examined it. "Rorik has an agreement with her. We may try to steal each other's cargo, but no blades and no death." He eyed her. "He gave you a knife since he most likely didn't think you'd actually use it. It was supposed to make you feel better. Safer. He thought he had a little Christian lamb, as the priest said, on his ship. Instead, he finds a shieldmaiden. Kaia will be so proud."

Looking at the departing ship, she sighed. She was no shield-maiden. That was for Kaia, Asa, and Alvida. All tall, beautiful, and fierce. Not her. In this strange world where princesses were pirates, men stole from each other by mutual agreement, and warriors fought for the simple joy of it, she was just . . .

Lost.

Chapter Ten

Vargfjell

Rorik rubbed the back of his head where a headache was starting. They approached his shoreline, and several new vessels were pulled onto the beach. Standing in the right rear of the ship, he turned the steering board to come in at the best angle beside them. Elfwynn stood in the bow, facing front, her back to him. As she had been the entire journey."Looks like the *Wind* is there," Galinn said. "Eirik traveled quickly. No doubt his shieldmaiden wife came along."

"Asa. Yes. She'll be an asset. I have a feeling my aunt, Lifa, has also come to see to any rune readings that the people may need here. And that means Nuallen, her bodyguard, or whatever he is, will be here as well."

"I saw you and him eyeing each other like two wolves when we were at Haardvik. I sailed with Kaia the last few summers, so I'm not certain how you know him."

Rorik nodded. "I attacked his holding in Northumbria a couple of years ago. He was injured and Eirik took him as a slave. I wanted to throw him overboard so he wouldn't use so many of our provisions if he was just going to die anyhow. The gods intervened and I had no choice but to let him live. Eirik freed him, but Nuallen didn't return to his land. I think he wants my aunt, but he'll have to rethink that if I have anything to say about it. For some reason, he resents me for it all." He couldn't keep the irony out of his voice.

"And now you bring back Elfwynn, a Northumbrian. He'll love you for that."

"If he's here. Lifa knows of the animosity between us."

He made a noncommittal sound. "The other ships are Eirik's. Or are they the ones he gave Magnus?"

"Yes, so that means he's here with a large number of men. Good." Perhaps Silvi also came, as a healer. Not that he didn't have his own, but she was gifted in so many ways. In that, Magnus was fortunate. Perhaps with both Lifa and Silvi here, his own keel would be deeper and steadier in a rough sea. And it *would* be rough.

None of them were going to appreciate the outcome with Elfwynn. The women of Vargfjell had already made their displeasure with him known before he'd left for Hedeby. What were they going to do when he brought her back? They would have to accept his decision regarding her. It was a strong hand that held the sword protecting them. He couldn't loosen it.

The ship drew closer to the docks. People gathered there to welcome them back and the ache in his head grew worse.

He'd snapped, there in Hedeby. He'd been able to keep the fires in his mind from burning for so long. Lifa and Silvi's love had given him that ability years ago. At the church in Hedeby, though, the priests had refused to pay him what he needed. He could take no less or it would appear he had bowed to them. Word would spread that he had crawled before the White Christ.

In frustration, he'd threatened them, which only angered them and they swore he'd never trade there again. Then he'd heard Elfwynn had disappeared into the town. There was no telling what might have happened to her. She could have been raped or killed. Or enslaved . . .

Exactly what he had tried to do to her. The pain blazed in his head and he rubbed the back of his neck harder. When he'd seen her near the church, and the priest had tried to shield her from him, all he could think of was that someone was keeping him from something he wanted. The damned priest dared to stand up to him, with half the town watching. A weakling priest, by the gods. And then Elfwynn hit him.

To be struck in battle was one thing. He expected it and could brace himself against the memories, use the rage to crush his opponent. This time was different. He hadn't seen it coming.

Everything had crashed down on him. The red haze had filled him. He hadn't seen anything else because of the rage. Then, Elfwynn said his name. She'd never done that before. It was as though the breath she'd used to speak it was a gentle breeze, dissipating the scarlet haze and the fires scorching everything he was.

The next thing he knew, that bastard, Ibrahim, was smacking his oily lips over her and she was looking up at him with tear-filled eyes. He'd realized what he'd done and panic had gripped him. He'd faced scores of armies, kings, fleets of warships, and none of it had seized him with fear. This had.

He studied her as he guided the ship across the bay. She stood straight, unmoving, her chin raised. But it was all a show. Ever since that instant in front of Ibrahim's house, she'd had a look in her eyes of sorrow, hopelessness, defeat.

His gut twisted. All he'd known was that he had to get her away from there. He couldn't lose her, not only to the Arab, but to anyone. He'd babbled something to the slaver, all the while praying to his gods he'd be able to keep hold of her long enough to make it to his ship. The flames in his mind had turned to ice as chills ran down his spine. He barely remembered how they got to the ship, but they had. And even though the officials from the Church and Horik were hard on their heels, he'd gotten away. By the time they could have found a ship to give chase, he'd been well out into the Schlei Fjord and heading for the islands south of the Kattegat where he could lose them.

He allowed himself a tiny smile. Then they'd run into Alvida. She was a formidable rival, and even, at times, an ally. Their relationship, for want of a better term, was a strange one, but it served them both well. It could be said they traded their goods with each other. Only it was with brawling, instead of bargaining. The men loved it. And he always hid the best of his cargo, like his wine, beneath the decking of his ship. She most likely did the same. Better it got wet than stolen.

When he'd seen the pirate creeping into Elfwynn's tent, he'd pushed three men into the water, including his own, to get to her. But they'd both come flying back out, she with her knife, and he'd had to pull her away before any real blood was shed. She was more shield-maiden than she knew.

He'd been so angry at all the havoc she'd wreaked in his life, that he'd told his men he planned on making her his slave to repay him. On the days-long journey, though, he'd come to his senses. But because, like an idiot, he'd announced it to them, he couldn't entirely go back on it. He'd lost enough face with his warriors that he couldn't afford to slip any further. Already, they gave him surly looks. His prestige was eroding. Men didn't follow a weak leader. He needed every man he had, especially now. Needed them and their respect.

He could, however, amend his pledge, and in a way Elfwynn might not mind. He grimaced. In the small ship, she'd heard his proclamation about her status. She'd turned away, tears on her cheeks. Those glistening drops had torn his heart a little more.

He'd keep his word, though, about making it right with her. He'd just have to balance it with what he needed to do to keep his reputation safe. That was the only way to keep his people safe as well. Of the two, the latter was far more important.

The men loosened the sail so the ship glided gently to the dock as he steadied the rudder. Others on the pier caught the lines they threw them, stopping the ship. Of course it was done perfectly. He paid a great price to have only the best warriors with him. And that price had just become steeper because of the harm he'd had to do to Elfwynn to ensure they continued to respect him.

Magnus, Eirik, and Leif waited on the shore. Asa and Silvi were with them, but Lifa wasn't there. He sighed in relief. Of all of them, her displeasure about Elfwynn would be the hardest for him to take. It was likely Asa had already told Magnus and Silvi about their meeting in Haardvik. It would be difficult enough explaining himself to Lifa as it was. He didn't need them outnumbering him too much.

Galinn helped Elfwynn onto the dock. Damn him. Rorik leaped off and stepped between them. "My thanks, Galinn. See to the cargo."

Galinn glanced between them, then nodded and jumped back onto the ship. Elfwynn stood still, her eyes moist and distant.

"So what shall I call you now? Master?" Her chin quivered as she raised it.

Call me Rorik, as you did once. "No. Whatever else you like."

"You wouldn't approve of what else I'd like to call you."

"I imagine not." If only he could take her in his arms, wipe away her tears, right here. Right now. But he had enough to do. His men would see to the cargo, but Eirik and the others waited for him. They were allies and family. They had to come first.

"Go to the longhouse. You know the small chamber next to mine? Go there and wait for me. I have to speak with you."

"Is that to be my prison, then? A tiny room? Is that where you keep your slaves?"

"No, I don't keep slaves and you know it. The chamber was my mother's, so she could nurse us and care for us in private when we were young. It's very comfortable. No prison. No locks. Elfwynn, look at me."

She didn't. Not for many moments. Then she raised her eyes to his. The pain in them was a sword driven straight into him.

"I told you I'll make this right. And so I will. You're not a slave and I think you'll be pleased with what I have in mind. Just go there and wait for me."

She dropped her gaze and nodded. As she walked to the path leading to the village, he followed her. She gave Asa and the others a slight nod, then continued on. Eirik frowned at him.

"What in Hel's name, Rorik? I thought she was going to her church in Hedeby."

Galinn walked past, carrying a crate. "No, she's his slave now." He wasn't smiling.

Eirik, Asa, Silvi, Magnus, and Leif all turned to him as one, their expressions dark. Asa put her hand on her seax, but Eirik grabbed her wrist. She clenched her jaw as she tried to free herself, but Eirik didn't move and didn't let go. Thank the gods.

Rorik held up his hand. "No, she's not. Plans changed a bit in Hedeby. It's been a long voyage and I'd like a cup of fresh ale. Let's go to the longhouse and I'll tell you everything."

After that, he'd be fortunate if Eirik didn't turn Asa loose on him. And if they all didn't join her.

The day was getting better and better.

Rorik sat alone at a table in the longhouse, sipping another ale. It was mid afternoon and few people were there. He'd had food and drink brought to Elfwynn. Now if only he could find the courage to talk with her.

His family hadn't been very understanding as he'd explained what had happened. True, they hadn't killed him. Asa had even settled down. Slightly. Eirik had offered to pay Elfwynn's ransom. He'd refused. The arguments had begun at that point and the situation had sunk faster than a ship full of cargo in the North Sea.

It also turned out that Lifa was there. Of course. She was reading runes for some of his people who lived further inland, but she would be back before the evening meal. With Nuallen.

He had enough trouble with the Northumbrian's hatred without adding Lifa's displeasure to the mix. Rorik didn't know what in the name of the gods that man was, but he was more shadow than flesh. It was said he could kill a man without his victim knowing it. If Lifa even looked wrong at Rorik, that would be excuse enough for Nuallen. Between one breath and the next, Rorik would find himself in Valhalla. When he died, he at least wanted to see who his slayer was, so he could find him again there and kill him over and over until Ragnarok took them all.

Though it was just his luck that Nuallen was a Christian and wouldn't have the honor of being in Valhalla.

He buried his aching head in his hands. His family would back him in this war. He had no doubt of that. But their relationship went further than the battlefield. The looks of disapproval and anger they'd given him settled inside him like a lump of glacial ice.

When Lifa heard about this, it would be even worse. At least he might not have to see her until tonight. But he had to face Elfwynn now. She'd waited on him long enough. He'd always thrown himself into the worst battles imaginable with fearless abandon, rode out the fiercest storms on the seas, and sailed into waters that no one else dared. None of it daunted him.

One little Christian did. If he'd failed in any of those other feats, he would lose only his life. It had to happen at some point. It was fated at his birth, so he might as well make a good show of it for the gods to enjoy.

If he failed at this, though, he would lose something more precious. He'd lose Elfwynn. If he hadn't already. At least this way, he had her here, near him, and he'd have the time to try to heal the grievous wound he'd caused within her.

He didn't want to look too deeply into why this was important to him. It might only be that, because he'd brought her here to begin with, he was responsible for her and he'd always taken such things seriously. He did the same for Vargfjell.

But what if it was something more? He downed the rest of his ale and rose from the table. One disaster at a time.

Like diving into freezing water in midwinter after a sauna, it was best to do it and get it over with. As he passed the weaving room, he glanced in. Each loom held a length of cloth, as it should. But the women were gone. They had to have spoken with Elfwynn and heard the story when she came into the longhouse. Even now, they were most likely spreading the word throughout the village that she was back. It was too much to hope everyone would be pleased by the circumstances. The day felt longer than the entire voyage from Hedeby.

He knocked on the door to the small chamber but got no answer. Had she fled? Concerned, he opened the door.

She was asleep on the bed, under a white fur cover. A half-eaten bowl of stew was on the small table and her bag of clothes lay unopened on the floor. The servants had kept this room in order, most likely in the hope that someday he'd have a wife who could come here to nurse her children and keep them close to the master chamber.

His mother had needed it to escape the horror of her life, to be safe with his sisters and him. But he would never risk another woman having to live in that nightmare. Or any children, for that matter.

Sitting on the bed, he watched her. Her curling hair was still wind-tossed from the voyage, spreading across the bed behind her. Long lashes swept her cheeks. Tear-stained cheeks. Lying in a tiny ball beneath the fur, she looked so defenseless and lost. Something inside him moved and he passed his hand over her hair but didn't touch it.

"I'm sorry." He whispered the words. "Everything went so wrong. If I were any other man, a better man, I'd let you go. But I'm not. I have to rule with my sword and my word. If I break either of them, I could lose all I have and all I am. And if I lose, then my people, my family, and my land, will be lost. They must come first. I just hope I haven't broken you in the process."

He lifted her hand from the pillow and squeezed it. "Elfwynn. Wake up. I have to speak with you."

She opened her eyes, dreams still floating in them. Then she saw him and sat up, clutching the fur to her, eyes wide. He didn't move, didn't want to alarm her. They were alone, on the bed, and he ruled here. No one would stop him and she knew it, so he stood and leaned against a wall to put some space between them. Anything to take the fear from her expression.

"I only want to speak with you. Was the stew enough for you?"

She nodded. "I was too tired to eat all of it."

"We'll have the evening meal in a short while. Perhaps you'll feel better then."

"I'll feel better when I know where I stand here. On the ship you said I was to be a slave, yet once we landed, you said not. Which is it?"

She was direct. He would be the same way if he didn't know his future.

"You're not. I spoke in anger on the ship." Not wanting to loom over her, he pulled up the one chair in the room and sat down, keeping his distance. She relaxed, but still eyed him and he couldn't blame her. It was important she listened to what he said, rather than worry about what he was going to do.

"You have to understand I suffered a great loss with the burning of my ship. They are almost living things to us. We never destroy them, even in a sea battle. They are too valuable and treasured, a symbol of what we are. You've said I wouldn't feel the cost of rebuilding it, and in that, you're right. The cost to me is more than gold. The Norse admire strength above all else. Everything we are is instilled with physical strength, political power, and reputation. Especially for a man in my position.

"In many ways, your father defeated me. Not only did he burn my flagship, but he attacked us and killed two of my men. That requires the payment of wergeld, their set value in gold."

"We have the same thing in Northumbria. A person's value is according to rank."

He nearly sighed in relief. At least this was familiar to her. "There must be some form of recompense to their families for their loss."

"Why can't you pay the families?"

"Because I didn't cause the loss. Your father did."

"And now you can't get the money from him, so you'll take it out on me." Her eyes flashed as she glared at him.

"Don't forget, you did offer yourself in exchange for my not destroying your keep to get the money."

"That was for the ransom."

"Yes, and it failed."

"Because you asked too much."

"The cost of a ship is what it is, and the wergeld is a set amount, as well. Earlier this summer, a man named Toke accused Magnus of an unlawful killing of his son. Because the son was an heir to property, it was a major offense. It wouldn't be considered murder, for it happened in the open with witnesses, but it was serious enough to be brought before the *thing*. If the free men there had voted Magnus guilty, then his entire family could have been devastated financially, for they all would have had to pay for what he had done. Fortunately, he was cleared of any wrongdoing.

"Your father killed two of my men in treachery. He has refused to pay me, so I must get it another way."

"And I, being of his family, must be the one to suffer for that."

"Not suffer, no. I never want to see that. But I can't let it go. If I do, word will spread that I'm weakening and I can't have that. I have to get the cost one way or the other so men will see I seek revenge from the earl."

"With his daughter."

"Yes."

"I see." She plucked at the fur. "And what is to be my fate? There is little I can offer you, except that which men have always taken from women." She flushed.

"With how you feel about me, it would be rape. I have killed my own men for that. It will not happen here." At her nod, he continued. "It will be more convenient for you to be in this room because you will see to my things. My chamber and clothing kept in order and clean. My sauna kept well stocked with water and wood. You'll serve my meals and my drink to me in the hall. It shouldn't take you long to do any of these things. I'm a simple man."

She gave him a doubtful look. "And how long will it take me to work off this debt at that pace? I'll be hobbling around here when I'm old and gray."

"That's not all I'll expect from you."

"Oh?" She bit her lip.

"A sail. You'll weave a sail for the ship replacing the one your father burned. When you've finished it, then you'll have repaid the debt of your family and you'll be free."

She blinked, her brows raised. "That's all? A sail?"

"It uses the same amount of material to clothe forty men. Make no mistake, it takes a long time, as long as to build the ship itself. And that's if several women work on it. You, and you alone, will weave it. It will likely take about four years."

He watched her consider it. It was the best solution he could think of, for his men would see he was getting recompense for his loss. Weaving was easy for her and she loved to do it. He would get a sail of the highest quality.

She'd live well with the best food, clothing, protection. He'd make certain of it. The same as the people here. Vargfjell already loved her, so they'd welcome her. At least they'd see she was doing what she enjoyed, so perhaps he wouldn't have a revolt on his hands. Perhaps. Meanwhile, he'd have the time to figure out what the strange attraction was she held for him.

"Do you agree?" He studied her.

She didn't look at him, but at the fur she was picking at. "I don't have much choice. It's not such a different life as I would have had at home with the washing and cleaning. Even though the men cook, the women still serve in the hall, so that's the same as well. And at least you have good looms here."

The tension in his shoulders loosened until she raised her head with a determined glint in her eyes. "I'll weave you a sail. But know this, Northman. It might take another woman four years to weave a sail, but none of them are as good or as fast as I am. I'll weave until my hands bleed and my arms cramp. I'll weave even if I can no longer stand at the looms and have to kneel. Though for some reason it be years, and though I grow old and blind, still I'll weave, until I'm free again."

Elfwynn let the stone weight drop, and the warp threads tightened perfectly. She ran her hand over the threads she'd strung already. In the morning, she could begin weaving.

She glanced out the door and into the hall. Rorik was still sitting at his table after the evening meal, talking with Eirik, Leif, and Magnus. Galinn and some of the other men sat in on their session as well. They must be planning for their war.

Her hand shook at she knotted more of the warp threads around the weight stones. Just the thought of war brought the fear upon her. Her father and Wulf weren't here, though, so why would that be?

No matter. She was just tired. She'd slept a bit more after Rorik had left, so she felt better than she had. But for the entire journey, the emotions churning through her and her uncertainty about her fate had taken their toll on her. When she'd awakened and saw him sitting beside her on the bed, she'd had an instant of fear. He was so strong, so masculine. Anything he wanted, he took. And if he'd wanted her . . .

Instead, he'd gone out of his way to reassure her, moving away and sitting down. He didn't have to do that, but he had. Her jaw tightened. She couldn't soften toward him. Rorik held her responsible for her father's perfidy. He had no right to do that. But his word was all that mattered here, not what was right or fair.

Still, it could have been far worse. She would have most likely spent her days weaving anyhow. It made little difference what the cloth would be used for. In the morning, before she started, she'd have to go to the docks to find a sail to study. She didn't want him to have an excuse to back out on his word because she'd used the wrong pattern.

Why did he want her here? Before they'd left for Hedeby, he'd tried to talk her into staying. Now, he ensconced her next to his room, rather than at Oslafa's house. One would think, with all the tension between them, he'd want her to stay far away from him.

"Elfwynn." Oslafa hurried into the room, Turold following her. "I was away for the day and just heard you were back and about what happened in Hedeby." She embraced her. "Everyone is talking about it."

Heat crept up her face. Everyone must have known what happened as soon as they saw her serving Rorik at the evening meal a short while ago, but it was disconcerting that they should be discussing her. So many people had greeted and hugged her during the meal. It had warmed her like nothing else had in a long time.

"It looks like I'm one of you," she said. "For a while, anyhow."

"We always considered you more than a guest." Turold gave her a quick embrace. "Now you are."

"You haven't gone back to the farmlands yet?" Elfwynn smiled up at him.

"Just before he left, I asked Rorik if I could stay here and work on the houses instead of the barns. He said yes."

She nudged him. "So you could be nearer to Finna."

"Yes, and it pays better. But I'm not certain it was wise. It will only make it more difficult to part when we eventually have to."

"We'll work on that while I'm here."

"I saw the cloth you gave my mother so she could sell it toward the bride-price." He took her hand. "I thank you. It will help, if Finna can keep from marrying someone else in the meantime."

Perhaps if she could teach the other women the more complex embroidery stitches she knew, they could all work on ribbons to sell. She hadn't thought she'd have the time before, but now, she did. With the Norse love of color and ornamentation, the ribbons would be worth a great deal. Somehow, they'd find a way.

As the young man released her hand, she glanced out the door into the hall. Rorik still sat at the table with the men, but he was watching her, his eyes narrowed. She answered his hard look with one of her own, then smiled at Turold. Let Rorik think what he wanted.

Oslafa leaned closer. "There are many people who are not happy with Rorik right now. They don't like what he's done to you, making you pay for what your father did. The men who went with you to Hedeby are especially displeased with him."

"I thought that was their way. Even we have similar laws at home."

"Rorik's all but a king. He can amend any law and make any judgment himself. A ruler, whether king or jarl, must please the people. It's not like in our land where kings say they rule by the will of God and none can go against that. Here, a king or jarl leads his people by their will. If they don't approve of him, they can vote against him and another will take his place. Likewise, his sons may follow after him, but only if they prove themselves. It's not a given. Any man who leads knows this, and has to take it into account. And right now, none of us are very pleased with him."

She wanted to take a small amount of vengeance on him. Even a tiny splinter could bother the strongest man. As she'd prepared the loom, she'd thought of small things she could do to antagonize him. But nothing like this. "Oslafa, I don't want any of you to fight my wars for me. Rorik has done too much for Vargfjell for any of you to turn against him. Not over me."

"We won't turn against him," she said. "We love him well and will always be loyal to him. But that doesn't mean we'll turn a blind eye to anything he does. It's our right to express our displeasure. And we will. In our own ways. You don't see any of the weavers in here, do you? We slowed our work before you left and we can do so again. We'll always make certain Vargfjell has what it needs, but we can put a bit of pressure in certain places and in certain ways that Rorik will notice."

She smiled with a twinkle in her eyes. "The food may not be quite as good. The ale may be a bit sour, the beer not as sweet. The servants might be a little slower and the men might not want to stay and drink quite so late. Or at all. Do you see anyone in the hall right now besides those with Rorik? When has it been empty this early in the evening?"

"I can't believe an entire village would do that for me."

"As you said, you're one of us now. When you first came here, you could have held yourself away, looked down on us. You didn't. Instead, you gave of yourself, your talents, and your kindness. All good Christian virtues." She grinned.

"If I were that good a Christian, I wouldn't have the thoughts I'm having about Rorik."

Oslafa gave her a teasing smile. "Oh?"

"Not like that." She blushed again. "Like how I can make him miserable without him killing me." She sighed. "Maybe that's not a good idea after all. I saw his temper in Hedeby and I'm not certain I want to see it again."

"You most likely won't either." Oslafa sobered as she glanced out the door at him. She lowered her voice. "Rorik has a darkness in him that stems from his past. His aunt, Lifa, taught him how to curb it when he was growing up. He's kept it under control for the most part. But it's said when something is being taken from him, something he holds as his or that he loves, the rage comes on him again. And it can last for days. When he heard you speak to him at Hedeby, it broke the grip on him." She studied Elfwynn, her expression thoughtful. "Something he holds and something he loves. And yet, when the rage came on him in Hedeby, all he was holding, and all he stood to lose, was you."

"Thinking of absconding with it and sailing back to Northumbria?"

Elfwynn jumped at the sound of Rorik's voice above her. Shielding her eyes with her hand, she looked up at him from the deck of the ship as he stood on the dock. He jumped down beside her. He made it look so easy, while she'd felt like she was going to capsize the whole thing when she got in. Or end up in the water herself.

"Just make certain not to sail all the way to the great inland sea that has no tides. Remember to take the North Sea instead. Go to the tip of our land, then southwest."

"Thank you. I'll remember that. Now all I have to do is bribe a crew, steal provisions, and learn how to wield a sword so I can fight pirates along the way. And figure out which way is southwest."

"You'll be a shieldmaiden, then." He grinned at her.

She didn't return the smile. "I've been studying the sail. It's a simple tabby weave, but you didn't tell me the sails were a double thickness."

"I didn't hide the fact. You could have seen it at any time while you were on the ships."

"I wasn't worried about the thickness of the sails when I was being hauled back and forth across the sea, trying to keep from drowning from all the water sloshing in."

"My ship was better sealed than the one you came from Northumbria in. There wasn't much water in it at all. As to the sails, our sheep have longer, larger hairs than most, so the wool is strong and light. Still, the double thickness is needed for even more strength. I'll have a piece of sailcloth brought to you so you can have a sample."

"So kind of you."

"I thought so." He stepped closer. "Make no mistake, little Christian. You're mine. Until you pay off this debt, I don't want anyone else encroaching on what belongs to me. Tell Turold to stay away from you. Or I'll tell him myself."

"I thought only slaves were owned and you've assured me I'm not one. Or will you go back on your word? I've heard that you become enraged like you did in Hedeby when someone tries to take something that's yours. You got angry when that slaver wanted me, and that would imply you think I'm yours. I'm not."

"You tried to run, to deprive me of the ransom. In my eyes, that's the same as stealing from me. And those who steal must repay the ones they take from."

"I'll repay you with the sail, as I said I would. But other than that, unless you make me your slave, I'm free to be with whomever I want, like a Norse woman would be. You can't go through life having tantrums because someone takes yours toys, Northman. One day, you'll hurt someone because of it."

He didn't say anything. Turning pale, he stared across the fjord. Then, without looking at her, he climbed off the ship and walked toward the village.

She watched him. He lacked his usual swagger, barely returning the greetings people gave him as they passed him. That was strange. The Norse, especially Rorik, would never step one foot from battle, as Kaia had said. And this was a battle between them. Of that, she had little doubt. He must know it as well.

Still, he had retreated from her without one of his teasing or suggestive remarks. He was most likely regrouping, as happened in battle, and was planning some other way of irritating her.

She frowned. Perhaps he wasn't regrouping. There had been something different about him when she'd spoken about his anger. Something distant and even fearful. With the haunted look she'd seen in his eyes, he appeared as though he'd had a nightmare long ago, and had never quite awakened from it.

Chapter Eleven

Rorik grimaced as he took a sip of the ale, then set the cup on the table.

Elfwynn held up the pitcher, giving him a sweet smile. "Would you like some more, Northman?"

He put his hand over the top of his cup so fast he nearly knocked it over. "No. It's fine. I'm fine. Everything's fine. I don't need any more. You can go for the rest of the evening."

"As you wish." She left, trying not to laugh. The ale was awful, the food over-spiced, and the beer, a normally slightly sweet beverage because of the fruit in it, was like mead. A week had passed since she'd come back, and Vargfjell was slightly off kilter. It couldn't be said that anything was horribly wrong. But nothing was right, either, and yet all through it Rorik just gritted his teeth and bore it.

Laundry floated down the fjord. Horses wound up in the longhouse one night. And that day, chickens had found their way into the rafters, making a mess with feathers everywhere. Rorik never said a word. He just shooed a protesting chicken off his seat when he sat down to dinner and plucked a feather off his plate. The cooking women used too much costly pepper in the stew and he'd quaffed a great deal of the sour ale, but he'd finished his food without comment.

"We can't keep this up." Oslafa met her at the door to the weaving room. Elfwynn rarely left it, except to do her chores. "At least not after Jarl Thorir comes, and he's due any day. We can't insult him and Vargfjell by serving less than the best."

"I know. It doesn't seem to be working anyhow. Rorik hasn't said anything about it."

"And that's odd. He's always demanded everything be a certain way. But he's tolerating it all."

"He's plotting something." Elfwynn went to her loom. "Some nefarious revenge. Or, this is his revenge. Keeping us guessing and wondering. He *is* the consummate strategist. I overheard the men planning this battle and they've said they can't let the king know just what their numbers are until they engage. Perhaps that's what he's doing. Not showing anything until he strikes. He's doing this, just to get at me." She splayed her hand on the warp strings.

Oslafa grinned. "I think it's working. He's making you more insane by not reacting than if he came right back at you. If he did, that would just arm you even further."

"I agree we can't continue this while the jarl is here. And the chickens have to go. I'll think of something more personal. Aimed only at him. That way, Thorir will see Vargfjell as it should be. But while they're planning their war, I'll be waging one of my own."

By the time Jarl Thorir came, everything was set to rights. The livestock were back where they belonged and the longhouse was immaculate. A few feathers still clung to the underside of the roof where no one could reach them, but other than that, the hall sparkled. Delicious aromas wafted from the cooking room.

Thorir walked in, his men flanking him. As Rorik strode across the longhouse to meet him, it felt as though he pushed a wave of power before him, like the bow of a great ship cutting through the sea. They grasped wrists in greeting, towering above the other men, their mutual strength palpable.

Elfwynn stared at them. She dared to try to stop Rorik from his heavy-handed ways with her? Biting her lip, she firmed her resolve. Living with his possessiveness was not an option. Now, if she truly belonged to him, and he to her, that might be different.

Her stomach dropped. What was she thinking? It could never be different. She was only a simple Christian woman in a strange land and he was . . . the lord of that land.

He stood with the other men, glittering with the gold jewelry he'd had her polish, and wearing the fine clothing she'd cleaned and laid out for him. He'd washed with the water she'd drawn and would sit down to a meal she'd serve him.

Yet here she was, watching him. And she would fall under his spell a little more, like so many other women had.

She'd thought to hate him, and perhaps she did. Her mother had once said she hated Edward for being so handsome, and desirable, and unattainable. Yet, she'd also said she loved him. The two weren't so different when love went unanswered. Perhaps she was more like her mother than she realized.

Her mother might have pined her life away, but she wouldn't. She'd keep fighting and weaving until she was free of Rorik forever. They said the Norns, as well as the Valkyries, wove men's fates in their magical looms. Her loom wasn't magical and she was no Valkyrie, so let them tangle the destinies of men in the threads of the *wyrd*.

She would weave her own fate.

The bag of runes sat untouched on the table in front of Lifa and Silvi. Sometimes they used them to draw out influences surrounding them. But they wouldn't need them tonight. Not when he was pouring his guts out all over the place as though he'd been sword struck.

Rorik had met with his aunt almost every night since he'd returned from that disastrous trip to Hedeby. At times, Silvi joined them. It took him back to the days when he was so young, when there had been a glimmer of light for the first time in his existence. Lifa was the radiant star guiding him.

Lifa picked up the bag and turned it over in her hand. He nodded to it. "Each night you bring it and yet you never cast them."

"I already have. They have shown me that this is a time of change for you."

His skin crawled, but he kept his voice light. "What did they tell you?"

"You have Tiwaz in the position of what is happening now. It's the warrior's rune, which comes as no surprise. It indicates a battle with yourself. This, I can sense. It also shows an increase of wealth."

"That's a given."

"There are many types of wealth, as Magnus has discovered. Tiwaz also shows a man in love."

He grimaced. "I like the portent of wealth better."

She gave a fleeting, troubled smile. "It indicates that you must cut away the old and await the *wyrd*, the fate. Ingwaz also shows this. As with birth, it is a dangerous time for you. Hagalaz, Othala reversed, and Thurisaz reversed. All of these you have. They say the same—a time of change and it could be anything from a gradual awareness to a ripping apart of all you know. Through your refusal to see clearly, you'll cause pain to others. Think of the pain you've caused that innocent Christian girl."

"I seek only to support my people, Aunt. To be what my cursed father was not. I obtain wealth and grow my power to attract the best warriors so I might protect Vargfjell and give its people the finest life I can. I will not waver."

She shot him a scalding look. "Thurisaz reversed means the person for whom it was cast will not heed its advice. I didn't need it to tell me that. Ever you have gone your own way."

"No." He touched her arm. "For you and Silvi are beside me always in my mind. I was little more than an animal when you fostered me. You both showed me there was more than pain and horror in the world. I'll always owe you for that."

"You owe nothing. You were a frightened, angry child, Rorik. Your sisters were the same. All of you will bear the scars brought by your father and the death of your mother, but at least the wounds no longer bleed. You have much wealth and power, but the greatest wealth of all is love. We tried to give you that."

"And so you have. But what I do with Elfwynn, I do for my people. My father brutalized the people here. Before he was killed, I abandoned them. I vow I will not fail them again. Because of Elfwynn's service to me, I will have recompense for what I have lost. My name will ring in the halls of kings again with the respect and honor I'm due. Vargfjell will continue to grow and prosper. Nothing will change."

"And yet, the runes have said it will. It already has. I see it in you, Rorik. The way you are with her, watching her as she moves through the longhouse, the tone in your voice as you speak with her."

"The only thing that's changed is how badly Vargfjell is being run. I know why, though."

"Why do you think that is?"

"My men weren't happy with me when I brought Elfwynn back. They weren't pleased that I didn't get any recompense for her and were giving me surly looks. No doubt, they persuaded their women to slack off in their chores. I've made my decision concerning her, though, and I can't back off on my word. They may not feel I tried hard enough in Hedeby and cheated myself, but they'll just have to accept it. I'll suffer through the bad ale, the over-seasoned food, and the chicken feathers in the stew. If I give in, I'll appear even weaker. My word is law here."

Lifa and Silvi looked at each other and smiled.

"And a refusal to see clearly," Silvi said.

"So true." Lifa shook her head.

"Don't both of you start." He frowned at them. "Talking with you about my loss of control in Hedeby is the only way I've had any peace of late."

"Is that truly the only time?" Lifa gave him a searching look.

"You never ask a question unless you know the answer. Tell me. What will I say?"

"You mentioned that, in front of Ibrahim's house, Elfwynn promised to play the harp for you and that helped bring you out of the rage. You said she played for you before you left. It was just an off-hand remark while we spoke, but I know what it must mean to you."

"It was a shock to hear the music," he said. "But it also brought me peace. Strange."

"Not so strange when you consider your past with it. Why don't you have her keep her promise?"

"To play it? I don't know if she would. It appeared to disturb her. In fact, she denied being able to play at first. Perhaps it holds memories for her she'd rather forget. I know what that's like. To dredge them all up might not be wise."

"Yours are far in the past and she's living hers now. The memories never die, Rorik. We bury them, but sometimes the best thing to do is to let them out. Like Asa did with Eirik. It's helping to heal her. If anyone here needs healing, it's Elfwynn. And you."

"I'm fine." He straightened. "I just needed to talk with you, ask for your wisdom about the rage coming on me again. I usually know why, like the loss of my ship. But this time was so intense, I couldn't even remember it."

"Perhaps because if you lost her, it would be worse than losing your ship."

"Nothing is worse than losing a ship. Especially my flagship. Then she scored a direct strike to every shield I have when she said I'd hurt someone because of it." He ground his teeth. "Was that just a lucky comment, or did someone tell her of the past here?"

"No one would do that," Silvi said. "That is only your tale to tell, if you choose to. Perhaps you should."

"No. She already thinks I'm a monster. Then she'd be certain." He played with the rune bag. "Maybe she's right. I've never hurt a woman so much in my life. And I don't know how to stop the damage."

Lifa put her hand over his. "You're not your father, and that fear lies inside you. You bear scars, as do your sisters."

"And we're all so upstanding and normal. I fly into uncontrollable rages. Kaia wants to kill everything. And Ellisif." He sucked in his breath. "She is the worst, I think, in many ways. Such a brilliant mind, and yet she hides it in the darkness of the forests and the shadows within herself."

"She was the youngest," Lifa said. "You took her into the woods to save her and she has chosen to retreat there to hide from the world. It's where she feels the safest."

"My huntsmen came across her a couple of days ago. She knows we have more people here now and need more meat. She's hunting. So we may see her soon."

"Good." Silvi smiled. "I was hoping she'd be here, no matter how briefly. She might stay for a day or two if we're here."

"She might. I know she feels the same way about you that I do. Lifa, the love you gave us was that of a mother, and Ivar's love was the first we'd known from a man. Eirik was as a brother, and Silvi, you were as a sister. Your love shone in our lives then, and still does."

"That love, as deep as it is for all of you, is as the twilit noon on a mid winter's day compared to what you could know with the right woman, Rorik. You're still living in that twilight." Lifa tilted her head to one side. "Ask Elfwynn to play the harp, even if it's for the village, as she did before. You often have music at the evening meals anyhow, especially while the jarl is here. Then you can ask her to play for you alone. Let it take you back, Rorik. It will help."

"I don't see how, but I'll think on it." He rose. "Sleep well. And thank you." Lifa nodded to him, then she drew the bag to her, and Silvi moved closer. They'd read the runes and probably plot against him. Or place the stones someplace for some nefarious purpose.

He smiled to himself as he walked past them, but it died as he saw Nuallen sitting at a table behind them. The Northumbrian hadn't been there earlier and Rorik had been facing in that direction. How did he do that? He gave him a brief nod and Nuallen returned it, his hard eyes those of a slayer. He knew as well as Nuallen did that eventually, there would come a reckoning between them. Not when it could hurt Lifa. But one day.

On the way to the front doors, he passed the weaving room. Elfwynn was there, as usual. Any time she wasn't working for him, she was weaving the sail. She had to rest sometime. He crossed to her.

"It's late. You should go to bed."

"No one has told me when to go to bed since I was a child." She didn't stop and he had to back up when she moved to his side of the loom. Her sweet scent filled him and he breathed deep of it.

"Then perhaps someone should."

She gave him a harsh look. "And I suppose you're going to volunteer?"

"I'd like to." He grinned at her. From her expression, she wasn't amused. "You're working too hard. You must be tired."

"I'm not tired. When I am, I'll go to sleep."

"I thought Christians were meek and mild. What is it you say? That the meek will inherit the earth?"

"You Northmen seem inclined to do so and you're welcome to it. Why would I want to inherit it? It's been nothing but trouble for me so far. And so are you."

It was all he could do not to laugh. She was in a fine mood tonight. "Then you'll love it even more when I make another request of you."

She put down the shuttle and faced him. "What else do you want of me?"

"I'd like you to play the harp at the feast I'm giving tomorrow night to see Thorir off. We've nearly finished our meetings and he's leaving the next morning to gather his men."

"Then it will be war."

"Yes."

When she picked up the shuttle, her hand shook. "Very well. I'll play."

He left before they got into another argument. He hadn't thought it would be that easy. She could be trying to soften him for some reason. He didn't quite trust her. But if she'd play without a fight, he'd take what small victories he could. These days, the gods knew, they were rare enough.

When he entered his chamber, the light from a dozen oil lamps filled it. As always. It was one of Elfwynn's duties. He never slept in the dark, whether he was alone or not. He wasn't alone.

Gunnhild rose from the bed where she'd been lying, naked, her glorious blonde hair cascading around her. His heart sank. He'd been all but ignoring his women this past week. His thoughts had been too dark. If his control slipped again and he hurt one of them, he'd never forgive himself.

Before, they'd always waited until he asked one of them to be with him. But this night, Gunnhild had taken it upon herself to come to him. She stopped before she reached him.

"Whenever you've seen me like this before, I had no doubt of your interest." She glanced down. "I can see I don't arouse you any longer."

"It's not that, Gunnhild." He went to her and gave her a brief kiss. "I've had many things on my mind since I returned."

"So many, you haven't even noticed that the others have left you?"

He thought back. None of them had been at the meals in the evenings, but then, many people hadn't. Magnus's, Eirik's and Thorir's warriors filled the hall these days, along with his own. Not many women, and he couldn't blame them.

She played with the gold bead holding his shirt closed, but didn't look at him. "Bótvi, Ethla, and Hrótha have caught the eyes of three of Thorir's men. Ragnvé likes one of Magnus's warriors and Sibba has spoken with one of Eirik's. None of the men want to sail in your waters, so to speak, but with your nod, they just might dip in their oars."

Had Eirik been right? "Have I been unfair to all of you, Gunnhild? Have I held you back from marrying and having families of your own?"

"We stayed of our own free will. You know that. I think as long as we were with you, we hoped there was a chance you'd choose one of us to marry. But we see the runes carved in the stone. Or at least, they do. I hoped, still. But when you kissed me just now, I knew it as well. Nothing was there for me. Ever since you brought home that little Christian woman, you've spent more time arguing with her than making love to us. She intrigues you. If I knew you wanted a fight, I'd have given you one. That which is too easy is least desirable."

He could find no argument to that. Elfwynn had intrigued him. She was the one woman who didn't want him. His looks, his wealth, his rank, all of it drew women to him like the shore drew the waves. But not her. She wanted no part of it, or him. She was a challenge and he had never been able to back down from a provocation.

"Gunnhild, it's a passing phase, a temporary allure. I've agreed that she'll leave when she finishes the sail. If I wanted her to stay, why would I have done that?"

"A sail. I may not have ever put a needle to thread, but even I know how long that takes. If you didn't want her here, why did you set such a long task for her? It's so you have the time to win her." Before he could reply, she put her finger on his lips. "I've loved you well, Rorik. And if I were more certain of myself and less certain of her, I'd fight her for you. But still, the choice would be yours and I don't want others to see me lose. Surely you, of all people, can understand that. Grant me the dignity of allowing me to be the one to walk away. With my head high." Her chin trembled as she lifted her moist eyes to him.

He brushed her hair back, his heart full. "I've never held any of you here. Perhaps I should have. Now it's too late."

With a short nod, she walked to the chair where her shift lay. She slipped it over her head and it fell around her, hiding the beautiful body he'd never see again. His chest tightened as she wrapped her dress around herself and fastened the brooches at her shoulders. He understood her need for dignity. He had his own, as well. They were Norse. They would not kneel or beg.

Gunnhild walked past him, but he touched her on the shoulder and she stopped. "You're part of Vargfjell. Will you remain here?"

She didn't look at him. "For now. I still have my beauty and there will be many fine warriors here because of the war. Once it's known that I'm free, I may find one of them. None will be you, but at least I'll know I did have a part of you for a while. Just don't do what I did, my love, and wait too long for what you want."

After she left, he sank down on the empty bed. He'd always held tight to everything, except what truly mattered. The women had been a part of his life for so long. Now they were gone and he was alone. He had his family, though, and Vargfjell, so at least they would be there for him. In the day.

Here, in the night, when the darkness around him matched the shadows within, there would be no one to bring the light of a smile, or a caress to comfort him. He couldn't bury himself in a soft body to forget or wake with loving arms around him. Those things had brought him a tiny flicker of radiance. But that spark was never enough to fully thaw the frozen winter that he was inside.

For fear that he would hurt a woman he loved, he had never loved. For his hatred of the dark, he had never slept without light filling the room. It didn't matter. He could buy all the oil in the north and light every lamp he owned. They would never banish the shadows in his mind.

Even in the best of times, with crowds and laughter and revelry, he had existed in a twilit realm, as Lifa had said. Perhaps it was time to illuminate, not the darkness without, but that within.

Perhaps it was time to love.

"We're agreed then?" Rorik looked at each of them in turn—Eirik, Magnus, and Thorir. Leif, Asa, and Kaia also sat in on the planning session in the hall. "Thorir will bring his ships here when his raiders come back from their journeys. They'll join all of ours, since my own will have returned by that time. Based on the information we'll have by then, we'll go to sea and hunt a king's fleet." They all raised their cups in affirmation. "Thorir, you and I will leave some of our men here and at your village to protect the women and children."

Thorir nodded. "My younger brother, Jóarr, will remain behind to carry on our line if I should fall. He'll protect my people with his warriors. If the jarls hear of our battle on the seas, they may try to attack our villages from the south before we return. We must be prepared for that."

"I have two ships patrolling the islands that lie south of the opening to the fjord, watching for any ships that might slip in here if the king tries to hem us in. They'll warn us," Rorik said. "I also have ships gathering information from those who live along the coast. They'll be back soon."

"It's difficult to guess how many warriors the king will send here by sea." Leif flipped a knife up and caught it by the hilt several times as he spoke. "It's difficult, obviously, and he doesn't know how strong we are. He'll most likely underestimate us. He may not have heard about the marriages combining Thorsfjell and Haardvik. It joins Vargfjell to us also. If he had, I doubt he'd try you, Rorik. It's a test and he's not going to expose too many of his own men to a possible defeat."

"I agree," Eirik said. "A defeat would make him appear weak and he can't afford that. Not while he's eyeing the Sogn region."

"They can't gauge our numbers on the seas." Magnus took a sip of his ale. "No one will know our true strength. It may help us next time. And there will be a next time."

"Unless we wipe them out completely now." Kaia's eyes were like steel blades. "Send his men's stripped carcasses in a ship back to the Vestfold where Halfdan is. Burn it in the fjord at Kaupang."

"Oh yes. That would make me even more welcome there." Rorik gave her a warning look. "We have to be careful. Don't let it be known we suspect Halfdan's presence in all this. All we're doing right now is attacking other ships on the seas. It happens all the time. Sending a flaming ship to the Vestfold would give away that we know it's Halfdan."

Magnus caught all of them in his gaze as he looked around the table. "I agree. Some of you make your living by raiding other lands and that's fine. I don't. I'm a merchant. I have to have access to the great markets to support my people. I need to be careful who I alienate. Even if Halfdan controls the Sogn region, I still have to sail through there going to and from Thorsfjell. You have the information I learned from the people along the fjord. And I left a ship there to watch for Halfdan's movements. I'll back you all the way with everything I have, Rorik, but I have to be circumspect about it."

Eirik drew a pattern in a puddle of spilled ale on the table. "At least if anyone sees Magnus's ships here, they'll think they still belong to me." He hesitated as he looked at the symbol he'd drawn. "I'm much closer to Halfdan than any of you. Just across the mountains, in fact. And the Sogn is just north of me. I don't see any real confrontation with him until the spring. By that time, my shipwrights will have several new ships ready for me if I have them work through the winter. I'll have back the men I loaned Magnus so my power will be at full strength."

"More men come to me every week wanting to fight for me," Magnus said. "I should have enough by winter to crew my ships and return your warriors to you, as we agreed."

"Don't forget," Rorik said, "any ships we capture are ours. We split them between us. If he sends as many as I think he will, and if we can get all of them, it will double our strength."

The men banged their mugs on the table in agreement.

"That's all well and good," Asa said. "But I agree with Kaia. We need to strike hard and send a message to all in the north. Not just to Halfdan. Blood sends the strongest message."

Rorik looked at Magnus. "How did the women in our families become more bloodthirsty than we are? This makes us look bad."

A glance passed between Kaia and Asa. "We learned from men," Kaia said. "In more ways than one. If you boys can't handle the battle, my shieldmaidens and I are more than ready to lead you into the fray."

"Just be certain to follow my orders, Kaia." Rorik stood. "I promise all of you, I intend to make my displeasure well known in the entire Trøndelag. And in Hålogaland, and the Sogn, and Hordaland, and all points south and east. Right up to Halfdan's front door. By the time this is all over, with the power that is in Lade now, and with what we'll show him we have, Halfdan will be begging us to treat with him and offering us titles and even more wealth. In another few years, this region will be among the most powerful in the north. And it all starts here, now, with us."

"Are you quite certain you won't let me pay the ransom for the Christian and take her with me when I leave in the morning?"

Rorik almost spit out his wine. He swallowed with an effort and glanced at Thorir. The jarl's face was serious, but there was a glint of humor in his eyes. Elfwynn was at the head of the hall, playing the harp after dinner, as he had asked. Even though other musicians played along with her, he had heard only her music. Through the evening, Thorir had to nudge him a few times to get his attention, he was so lured by her playing. He was being too obvious. That exposed a weakness and he couldn't afford to be weak in front of anyone. Thorir had already focused on it.

"I've told you about her temper. As a friend and ally, I'd be wrong to saddle you with her. Besides, she's earning the money back by weaving me a sail."

"So I've heard. You waste her, Rorik. All day, everyday, when she's not cleaning up after you, she's been with her loom instead of with a man who appreciates her. You've made her all but a slave. I'd make her all but a queen."

"Slave or queen, I doubt it would matter to her since she's not home." He eyed Thorir. "You would keep her for yourself, then."

"Yes."

"And I have promised her she'll go home after this."

"She would not want to leave *me*."

A slow fire started in his mind. He concentrated on Elfwynn's music, letting its beauty enter him, soothe him. The flames subsided. If he heard this every night as he went to sleep, the darkness could never enter the room. Her music would drive it away better than any lamp.

He took a sip of mead. "I have made a promise and I intend to honor it."

"I wonder. You could send her back now and no one would think any less of you. No warrior would forsake you, no shipwright leave a vessel unfinished. None of your people would turn their backs on you, and you know that. They are too loyal. Yet you use that as an excuse to keep her here."

"It's not an excuse. You know how important our reputations are, if not to my people, then to the world."

"And you must hold to what you have or get recompense for it. In our land, we can't weaken or let another sway us in our resolve. I understand that. But take this word from me, my friend. I have a few years on you and I was married to a woman I loved and lost. Before this, you've never loved. There will come a time when what you want and what the world wants no longer matters. All that will be important is her. What she wants, what makes her happy. When that occurs, you'll know what love is. Only then, will you be able to let her go."

Elfwynn poured out her silver and gold coins into her palm. She'd worked so long at home to earn these, and it was almost enough to take her mother and her to Strathclyde and away from Edward. Just a little more time and she would have been gone and never seen or heard of Rorik of Vargfjell.

It was too little, too late. She didn't need the money now. Even if she made it home one day, it would be a long time from now. She could always sell her loom and her harp to raise the money again.

There was another need for the coins, one more imminent. She slipped the pouch in a pocket she'd made in her skirt and walked to Oslafa's house. As she'd hoped, Turold was there with his mother, speaking with her outside.

She embraced Oslafa. "I'd hoped to find you both here. I've heard Finna's father is making noise again about her marrying."

"Yes," Oslafa said. "The word has spread that Rorik's women have left him to marry other men. Finna's father is taking this as a sign he would be more amenable to wed now."

Elfwynn tried to keep her jaw from dropping. They'd left him? Why? His bed hadn't been quite as rumpled in the mornings of late, but she hadn't thought anything of it. What woman in her right mind would leave him? Besides her?

She gathered herself. "I'd heard her father was pressuring her again, but not why. Turold, I want to give you this." She pulled out the pouch and handed it to him. "I had it with me when I came here, but I don't need it any longer. Perhaps it will help."

He looked inside the bag and his eyes widened. "I can't take this." He tried to hand it back. "You've already done too much with weaving the cloth. I want to work for the bride-price."

She put her hands behind her back so he couldn't press it on her. "And end up losing her. If he can't get Rorik to marry her, it will be someone else. With this war coming, there'll be more men here and more chances for him to speak to some of them. Is this enough?"

Oslafa took the bag and looked inside. "Oh my. If it isn't, it's close. But the other problem is that he wants her to wed someone of higher rank than Turold."

"You work here now, on the houses in the village instead of on the farms. That must be better work."

"It is," he said. "It pays more, but it's still not good enough. If only I could be a shipwright. That's prestigious work and I could do it. But I haven't had the chance."

"Keep that." She nodded toward the bag Oslafa held. "Add it to what you already have. We'll figure something out."

"I'll make this up to you," Turold said. "I'll make you something beautiful. A carved cross of sea-ivory, perhaps. I can do it. If I can get the ivory." He embraced her. "I'll pray to God each night for you. Surely He knows the good works you've done here and will bless you."

Too late. "Your prayers are more than enough." She reached up and touched his cheek. Such a fine young man should have the one he loved beside him. "I have to head back to the longhouse. I didn't draw the water for Rorik's sauna yet. I wanted to be certain to find you before you went to work."

After they went into the house, she left, lighter of heart. Of course, it wasn't because Rorik's women were gone. It was because the money would go toward a better use now, and perhaps it would bring some happiness. Smiling, she lifted her head and stopped. Rorik stood in the road, his arms crossed, his eyes dark.

"It's not like you to leave things undone, Elfwynn," he said. "When I wanted my morning sauna and there was no water and no wood, I thought something might be wrong. It is, but not because of the sauna."

"I don't know what you mean, Northman. Nothing's wrong. You were seeing Thorir off and I thought you'd be gone longer. I'll see to your water now." She walked past him.

He caught her by the arm. "I told you to stay away from Turold and then I see you and he embracing. You caressed his face. I'm not pleased at your disobedience."

"Disobedience?" She snatched her arm away. "What am I? A dog to come when you call and obey your every command? I think not. As long as I do what I agreed to, I can embrace a shipload of warriors and it shouldn't matter to you." She continued down the road.

He followed her. "Try it again, Elfwynn, and you'll see what matters to me."

"I already know the answer to that, Northman. Your ships and your wealth." She whirled around to face him. "Oh, and let's not forget your status and reputation that lets you trample over everyone's life while you sit in your hall, untouched by anything and anyone. All your women left you, and yet you drank and laughed at the feast last night like nothing happened. Because in your eyes, nothing did." She spun and walked toward the longhouse, silence behind her.

As she entered the front door, she glanced back. He stood in the road, staring at her, probably shocked anyone would speak to him that way. She wasn't one of his simpering women and he should know that by now.

She went to the well at the back of the longhouse and drew some water. As she picked up a bucket to pour it into, a tiny snake moved. It had been coiled up beneath the bucket and she had disturbed it. It was a harmless thing, and she watched it for a moment. Then she smiled. *A private little war.* That was what she had promised Oslafa she would wage and that was what would happen between Rorik and her.

That evening, when she went into Rorik's chamber to light the lamps, she brought the tiny creature with her. She lifted the lid of the small basket she'd put it into and let it crawl out onto the down mattress. After flipping the furs and blankets over it, she tucked them under the mattress and arranged the pillows at the head of the bed. Nice and cozy.

She finished up and went into her room. Sometimes she wove into the night, at other times, she talked with the women in the hall she'd made friends with. But tonight she didn't want to risk being anywhere in Rorik's sight when he met the snake, so she remained in her room and embroidered for a while.

When she grew tired, she went to bed. She lay awake, waiting for him to retire for the night. When his door opened and closed, she sat up, listening.

A muffled yell from his room started her laughing. To keep quiet, she shoved her face into her pillow, her body shaking with mirth. At the sound of his footsteps, she rose and cracked her door open. He was walking toward the front doorway, muttering to himself, holding the small snake in his hand. She eased the door shut and went back to bed, smiling.

The war had begun.

Chapter Twelve

How long was he going to stand in the doorway and watch her weave?

Elfwynn ignored Rorik. She had more important things to do than rise to whatever bait he was trying to toss her way. When she'd served him his breakfast that morning, he'd acted quite normal, but an understanding had passed between them as he'd thanked her. The game was on. Her only concern was that he was so much better armed than she was.

He sauntered over to her loom and leaned on the next one over, his arms crossed. No one else was in the room yet and it made her uneasy.

"I thought I should warn you that the snakes in the area are very active during this warm time of year."

"I'll keep that in mind."

"I found one in my bed last night."

"Oh?"

"Yes. It was small and harmless. Still, one wonders how it could have climbed up there and under the tucked-in covers. Often where there's one, there's more. I've heard that sound will drive them away."

"So it does." Where was he going with this?

"To be certain I don't have any others in the room, I'd like you to come in and play your harp for me when I retire. As a precaution."

She did look at him, then. "I don't think so, Northman. It's not what we agreed on."

"It is, however, what you promised."

"What are you talking about?" She stopped weaving and faced him.

"In front of the Arab's house, you spoke to me to calm me. I remember you said you'd play for me every night."

He *would* remember that. "I said anything I could think of to try to reach you. That's all."

"So you go back on a promise?"

"It wasn't a promise."

"And yet, you said it, didn't you?"

"I can't do that. Don't you know what that will do to my reputation when I'm seen going in there with you?"

"First, it's well known you don't think much of me. No one who has heard you speak to me can doubt that. Second, it's also known I don't touch a woman unless she's willing. Third, everyone knows you're not willing. Therefore, your reputation will be safe. Fourth, anyone would be able to hear the music through the door. As long as you continue playing, what you're doing will be obvious."

What *he* was doing was obvious. Taking revenge. When they were alone, her hands were occupied, and she couldn't stop playing, what would he do to her?

Warmth crept over her, unfurling like a flower opening within her. She'd be at his mercy and, as a Northman, he wouldn't have any. Still, he'd never force a woman, so she should be safe. If she stopped him, he wouldn't take her. *If* she stopped him. With his history, he must be a master of seduction. There was a great difference between force and enticement.

God forgive her, but he was enticing. Even with how much she resented him, she couldn't deny it. She would just have to trust in his code and her determination to stop anything from happening.

"Very well. I'll play the harp for you. But if you come near me, it's over. Agreed?"

He smiled down at her in his heart-stopping way, the very devil in his eyes. "Agreed. I'll see you this evening, little Christian."

Biting her lip, she turned back to the loom. What had she done? This was a battle and she had just stepped into his territory where he would have the advantage. He might stay away from her, but not all fighting was done toe to toe. There were spears and arrows, ways to engage from a distance without ever touching the enemy.

She ran her hand down the thick woolen cloth. It was said he could catch a spear in flight and hurl it back at the thrower. Against weapon-skills like that, there was no defense. This plan was foolish.

She stood no chance against him. Perhaps it would be better to back out now, before this went too far.

But the teasing look he'd given her had raised her hackles. He was too high-handed, too arrogant. It would bring him down a few notches if he tried anything with her and failed. He needed to experience defeat once in his life.

If she remained strong, she would be the one to hand it to him.

At least he'd waited until it was so late, most of the people had left the hall for the night before he sought his chamber. There were fewer people to see her pick up the harp and follow him.

When she entered, he had already pulled off his tunic. He stood with his back to her, clad only in his shirt and trousers. She stopped at the door.

"You're not going to undress, are you? If so, I'm leaving."

He smiled over his shoulder. "You don't expect me to sleep fully clothed, do you? I'll remain decent so as not to offend your delicate sensibilities."

"The day you're decent is the day I'll see your gods come down and walk among us."

"Take care what you say. Sometimes they do. Ask my sister Ellisif." He drew off his shirt. The muscles in his back rippled as he moved. His ebony hair flowed to his waist, gleaming in the lamplight.

She busied herself drawing a chair to the wall near the door, and as far from the bed as possible. It appeared he wanted her to play until he fell asleep. Strange, but perhaps without his women with him, he needed something else to relax him. That, she could do. Then she'd leave immediately.

He walked to the bed and pulled back the furs, checking underneath them. She took the chance to peek at him. His chest was broad and his stomach flat, each ridge defined under his skin. Cords of muscle ran along his shoulders. Scars crossed his upper body, just as she expected of a warrior and a raider. None of those marks were severe. They showed his prowess in war, proving that the tales of his battle-skills were true.

She raised her eyes. He straightened, smiling at her, and shook his hair back, giving her a better view. "Like what you see, little Christian?"

"You're a man, like any other. I've seen many of my father's warriors in various stages of undress as they trained. It is of no matter to me." Setting her fingers to the strings, she tested the tuning. Her body awoke, warming deep within. She'd suspected he could wield his body like a weapon and he'd just cast the first volley.

He chuckled and slid onto the bed. Instead of pulling up the covers, he lay on top of them, his arms folded behind his head. The light bathed his long body in a golden glow. Biting her lip, she concentrated on the harp, making certain all the strings were in tune.

She played a soft melody, one she often used to help her mother go to sleep. It might work on him as well, and then she could leave. As she played the first notes, it was so easy to forget he was there, to forget where she was. Closing her eyes, she let the music take her.

Free. Free of the memories of her father's betrayal, her mother's pain, her own loneliness. Free from this foreign land and its lord who made her feel both anger and longing as no other ever had. She was the music, soaring and beautiful. The vibrations from the harp entered her, then left her again in the song, wafting into the air, leaving everything behind.

She continued, song after song, until her fingers ached and the skin on their tips was tender. The discomfort brought her back and she rested her hand on the strings to mute them. She glanced at Rorik.

He was on his side, facing her, his eyes closed, his breathing deep. He looked almost innocent, without the teasing sparkle in his eyes, or the arrogant curl at the sides of his sensuous mouth. His body was like a sculpture she had seen once in an ancient building that a great army had built long ago in her land. The statue was of one of their gods, carved in white marble, perfect and glorious.

His hair spread like spilled ink across the pillow, contrasting with his pale skin. What would it be like to join him there? To lie beside him and let his sensual power wash over her? To give up and give in—to him?

Troubled, she rose and went to the door to escape him. And her own thoughts.

"Sleep well, little Christian."

She jumped and looked back at him. He hadn't opened his eyes, but his lips curved up in a slight smile. "Be careful of your own bed, though. As I said, there was a snake in here last night and where there's one, there's often more."

She didn't answer, but hurried out. Not bothering to put the harp back in its corner in the hall, she went into her own room and sighed in relief. She lit a lamp, then eyed the bed. Why had he warned her about more snakes? It would be like him to retaliate in kind. Had he kept the snake from last night? Did he put something even worse beneath her blankets?

She set the harp aside and approached the bed. Staying back as far as she could, she hit the cover in several places. Nothing moved. There was no choice but to face whatever he had done. Holding her breath, she threw back the cover.

A gold necklace lay on the sheets. It was about the same thickness and length as the snake. She picked it up and sat down as a shudder ran through her. It was very heavy and worth a fortune, enough to pay for passage to Northumbria and then to Strathclyde. And let her mother and her live in comfort for a very long time.

Why had he done this? Did he think giving her baubles would soften her toward him? This was far more than a bauble, but to a man of his wealth, it would be negligible. He'd probably stolen it, anyhow. After all, that was what he did.

She turned it in the thin light of the oil lamp. He likely thought to buy her respect with this. Or buy her. A slow anger built in her. She wasn't one of his glittering women who thought only of ways to please him, attract him, and entice him. Who could be bought with pretty things. They were all gone now, so he must be looking for others to take their places.

She wouldn't be among them.

It would be foolish to throw it back at him, for she might need it one day. She hid the necklace under the mattress then undressed, leaving her shift on, and climbed into bed. The Northman might be trying to declare a truce between them, but she doubted that. Far be it from him to parley. He raided, conquered, and then took what he wanted. He'd do the same to her. He could have punished her, enslaved her for disrespecting him the way she did. And yet, he hadn't.

Could it be he had a heart after all? She turned onto her side and pounded the pillow. He was accomplishing just what he wanted— softening her toward him. It wouldn't work. He might have a heart, but it was only an organ, like any other. It felt nothing, loved nothing, the same as he. If she made his life miserable, he'd either leave her alone altogether, or let her leave Vargfjell. Then she'd never have to see him again.

She stared into the night. If the heart was just an organ, why did it feel like hers was breaking?

He'd done it again. Was there no way to win against him?

Elfwynn fingered the beautiful dress. It was a golden tan color with white insets and beading on the long double sleeves and intricate neckline. Its skirt was split in the front, revealing a white underskirt. The workmanship was unlike any she'd ever seen and he'd no doubt stolen it from somewhere.

The day after she'd found the necklace, she'd put something very foul that she'd found in the pigsty into one of his shoes. That afternoon, when she went into her room, she'd found a new pair of finely crafted shoes there. A bottle of rare perfume was resting in one of them. Then, yesterday, she'd put Spurge Olive dust into one of his shirts and laid it out for him to change into when he was finished training. It would make his skin itch and redden. When she served him his evening meal, he'd scratched his chest while he'd leveled a stare at her, but never said a word about it.

Now, she'd found this exquisite dress in her chest. It almost made her feel bad that she'd cut the girth on his saddle that morning. Almost.

She put the dress back into her chest. It wasn't as though she'd have any occasion to wear it. It was a dress fit for a jarl's wife, not her. She was little more than a bondservant here, paying off a debt. Servants didn't wear gold necklaces, fine shoes, or dresses covered in beading while they did laundry and cleaned rooms. It didn't make sense.

But the laundry wouldn't get done if she was sitting here, no matter what she wore. She grabbed the basket filled with his clothes and walked out of the longhouse. It was a beautiful day and a walk to the fjord would clear her mind.

The Northman and his men had gathered to ride to the south, to look for signs of encroachment. Turold was walking in as she came out.

He stopped her with a hand on her arm. "Elfwynn, is Finna in the weaving room?"

"I didn't see her."

"I think her father is making her stay home rather than helping with the weaving so she doesn't speak to me. I'm worried he's becoming frustrated that Rorik isn't showing any interest in her. I'd hoped to speak with her, but I suppose I won't be able to today."

"If I see her, I'll let her know you're trying to find her. Maybe we can plan for you to be with her later."

"My thanks. If you ask her to help you, he'll let her go then."

She nodded and walked toward the group of men. As she approached, Rorik swung up on his horse. The saddle slid to the side and both it and he landed on the ground in a heap. The well-trained horse stood still, staring back at him with a curious look.

She walked past. "Trouble mounting?"

He sat up, rested his elbows on his knees, and glared at her. "Not until now. Though I'd be glad to demonstrate to you just how good I am at it." The horse nibbled the top of Rorik's hair.

"At least your horse knows how skilled you are." The laughter of the men followed her down the path to the water.

When she reached the shore, she tucked her skirt in her belt and took one of the shirts out of the basket. If she didn't have to do these chores, and play music for him every night, she'd have much more of the sail woven than she did. It was as though he was trying to stall her, keep her from working on it. She gritted her teeth as she rinsed out the shirt. Perhaps cutting the girth was unwise. There would be hell to pay this time. But it was worth every coin.

"Elfwynn."

And he'd come to collect. She didn't look up, but continued working.

"You went too far this time, Elfwynn. I could have gotten hurt."

"I think not, Northman. You've spent your life in battle and raiding, cutting and slashing your way through the world. And you managed to stay alive while balancing all those women at the same time. That is truly a feat for the sagas. I don't believe a fall from a horse would hurt you. Nothing does."

He was silent for a time. "You know, we have washing women to do that."

"Really? They would treat this embroidered shirt like they do the wool blankets. They'd destroy it. I don't want to see that." She swirled it in the water.

"Don't tell me you're worried that I might miss one of my good shirts."

"Of course not. I do care about the shirt. About the weaver who made the cloth, the woman who sewed it, and the embroiderer who did the stitching. I care about all the work that went into it since I'm like them. Not like you. Them. Like Oslafa, Finna, Kolla, and Turold. They live to toil for you so you can have the best of everything. The best clothes, the best houses, the best food."

"And I protect them with my life." He crossed his arms. "Speaking of Turold, once again you've gone against my word. I saw him touch you. I forbade it. I'll speak to him about it and it won't be pleasant."

Speaking to you never is. She squeezed the material to remove the water. "You'll do as you want anyhow. Your word is the law here and everyone has to jump to appease your every whim."

He strode into the water to where she stood. She straightened and met his glare. "That's right, little Christian. Everyone does what I say. Except you. Always you tax me, always you defy me. Always you keep meeting with your lover."

"He's not my lover." She threw the wet shirt at him. It hit him in the chest with a splat then fell into the water.

"And now you attack me?"

She almost laughed. "First it's a fall from a horse, now it's a wet shirt that will bring about your untimely demise? I always thought you were harder than that, Northman."

"I'll show you how hard I am." He pulled her to him, his hands on her shoulders. She twisted to get free, but he put his arms around her and there was no escape. "No woman has ever spoken to me as you do. Ever since the day I met you, I've had nothing but havoc in my life. Perhaps my gods have cursed me for taking you."

"No, perhaps *my* God cursed you for taking me."

He stared at her for a moment. "Whichever it is, nothing is the same. I should just gag you and keep you quiet and subdued. Maybe I'd have peace again. But I can think of a better way to keep you silent."

He kissed her. It was the heat of fire and the hardness of steel. It was power and arrogance and total command over her. She couldn't escape. She didn't even try.

This had been coming between them, in the same way Ragnarok was inevitable for their gods. The death of everything that came before. Complete devastation. Her traitorous body leaned into him and he gathered her closer, making her open to him in ways she'd never dreamed of. He tasted of wine and fruit, his scent was of the wind and the sea. His arms were warm and strong around her. She ran her hands along his back, feeling the muscles she'd seen a few nights before.

He breathed into her mouth and filled her with him. Then he lifted his head and looked down at her. Victory sparkled in his silver-green eyes as he loosened his hold on her.

He thought he'd won? That she was just another conquest?

She shoved him hard. He lost his balance and tipped backwards, but as he fell, he grabbed her hand and took her down with him. She shrieked as the cold water closed in over her. Laughing, he pulled her up with him, both of them sodden and filthy from the mud their floundering had stirred up. She pushed him away.

"You idiot." She splashed him. "Now your shirt is gone."

He splashed her back. "Forget the damned shirt. You liked me kissing you. Admit it."

"I'll do no such thing. You had no right to do that. I thought you didn't force women." She smacked the water toward him several times as he ducked, grinning.

"That wasn't force and you know it. At least now you've been kissed by a man, not a boy like Turold." He sent a wave of water over her.

She sputtered. "I've never been kissed by anyone, Northman. And I've told you, Turold doesn't love me. He loves Finna."

He stopped. "Finna? Orri's daughter?"

"Yes, Finna, Orri's daughter."

"Why aren't they together, then? Doesn't she favor him?"

"Yes." She searched through the water for the shirt. In her anger, she'd blurted out the truth. There was no help for it now. "She does. They love each other. But her father won't let him marry her."

"Why not? He's a fine young man."

She almost reminded him that he hadn't thought so earlier, but it wouldn't be wise to antagonize him about this. She'd hold her tongue for their sakes.

"He won't let them marry because Orri hopes you'll be attracted to her and wed her."

"Me?" He cast through the water, helping her look for the lost shirt.

She hid her smile at the sight of the great Rorik of Vargfjell, stooping to rake his hands through the mud. "You. And he's raised the bride-price so high, no one but you could afford it. He doesn't think Turold is good enough for her because he's only a wood worker. Oslafa and he have a good amount of money, but not enough." She wouldn't mention the money she'd given them.

"I wondered why she wasn't married yet, a pretty girl like her. I never knew."

"They didn't want anyone to know. Apparently, in your culture, you frown on courtships. They were afraid Orri would take revenge on Turold and force Finna to marry someone else."

"No woman is forced to marry anyone here," he said. "Ah." He came up with the shirt, but didn't give it to her when she reached for it. "Never mind about all this. You're cold. Go have a sauna to warm up. The washing women can do this and I'll warn them that you'll come after them if they ruin the stitching. That should put the fear of the gods into them."

She drew herself up to make a retort, but at the humor in his eyes, she had to smile. Lowering her head, she tried to hide it, but he had caught it and grinned with her. A laugh welled up in her that she couldn't hold back and he joined in.

He was truly dangerous, and not as the world knew it. His weapons lay in his sparkling eyes and wicked smile, his teasing and his humor. They hit her like a shield wall, battering at her until she couldn't resist any longer.

She shivered and it wasn't entirely from the cold water. His gaze swept her. And lingered. She glanced down at herself and turned away from him, heat rising into her cheeks. Her soaked dress clung to her like a second skin, the fjord water drawing the tips of her breasts tight. Everything showed. Wrapping her arms around herself, she sloshed onto the shore with as much dignity as she could, though her skirt had come out of her belt and wrapped around her legs in a sodden mass.

She put her shoes in the laundry basket, picked it up to have something to hide behind, and took the path to the longhouse. He was following her, God take him. Probably looking at her rear with the dress plastered against it.

"The men will be in the sauna now, so use mine."

"I don't think so."

"Getting you warm is more important than your modesty, or my interest in what hides behind that modesty. Go. I swear I won't peek. When you come out, there'll be a robe for you. Leave the dress. The washing women will see to it."

She didn't reply. She hurried through the longhouse that, mercifully, was empty. As she set the laundry basket down in her room, he followed her in.

"What are you doing? Leave me alone."

"No." He took her hand and led her out of the room and toward the back door. "I'm making certain you do as I say. For once." She had no choice but to walk with him to the sauna. When they stood in front of the building, he released her hand. "Go in. Get warm." He returned to the longhouse.

Sighing, she went inside. Steam already filled the inner room. Warm, relaxing steam. She dropped her clothes on the floor and entered it. How did the servants know he'd need this? Part of her duties was to be certain there was water and wood, but the servants didn't start the fire until he was ready for it. She dumped water on the hot rocks and sat down.

Something had changed between them, but she wasn't certain what it was. A shifting in positions of two adversaries who had realized that, perhaps, they were too equally matched? She'd been butting her head against him all this time, yet he'd never come back at her the way he would any other enemy. Why? It would have been better if he had. Then she'd have a target to aim at. Instead, he was as changeable as the wind, and as difficult to hit. She'd done terrible things to him, yet he'd repaid her with beautiful gifts.

Like he was courting her.

As though he'd do that. Then again, there'd been the kiss. Was it just a way to conquer her, get her to acquiesce to his wishes? Soften her up? It'd certainly worked. At least, for that moment. She couldn't let down her guard again. He was too wily, too much the strategist. To him, it was all a game. To her, it was her future.

He had quickly lost interest in Turold and Finna, changing the subject as he had. So much for his compassion toward his people.

Sighing, she rinsed and went to the outer room. A warm, woolen robe lay on the bench and her soaked dress was gone. She wrapped her hair in a towel, put on the robe, and went to her room, seeing no one. The basket of laundry was gone. On the bed, lay a beautiful new dress with embroidery on the sleeves and bodice, and a soft linen shift.

There was an ivory comb, inset with gems, beside it. Once again, at his mere word, lovely things appeared out of nowhere. His every desire was anticipated. It was as though he need only think of something and it was done for him. All he'd ever known was luxury and wealth. The world changed to honor his wishes, bowing to him as he stood eye to eye with his gods.

No doubt, he thought if he gave her all these things, she would bow, as well. Something had shifted between them and he must feel it. But it wasn't because of his gifts, or his wealth, or even the power of his kiss.

It was because they had laughed together for the first time, shivering in the freezing water of the fjord. And in that moment, perhaps the entire world didn't change.

But hers certainly had.

Chapter Thirteen

"Finna, would you come with me?" Rorik smiled to ease the awed look she gave him. The other women in the weaving room whispered and stared. Elfwynn wasn't there. Unfortunately. When he didn't see her, he couldn't be certain what plots she was carrying out against him.

The young woman walked outside with him, a questioning look on her face. "Did I do anything wrong, Rorik?"

"Not at all. We're going to your house so I can speak with your father. Here's what I want you to say." As he spoke to her, she nodded, her expression lightening. When he was certain she understood what she was to do, they headed for her house.

He glanced around to see if Elfwynn was nearby. He didn't trust her. He thought the kiss yesterday would have made her less inclined to try to maim him in some way. But it hadn't. While it was true he hadn't found anything wrong, so far, she wasn't pleased with him.

She hadn't met his eye when she'd served him last night, and when she played for him, her music was off, as though she couldn't concentrate. Was it her resentment of him? Or was it the kiss?

He had thought to control her, show her he was in command. Instead, she had taken over his senses. Her sweet scent, the feel of her in his arms, her soft breath entering his mouth, all of it had consumed him. With other women, he had taken and given back only what he chose. But that kiss stripped his thoughts away, leaving him bare. She had to have felt the connection between them. When he'd ended it, he'd looked down at her to let her see his pleasure and joy.

Another woman would have melted. Gazed at him with adoring eyes. Begged for more as she gave in to his every wish.

Elfwynn had shoved him into the water.

He winced. It was no surprise she reacted that way. It was part of what made her so intriguing, if a bit hard on his clothes, saddles, and him. All he ever heard from other women was, *Yes, Rorik. If that's what you desire, Rorik. Whatever you say, Rorik.* It all sounded the same after a while, like the humming of bees. With Elfwynn, he could never be certain where she was going to swing her verbal sword. Or how to parry it.

That was what made life worth living—the thrill of battle and standing steel to steel against a worthy adversary. The blood raging in his veins, the battle cry tearing from his throat, the thrill of triumph as he raised his sword high to the gods, his enemies at his feet.

In some ways, Elfwynn gave him that. Every victory with her was that much sweeter for being so hard-won. He could buy the smile of any woman, except her.

She hadn't worn the expensive dress or the necklace or the new shoes he'd given her. But then, why should she? All she did was clean up after him and serve him. When he'd seen her in the fjord, washing his shirt, something had twisted in him. It wasn't right. She was too fine for that. When he got back to the longhouse, he'd tell her she wasn't to serve him any longer. She could spend the time as she wished.

That would most likely be weaving. Which meant she'd finish the sail sooner and he'd never see her again. Unless he won her affection before that. Thorir had said if she were his, she wouldn't want to leave him. Over his dead body.

It would be his pleasure to make her feel that way about him, if he survived it.

Orri was working in the small garden beside the house when Finna and he walked up. The older man saw them together, and his eyes widened. He smiled as he wiped his hands and came to greet them. "Rorik, welcome. What brings you here with my daughter?" He looked back and forth between them both, his grin spreading.

This was going to be entertaining. "A question of marriage, Orri. I hear you wish for Finna to marry."

"Oh yes, Rorik. She's a sweet girl. Pretty. Talented. She'll make an excellent wife for a good man."

"I agree. Unfortunately, other men have been courting her and she doesn't want to give offense by choosing another who came later, over them."

"Young girls often don't know what's the best for them, do they Rorik?" He kept up his smile, but it was strained. "We men have to decide these things."

"Yes, but it doesn't sit well with me to force a woman to marry against her wishes. You know that, Orri." He gave him a hard look. "I would hear what she has to say."

"Of course. Of course. Well, girl, what do you say to all this?"

She glanced down as though she was flustered. "I don't know, Father. Alfarr has spoken to me quite nicely. And he's handsome."

"Not him. I won't have you marrying a boy younger than you."

"You're right, Father. That wouldn't work well." She paused as though considering and Rorik quashed a smile. She should be a skald, telling tales for the people's enjoyment.

He put his arm around her shoulders. "Who else, Finna?"

"There's Dagrun. He gives me flowers and nice things."

"When did he do this? I'll teach him to try to bribe my daughter into his bed. You're not marrying him."

Rorik almost rolled his eyes. Fathers. No wonder courtship was one of the most dangerous times for any man. Just a hint of impropriety could mean death to the suitor.

"Is there anyone else?" Rorik drew her closer and smiled down at her. She gazed up at him, her eyes wide and dreamy.

"Yes, Rorik. I favor . . ." She hesitated and Orri leaned closer.

"Yes, girl? Who is it?"

"Turold."

"What?" He threw up his hands. "I told you that whelp wasn't to come near you. I forbid it. He doesn't have enough for the bride-price and he's only a wood worker. Nothing."

"Now just wait, Orri." Rorik released Finna and stepped up to him. "According to our customs, a father can refuse two suitors that his daughter names. The third one, he has to accept. That would be Turold." He'd spoken with Osalfa this morning and she'd told him the *mundr* Orri wanted. "Your bride-price is three times what it should be. Lower it. The young man has the money for that. As for his being a wood worker, he's so skilled, I'm making him a ship-wright's apprentice. I'm increasing my fleet, so he'll be very busy. It pays well and holds a prestigious place among our people. Most important of all, Finna will be happy. As a father, you cannot ask for more than that."

"I suppose not, Rorik." He sighed as Rorik crossed his arms and glared at him. "I agree, Finna. Marry Turold if he's who you want."

"Thank you, Father." She embraced him.

"I was only looking after you, girl. To be sure you'd have a man who can take care of you. You know that." His voice was gruff.

"I must return to the longhouse," Rorik said. "We leave for battle tomorrow and I have much to do. We'll have the *handsal* tonight."

Finna left her father and stood before him. Her eyes were bright with happy tears. "Thank you, Rorik. I'll never forget this."

"It's nothing. Let me know when you wish to marry and we'll have a grand celebration." He walked back to the village. At least that was done and he had witnessed it. That was why he'd seen to it himself, so Orri couldn't deny it. Turold wouldn't have a reason to sniff around Elfwynn any longer. And it pleased him to see to the happiness of each of his people.

Oslafa had told him some interesting things that morning about Elfwynn, including the role she'd played in getting Finna and Turold together. He needed to speak with Elfwynn about that.

She was in the weaving room, no doubt having gone there after he'd left with Finna. He went to her loom and examined the cloth she was making for the sail. It was of the highest quality, tight and thick, the weft straight and even.

She said nothing to him, only continuing her work even though she came close to bumping into him as she moved to the right side of the frame.

"Elfwynn, I need to speak to you. Will you walk with me?"

"I have much to do, Northman. I don't have time for pleasantries like some do."

"Please?"

She stopped weaving and stared at him, shock on her face. The word sounded strange to him, as well. Then, pressing her lips together, she nodded. He led her outside and down to the fjord. There were benches along part of the shore for people who wished to enjoy the water and watch the ships at the nearby docks. His new ship, the one to replace *The Sword of the Waves*, was taking shape on top of blocks a short distance off. Other vessels were on the beach, including Eirik's and Magnus's.

The ships that had been out patrolling and gathering information had returned. There was a large fleet heading north from the Sognefjorden. He was uncertain where they'd put in to unload the men who would help the jarls. Tomorrow, he'd start out with the ships once Thorir arrived. One never knew what the Norns had woven into one's destiny, so he wanted to make things right with Elfwynn before he left.

He indicated one of the benches and she sank down on it. He sat beside her. "I thought you'd like to know that Turold and Finna are getting married. I spoke with her father and he agreed."

She smiled as she looked out at the fjord. "I'm so happy for them. When you didn't say anything more about them yesterday, I thought you didn't care."

"I care about all my people. I had already formed a plan in my mind, but I had to talk with Oslafa and Turold about it. I did so this morning. She also told me some interesting things about what you did for them. The cloth you wove before we went to Hedeby, for instance. You gave it to them to raise silver for the bride-price."

"I wanted to help and it was all I could think of to do."

"And then, you and Turold made it seem as though you were interested in each other to throw Orri off the scent."

"They didn't want me to say anything about it, so I couldn't tell you. Though in the end, I did." She blushed.

"And it all worked out. But there is one more thing." He drew out of his belt pouch the bag she'd given them with her silver and gold in it. "You gave them this money. Why?"

She looked at the bag, everything she had in the world, held in one of his hands. "I'd been saving it for a long time and I had it with me when you took me. Now I'm stuck here, and by the time I leave, it most likely won't matter any longer. I didn't need it and they do."

"They don't need it either." He took her hand, put the bag in it and folded her fingers over it. "This is yours. I made Orri lower the bride-price to what it should be. Turold has more than enough and now he'll start working on my ships. So he'll be quite well off and Oslafa insisted that this be returned to you."

She nodded, not looking at him. "Is that all you wanted? I should go back to work."

No, he wanted her, and if she were any other woman, he could tell her that. But it would never be. She'd rejected all his gifts, and him, but there was still something he could give her. Not her freedom to return home, for there was the issue of compensation for his lost ship, and upholding his reputation. However, he could still please her. He might be cutting his own throat by doing this, but if it made her happy, he'd wield the knife.

"About your work. I don't want you cleaning up after me any longer. I have servants for that. By making things off kilter around here, my men and people have been letting me know their displeasure at not getting enough recompense for my burned ship, but I don't care."

"Did you ever consider they were doing it, not because they thought you didn't go far enough, but because you went too far? They felt for me. Weaving a sail is one thing, for I love to weave anyhow, but they didn't like that I was treated like a servant."

He laughed. "So that's what it was. In that case, to keep the village intact, you're free to do as you want, including weaving the entire day. I still must get something for the ship, but I think this is agreeable to both of us."

"Thank you." Her eyes sparkled with joy. "It will still take a long time, but at least nothing will interfere with my work. I'll finish the sail that much sooner." She quieted.

The unspoken words hung in the air between them. *And leave here that much sooner.*

He was never one to step back from battle. "As I told you before, you could always stay here."

She gazed across the water as though she saw something far away. "No. I can't."

He ran his fingers through his hair in frustration. "Why not? What do you have there besides a bastard of a father?"

Instead of flaying him alive for the comment, she spoke so quietly, he almost didn't hear her. "My half brother, Wulf. He'll be searching for me. He won't give up unless he knows I'm dead. My mother. She's ill and needs me. I have to get home for them, if for nothing else."

Her mother? "Why didn't you tell me about your mother before?"

A slow, sad smile touched her lips. "Would it have mattered to you? Would one Northumbrian woman matter to the great Rorik of Vargfjell?"

He touched her cheek. "One Northumbrian woman does matter to me. You."

"But they matter more." She nodded to the ships. "And your reputation as unrelenting and merciless. It's all right. In a way, I understand. And in a way, that makes it even harder. It means you're not the cold, heartless man I once thought you were. You need all that to protect your people. I know that now, and I respect it. My father is much the same way as you are. I suppose all men of power must be so. But sometimes, in holding on so tightly to that power, you squeeze those who love you until they cannot breathe any longer. They die inside. I've seen it happen to my mother because of her love for my father. I will not let it happen to me."

She rose and walked back up the path toward the longhouse. He stared after her, his mind ringing as though she'd hit his skull with a war axe. Had she just said what he thought he'd heard? That she loved him? Or she *would* love him if he weren't so much like the father who betrayed and hurt her.

He'd called the earl a bastard, and yet wasn't he one himself? If she had told him first off about her ill mother, would it have stopped him from taking her? Probably not. Now that he knew, he understood a little better her anger at being here. Her life could not have been good under a father who didn't care about her. He should know. But it hadn't been without love. He'd met her half brother when he was bargaining with Edward and he seemed a good man. If someone had sailed in here and taken one of his sisters, he'd never give up trying to find her either. If she didn't kill the idiot first.

If Edward didn't care about Elfwynn, he most likely didn't care about the mother, either. Was she getting the help she needed? Was her daughter the only one who looked after her? Rorik closed his hands in tight fists as the pain seared through him. He hadn't been able to save his mother so long ago. The agony of that still tormented him. Did Elfwynn's inability to be there for her mother haunt her as well?

He rubbed his hand over his face. This complicated things. He had some decisions to make. After the battle. The men were sharpening their weapons, and Thorir would be here in the morning. This was the very survival of Vargfjell and its people. Elfwynn would understand.

But afterward, he'd make certain she understood so much more.

The *handsal* for the marriage between Finna and Turold had gone well with Orri. He'd insisted on the formal agreement to be certain that if anything happened to him in the coming battle, the couple could still wed.

Rorik set down his empty cup and rose to go to his room for the night. One had to prepare for all eventualities before war and he'd made certain Vargfjell would be in good hands. If Eirik survived, he'd take over as the closest kin until one of his heirs could rule here. Like Ivar had done after his own father's death until Rorik was old enough to return. He had family in the far north on his father's side, but he didn't know them and didn't want to. They might cause a problem with the claim, but with Eirik's power, they wouldn't prevail.

Elfwynn would be returned to her homeland. Magnus had promised to take her there should it be necessary. That would make her happy. He put his hand on the door's latch. If only he could hear her laugh one more time, as she had when they'd stood dripping wet in the fjord. She'd never laughed with him before, and now, it might never happen again.

She was there, waiting for him with her harp. All the lamps were lit and the glow shone in her honey-colored hair. He closed the door and leaned back against it.

"I said you don't have to serve me any longer. That includes playing for me each night."

"It's the night before you leave for battle." She spread her fingers on the strings, but didn't move them. "Wulf and my father were always tense before they left for war. Sometimes I played for them. They said it soothed them. I thought it might help you as it did them."

"It will." He walked farther into the room and unfastened the belt over his tunic. "I go over and over everything I think will happen, what I hope will happen, and what I fear will happen. It doesn't make for a restful night."

Often, he had buried himself inside a woman the night before, so as not to think. Only feel. But while that had exhausted his body and his mind, it had done nothing for his spirit. This would. Her music awakened a part of him he'd thought dead when his mother had died. Elfwynn touched him on that same level. She was a comfort to him, an easing of his pain, the music that had been too long silenced coming to life. An awakening to a distant dream of the only time in his youth he'd been safe and loved.

She played a lilting, beautiful song. Instead of lying down, he sat on the edge of the bed and watched her. Strumming the strings with her right hand, she muted the ones she didn't want to sound with her left. She bent her head to the harp, and her hair fell over her arms, cascading around her in spiraling curls. Closing her beautiful eyes, she swayed to the melody, lost to the song, bringing him with her.

The last notes faded. She looked at him as though only realizing he wasn't reclining.

"Is the music not to your liking?"

"It is. Very much so. But I'm not tired and I'd rather watch you play. It takes me to a time I thought I'd forgotten."

"Is it a time you want to remember?"

"It is and it isn't." He looked at the harp. "That belonged to my mother. She was the only one who could play it. The music brings many memories to me of her. No one else has played it since the day she died."

"It's a fine instrument. So like the one my father had made for me." She gave him a slight smile as she ran her fingers over the strings. "The music has both good and bad memories for me as well."

"For both of us." Catching her gaze, he held it, willing her to feel the same connection he did. "Please, continue."

She did. As the song spun out from the harp, he listened to the passion with which she played and watched the rapture on her face. Her elegant hands moved with grace and strength, like she did. What would it feel like to have her touch him like that?

If only he could make her feel what the music did to him. If only she could look like that because of his touch and his words when he whispered them to her as he made love to her. He had to taste her one more time, take the memory of her scent and the sensation of her skin on his lips into battle with him. Perhaps even into Valhalla.

He went to her and knelt by her side. She opened her eyes and her fingers hesitated on the strings as she looked at him.

"Don't stop. For anything. Not even this." He kissed the side of her chin. "We don't want anyone in the hall to hear you cease, do we?"

She swallowed and shook her head. Her hands trembled as she tried to start another song. He moved his mouth to her jaw, nibbling and kissing her tender skin. Taking her ear lobe between his teeth, he bit gently and let it slide free. She shuddered and missed a chord.

Her scent was that of flowers and light. He breathed deep of it, carrying her essence into his body. Moving her hair around to her far shoulder, he ran his tongue over the nape of her neck, then blew on it. She bent her head, exposing it, surrendering to him.

He smoothed his hands over her back and her flat stomach, then upward. Combing his right hand beneath her hair, he held her as he slid his other hand over her breast and up her neck. Taking her jaw, he tilted her head back until she met his gaze. Her fingers stilled.

"You've stopping playing." He looked into her eyes and found no fear or anger. Only desire.

"I know." She set the harp aside.

He gathered her to him and slanted his mouth over hers. She clung to him, opening to his demand, accepting his mastery of her. It fired him. He had to know the feel of her under him, to bathe himself in her warmth. He needed to wrap himself in her glorious hair and taste her on his mouth.

She was his, in all ways, and he never had to let her go now. She'd stay with him, and her innocence would be his.

He held her to him. If he took her tonight and died tomorrow, her future would be ruined. And if there were a child, it would grow up in a foreign land, never knowing of him or its true heritage—Vargfjell. He'd always been careful with his other women, but with Elfwynn, he didn't want to be.

He desired a child with her. That had never happened before and it made all the difference.

He loved her.

Burying his face in her hair, he gritted his teeth. He'd never denied himself with a willing woman, and she was willing. He drew in her essence for what might be the last time. Then he pulled away to look into her eyes. She gazed back at him with trust and he gave her a gentle kiss.

"You'd better go, little Christian. Your god is already angry enough with me and I need all the luck I can have in the coming days. I don't want him arguing with my gods about my fate."

"I thought the Norns already decided your fate." She gave him a shy smile. "Though knowing you, even if the Valkyries came for you, you'd charm your way out of their grasp and return here."

"If I had you to come back to, I would." He kissed her again.

When he sat back on his heels, she looked down at her hands. "I'm afraid of the coming days, and of what will happen."

He took her wrists and kissed her palms. "I've made certain

you'll be safe. Galinn is remaining here and will take you and all the women and children to a waiting ship at the first sign of trouble. You'll be safe out on the seas. And if anything happens to me, Magnus or Eirik will take you home."

"That's not what I meant. I fear for you. That I'll never see you again." She broke away from him and ran out of the room before he could stop her.

He knelt there, looking at the closed door. If he went after her, what would he say? That he loved her? It would be best if she didn't know it in the event he didn't return. Then she'd go home, and he'd be nothing more than an unpleasant memory for her.

But if he did return? They still didn't have a future. Either she'd finish the sail and he'd have to send her home, or he would send her home anyhow. Because, like Thorir had told him, it was what she wanted and he had to put her happiness over his own.

Because he loved her.

Redbank, the keep of Earl Edward
Kingdom of Northumbria

"My lord." A guard ran into the hall, out of breath.

Wulf and his father stood up from the table where they'd been drinking ale. Their men also rose, their hands going to their swords.

"I was patrolling and saw Northmen along the shore, very close to us."

"Is it an attack force?" Edward walked around the table, his face grim.

"No. It's only two or three of them. But they're not bothering to hide themselves. It's as though they wanted me to see them. I thought you should know."

"I do. Gather more men and go out—"

"I'll go." Wulf put his hand on his father's arm. "Let me see what the situation is. One man may go more quietly than several."

Edward studied him. "Very well. Go." He sent him a grave smile. "See what news your contact brings to us."

Wulf opened his mouth to deny it, then closed it again. It wasn't surprising his father knew he spoke to the Northmen on occasion.

When it came to the safety of his keep, he knew everything. Chuckling, he nodded to his father and left, calling for his horse.

As he waited outside, his heart sped up. Brandr. He had to have information for him, though whether it was about Elfwynn or not, he couldn't say. In all the weeks since she'd been missing, there had been no sign of her anywhere, anyplace. Maybe, finally, he'd heard something.

He leaped on his horse and rode out of the keep as though an army of Northmen were after him. Heading west along the shore of the river, he urged his horse on until he saw Brandr's men. He stopped in the midst of them.

"Brandr wants to see you."

He didn't wait to reply. Riding hard along the bank, he scanned the water as he had so many times before. He'd searched and searched for any sign of her, any clue as to what had happened to her—a scrap of clothing, a shoe. A body. Nothing. Oddly enough, it gave him hope, though lately that had begun to dwindle. Now it kindled in his chest once again and even when he reached the camp, he didn't slow down.

He reined in his horse in front of Brandr's tent and jumped off. The large raider strode toward him, and they gripped each other's wrists in greeting.

"News?"

Brandr shrugged. "Perhaps, perhaps not. But it's possible." He took a pitcher from a waiting man and poured two cups of ale. He handed one to Wulf as they sat. "Rorik of Vargfjell was seen recently in Hedeby. He was trying to ransom a young woman to the church there. A woman who spoke Northumbrian."

He leaned forward, his pulse racing. "Did they pay?"

Brandr held up his hand. "From what I've heard, they didn't. He wanted too much. The price of a longship and the wergeld for two warriors. The church there simply didn't have it. The woman tried to escape and went to a priest, but before she could get to safety, Rorik found her." He laughed. "Half the town heard them arguing and the other half heard about it later. He tried to sell her to a slaver there, but she came at him with a knife when she realized it. Seems she has a bit of a temper."

"That must be Elfwynn. Rorik lost a ship and two men while he was here the first time. He must want recompense for them, but why didn't he try to get it from my father? That would make more sense. Did the slaver take her?" He held his breath. If that were so, then there was no hope of ever finding her.

"No. When she attacked Rorik, he said she wasn't worthy and that he would bring her back when he had properly tamed her. The Arab wasn't pleased and Rorik got out of there with her on his shoulder and the Church on his heels. Turns out from what I've heard, the priest went to the bishop, who went to the king, who happened to be there. Horik sent the money, but by the time they got to the docks, Rorik was already leaving. They got away."

"Oh, God." He buried his face in his hands. "He could have taken her anywhere, even the Eastern slave markets."

"The word is he had a confrontation later that day with the pirate Alvida. The tale was told over many cups of ale that one of her men tried to rape the Northumbrian woman. She didn't take well to that and came after him with the same knife. Rorik tossed him overboard. When Alvida found out, she threw the pirate off the other side of the ship. What is important here is that they were in the Kattegat, so he was headed to the North Sea." He met Wulf's hopeful gaze. "He was going home to Vargfjell. With her."

Wulf closed his eyes. *Thank you, Lord.* There was still hope. If he could get there in time. If the bastard, Rorik, was trying to 'tame' Elfwynn he'd have his hands full. But then, he could harm her, or even kill her if Elfwynn didn't comply. And she probably wouldn't.

He opened his eyes. Brandr was regarding him over the rim of his cup as he took a long drink.

"How much to take me to Vargfjell?"

He let out a belch. "Because you're a friend and ally, I won't cheat you too much. And I have some goods I can trade while I'm there." He poured them more ale. "But if Rorik wants the price of a longship and the wergeld in exchange for your sister, you'd better bring plenty of gold and even more silver. You're going to need it."

Chapter Fourteen

Vargfjell

Elfwynn stood in the village, overlooking the shoreline. The ships lined the beach, packed so close together there was barely enough room to walk between them. At the docks, they were tied two and three deep. Thorir's fleet of ten was anchored in the fjord and he stood on the beach, talking with Rorik.

She touched her lips where Rorik had kissed her last night. When she had taken the harp into his room and waited for him, she'd known what might happen. She'd gone anyway. Little by little, he was opening to her, like when he'd told her about his mother's harp. As she'd played it, she'd felt closer to him, as though she could be a part of his life. But it couldn't be.

It wasn't only because of what awaited her at home. She wouldn't be one of many women he bedded, and she couldn't live with the sight of him being with others. He was alone now, and perhaps that explained why he was attracted to her. Eventually, it would change. Right now, he was preoccupied with this battle. Afterward, he'd look for others to replace those who had left him. Like worn out pieces of furniture.

The battle. She bit her lip as fear hit her. They hadn't even left yet, and already she was shaking, her throat closing. Who knew how long they'd be gone? She couldn't live like this for days or weeks. And why did she feel it at all?

Always when she got the choking feeling, the sweating, and the pain in her chest, it was because someone she loved had gone to war. It had started when she lost her brother, then her cousin. Each time Wulf and her father had ridden out, she'd endured the fear until they returned. She loved them and that was the connection.

Now Rorik was leaving. Her stomach gripped her with nausea as he and Thorir walked up the path toward the village. Early this morning, Lifa had read strange inscriptions on some flat stones she'd cast and had said the gods looked favorably on this voyage. But the priests always said God blessed the warriors as they left also. They weren't always right. All around her, men gathered to speak to their families, friends, and lovers, perhaps for the last time.

The familiar sense that she wasn't truly there overwhelmed her. It was part of the fear. She looked at all of them as though she were on a mountain, very far away.

She focused her attention on Rorik. He was an anchor keeping her from drifting in an unknown current. He smiled at her, but then a commotion drew his attention to the crowd.

The people parted, murmuring. A tall, very beautiful woman walked toward them. Her light blonde hair was caught in a tight braid down her back and her silver-green eyes were slanted, with a very deep intelligence in them. She carried a bow slung behind her and was dressed in leathers and furs. Carrying herself with an obvious sense of pride, she moved with purpose, grace, and strength.

As she drew closer, the reason for the crowd's reaction was evident. Two wolves trailed her, one white and one black. They were massive, their golden eyes scanning the people on either side of them. She must be Rorik's sister, the one who stayed alone in the woods. Wasn't anyone in this family normal?

Rorik strode forward without hesitation and embraced her as the white wolf sat against her leg, its tongue lolling out in a predator's grin. The black one remained standing on her other side, watchful and still. "Ellisif. I thought you might come here eventually."

She leveled her sharp gaze at him. "I have seen the movements of your men and those of the jarls' men in the south. They have come onto our lands and have gathered at their villages. I have also seen Eirik's ships in the harbor and strange warriors here. You go to war."

"Yes. We believe Halfdan the Black is backing Oddr and Kolbienn. He wants to test me to see how strong I am and if I pose a threat to him. I'm sending him the message that I do."

"With a sea battle. You will stop the men on the seas before they get here, so close to Vargfjell. And, if I know you, obtain more ships."

He laughed. "Of course. Not just any ships, though. King's ships."

"For a man who is all but a king in name."

He slashed the air with his hand. "King, jarl, no matter what you call it, I don't want the responsibility."

"No matter what *you* call it, it is what you are. And one day, soon, when you accept all that you are to your people, you will allow them to speak the title." She shifted the bow on her back. "I have come to offer my skills as an archer. You will make the first attack with arrows before you engage the men directly, ship to ship. I never miss. I would be an asset to you."

Kaia stepped over to them. "Yes, you would, Sister. But I am going and we cannot risk all of us in battle. If we're defeated, someone must live to perhaps continue our bloodline."

"Is our bloodline so blessed of the gods that it should be continued?" Ellisif tilted her head to one side. "It's no secret that I won't marry, and yet you have allowed that you might. If any man can best you in battle. It would make more sense for me to go. There is no loss if I fall."

"There will be loss if any of us fall," Rorik said. "To each other, if no one else."

"True." Ellisif's serene expression never changed. "But the Norns have decreed the moment of our deaths, so even if I remain home, I will still die if it is my time."

"We'll fight hand to hand after that." Kaia gripped the hilt of her sword. "That's not what you do."

"I may not make it my life's work to fight." Ellisif pointed to the distant trees. "But I face animals, men, and the gods themselves out there, for I often see Odin walking over the mountains and speak with him. Thor passes me in the storms. I've survived. Don't doubt my skill in slaying when it's needed."

They spoke of death and their gods so lightly, as though they mentioned the weather. Ellisif stood very still, her face never changing. It was easy to see why she was such a skilled hunter. Patience and a calm astuteness surrounded her. She was like no one Elfwynn had ever seen.

"I'm Jarl Thorir." He'd remained where Rorik left him when he'd greeted his sister. He made a slight bow, his eyes never leaving her. "Rorik has mentioned you. I'm glad to meet the sister of such a great ally."

She narrowed her gaze on him, unmoving. "You live to the east. I've seen your hunters when they pass close to us."

"Then you must be within my boundaries."

"The animals I run with know no boundaries and neither do I." She put her hands on the wolves' heads and looked at Rorik. "You must have been speaking of how to secure your alliance. Look elsewhere other than at me, Rorik. I have my life in the forests and it suits me."

Without waiting for Rorik's agreement, she stalked toward the ships. The two wolves trotted away from her and settled themselves in front of the longhouse. Were they going to wait for her there? The entire time she was gone?

"I suppose that answers that." Rorik shook his head as he watched her.

"She was always stubborn," Kaia said.

"And that's the sail deriding the clouds because the wind pushes them."

She shot her brother a sour look, then followed Ellisif to the beach.

Rorik crossed his arms. "I knew this would happen. I had hoped to be away from here before Ellisif came, but I should have known better. She sees everything, and knows even more. It's not enough I must worry about one sister, now I have to watch over two of them."

"It may well be." Thorir clapped him on the shoulder. "But I have a feeling they'll be the ones watching over you." He also left for the shoreline.

Rorik inclined his head to Lifa and Silvi. "I hope not to bring too many wounded to you afterwards."

"However many you bring, we'll be here," Lifa said. "May the gods grant we'll have little to do."

Nuallen stood behind them and their eyes met. "If anything goes wrong here, Galinn will take my aunt, cousin, and Elfwynn to the seas for safety. Watch over them with him."

"Always." His eyes were cold, but they softened as he looked at Lifa.

Rorik tensed, but Nuallen left with Lifa without saying anything further. He gave Elfwynn a slight smile as his men moved out. "I don't know how long we'll be. It could be days or it could be weeks. It all depends on where and when we come across the king's ships."

"It doesn't sound too wise, warring with kings." She couldn't imagine her own father doing it. But then again, he did fight to keep Kenneth MacAlpin, king of the Picts, from invading the north. So perhaps it wasn't much different.

"With so many kings in our lands, it's bound to happen sooner or later. I'm just doing it under my terms, in my time." He looked at all the villagers gathered there. "Galinn and many of my best men are staying here to guard all of you. Expect me back only when you see me." His eyes, so silver and green, sought hers. He hesitated, then bent and kissed her, very fast. Studying her face, as though he was trying to remember it, he stayed for a moment longer, then followed the column of men and shieldmaidens down the path. She tasted him on her lips, shocked that he would do that in front of his people. She glanced around her, but everyone was watching the ships leave.

The men pushed the vessels off the shore, climbing in once they were afloat. The larger ships were at the docks and Rorik jumped into the *Wind*. It was the most impressive, and would be his flagship.

The crews hoisted the yardarms, the sails catching the favorable wind, a good omen. Rorik's ship moved out ahead of all the others as he led the way into the main part of the fjord. Oslafa, Turold, and Finna joined her on the rise as they watched them leave. Turold had his arm around Finna, now that they were betrothed. At least they could show their affection.

"He'll return," Oslafa said. "He always does."

As the lead ship, the *Wind* was the first to round the bend in the fjord and disappear. One by one, the others followed until the last one was no longer visible. The people turned away, going about their business, but Elfwynn stood looking at the waters, the breeze playing on her skin. Those same waters and wind would carry him into war and into a destiny she could never share.

She looked up at the clear sky. *Lord, it is said that all people are your children. Even though Rorik doesn't hear your words, protect him. Let him come back to Vargfjell. And me.*

At home, when Wulf and her father went to fight, the only thing that kept her from going mad was weaving. She stayed at the loom day and night until, exhausted, she fell asleep. That way, she wouldn't think too much, wouldn't feel too much.

But here, it wouldn't help her. The more she wove, the sooner she'd finish the sail. And when the sail was complete, she'd leave him forever. There was an ancient tale of a woman who wove all day, only to unravel it at night, so she never finished what she wove. But that wouldn't help her. If Rorik didn't love her, she couldn't remain here.

If only she could be like their Norns who wove the destinies of men. She'd weave the threads of her life into his so tightly, they'd never unravel.

She walked to the longhouse and into the weaving room. Running her hands over the cloth she'd woven, she loosened the bottom weft thread. It would be so easy to destroy what she had done, to make it take longer than it should.

Weaving was the only thing she could do to keep the fear at bay, the only thing that would calm her, and make the waiting bearable. But it would also take her from Vargfjell that much sooner.

Unless . . . She went to the shelves and picked out very fine, soft wool. It was a darker gray, natural to the sheep, and would set off Rorik's coloring. While he was gone, if she wove this, it would keep her busy, and when she was finished, she'd ask Oslafa to make a shirt for him from the cloth. The sail would take longer this way, but that was the idea.

Otherwise, the weaving she loved would take her all too soon from the man she loved.

Off the coast of Norway
Just north of the Moldefjorden

The gods favored them.

Rorik stood on the deck of the *Wind*, his hand shielding his eyes from the glare of the sun as he peered across the water. Anchored close to shore, just in his sight, one of his smaller ships had waited. No one would think anything of it, for ships often stayed in the calmer waters between the islands for any number of reasons. But it was crucial. He'd positioned it there to give him information on the fleet since the islands his fleet hid behind blocked his direct view.

It raised a flag, a signal to tell him they'd spotted the king's fleet moving north along the coast. It was almost the final piece of evidence he needed to know that Halfdan was, indeed, backing the two jarls. Before this, it had just been a feeling in his gut. Something that had saved him many times. He was, after all, related to Lifa, Silvi and Eirik. The gods gave such powers to families, whether related by blood or not.

He moved the great ship farther behind the line of islands where he'd hidden his fleet and gave the signal to lay the masts down on the overhead supports. There was too much danger if they fell during the battle, and sails could catch on fire. They didn't need them for fighting in such close quarters. Oars were more practical and they could turn with more precision.

As the men worked, he studied the winds and currents. "Thor blows the winds with us, and Njord makes the seas flow north."

Eirik grinned. "As Lifa said they would. Just right for letting them pass us."

"When we come out from behind the islands," Ellisif said, "you'll let the winds and waters take us toward them, while they'll have to row to meet us. We can use all our men for attack, while they'll have to use many of their own to maneuver their ships. It is a wise move."

He didn't reply. She didn't expect him to. Speaking of her observations was her way of understanding, though there wasn't much she didn't know about. Rorik had insisted both of his sisters stay on the *Wind*. He could keep a closer eye on them. Since Eirik was with him, Asa, of course, was there as well. Three shieldmaidens on one ship. He sighed. At least the others were spread throughout the fleet. Once he got to the commander's ship, it would be a rout and there were few fighters more vicious than a shieldmaiden. They'd be assets, even though it was one more thing he had to worry about.

Halfdan's fleet was keeping close to land instead of using the sea routes, passing between the shore and the islands, which was even better. The seas were calmer there and they'd be trapped between him and the land. If possible, he wanted to drive them onto the shore. This region was just north of the Sogn, where Magnus was well respected. Fighting in friendly territories would be to their advantage. Often the local men gave help to those they knew by killing off an enemy crew. They knew Magnus and Leif well.

He also had contacts there and they were watching the outcome of this confrontation from the land. Over the past days, while they'd been waiting, they'd spoken with the local men and those discussions had paid off. If the king's men tried to escape overland, they'd find a nasty surprise waiting for them.

A sharp cry drew his attention to the skies. Two ravens circled overhead, staying over their ships. They dipped and turned, their glossy black wings shining against the bright sky.

"There are Hugin and Munin," Ellisif said, raising her head to them. "They will watch us and tell Odin of our victory this day."

The ravens of Odin wheeled again, then flew over the island in the direction the battle would be. Rorik grinned. The god had sent them to show his support. It was a good omen and the men cheered.

The ship that had anchored to the east of the islands raised another flag. The fleet was in position, passing them now. He nodded to Thorir who was aboard his own flagship. One by one, the crews of each ship passed the word to the next vessel to move out from behind the line of islands. They all rowed out, in formation, the ships in the south heading out first. They came at an angle, so they would swing around and approach from the south, with the wind and currents.

The enemy's ships were large, beautiful, and well maintained. Each had a dragon on the forestem, proving they belonged to a jarl or a king. In this case, it was a king. Rorik had seen a few of them before and they were Halfdan's. A warrior named Glóthi the Bloody-Handed usually led the crews. If he was commanding the fleet, they were in for a fight.

Halfdan's men cried an alarm and turned their ships around to face Rorik's fleet. They couldn't outrun Rorik since men filled the ships, making the vessels unseaworthy and difficult to maneuver. They were too spread out to form a line quickly, so they drew their ships together in twos and threes, all the while moving closer to gather into a longer line of defense.

They had to row against the current while trying to lower their sails. It left few men to prepare for battle and as soon as Rorik's ships grew close enough, he threw a spear over the heads of the enemy, making the first strike of the battle.

"Odin owns you all!"

He signaled his archers. They shot a volley of arrows into the scrambling crews. Amid the screams, men raised shields to protect the rowers, but it left even fewer to return the fire.

Rorik nodded to Ellisif. She raised her bow, her face dispassionate, and let loose arrow after arrow. All found their mark. Even on the deck of a ship, she was as still and solid as the land itself. Her eyes never left their target, her hand was always steady. An arrow missed her by a hand's breadth and still she shot without ceasing. One of

Rorik's men covered her with his shield. Acknowledging it with a brief nod, she continued her assault.

Their father's cold-bloodedness and their mother's brutal death had stripped all emotion from her at a very young age. In its place were the strategic ways and calm mind of the consummate hunter. And now, she hunted men.

Rorik hung back. Normally, he'd be the first one into the fray. But Glóthi would be in the center ship, the largest one, and the *Wind* was the only ship massive enough to take it on. Rorik wanted to pressure him and let him see his death coming before granting it to him.

Magnus's and Leif's ships split off, each taking several others with them. Smaller vessels in the king's fleet veered off and attacked them, but Magnus and Leif guided their ships through the fray and toward the two ends of the forming line. Because of the oars, they came in bow to bow at the same time and the king's warriors rushed to defend their flanks.

The twins had two of the larger ships and even though the enemy's bows were high, theirs were higher. It gave them the advantage. Their men threw large rocks and spears down into the boats. The opposing crews had to defend upward.

As though they were of one mind, Magnus and Leif simultaneously grappled their bows to that of the enemy's and their crews poured onto the decks. Several of Rorik's other ships pulled up behind them. His men jumped to the twins' ships and followed them and their men to engage the defenders.

As his men defeated the other crew and drove them toward the center, they took control of each ship. They untied it and a few men rowed them away, like peeling an onion from each end. The king's men jumped into the water, surrendering and trying to swim to shore. The crews in Rorik's smaller boats killed them off. Most of those who reached land met similar fates at the hands of their allies watching from the beaches.

"It is time." Rorik held up his hand and the men dipped the *Wind's* oars into the water.

"I was beginning to think we'd miss all the fun." Kaia unsheathed her sword. "You waited long enough."

"He did the right thing." Eirik checked his blade. "We had to wait for Thorir to get around the line so he can come in at the same time from the other side. The most important men are in the center with their best warriors. Our attack leaves them vulnerable from the front and the rear, which is where Thorir is coming from. We'll hit them at the same time as Magnus and Leif get there."

"No place to go." Asa smiled. "Once we kill the commander, his men will give up."

"And die." Kaia bared her teeth in a grim smile.

"And we all get more ships," Rorik said.

Kaia rolled her eyes. "You and your ships. As long as I finally get one of my own, I'll be happy."

"As long as you're killing someone, you're happy." Ellisif set another arrow to her bow. "I'll guard all of you as you board."

"Just stay here and pick them off." Rorik gave her a long look. "You don't have the sword skill we do."

"How would you know?"

He didn't answer. The ships were very close now and he moved with the others to the bow. He scanned the ship ahead of them. A large, red-haired man fought some of the men who had boarded his ship, shouting orders as the main battle came closer. On the other side of the line, Thorir also closed on him.

Rorik studied the situation. The melee was concentrated in the center now, the flanking ships having been taken. Just as he'd planned. He climbed up behind the dragonhead ornament. To his left, Ellisif took up her position to guard him while he boarded the other vessel.

The steersman guided the *Wind* to the left of the command vessel, between it and the next one. Rorik didn't wait for them to touch. Hefting his shield, he leaped across and into the midst of the conflict. A man came at him, but one of Ellisif's arrows took him before Rorik could engage. She killed another man before he could meet him.

He glanced over his shoulder at her. "Odin's eye, Elli, leave me someone to kill."

"I'm just clearing the way for you." She nodded to his right. The commander was still shouting orders while he fought and hadn't seen him yet.

Eirik leaped past him, Asa following. Kaia was already fighting, grinning as she slew a man. Thorir leaped aboard from the other side, a sword in each hand. His men flooded in after him. They fought outward, meeting the king's men who still remained. Those men had been facing Magnus's and Leif's forces, but now they were surrounded on each side of the command ship. Some continued to fight, but many jumped overboard to try to escape their fate. Between Rorik's archers and the patrolling ships, they weren't successful.

Rorik blocked an overhead strike with his shield, sweeping the sword aside. A warrior wearing expensive mail struck him with his own shield, knocking him back. Rorik slipped on a rope on the deck. The man's sword sliced toward him.

Ellisif barreled into the warrior, sending them both flying. She moved so fast, she was little more than a blur. Spinning, she leaped onto him, her seax flashing downward through his mail and into his chest. She slashed it again across his throat, then stood and came to Rorik. He hadn't even had time to rise.

"No sword skills, perhaps," she said. "But a seax is another matter."

The warrior she'd killed still gripped his sword and it was one of the finest Rorik had seen. Only a man of great rank would have a weapon like that. His skin chilled. "Get back on our ship." He took her arm and pushed her toward the bow. "You've just taken down an important man. That will make you a target. You shouldn't be here."

"If I weren't, you wouldn't be here either." Her eyes widened. "Behind."

He pivoted and swept the spear aside with his shield, thrusting at the same time with his sword. He pulled it from the man's gut as he fell, and looked for Ellisif. She had gone.

Moving toward the commander, he glanced around to gauge the battle. Thorir fought with his two blades just a few steps from him. He blocked with one, while striking with the other. The bodies of three men lay around him. Eirik had fought his way onto the flagship, his every movement fast and unceasing. Asa guarded his back. Beyond the commander, Leif leaped up as a man thrust his spear at him, clearing it. He smashed the spear aside with his shield, then rammed the warrior and sliced his stomach open.

The metallic odor of blood filled Rorik's nostrils. It dripped down his body and pooled on the deck, but none of it was his. He hoped.

Rorik slew two more men as he made his way closer to Glóthi. A circle of survivors joined the commander. If he could get past them and slay him, it would end the battle.

One of the men who stood with Glóthi aimed his spear at Thorir. The jarl had slain another man and was walking toward Rorik as he looked around himself for another fight. The guard hurled the spear.

Rorik dropped his shield and leaped toward Thorir. As the spear passed him, he caught it, spun, and threw it. It hit the guard, impaling him through the chest, and he fell in a gush of blood.

Thorir laughed. "You have to teach me that one day. But right now, we have the king's men to slay."

"Agreed." He picked his shield up from the bloody deck. Eirik, Asa, Kaia, and Magnus joined them with their men. Leif stood on the far ship, his warriors with him. They'd fought their way into the center. The commander was surrounded.

An arrow struck another of Glóthi's men in the eye and he went down. As the other guards raised their shields, Rorik looked behind him. Ellisif had gone back to the *Wind* as he had told her to, but she was wrapped around the dragonhead, still taking shots. Rorik held up his hand to stop her. She had already saved him once today. He wasn't going to let her kill the rest of them while he stood by and did nothing.

He jumped onto the commander's deck. "A bit out of Halfdan's territory, aren't you? I believe you belong in the Vestfold. It's to the south, and yet you headed north. Lost, are you?"

"What makes you think we're his men?"

"Because I know of you, Glóthi. And I never forget a ship. I've seen some of these in Kaupang. They belong to him."

"So you admit to knowingly ambushing and attacking the king's ships?"

"First, he's a king, not my king. Second, you had so many men on board the vessels, they were barely seaworthy. Made it hard to maneuver them. You don't load down warships with this many men to go on a pleasure cruise up the coast. You were bringing an army to attack Vargfjell from the south to test my strength. Where were you going to land? The Hemnefjorden? Then move inland from there? You forget, my allies are many and might not appreciate an invasion by a foreign king. You thought you could just walk through there. You didn't expect me to meet you first."

He looked him up and down. "Rorik of Vargfjell. Your reputation is far-reaching."

Rorik glanced at Thorir and Eirik. They'd been right. In calling him by name, Glóthi had just admitted he knew him. The king had, indeed, sent them to attack him.

"I'd let you live to tell Halfdan of my strength, since he's so curious, but I think he'll have his answer when few of you return, and when I'm seen with this vessel as my flagship. I need a new one anyhow. Now I won't have to wait for one to be built."

"You'll have to get through me first."

Raising his sword, he grinned. "Thank you for the invitation." He charged him while Magnus and Thorir headed for the guards. Eirik and Asa split, darting around them while Leif rushed at them from the opposite side. They all met in a clash of steel, but Rorik went straight for Glóthi. They collided, swords to shields.

The man was as large and as powerful as Rorik. Neither moved, their weapons straining against each other. Rorik held his stare, an unspoken agreement passing between them. Nothing short of death. Then they broke apart and clashed again. Glóthi tried an overhead strike. Rorik blocked it with his blade and hit him in the stomach with the edge of his shield. The commander staggered back, then leaped forward again. His sword swept toward him. Rorik threw himself down, then cut with his own blade, slicing Glóthi's shin.

He rolled to his feet, keeping his shield pressed hard against his shoulder and arm, his head tucked behind it. Glóthi stabbed downward, the point of his sword breaking through the wood. It sliced his bicep. Rorik twisted the shield to trap and bend the sword, but the commander jerked it out.

Rorik moved across the deck, slipping on blood, avoiding bodies and ropes. Glóthi was skilled, a relentless fighter. He showed no signs of tiring. Already Rorik's shield had split and it wouldn't hold much longer. He lunged, swinging his sword for a killing stroke.

Glóthi ducked. The sword passed over him and bit hard into the mast. It stuck fast. Rorik yanked at it, then had to abandon it as the commander came at him. He held his shield with both hands, using it as both defense and a weapon. Holding it straight up, he pounded at the large man, driving him back, not giving him a chance to strike. Glóthi's shield splintered.

Dropping it, he rammed Rorik with his shoulder, and drove him into the mast. Rorik's head cracked into it and stars burst in his mind. Pain speared through his skull, almost driving his thoughts from him as he shoved Góthi back, hard. The commander fell over a corpse, but rose again, his teeth bared. Leaning on the mast behind him, Rorik forced his focus on his enemy. If he passed out, he was dead. The world swam, but steadied as he glanced down at his damaged shield. It wouldn't hold against another blade strike, but he had nothing else.

He couldn't leave Elfwynn like this. Not when he had just found what he'd always searched for. Not when he hadn't told her of his love. He gritted his teeth and lifted the splintered shield. The wood was weak, but the metal edge wasn't. If he missed, he'd have nothing left.

Sometimes, the only recourse was to let go of what one needed most.

Glóthi came at him, his sword raised over his head, death in his eyes. Rorik grasped his damaged shield with both hands and threw it, edge first. The metal struck Glóthi in his exposed throat. He dropped his sword, clutching at his neck. Rorik staggered to him, grabbed his head and jerked sideways. There was a sickening crack. He sank to the deck and lay still. Rorik grabbed the commander's sword and checked his surroundings. Glóthi's death had brought the fighting around him to a stop.

Some of the king's men leaped overboard and swam toward shore, but most of them dropped their weapons and knelt on the gory deck. At the stern, one of the fallen warriors lifted a seax, aiming it at Kaia's turned back. Rorik lunged for her, yelling. Before he could reach him, the man lurched and fell dead, an arrow through his chest. As Kaia spun around, Rorik looked over his shoulder. Ellisif, still hanging onto the dragonhead of the *Wind*, inclined her head to them. One corner of her mouth lifted in a slight smile.

Rorik looked at all of them, Eirik and Asa, Magnus, Leif, Thorir, Ellisif, and Kaia. They raised their weapons and, along with their men, shouted in victory. Their warriors on the ships around them joined in celebration and along the shoreline, their allies raised their arms, waving to them. A breeze circled the ships, then vanished. The two ravens sped away toward the distant mountains to tell Odin that he needed to make places in Valhalla for many valiant warriors this day.

Even the gods heard their triumph. Rorik smiled. And Halfdan would know of it, as well. They couldn't hope to have killed all his men who had fled and some had likely escaped to report back to him.

Eirik drew Asa against him. "From here to the Vestfold, and even beyond, the tale will be told of how we came up against a king and won. Rorik truly is the Lord of the Seas."

They raised their voices again, their swords against the sky. Rorik looked around them. So many ships waited for them. Not only his twenty-three, Magnus's four, Thorir's ten, and Eirik's great ship, but now they had a large part of Halfdan's fleet. He counted twenty-five of them. This one, he'd keep for himself to replace the flagship he'd lost in Northumbria. Then they'd split the others between them. As allies, they'd be invincible, at least on the water. The king had been concerned that Rorik was too powerful. By attacking him, he'd only succeeded in making him even stronger.

If there was to be a reckoning with Halfdan in the future, it likely wouldn't be by sea. No one would dare to threaten him there now. But with this many ships and this victory, men would flock to him and his family, wanting to align themselves with the strongest jarls.

He winced. With the additional power he wielded now, he was going to have to be a jarl, whether he wanted the title or not. His men moved from ship to ship, clearing the decks of the debris of war, tossing the bodies of the king's men overboard after taking their weapons, jewelry and mail from them. He'd have his own fallen taken to shore, pyres built for them, and then he'd send them off to Valhalla in splendor. It was what jarls did.

The ships that had fought away from the line moved toward the shore. They'd all meet there to assess the damage, drink to the dead, and divide the spoils. But no matter how long the others chose to remain, he'd sail for Vargfjell tomorrow to take the wounded there and let his people know he had won.

And now that he had survived, he'd let Elfwynn know she had also won—his heart.

Chapter Fifteen

Vargfjell

Rorik sighed in relief when he saw the light of the bonfires on the beach. No one else would have risked the twists and turns of the fjord at night except for him. He navigated the waters as easily as he walked through his longhouse, no matter if it was day or night. Knowing this, whenever he was gone, his people left fires lit from dusk until dawn in the event he returned in the dark.

All the other ships in the vast fleet had remained behind, anchored beyond the mouth of the fjord. They would make the journey in the morning. He couldn't wait that long. the *Wind* carried the wounded and he wanted to get them to the healers as quickly as possible. Most of his men could cauterize a wound and other such simple procedures, but some injuries needed more. They needed Lifa and Silvi. They'd add their talents to his skilled healers, but he had to get the men to them first.

He nodded to his steersman as he guided the ship to the dock closest to the path. If his guards were alert, they'd spot him very soon. The massive vessel glided silent and smooth on the glassy waters, but they should see its outline in the moon's reflection the same way he navigated at night. There was activity on the shoreline and someone ran to the longhouse. His men had seen them.

As they eased into the pier, a crowd came down from the village. He jumped onto the dock and people swarmed him, asking him of the battle.

"We were victorious. The king's ships are ours and even now, the fleet lies anchored off the fjord. They'll be here at first light."

As the people cheered, he searched for one face among them.

Elfwynn wasn't there. Had something happened to her? He strode through the crowd, smiling as they touched and praised him. Galinn came to him and reported that all was well in his absence. It meant she was still there, but where?

He ran along the path, but stopped as he came into the light of the fires outside the longhouse and looked down at himself. He'd washed off the blood of war days ago in the ocean, but salt still clung to him and his clothes were badly stained. This wasn't how he wanted to go to her.

The door to her chamber was closed as he passed it going to the back door and his sauna. Servants had already laid clean clothes out for him and the water was warm. He didn't have the time for a full sauna, so he upended the buckets of water over himself. After washing his hair and his body, he felt almost human, though he was sore from the fighting and his head still ached a bit. He wasn't as young as he used to be. But then, he hadn't fought much this summer, so perhaps he was getting soft. He paused. It was true he didn't miss it like he once might have. He must be getting old. Next thing he knew, he'd be sitting in his hall with a blanket over his legs, gumming porridge.

But not yet.

When he entered the longhouse, Lifa and Silvi were there, setting up tables to place the wounded on once the men carried them up on their shields. His healers helped them as Lifa walked to him.

"How many?"

"Twenty who are serious. There are at least thirty who aren't so critical. Those who could wait will come tomorrow on the other ships. We did what we could afterward, but there is only so much we know."

"That's why we're here." She looked at the other healers. "We'll take care of them, though it is the Norns who weave their destinies."

"I know, but you can make a difference in how well the survivors live after this." He gave her shoulder a light squeeze and headed for Elfwynn's chamber.

"Speaking of weaving, she's not in her room."

He looked back at Lifa. "Then is she at Oslafa's house?" It would explain why she hadn't heard the noise of his return.

"No. She's there." She nodded at the weaving room. The door was open. She should hear them. Lifa came to him, concern in her eyes. "She's finally sleeping because I gave her an herb in her drink. I didn't have the heart to wake her to move her to her room."

"I don't understand. Is she unwell?"

"Not in the body. But in her mind. She has a great fear of war, of losing those she loves to it. I tried to speak with her and she would only say that she lost her brother and a cousin to war. She hasn't slept since you left, and she's barely eaten anything. She's exhausted. All she has done is weave. It calms her."

"You said she feels this fear when someone she loves goes to battle."

She smiled. "It is what she told me."

He couldn't help but return it. "Then I'll have to reassure her, won't I? If I can wake her up. I know too well about your herbs."

"I gave it to her earlier today, so she should be fine once she wakes. Though I imagine the sight of you will cure her better than any herb."

"Take care of my men. Eirik is below helping organize the wounded."

She gave him a little push toward the weaving room. "We have dealt with men coming home from battle before, Rorik. Don't worry about us. Go to her. We won't need you until morning."

He wanted to tell her it wasn't that way between them, and might never be. But she walked away as the first of the wounded men was carried in on a shield. He crossed to the weaving room door and looked inside.

Elfwynn was asleep at the loom. But it wasn't the one with the sail. The cloth was of a darker gray color, very expensive and fine. The sail didn't look like she'd worked on it at all. She'd wanted to finish it as soon as possible so as to leave here. Did this mean she didn't want to go?

He went to her. Her cheeks were damp, as though she still wept in her sleep and his chest tightened. With great care, he picked her up, trying not to awaken her, and carried her through the longhouse to her room. More men had been brought in and the healers were busy unwrapping bandages and cutting away bloodstained clothing. They were in the best hands imaginable.

The chamber was dark, but with the light coming through the doorway, he found the bed and laid her down. He went out to the hearth and lit a lamp, brought it into the room, then paused. Should he just leave and let her sleep? Or should he let her know he was there?

After all the death and blood and pain, he needed to hear her voice, even if she got angry with him for being in here alone with her.

"Elfwynn." He sat beside her and touched her face, stroking her soft skin. It felt damp from her tears. "Wake up, little Christian."

She stirred, and opened her beautiful eyes. Dreams still drifted there, but then she focused on him and a soft smile came to her lips. With the love he saw, it might well be that he was the one who dreamed now. If that was so, he never wanted to awaken.

"You're safe." She laid her hand on his chest, just to feel if he existed or not. In the past days, she'd heard his voice in the place that lay between waking and sleeping. She scarcely dared to breathe for fear she was still dreaming. Now, he was hard and solid and so very real.

He took her hand and kissed the palm. "The gods granted us victory."

"And the rest of your family?"

"Odin smiled on all of us." He chuckled as she narrowed her eyes at him. "And I suppose you'll say your god had something to do with it, as well."

"He did if He heard my prayers." She looked away, her cheeks heating.

He turned her face back to him. "Why would you have prayed for me, Elfwynn? You knew if I died, Magnus or Eirik would have taken you back home. And why haven't you worked on the sail? You weave a different piece of cloth now."

"I'm weaving it for a shirt for you." She looked toward the lamp, anywhere but into his sharp eyes. "I got bored with plain white, coarse wool. I wanted to do something different. I still have a long way to go with the sail, so I didn't think a few days one way or the other would matter."

"Are you quite certain that's the reason?" He leaned over her, his gaze boring into her.

"What other reason could there be?" She tried to retreat into her pillow, but there was no escape.

"Perhaps that you didn't want to finish it so soon. Perhaps because you don't want to leave after all." He looked at her mouth, his steel-colored eyes darkening.

"I—I have to return home." Her pounding heart made it hard to think straight. Or was it his clean, wild scent?

"Do you?" He was so close, his breath and hers were one.

She gave a tiny nod, unable to speak for his closeness and her own sudden uncertainty. Northumbria was so very far away now. In more ways than just distance.

"Tell me once, Elfwynn, and I'll never ask again. Can you leave me? Can you leave this?"

He closed the tiny distance between their lips and kissed her. She wrapped her arms around his neck as he gathered her to him. His ebony hair fell like the night around them and she combed her fingers through it. It was still damp, so he must have just washed it, and its coolness soothed the heat building within her.

His possession was complete and she gave in to it, letting herself relax in his grip. Surrendering to him. Tightening his hold on her, he took her mouth as he took everything in his world, with certainty and confidence. With the knowledge that he had every right to what he wanted. It was what she desired, as well, and she told him without words as she answered his kiss.

He ran his hand over her breast. It sent fire throughout her body and she leaned into his touch. He could do this with just a brush of his fingers. If they came together, skin to skin, body to body, what else could he do to her? Taking his hand in hers, she pressed it to her breast and met his questioning gaze without retreating as she had so often. To not step one foot from the challenge that he was. She smiled at him. He took a shuddering breath, closing his eyes.

A slight smile, filled with regret, touched his lips. "I should go, little Christian. If I were to stay—"

She cupped his face in her hands. "Stay."

His brows knitted together. "Do you know what you're asking?"

"Yes, Rorik. I do."

He straightened, bringing her with him. "Do you know what might come of this?"

"No. All that is certain is that we have this night. I have seen how quickly life can fade. None of us can say we have tomorrow. As a warrior, you know we must take what we can, while we can."

"And as a warrior, if I take you, I may not let you go." He kissed her again and got off the bed. His gaze never leaving hers, he pulled off his tunic.

Her blood heated. She looked into his eyes and he gave her a knowing smile as he slipped off his trousers and silk shirt. His hard chest and chiseled abdomen gleamed in the soft lamplight. Soon, he would wrap that strength around her.

Standing like the warrior he was, he allowed her to drink in the sight of him. The old scars and the new partially healed wounds on his body only accentuated his power, signs of his prowess in battle. His erection was already hard and heavy. Warmth blossomed between her legs. With his long black hair and the strength he exuded from every part of his body, he was like one of his gods come to earth. But he was no mere god. He was hers, if only for this night.

He took her hands and helped her stand. He was so tall she barely came to the base of his throat. With a gentle hand, he unfastened the brooches holding her gown and tossed them aside. He unwrapped her dress. She stood before him clad in only her linen shift. Unable to stop herself, she crossed her arms in front of her, guarding what was left of her heart.

"If you ever want to wear this again, it will have to come off. It won't protect you and I can't promise what it will look like if you don't." He untied the string of the neckline. Heat rose into her face as he lifted it over her head. This was so new. *He* was so new. Awe touched her, knowing that such a man would want her.

Raising her arms to cover herself, she bowed her head, mortified that she should be standing here, naked before him. He took her hands and lowered them to her sides. Still holding them, he gazed at her. She tried to pull away, but he didn't allow it.

"Don't think to hide your beauty from me, Elfwynn. It is nothing I haven't seen before in my dreams of you."

She gave him a sharp look and he smiled. Women all over the known world had melted at that smile. She was not immune. Not anymore. A sensation of wanting, of needing, shot through her.

He must have sensed it, for he guided her to the bed and laid her down. As he drew her under him, his hardness lay along her thigh. Kissing her, he cupped both her breasts in his hands, thumbing their tips. Fire swelled deep inside her. She gasped, arching up toward him.

"So beautiful and so passionate." He nipped her throat and she writhed beneath him. He was like the storm. Primal, dangerous, and yet one couldn't help but watch it, caught up in the wind as it whipped past. Lowering his mouth to her breast, he took it as his. His tongue rasped her skin. She wrapped her arms around his neck, crying out her need as she held him to her.

He lifted his head and his deep, commanding voice streamed into her. "You taste like the finest wine from the south. In nights to come, I'll pour it over your body and drink it from your skin."

Oh, Lord. Her hips surged forward toward his erection. She tilted her head back, offering herself to him to take as he pleased. Caging his arms around her to hold her upward, he kissed his way down her body.

"Mine, always." He slid his hands to her hips, tasting and nipping her, paying careful attention to her inner thighs as he spread them, and her most private place.

He could kiss her *there*? She clutched the bedding to hold herself in the real world as he parted her folds with his mouth, his wide shoulders keeping her legs open for him. The muscles deep within her, that she didn't even know she had, relaxed under his tongue. His mouth was hot and wicked, seductive and magical. Warmth spread throughout her and she grew weak, unable to move her legs. Grabbing his hair, she moaned. He could kiss her there anytime he wanted.

Then he left her and she almost yanked his hair in frustration. But he only nibbled her flat stomach and sensitive ribs, then tasted her arms and shoulders, his teeth scraping her skin as he stretched himself over her again.

Holding her with his gaze, he pressed his fingers into her, piercing her deep inside. She jumped and tried to wriggle away.

"Stay with me, Elfwynn. I only want to make this easier on you. When we truly come together, I want there to be pleasure for both of us. This way, the worst will be over."

She quieted, but as he moved his hand there was a tiny pinch, then a driving hunger built in her core. She needed him. It was all she knew. He withdrew his hand, leaving her wanting something. *More.* Wrapping her legs around him, she tilted her hips up to him. He took her hands in his and held them down beside her head.

"We have all night, Elfwynn."

"Don't you dare make me wait until morning. I won't survive it." She tried to pull her hands from his, but he didn't allow it. Still, the inferno built inside her and, with desire driving her, she bit his shoulder. Hard.

He reared up, much of his weight on the hands that held hers. It didn't hurt. The bed was soft beneath them and gave under the pressure. His gaze burned down upon her, but she raised her chin and met it with defiance. She wanted to scream with frustration, but she wouldn't give him that weapon.

"Obstinate, aren't you?"

"You've known that since the day we met."

He stared down at her for a moment, then a corner of his mouth twitched. Finally, he laughed. "Then don't let me arouse that infamous temper of yours. There are more pleasant things I'd rather arouse." His voice was as warm as the richest wine and it poured into her. Still holding her hands, he slid into her in one smooth motion.

She tensed. It should hurt, but it didn't. He had spoken the truth and made it as easy for her as he could.

He held still. "Are you all right?"

"I will be. Now." She gave him a pointed look.

Lowering himself onto her, he released her hands and held her shoulders. She was more than ready and met his thrusts with her own urgency. Heat lightning spread out in her, as in a distant storm. His hair flowed down around them both, like the darkness of that tempest, and his eyes were the color of the swirling clouds.

"Look at me, Elfwynn." He held her in his gaze as he moved. Her muscles tightened along his length, something within her clenching.

He slowed, and she almost bit him again as the pressure soared inside her.

"Say you're mine. Every part of you. Mine."

She gripped his arms, unable to deny him. "Yes. Everything. Yours." For now, at least.

He slammed into her. Her mind fractured and he held her as she flew, her entire world quaking. Then he withdrew and found his own release. Collapsing onto her, he kissed her shoulder. They lay together, his weight still on her, but she welcomed it. It kept her from flying away forever. He shifted off of her and she missed his solid warmth. But he held her to him, her head on his chest as their breathing slowed.

"Is it always like this?" She lifted her head to look at him.

"No. But I'm willing to do all I can to find out if it will be so between us." He sent her a weak grin and she gave him a light hit on his shoulder. He brought her hand to his mouth and kissed it.

The sleepless days and little food took their toll on her and she closed her eyes, snuggling against him. He tossed the soiled covers onto the floor, pulled the furs over them, and settled her in his arms.

Then she remembered. "There's only one lamp lit in here. I know you like many of them when you sleep. Is it too dark for you?"

"Not with you here beside me. You're all the light I need. Now and always." He kissed her hair and relaxed against her.

Opening her eyes, she watched him drift into sleep. There wouldn't be an always for them. Just this time. He spoke as though they had a future, but they didn't. Even if she didn't have Wulf and her mother at home, and wanted to stay with him, it was all too clear what it would be like. He raided and fought. It was his way of life. At times, he was gone for weeks, perhaps even all summer. She wouldn't survive it. Look what it had done to her this time, and he had been gone only a bit over a week.

No. This would have to end when the sail was finished. He'd made certain there wouldn't be a child. If he hadn't done that, and she did conceive, it would bind her to him as surely as chains would. She understood him well enough to know he'd never let his heir leave, and she'd certainly never part with her babe.

As it was, when the time came, she'd return home to her mother, and together, they'd go to where they could finally find peace, away from the men who could never return their love.

What had she done?

Elfwynn buried her head in the pillow, not wanting to face the world, a world that was very different now. She'd been with a Northman. Not just any Northman. Rorik of Vargfjell. The most powerful, most feared, and now, the richest of all of them. With this victory, people would flock to him, and not just warriors. They'd bring their sisters and daughters, all Norse, so many of them blonde and beautiful and strong. Just what he liked, and not what she was.

A gentle hand turned her over and she opened her eyes. He moved on top of her and greeted her with a soft kiss, then worked his way down her throat. Tilting her head back, she gave herself up to him as he nipped the inside curve of her breast.

He raised his head and smiled down at her. "Good morning to you.

At least, I think it's morning. By the light, though, it may be later than we think."

"You needed the sleep, I'm certain."

"And so did you, I hear. Lifa said you were afraid while we were gone. A fear comes on you when someone you love is fighting."

She shouldn't have said anything. But Lifa was so comforting and easy to speak to, when she'd asked about why she was trembling and not eating, she'd told her.

"It was just the uncertainty. I've grown to know many of you. It upset me to think any of you were in danger."

"That's not what you told my aunt. You said 'love'." He held her gaze. "Love."

She shook her head. "It makes no difference, Rorik. You're safe now and I still must leave when I'm finished with the sail."

"Even after last night, you insist on leaving?" Putting his weight on his elbows, he cupped her face in his hands.

"My mother and Wulf don't even know I'm all right. I cannot let that continue. As much as I miss them, I know they're alive." She paused. "At least, I think they are. My mother may have pined away for me and Wulf may have died searching for me or in a battle."

"And what if I were to send a ship there with a message that you live and are well? Can you write?"

"Yes." She smiled up at him. "In our society, there's little difference in the education of men and women. My father thought we all should know how to read and write so no one could take advantage of us. He believes in improving the mind as well as the body so as to be prepared to face this world."

"A wise man, even if he is a bastard. Still, if you were to write to them and I had it taken there, would they know it was from you? We don't usually have the things you write with in other parts of the world, but I've taken them in raids over the years. You could include something that only you would remember. Then at least, they'd have that relief."

Could that work? Where she had been harboring a dark, nagging concern for those at home, now a tiny flicker of light grew in her. But there was still the matter of his leaving for raiding and war. And the inevitable women. She wasn't going to lie to herself about her ability to hold his interest. There were too many beautiful women in the world. And he'd be traveling that world.

"Let me think on it." One thing at a time. If he sent a message, it would, at least, buy her some time to decide. But was it her decision? "You hold all the power here, Rorik. If you want me to stay, you have but to say it. It would be as you please."

He rested his forehead against hers. "No. It will be as *you* please. Though if you want me to take the decision from you, I will." Raising his head to look at her, he moved his hands to hers and curled his fingers through hers. "I could tell you that you're mine and that I'll never let you leave me. I could keep you whether you willed it or not."

It was so tempting, to have the choice taken from her. Then the onus wouldn't be on her. There was a strange comfort in letting him control her, knowing she couldn't get away from him. But she'd found, to her surprise, that wasn't who he was. Nor was it the way she was. "I once believed that about you, but not any longer. I think it may be a decision we both make. Together."

"So it is." He kissed her again. "Right now, I think we'll agree we need to eat. As much as I'd like to enjoy you again, you need to heal and I'm starved."

She was, as well. Now that he was home, her appetite had awakened. It was most likely well past the morning meal, but all he had to do was speak the word and the servants would have food ready for him. It was probably already on the tables in the hall.

As they dressed, she sighed in relief. Judging by the light in the small window, it was midday. Most people would be about their work elsewhere. The fewer people who saw them come out of her room, the better. It would be mortifying if the village knew where he'd slept last night. With his reputation, there could be no doubt about what they'd done.

He opened the door and walked out first. In their culture, one could never be certain what lay on the other side and it was safer that way. As she followed him, a great shout went up and she jumped.

"Hail Jarl Rorik!" The hall shook with all the people yelling his name. Everyone in Vargfjell seemed to be there and they were all smiling at Rorik and her, shouting and banging their weapons, plates, and cups. Magnus, Leif, and Eirik stood in the front with Silvi and Asa. The other ships must have come in during the morning, so all the warriors joined the crowd.

Her face burning, she hid behind Rorik. Oh Lord. *Now* they chose to honor him? He pulled her out from behind him and held her at his side.

"I thank you, people of Vargfjell." They quieted as he spoke. "But you know I've never accepted the title of jarl. It is not something I feel I've earned or wanted."

They all shouted again, and cries of "Jarl, Jarl, Jarl" echoed through the building.

Galinn stepped forward. "Rorik, you've faced a king to protect us and won. You've brought back great wealth in ships and weapons and jewelry. Your power will only grow as more warriors seek to fight for you. There is no one who can stand against you. Your allies and family honor you, your people revere you, and all on the seas fear you. You will not call yourself a king, and yet, if you are not at least a jarl, then who is? We've prepared your seat for you."

The crowd parted. At the head of the room two chairs stood on a dais. Elfwynn had never seen anyone sit in them, but they must have been for the jarl and his wife. Now, the pelts of white bears were draped over them and a fortune in furs covered the ground beneath them.

Rorik's hand tightened on hers and a muscle in his jaw jumped. She was the only one close enough to see it and she pressed his hand in support. Why did it so upset him to see them that way?

"Men lead by consensus," Galinn said. "By the consent of all. Even kings. We have agreed that you, Rorik, are the jarl of Vargfjell. Would you go against the will of your people?"

Rorik's shoulders fell, as though he had tightened them for battle, but then surrendered to the inevitable. He looked at all of them. "It is said the gods write in runes the destinies of those who rule. The people are the chisels that carve those runes. If it is your will, then I agree."

He turned to her and she nodded with an encouraging smile. He kissed her palm, then left her and walked to the dais. Closing his eyes, he hesitated in front of the chairs. For the first time since she'd met him, he appeared uncertain of himself.

Lifa stepped from the crowd. She wore a blue gown, hemmed with gemstones, and carried a long staff carved with strange symbols. "As it is the will of the people, so have the runes spoken. It is time, Rorik of Vargfjell, to take your place as jarl, as a ruler of men, with all the wisdom, power, and responsibilities of that rank. This, you have earned. Not from your father, or from those who have gone before, but from your own strength, courage, and honor. You have won this by your sword and your heart. None, past or present, shall wrest this from you. So have the gods said." She banged her staff on the floor.

He stared at Lifa, as though drawing strength from her. Then he inclined his head and sat on the larger chair. A cry went up again, from those gathered there as he gazed out over them. So proud and magnificent, he outshone any man she had ever seen. He was so far beyond her, she might as well be back home already.

She skirted the celebrating crowd as they broke out the wine, beer, and mead, and escaped outside. Walking down the path to the shoreline, she looked at the waters.

Ships lined the beach and the docks, and more were anchored further out. She'd never before seen so many in one place. They were all beautiful, sleek, and deadly. When she'd watched Rorik's ship burning on the riverbank, she'd thought they were ugly. But now, she saw their beauty, and the skill it took to build them.

And one of them would have to take her home as soon as possible. She sank down on a bench. It had been a mistake to take the time to make the cloth for a shirt for him. Now she was that much further behind. It was a foolish dream to consider staying, even if he sent a message to Wulf. It didn't solve their biggest problems. His raiding. His desire for so many women. And now, his rank.

She was the illegitimate daughter of a foreign earl and a village woman. No one special. If he ever married, he needed a wife who could bring him allies, political power, and prestige. She could bring him nothing.

"Elfwynn?"

She closed her eyes. Why did he have to come here, just when she was gaining the strength she needed to refuse him?

He sat next to her. "I looked for you, but you weren't there. Leif said he saw you leave."

"The celebration is for you and your people." She continued studying the ships.

"Here. I know you must be hungry." He held out a cloth with bread and cheese in it.

She took it, but placed it in her lap. "You should be in there with them, celebrating."

He had another piece of cloth and opened it. Taking a bite of his own meal, he leaned back. "I prefer this, sitting here with you, watching the ships and the water. It's where I'm most comfortable. Besides, with all the drink that's flowing, they won't even notice I'm gone."

They sat in quiet closeness for a time, watching the breeze play over the fjord. If only it could be this way between them forever. Only the two of them. No crowds, no war, no responsibilities tugging them toward different sides of the world.

Above them in the village, the sounds of a drunken brawl erupted. Rorik rubbed his hands over his face. "I'd better go up there before I have another battle to contend with. Where will I find you later?"

Her eyes met his. "In the weaving room."

"I see." His jaw tightened. "So you still intend to finish the sail?"

"Yes. I agreed to do so."

He nodded. "And after that?"

"It must be as *you* agreed. I must return home."

Something in his eyes hardened, like the implacable warrior she'd first thought him to be. Or the jarl he now was. "And if I decide to keep you here?"

Deep inside, her body clenched. "Then I'll have no choice, now will I?"

He stood. "I'll come to you tonight." Without looking back at her, he strode up the path.

She set her meal aside and tucked her feet up on the bench, curling into herself. Perhaps that would solve all of her problems. If she had to live here with the pain of loving him, seeing him with other lovers, and watching him leave on his voyages, eventually resentment would kill her feelings for him. Then nothing could ever hurt her again.

Chapter Sixteen

All that day and through the evening, he'd celebrated with his people. He'd made all the right toasts, served his finest wine like it was ale, and feasted as though it were his last night.

It might as well be. Elfwynn gave him the peace he longed for. An emptiness had been within him for so long, he hadn't been aware of it until she'd filled it. It wasn't just her music and her wit. She was the only person he could simply be with. They'd sat together down by the fjord and he'd never been so content. With her by his side, he'd never feel the need to wonder if what he'd been looking for all his life was just over the horizon. It was here, with her.

How could he send her back to that bastard of a father? A message to her brother should be good enough, and if it wasn't, he'd bring her mother here to live. Then she'd have nothing more holding her in Northumbria.

This night, he'd be with her, love her, show her how he felt. He set down his cup. Suddenly a nasty little feeling twirled in his gut and it made his blood chill. *Something comes.*

Nothing could touch him now. The southern jarls waited for an army that would never arrive. Halfdan was weakened by the loss of men and ships, though he didn't know it yet. Even now, the story was spreading throughout the lands about his victory. So what was it?

Lifa sat within his sight, watching him. When he'd stood on the dais, she'd been his anchor in the rough seas his own people had thrown him into that day. Just seeing the love in her eyes had brought back all that she and Ivar had done for him so many years ago. Their guidance and acceptance of what he was had prepared him for this very day when he would become who he was born to be. She smiled at him and tilted her head to the weaving room. He glanced at the door.

Elfwynn left the room and went to her chamber. Lifa raised her cup to him and drank. Finishing his wine, he gave Elfwynn a short time to prepare for bed, then rose and went to her door. He knocked once before entering.

A single lamp burned on the table beside the bed. She lay there, the covers up around her shoulders, her hair curling over the pillows. His body tightened as he went to the side of the bed and looked down at her. She stared up at him, but he couldn't read what was in her eyes. Fear? He'd never want that. Uncertainty? Perhaps. He had been short with her by the fjord that afternoon. He was on such a tight leash now, he didn't dare let it, or himself, loose.

Not leaving the side of the bed, he removed his clothing and slid under the blankets. She was still in her shift, warm, soft, and so inviting. He wanted to sink into her, lose himself in her peace and beauty. He moved over her and took her in his arms. But as he kissed her, she trembled and turned her head.

He continued to rain tiny kisses over her cheek. It was damp. Touching it with the tip of his finger, he searched her eyes.

"Why, Elfwynn?"

"It is who you are. What you are. And I must leave here because of it."

"I don't understand."

"You're a raider, gone to the ends of the world, leaving everything behind. Including me. They say you always return, but one day, you might not. I'd never know what happened to you. I cannot live with that fear, Rorik. You're a jarl now, so powerful you topple kings. I bring you nothing, and yet you are everything."

"I'm the same as I was last night when you said you'd consider staying here."

"But then today happened."

"I know, but it's never been what I wanted. My father was jarl here and I can't be anything that he is."

"Any man would want to be what you are. Wealthy, respected, strong. You walk through this world like you own it, never doubting, never uncertain of your place in it. And now, you would own me, as well."

"That's where you're wrong." He slid off of her, and gathered her to him so that her head rested on his chest. "I don't want to own you, Elfwynn. I want you at my side, free and proud. Your fire and spirit is what attracted me to you. Why would I want to chain that? But it's more than that. It's the peace you bring me. With you, there's no need for lamps or light. You are my light."

"You've said something like that before. Why do you need the light at night, Rorik? You speak of needing peace and not wanting your heritage." She put her hand on his chest. "Let me understand you. Only then can I make the right decision about what to do."

He remained silent, as afraid as he had been during his first battle. What if she learned the truth about him and what he was? She would leave him in disgust then, and never come back. Was this the danger he had felt a short time ago? A turning point in his life? A ripping apart of all he knew, as Lifa had seen in the runes? He had never stepped back from battle, never shirked what he must do.

It was said that when Asa told Eirik of her past, it released the pain she had been carrying all those years. She was so happy now with Eirik. Could it be the same for him? Lifa thought so. She'd always said it was better to cut open a half-healed wound than let it fester, to let the poison out so the wound could heal inside as well.

The people of Vargfjell knew, for they had lived it with him. But they didn't know what it had done to him. Only his sisters did, for they were the same as he. Lifa, Eirik, and Silvi knew. If it weren't for them, he'd be dead. Or worse, like his father.

Perhaps it was time. If he wanted to give Elfwynn his future, he first had to give her his past.

"My father's name was Kolr and my mother was Gudrid. She was the sister of Eirik's father, Ivar. By all accounts, when they married at a young age, Kolr was a fine man. His ancestors were from north of Hålogaland near the Malengenfjord. They came south with the ancestors of our neighbors in Lade and conquered this area. Vargfjell was his, though at that time it was called by a different name. I was born soon after they married.

"When I was only a few years old, Kolr and his men fought the enemy of his family. They were taken captive. They say he was forced to watch his warriors die one by one, in horrible ways. He, too, was tortured. But death was too good for him, they said. Too easy. They set him free to return home, but he brought with him the memories. Little by little, they chipped away at him until, like a stone that is carved too much, his mind cracked and broke apart.

"Among our warriors, we have those who are called berserkers. They eat a mushroom that makes them fearless and overly violent in battle. They chew their shields and are the first to engage the enemy. They are mad for a time. He became like that all the time. He killed many of the farmers and raped the women of the village. The good men who could escape with their families did, and others who wanted only to destroy and pillage came to join with him. He became the scourge of the lands here."

He swallowed and glanced down at her. She kept her wide, beautiful eyes on him, never wavering. "He brutalized and raped my mother repeatedly and she couldn't escape. That's where my two sisters came from. She would have had even more children, but she lost many of them due to his beatings. Often, he locked me in a dark place while he assaulted her and my sisters. Ellisif and Kaia were only infants. I had to listen to it, unable to do anything about it."

"That's why you don't like the darkness."

"I don't fear the dark, itself. I see him there. And hear their cries. I still do, in my dreams, but at least when I wake, I see the bright room around me and know it's a dream. If it's dark, the nightmare continues."

She placed her hand over his heart. "What happened to them?"

"My mother found two good men here. She sent them to Haardvik to tell Ivar what was happening. They couldn't take a ship. They had to travel overland and it took months. My father eventually figured out where they had gone. In a rage, he dragged my sisters and me outside and stabbed my mother in front of us. He did it in a place on her body so she wouldn't die quickly, but bleed to death over a time. We were held there to watch. The last thing she said to me was, *Run.* With the last of her strength, she threw herself on him and tried to kill him. In the chaos, I grabbed a seax from the belt of the man who held me and slew him. As my father slaughtered my mother, I took my sisters, escaped to the forest, and hid them there."

"Oh my God." Her tears fell on his skin. "How old were you?"

"Seven winters. Kaia was five and Ellisif was four."

"So young, and you killed a man?"

"In this land, there are accounts of children as young as six winters who have carried out blood feuds, slaughtering entire families."

She paled. "How did you survive?"

"Some of the women from the village brought us food and supplies. We lived there for a long time, alone. It is why Ellisif still stays there. She was so young, all she knew was the safety of the woods. She was so hurt, all the emotion was stripped from her. She thinks that if she doesn't feel, the memories won't control her. Kaia just hates everything. She carries a great deal of anger within her."

"So she became a shieldmaiden. Did the men reach your uncle?"

"Yes. When they told Ivar about Kolr, he called together all his ships and those of his allies and came here. He slew my father and the men who followed him, then he had the women find us and bring us back. We saw our father lying bloody and broken on the ground. I took his sword from his dead hand to try to prevent him from going to Valhalla.

"We all were little more than angry, wild animals by that time. Ivar brought us to the best healer he knew—Lifa. She touched us and we felt her love. Ivar left men here as regents until I came of age. They rebuilt the village. Most of the people who had left came back. In the meantime, we lived at Haardvik. My uncle taught us of honor, respect, and self-discipline. Lifa taught us of love, control, and empathy." He gave a dry smile. "I think they were only partly successful, but at least we could rejoin society."

"I think they were very successful. Look at all you've done here."

"When I returned, I vowed I would not be my father, would not even take his title or his name. That's why I'm known as Rorik of Vargfjell, not Rorik Kolrson. I wanted to make it up to the people here for all the atrocities he committed. I know in my mind it wasn't my fault, but in my heart, I still feel that it is. If only I had done more to stop him. Instead, I ran." In spite of himself, his voice shook.

She lifted her head. "You were seven years old, Rorik. What else could you have done? You kept your sisters safe, and that's remarkable for so young a child."

"I don't think I was ever a child. Not in the sense that you would know. I've tried to give my people the best of everything. The best food, houses, protection. I scour the world to bring back luxuries for them to enjoy. I trade for the finest cloth, the rarest wines, everything

I can so they want for nothing. Still, I'm driven to search for more, to do more. My blood is tainted and I can never change that, not even for them."

"You're not your father, Rorik."

"Aren't I? Look at the rage that comes on me. Look at what I nearly did to you in Hedeby. That is why I won't marry. If I break like he did, I won't do the same thing to a woman I'm supposed to protect and love. If I don't have children, I can't pass this curse on to them."

"That's why you pulled out before you found your pleasure last night."

He nodded. "I've always been careful that way. The bloodline ends with me."

She sat up, wearing only her thin shift. The front was unfastened and it loosened the neckline so that it slipped off one shoulder. She was so beautiful, he almost groaned.

"Don't you see? His sickness didn't come from his blood. It came from something that happened to him, that his enemies did to him. We don't pass the things that happen to us to our children. Your rage is because of what he did to you, what you endured when you were so young. It still lives within you. It might happen to anyone. Perhaps, by speaking of this, it will help you."

"In the north," he said, "we value strength above all else. He was weak, flawed. Who's to say I don't carry that same flaw within me? Once, you told me if I wasn't careful, I would harm someone with my temper. It shook me when you said that. Losing control is my greatest fear. It's why I don't become close to anyone, except my family. They saved me, especially the women. My mother gave her life for us. Lifa and, eventually, Silvi healed us. And the wives of the village risked their lives to bring us food in the forest. Because of them, I respect women and have always done all I can to protect them.

"But look what I did to you. I took you from everything you loved for something that wasn't your fault. I made you all but a slave. Then, when the rage was on me, I tried to sell you."

"But you didn't."

"No. Because I heard your voice and it brought me back. You're much like my aunt and Silvi in that respect. You bring me peace."

"Even when I'm talking back to you?" She gave him a shy smile.

"Even then. In a way, it was refreshing. In my world, everyone is so careful around me, partly because of the rage, but also because of who I am. Men follow my power, merchants want my money, and women desire my body. But none of that mattered to you. You gave me a smack upside the head with your sharp wit and sharper tongue and it intrigued me. It had never happened before. Everyone is too afraid of me for one reason or another. Not you."

He took her hands and kissed them. "I find peace with you. The peace to be what I am. Not Rorik of Vargfjell, not the raider the world fears, and not the consummate lover who must be perfect. Just me. Will you stay with me? With all my flaws and tempers and imperfections? Will you be my light so I'll see you when I wake and know the night-mares are no more?"

Her smile was a balm to his torn heart. "When you look at the scars in your mind, you see only the wounds that caused them. I see them as evidence of the strength it took to overcome those wounds. You've healed, not only yourself, but everything around you. You're all that is strong and honorable. Men respect you, and your people love you for yourself. Perhaps one day, you'll see this. You're every-thing I could ever desire. Just for what you are. If you want me, just for what I am, I'll stay here with you."

He pulled her across him and kissed her. His heart was already lighter, and a calm acceptance of the past ran through his veins. Once again, she had gifted him with that.

She lay down beside him, trusting him in spite of all he had told her. He'd opened himself to her with all his darkness and rage and bloody wounds, and still she would remain here. With him.

Rising on his elbow, he blew out the oil lamp on the table beside the bed. He gathered her to him and closed his eyes. With her in his arms, the darkness had no more power over him. As long as she was there, it never would.

Rorik yawned into his cup of ale. At least the longhouse was quiet in the late morning. Elfwynn was still asleep and he didn't want her disturbed, so he'd all but kicked everyone out. They had work to do.

He hadn't slept much after he'd told her of his past. He'd made long, lazy love to her, then had lain awake as she slept beside him. The past had played over in his mind, but this time, he'd viewed it as though he stood on a mountain above it, no longer in the valley.

The anxious feeling roiling in him since yesterday had become stronger. He'd thought of asking Lifa to read the runes for him, but she was busy tending the wounded. That was more important. And, if he was truthful with himself, he didn't want to know. Whatever the gods had in store would come soon enough.

Galinn came in the front door and strode toward him."Jarl."

A chill passed through him. Why? Was it hearing that title spoken again in this hall, or something else? "Just Rorik, old friend. What is it?"

"A ship has come in from the fjord and is signaling that they want to land."

"Do you recognize it?" He stood.

"No. It holds about thirty or forty men."

A good size, but not large enough to be a threat. "Give them permission. Have them go to the docks and tie up alongside one of the other ships. I'll be there right after you."

As Galinn left, Rorik checked on Elfwynn. She was just stirring, her eyes sleepy. He watched her as she stretched. Why did it feel as though he'd never see this again? Sitting on the bed, he kissed her. She smiled up at him.

He brushed back her hair. "There's a strange ship coming to the docks. I don't know what will come of it. They may only want to trade, but it would be best if you got dressed."

"I will." She started to rise, but he pushed her back on the bed and took her mouth with his. He kissed her, clinging to this time as long as he could. Perhaps this dread was an omen, such as Silvi got. Or perhaps it was because he'd finally found what he'd been searching for and feared losing it. Either way, he didn't want to leave her, but he had to see what this ship was about.

He gave her a brief caress and left. As he walked down the path to the shore, he peered out at the vessel just making its way toward the docks. He never forgot a longship. He remembered this one, from the markets. And Northumbria. The Danes were camped on the riverbank there and when he'd left the earl's keep, he'd passed it on the shore not far to the east. His heart sped up.

As he stepped onto the dock, he stopped. A man jumped onto the pier before the ship had fully landed. Even if he didn't recognize him from the meeting with Edward, his resemblance to Elfwynn left no doubt. He was her half brother and was headed straight for him, a determined look on his face.

His stomach dropped as they walked toward each other. There could be only one reason he was here. They met midway on the pier.

Rorik inclined his head. "Wulfric of Redbank. Welcome to Vargf-jell."

His gaze never wavered. "Where is Elfwynn?"

"In the longhouse above."

Wulfric blinked as though he hadn't expected that answer. "I want to see her."

"Of course. Come this way. I'll have food and drink prepared for all of you. Whose ship is that?"

"The Dane, Brandr."

He'd heard of him, but didn't know him personally. He glanced at the ship and saw a large, dark-haired man giving orders as they tied the ship to another. How had all this come about?

When they entered the longhouse, he told the servants to bring his best wine and ale, serve the finest food, and prepare the saunas for those who wished to use them after so many days at sea.

He handed Wulfric a cup of wine and raised it to him. "Skoal." They drank. "How did you know she is here?"

"I want to see her first. To make certain she's all right."

Rorik nodded, setting down his cup. He had to step with care around this. When he opened the door to Elfwynn's room, she was just finishing dressing. Her hair was combed and flowed free, shining in the soft light. She looked at him, her luminous eyes questioning.

"We have a visitor. You'll want to come out here."

"We?" She frowned as she approached him.

He nodded, the sick feeling in his stomach growing. Opening the door farther, he let her walk out past him. She stopped short as Wulfric came toward her.

"Wulf?" She barely spoke the name, but it lanced straight through him like a spear thrust into his heart.

With that one word, he had just lost her.

She couldn't move, couldn't even think. Then Wulf grabbed her to him and enfolded her in his strong arms. His scent, like that of home, surrounded her, and all the sorrow, fears, and frustrations that had stewed in her let loose.

She sobbed so hard she couldn't breathe. He had always been her great shield against the world and now he was here. Taking in gulps of air, she tried to look at him, to make certain he was real, but the tears and the sobs wouldn't stop.

"It's all right, Elfwynn." His deep voice soothed her. "It's all over now. I'm bringing you home where you belong."

Home. The place she'd dreamed of all this time. Except now. Only last night, she'd decided to make Vargfjell her home. Sniffing, she looked at Rorik. He stood nearby, his arms crossed, his face implacable.

"I think we need to talk." His voice was rough and his silver eyes glittered. "This is no one else's business. Come this way."

With Wulf's arm still around her, they went into Rorik's chamber. It was large and had a table with four chairs near the wall. She sank into one of the chairs before her legs gave out. They joined her, facing each other. Wulf held her hand across the table, giving it a reassuring squeeze.

Rorik eyed their hands, then focused on Wulf. "How did you know she was here?"

"There was an altercation between you and a Northumbrian woman in your market town of Hedeby. Word spread. I have contact with Brandr to keep the lines of communication open between us and the Danes who camp in our region. I went to him when Elfwynn first disappeared to see if he'd heard anything about her fate. I suspected you had taken her. He agreed. He's kept his ears open for me. When he heard about Hedeby, he contacted me."

She looked at Rorik. Why was there any doubt about what had happened to her?

"Wait." Rorik held his hand up. "You must have known I took her. Why would you have gone to Brandr to question it?"

"All we had to go on was that you might have wanted revenge for burning your ship. It made the most sense."

"And the ransom demand didn't tip you off?"

He frowned. "What ransom demand?"

"The one your father refused to pay because she is baseborn and, therefore of no value."

Wulf stood. "What lies do you tell? My father wouldn't think that of Elfwynn. He has been half a man since she vanished. He'd have given everything he owns to save her."

She put her hand on his arm. "Please, Wulf. Just sit." The last thing she needed was a fight between the two men she loved the most, especially while her own head spun. What was Wulf saying?

He sank down. "When did you send this demand?"

"The day we took her. She would have been home that evening had it been paid."

Wulf shook his head. "We weren't there when it happened. My father and I were many days' ride from the keep."

"I know you weren't home, Wulf," she said. "But Father was there."

"No. He came with me at the last minute. Neither of us was there. We didn't know of your abduction until we returned and by then, much time had passed."

Elfwynn met Wulf's eyes. "No one was there, then. Except your mother."

"Surely even she wouldn't be that hateful, Elfwynn. It just couldn't be."

"Couldn't it? She's despised my mother and me for as long as I remember. You and the women at the keep live in different worlds. You don't know."

"Hating is not enough of a motive to send someone to almost certain death," Rorik said. "There had to be more than that."

"There is." Wulf's face was grim. "By our laws, a baseborn child may inherit if the mother is freeborn, which Elfwynn's mother Rohesia is, and if the father acknowledges the child. Which our father did with Elfwynn. She stood to inherit a full third of my father's estate if he should die."

"And that doesn't bother you?" Rorik studied him. "Men have killed for far less than that."

"I mean to make my own way in the world," Wulf said. "I can't speak for my sister, but as far as I was concerned if it gave Elfwynn more of a chance to lead a secure life, I welcomed it. We weren't certain she could make an advantageous marriage, so this would ensure she'd have a place in the world."

She wanted to be sick, but she had to keep thinking. "Rorik, who did your man meet with that day? Can he describe him?"

"He made jokes about him because he was so scrawny. Said he had small eyes, like pig's eyes, and thin hair."

"Wigberht." She and Wulf said it together.

"Who is that?" Rorik's eyes narrowed.

"My mother brought him with her when she married my father," Wulf said. "He was one of the fighting men who were part of her dowry, even though he never fought. He doesn't stray far from her and I've always suspected he was not all he seems. But no one has caught them doing anything improper. We wish it were so, for then my father would have reason to divorce her."

"But she could never have planned this out," Elfwynn said.

"No, but she could have taken advantage of the situation when it occurred. When Rorik sent his ransom demand, Wigberht may have intercepted it and told her. She set the wheels in motion."

"She sent me on an errand. I didn't think much of it, for she's done that before. Two of father's guards went with me. They would know."

He shook his head. "They disappeared the same time you did. We thought Rorik had killed them to take you."

"I never saw them after they abandoned Elfwynn. This gets deeper and deeper. Was anyone else there who might have known what happened?" Rorik's expression was hard.

"Only my sister, Rowena." Wulf paused. "But I haven't seen her since then. As Elfwynn said, we move in different worlds, so it's not unusual for me not to see her for weeks or even months at a time. And my mother said she was disobedient and was being punished in her room. Then she said she was afraid Rowena would be taken like Elfwynn was and wanted to keep her safe."

"And quiet." Elfwynn held down a sob as her world reeled. Oh God. All this time, she had thought . . . "Father didn't abandon me. He didn't refuse to pay the ransom, because he never heard about it."

Wulf took both of her hands. "He's been sick with worry and grief. I've never seen a man so haunted. He loves you so, Elfwynn. This has almost destroyed him."

She almost couldn't form the words. "Mother. How is she?"

"I had her moved within the village. I have a woman with her all the time, seeing to her. She lives, but this has taken much from her. When I heard about Hedeby, I told her and that gave her hope. I promised to bring you home to her."

She sighed, her muscles unknotting. Her mother lived and it wasn't too late.

Wulf turned to Rorik. "I'm prepared to pay any ransom for her.

I'm told it's the price of a longship and the wergeld of two warriors. There would be no further reason for her to remain here."

No further reason, except for Rorik.

He regarded her with utter calm, but it was deceptive. Especially with what she now knew about him. His revelations last night had stunned her, and yet they explained so much. Everything he was and all he did sprang from that horrendous beginning. He presented a hard face to the world, but inside, he was still mourning for the child he'd never been. How could she leave him now, knowing she might be the one island of peace in his turbulent world?

"Wulf, I need to speak to Rorik. Alone."

He studied her. "What could you have to say to him? He took you against your will, forced you to stay here, and—"

Heat rose in her cheeks and Wulf's jaw dropped. "You? And Rorik?"

"She. And I." Rorik gave him a pointed look. "Now may I speak with her alone?"

Wulf pressed her hand. "Elfwynn? You're certain of this?"

She nodded. "I am, Wulf. I'll meet you in the hall and we can talk. Please." She didn't want him to leave. It was so good to be with him again. But there were things that had to be said.

Nodding, he stood. He gave her a kiss on the top of her head and left with a backward glance at Rorik. A warning glance.

When the door closed, she met his level stare. "My father didn't betray me."

"It would seem not. I imagine this changes everything."

"Not the way I feel for you. But I have to go back to him. To my mother. Even if it's only to let them know I'm well."

"I see. When I first realized I had to take you with me or risk my reputation, I told myself I was likely doing you a favor by saving you from a father who didn't care about you. It's what I kept believing. That this was better for you. Now I see that's not the way it is." He looked away. "It is not your leaving that concerns me. I agree you need to go back to your father so you both can heal. I never had that with mine.

"When men are dealt a death blow, with their last breath, they often see their lives very clearly. I sometimes wonder if, when he lay dying after Ivar attacked him, my father didn't have an instant of regret for all he'd done and I wasn't there to see it. Perhaps he could have said or done something that would have made it right." He gave her a wistful smile. "Perhaps not. But I still wonder."

He came around the table and knelt by her. Taking her hands in his, he looked down at them. "I don't want you to wonder. Even if Wulf were to go back and tell of how it is here for you, it wouldn't be the same. You need to see him, speak with him, feel his love. It has been a wound within you and it needs to heal. I think only his touch can do that.

"It is what will happen afterward that troubles me. You'll be back at home, with all those you love. Vargfell will be a distant memory, an unpleasant one in many ways. There's nothing to bring you back to me."

"I imagine one of your ships could do that." She tried to smile.

"Your father would burn it again. Do you think he would allow you to come back here, once he has you home again? He'll lock you away so far within the keep that even if I brought all my ships and men, I'd never find you."

"You seem to forget one thing, Northman. I have to return here. I still owe you a sail and I always honor my promises."

He drew her to him and kissed her. "Forget the damned sail. You owe me nothing. But your father does. Come with me."

He took her hand and led her out into the hall. Wulf was sitting with other men. He rose as they walked to him.

"Elfwynn has decided to return home," Rorik said. "And I ask for no gold or silver now. I have one stipulation, though."

"What is that?" Wulf tensed.

Rorik brought her hand to his lips and kissed it, then turned to Wulf. "Edward still owes me, but I intend to collect from him personally. Besides, I don't trust Elfwynn's safety with anyone else on the seas. Whenever you wish to leave for Northumbria, I'm taking you there myself."

Chapter Seventeen

On the shore of the Humber River near Redbank
Kingdom of Northumbria

Elfwynn watched the currents in the water of the river. Eight long-ships were beached to her left. Once, they would have struck fear into her. Now, they gave her a small bit of comfort, for they meant Rorik was here. If anything went wrong with this meeting with her father, he'd have a way to escape. Of course, he'd planned it that way. The Norse were never far from their ships at home or in battle.

Wulf had gone on to the keep. He'd said he didn't want her walking all that way. She shook her head. She'd spent her life on foot, traveling the roads and shoreline. It wasn't as though she was some delicate flower who had to ride in a cart everywhere. Still, it showed his concern for her.

They'd left Vargfjell days ago with all of Magnus's and Eirik's ships, and eight of Rorik's. Magnus, with Silvi, had peeled off first, at the mouth of the Sognefjorden, to head back to Thorsfjell. Then Eirik and Asa, along with Lifa, had turned for home at the Hardangerfjorden to return to Haardvik. Leif remained with them, saying things were more interesting with Rorik than with his brother. Only Rorik's warships remained after that and they'd made the crossing with no problems.

She hadn't spoken much to him during the daytime. He was busy with his navigation and handling the ship. But at night, though they hadn't slept together because of Wulf's vigilance, they had watched the stars and the light of the moon racing across the waves. There was little point in speaking of the future until she saw her father again. He still ruled her life and if he refused to allow them to be together, there wouldn't be much she could do about it.

And Rorik had never mentioned marriage at all to her. Or love, for that matter. That made her uneasy. Could she live with him without either of them?

Rorik came up behind her and drew her back against his chest. "My watch has said a group of warriors approaches. It must be your father with Wulf."

She turned around in his arms and rested her head on his chest. "I'm afraid, Rorik. I thought I'd be so happy to see him. And I am. But in another way, I feel this might be the last time I see you."

He pulled back and tilted her head up with a gentle hand beneath her chin. "It won't be. I promise you that. I have business with him, remember?"

"You said he still owes you, and yet you turned down the gold Wulf brought. What more is there?"

He smiled. "Let's go meet him."

She started to demand he answer her question, but he kissed her, silencing her. Then he took her hand and they walked to the clearing near the shore where Wulf had said they'd meet. His warriors followed them and when they reached the place, a group of men waited for them on horseback.

Her father was there, in the front with Wulf. He was thinner than she remembered, and his face was more lined, but it was still the face she'd loved all her life.

He rode forward, then stopped. "Elfwynn."

"Go to him." Rorik released her hand. She hesitated, and he urged her forward. "Go. Before I change my mind and abduct you again."

She walked toward her father and he jumped off his horse. Then she was in his arms and he buried his face in her hair.

"Elfwynn, my child. My precious child." His voice broke. She looked up at him. His eyes shone as he brushed back her hair. "I thought you dead. But God has been merciful and brought you home to me."

She choked back a sob. "I thought—I thought you didn't love me. All this time."

"How could you doubt it? You are more dear to me than anything I have." He kissed her forehead, then looked beyond her to Rorik. She faced him, her father's arm around her. "During our ride here, my son told me what happened and the suspicions all of you have toward Mildburg. I cannot discount it myself. When I return to the keep, I will find out the truth."

"I know," Rorik said. "Because I request that I be there also, under a banner of truce."

"This matter doesn't involve you."

"Doesn't it? I am still owed recompense for the price of a ship and wergeld."

"You refused the gold my son offered you."

"The price has risen considerably. Elfwynn assures me you would not have behaved with such dishonor and ordered my ships burned when we were in negotiations. At first, I thought if you would refuse to pay a ransom for your daughter, you were also capable of such perfidy. But with what has come to light, I believe her. I have the right to know who did order it, though. And I think you'd want to know, as well. I have a feeling both incidents are connected."

He studied Rorik, and Elfwynn held her breath. Rorik was up to something. Edward nodded. "I agree. You may bring ten of your men with you. No swords."

"Seaxes then."

"Accepted." Edward motioned to a group of his men. "Let them have your horses. I want to get back as soon as possible. I don't want any forewarning of this meeting to get back to my wife before I question her. Elfwynn, you'll ride with me. I'll not take the chance that anyone will ever separate us again."

He glared at Rorik as he spoke. The enmity between the two men crackled like lightning, and she was caught in the middle. But she was no prize to be fought over. If they insisted on hitting her with their sparks, she would just have to strike back.

"Rowena, sit up straight when you embroider. Your stomach looks fat that way. Are you gaining weight? You look slovenly."

"Yes, Mother."

She wasn't getting fat, though with the little exercise she'd had, it would be no surprise if she were. Ever since she'd overheard her mother and Wigberht plotting against Elfwynn, she'd been locked in her room. The only time she was allowed out was to come into her mother's private chamber to sew. She'd seen no one, spoken to no one, and hadn't been able to tell what she knew about Elfwynn. It wouldn't do any good anyhow. Her half sister was gone forever. And if she spoke up, her mother would make good on the promise to give her to the East Anglian earl who, it was said, murdered his wives.

Her mother couldn't keep this up forever. Eventually, she'd slip and that was all she'd need. It hurt, though, that apparently her father hadn't even noticed she wasn't at the meals. There was no telling what lie her mother had told about her, so perhaps it wasn't his fault.

Sitting beside the window, she'd seen her father ride out with Wulf earlier. Her brother had been gone for weeks and must have just returned. If only she had the freedom he did.

She looked up at a noise in the courtyard. They were riding in with a group of hard-looking men mounted on their horses. Hiding behind the fall of her hair to keep her mother from noticing, she tried to see who they were. Her father turned his horse as he slowed it. A woman rode behind him. She leaned forward to see better. It was Elfwynn. She was home.

A man with long black hair rode alongside them. She squinted to focus on him. He was the handsome Northman with whom her father had negotiated and who had tried to ransom Elfwynn. This was interesting. Now, perhaps, the story could be told and her mother's plot revealed.

She said nothing, not wanting to warn her mother. But Mildburg heard the horses and raised her head from her work.

"Who is that, Rowena?"

"Just Father and Wulf returning from wherever they went earlier."

The comings and goings of the men didn't interest her mother, so she continued her embroidery. Rowena bit her lip. *Please let them summon her. Please.* But just because they called for her mother, didn't mean she could find a way to tell them what she knew. She had to think, and be prepared to act.

At a knock on the door, Mildburg set aside her sewing and made certain her clothing was presentable. "Yes?"

Her guard opened the door. "My lady, Earl Edward has requested you attend him in the hall."

Pressing her lips together, she rose. "Very well. Take my daughter to her room and see that she stays there."

"Yes, my lady."

Her mother swept out, leaving just the two of them. This might be her only chance. She stood and followed him into the corridor. "I saw

Father ride in. He had people with him, but I couldn't see who they were."

"They are Northmen, my lady."

"One of them was a woman, was it not?"

He nodded with a sneer. "Elfwynn. She's come back."

She stared at him as though she was surprised. "Elfwynn? My dear sister? But we all thought she was dead." She put her hand to her forehead and leaned against the wall. "Elfwynn is back from the dead. Oh, this is such a shock. I feel faint." She closed her eyes.

"My lady? Can I help you?" He came to her.

"I need my maid. Get her for me."

"I dare not leave you, my lady. Let me help you to your room."

She moaned and sank onto the floor. "Everything is fading. Get my maid. She'll know what to do. I'm going to be sick." She doubled over, near his shoes.

At that, he straightened. "I'll bring help."

As soon as he ran off, she stood and rushed in the other direction. There was more than one entrance into the hall and she didn't want to risk coming across her mother so she ran a different way. As she neared the hall, she heard the voices of her father and Wulf. Another deep voice joined them, strangely accented. She darted into an alcove near the door and peeked around the corner.

They stood in the center of the large room along with ten northern warriors. The tall Northman was with them, along with Elfwynn. She was beautiful, not starved or harmed. The dress she wore was very fine, with silver brooches fastened at the shoulders.

Apparently, her father had also sent for Wigberht, for he was there, looking nervous. When he saw her, he'd have a reason to be fearful. She'd wait to see what her mother would say before she made her presence known. But she didn't have long before the guard discovered her missing.

Mildburg swept into the room, looking impeccable as always, a serene smile on her lips. "You wished to see me, my lord?" She stopped as Elfwynn moved nearer to Edward. "Elfwynn?" Her smile wavered. "Elfwynn, dear girl. You've come home."

"I called you here because I thought you might want to join in our celebration," Edward said. "It turns out that it was all just a misunderstanding. Jarl Rorik sent a ransom demand for her, but it seems I refused to pay it. Even though I wasn't here. Odd, that."

"Very much so, my lord." She looked at Elfwynn. "Welcome home, dear. I'm certain your mother was very glad to see you."

"They haven't seen each other yet, but Rohesia's coming here now," Edward said.

"Then I won't stand in the way of their happy reunion. I have work to do."

Edward lowered his head and tapped his front teeth, thinking. "Just one thing before you go, Mildburg. Jarl Rorik's warrior here has identified Wigberht as the man he told of the ransom demand. You and he go back a long way and you're together quite often. Do you know anything about this?"

She drew herself up. "I assure you, my lord, I have no interest in the affairs of men."

Rorik fastened his gaze on Wigberht. "You have not yet answered my man's account of the ransom demand."

He shook, his eyes darting toward Mildburg, then Edward. "My lord, I—I don't know what they're talking about. The man lies. They're nothing but barbarians. You'd take the word of a pagan over that of a righteous Christian?"

Rorik crossed the hall to Wigberht and glared down at him. "Not all Christians are righteous. We don't cling to notions of good and evil that are created by priests who profess to have the ears of a distant god. Our gods walk among us and judge us by what they see and hear. We have only strength and honor. And that honor outlives us all in the memories of men. In my culture, if anyone slanders another, it is lawful to kill him." He gripped his seax's hilt. "You have slandered my warrior."

Wigberht broke out in a sweat and licked his lips. Rorik pulled his blade from its sheath by a finger's width. The small man cowered. "She told me to do it. I overheard you talking about taking one of the earl's daughters and I told her of it, thinking to alert the keep. The Lady Mildburg told me to be quiet about it and to make certain the Northmen found Elfwynn."

Mildburg paled. "You never told me this, you little worm. You took it upon yourself to do this."

Rorik never looked at her. Instead, he caressed the hilt of his seax. "And?"

"And then, she said I was to intercept the ransom demand so that they would kill the girl."

Edward crossed his arms. "Did this happen as planned?"

Wigberht nodded, keeping his eyes on Rorik's blade. "I did this, my lord. What choice did I have? She's my lady."

"But why would you have gone to her to begin with?" Edward stood beside Rorik. "You should have gone to the man I left in charge of the keep's defense. Because you neglected to tell him, he would not have had time to prepare had the Northmen attacked."

"And we would have," Rorik said to Edward. "I was making preparations for war, but Elfwynn sacrificed herself for all of you. She offered to stay with me if I did not attack you. She asked that, instead, I take her to a church that would pay the money for her, and I agreed. The recompense for the burning of my ship wouldn't have come from you, but I would have had it. She alone saved your keep, Earl."

Edward looked at Elfwynn. She blushed, lowering her head.

Rorik pinned the little man with his gaze. "Who ordered the destruction of my ship when I was here earlier in the summer?"

"Lady Mildburg ordered the ships burned." Wigberht pointed at her. "She hates the Northmen for invading her lands when she was young. She wanted their ships destroyed so they'd have no escape. Then, Earl Edward could slay them."

Edward curled his lip in distaste. "What you did was treason. It only remains to be seen how far that treason extends."

"I am innocent in all this, my husband." Mildburg went to him and put her hands on his arm, clinging to him. "Why would I have endangered this keep and all in it, including myself?"

"It is not true, my lord." Wigberht knelt on the floor. "I swear it."

"There is a truth here." Edward said. "But with each blaming the other, I cannot say what it is."

Rowena stepped out from the alcove where she had hidden. Before she could move into the hall, a man grabbed her from behind and a hand came over her mouth.

"There you are. You got away from me once, but not again." The guard pulled her back, away from the door.

She tried to shake her head, but he was too strong and he pressed even harder so her teeth sliced into her lip. Using that pressure, she threw her head back and slammed it into his face. He yelled and she broke away from him. Blood streamed from his nose as he lunged for her again. His hand closed around her arm and she screamed.

"What is this?" Edward stormed into the hallway, Rorik behind him.

"I know what happened, Father." She jerked her arm away from the guard. "He's trying to stop me, to lock me in my room again. Mother had me imprisoned ever since I saw her and Wigberht plotting this. They didn't want me saying anything to you."

"It was the Lady Mildburg, my lord. She—"

Edward struck the guard with his fist, adding to the blood on his face. "Get out. Leave this keep and my lands and never show yourself here. I won't have you killed if you followed her orders, but get from my sight before I change my mind."

As the guard hurried away, her father turned to her. "Rowena, you saw your mother and Wigberht planning this?" At her nod, he gently took her hand. "Come with me."

They went into the hall. Both Rorik's warriors and Edward's guards had circled the two conspirators to ensure they didn't escape.

Mildburg's eyes grew large as she saw her daughter. "My lord, she'll lie. She's angry with me because I punished her for being disobedient. I—"

"Be silent. Rowena, tell me."

She repeated what she had heard them say about the ransom. "They meant for the Northman to find Elfwynn. And then, when the two guards left her on purpose, Wigberht killed them so they wouldn't talk. The Northmen didn't do it." She met her mother's glare. "And then she was going to reward him with herself. She's kept me locked in my room all this time so I couldn't say anything. She threatened me with marriage to the earl who murders his wives, so I was afraid." Her eyes filled. "None of you even noticed I was gone, but I speak the truth."

A tall Northman with light streaks in his dark hair nodded to Rorik and he spoke to her father. "Leif has an eye for the truth and he is satisfied that what she says is so."

"I, also, believe my daughter," Edward said. Rowena relaxed in relief. "And no daughter of mine will wed where she is unwilling."

He motioned to his guards and they held Wigberht. "For the crime of treason and for endangering this keep, I sentence you to death. Take him away."

Wigberht yelled as the guards dragged him out. As his cries faded, Edward regarded Mildburg. She fell to her knees, weeping. He stood firm. "Because you are a woman and the mother of my children, I'll not take your life. In fact, I'll give you a choice."

She shook, tears running down her face. "What choice, my lord?"

"For treason, the punishment is death, but I'll forgo that. For adultery, the punishment is mutilation. Cutting off the nose and ears. Then I will divorce you. You will choose between that or banishment to a convent and divorce. Which will it be?"

She hung her head, defeated. "The convent, my lord."

"Then you'll be locked in your chambers until arrangements can be made for your journey." He gestured and two guards helped her to her feet. She did not look back as they led her away.

Edward addressed Wulf and Rowena. "I am sorry to have to do that to your mother. But it was long in coming. I knew she was unfaithful, but I could never catch her at it. Now I have."

"She chose to be what she is, Father," Wulf said. "Perhaps now, in the convent, she can find peace."

"And so can we." Rowena said. No longer would she have to endure her mother's insults and threats. Now, she was free.

Chapter Eighteen

"You said the price for your lost ship and men has gone up, Jarl. What do you want now to make peace between us?"

Rorik settled himself across the table in the earl's meeting room. The man was nothing if not direct. They hadn't even had a sip of the ale he had poured for them. He could be just as direct.

"Your daughter. I want Elfwynn."

Edward's fingers tightened around his silver goblet. "You could have just kept her for yourself instead of bringing her back here."

"That's not how I am with women. I didn't want to take her to begin with, but circumstances forced my hand. Also, at the time, I thought you were a bastard who didn't care about your own daughter. I figured her life would be better at Vargfjell than here. When she learned you hadn't betrayed her, I knew she had to come back to see you. Her happiness is the most important thing to me."

Edward snorted. "You think living in your caves and burrows under the ice is better than this?" He waved his hand around the comfortable room.

Rorik chuckled. "Ask Elfwynn or your son about the cave I live in. They'll tell you all about it. At least, I have glass in my windows." He took a sip of ale. "I can bring you alliances and protection. I'm the shield you need in this region. No one will dare to attack you if you're related to me by marriage."

"Marriage?"

"Yes. I'm asking for her in marriage." If it meant he could be with her, he would do whatever was necessary to gain Edward's agreement. The earl would accept no less and neither would Elfwynn. He wanted it, as well. The long voyage here had given him time to think and he'd realized he couldn't give her up. He wouldn't disgrace her in both her culture and his by taking her as a concubine. Because of her, he was finally ready to leave the past behind.

Edward raised his head. "Why would I allow my daughter to marry into a people who do nothing but fight and raid? You have attacked our sacred houses, drowned our priests, taken all the gold and silver offerings there. All you do is make war on other innocent places."

"Are you any different? Look at all the wars in your own lands. You're so busy attacking each other, especially in Ireland, that you can't mount a defense against us. Northumbria, Wessex, East Anglia, Mercia, Strathclyde, the Picts—all of you are so blinded by your political squabbles that you don't see us sailing to your shores until it's too late."

"We have the right to defend ourselves."

"Defend, yes. But what of the Frankish king, Charlemagne? In our forefathers' day, he raged across the northern regions of the great continent, expanding his kingdom by conquest. He forced the peoples in those villages to become baptized, then he slaughtered them. In one instance, over four thousand were baptized and died in a single day. Our forebears saw that he was heading for our lands. They wanted to show him what he'd be up against if he chose to invade us. So they attacked you and, yes, drowned priests to avenge those who were forcibly baptized and killed." He leaned forward. "And do you know what? It worked. Our lands have never been invaded."

"He wanted to save the souls of those poor pagans."

"He wanted the spoils of conquest. As do we, only we don't dress it up in the vestments of religion. When our ancestors attacked the churches, they found the riches your people had used to try to buy the favor of your god. From then on, we did raid for treasure. But we are no worse and no better than your own armies who invade a village. In fact, your warriors do far more raping and slaughtering than we do. We mainly just want the gold and silver. But it's the priests who write the accounts, and we do not. So they make us out to be evil, while we are no different than you in so many ways."

Edward half stood, leaning across the table. "*We* are good Christians here, Northman. I'll not jeopardize her soul by giving her to you. I don't care what alliances you'd bring me, I'll not make a deal with the devil."

The earl wanted a devil? He could oblige him so very easily. His muscles tensed. The rage simmered, like water that was just starting to boil. He held it down as Lifa had taught him, gritting his teeth to keep himself under control. For Elfwynn's sake. The thought of her calmed him. A bit.

"You have no idea what the devil is. And we have a supreme god, much the same as yours."

"What? Your Odin?"

"No. Older than that. In our beginning, there was nothing, just endless space. But there was a creator. He made our gods and everything there is. He has no beginning, and rules everything. Does that sound familiar? We don't deny your god exists. In fact, in some places, we've welcomed him along with our own. In the future, that may not bode well for our culture. Where something is too easily accepted, it tends to take over."

He drained his cup and rose. "You don't want to get on my bad side, Earl Edward. I'm returning to my ships, but this isn't done between us. Why don't you ask Elfwynn what she wants? That's what we do in my land. Are we, huddled in our caves and burrows, more civilized toward our daughters than you are?"

He strode out before he started a real war with Edward.

His men followed him and they mounted the horses they'd borrowed. No one stopped them. He studied the defenses as he rode from the bailey. If the earl wanted to see just how vulnerable he was to the fury of the Northmen, he'd be pleased to show him. Nothing would stop him from getting Elfwynn back.

Even if he had to abduct her all over again.

Her mother was as delicate and translucent as a glass statue, but she clung to Elfwynn with a strength that belied her appearance.

"All I thought of was what you were going through," Elfwynn said as Rohesia wept with soft sobs.

"And I thought the same of you." She pulled back. "Living in that frozen land with those unwashed barbarians. How you must have suffered."

She smiled. "It's not as cold as you think. There's a current that runs along their coast from the south. It keeps them warm. The land is quite beautiful and majestic. And they're cleaner than many of our people are. We see them here after days at sea, so they're in need of baths. But in their own homes, they bathe often and they have something called a sauna. You steam yourself clean. Rorik's longhouse is bigger than the keep. Its walls are hung with weavings and they eat from silver and gold plates there. And the food is good and plentiful. I don't think they all live as Rorik does, but life with him wasn't so bad."

"With him?" The side of her mouth curved up. "Not with them?"

Her face heated and Rohesia laughed. "I thought that might be how it is."

"That is a sound I've not heard in a long time, Rohesia." Edward came into the house. "Your laughter."

Rohesia lowered her gaze. "It's so wonderful to have Elfwynn back. I feel strong again."

"You look better already." He sat down with them. "Rohesia, it's good that Elfwynn is here with us. I want to speak with you. You have heard what happened with Mildburg and Wigberht today?"

"Elfwynn told me."

"I have suspected my wife was being unfaithful to me. While it's true that I was with you for a time, I had to stop long ago so she would have no cause for divorcing me. If she had, by our laws, she could have taken a third of everything. That wouldn't bother me so much except she could have taken Wulf and Rowena away from me. Who knows how they would have suffered with her? I couldn't do it."

"I understand, Edward. I always have, though it's been difficult."

Elfwynn swallowed. She'd assumed all this time her mother had only been a convenience for him. But that hadn't been the case.

He took her hand. "I must wait for the divorce to be final. But after that, Rohesia, I want to be with you. I want you as my wife."

She put her hand over her mouth. "I'm not of your rank, Edward. I'm only a village woman and you're an earl. Nobility."

"Who will deny me my heart? Especially at our age. The king will not. He needs me in the wars and won't want to displease me. I don't think our people will object. So many of those who shunned you through the years were doing so because of Mildburg's hatred. They didn't want to risk her wrath. Now, they won't want to risk mine.

"Word is also spreading of how our daughter saved us from attack by going with the Northmen. Now, the people who turned their backs on her are cheering her sacrifice."

Elfwynn closed her eyes for a moment. She wanted to weep.

"I will be happy to be your wife, Edward."

He embraced her. Tears ran down her thin cheeks, but already she had a glow about her, a blossoming of the joy filling her.

Edward sat back and regarded Elfwynn. "Rorik has gone back to his ships."

Her heart stuttered. Was he leaving? Would he not say goodbye to her?

"He wanted you, Elfwynn. As his wife."

She gasped. Wife? Only she knew what that meant. "What did you answer, Father?"

"I told him no."

"And now he's leaving?" All the life seemed to drain from her.

"No. He became very angry, though he hid it well. He said this wasn't over yet."

Oh God. The rage. If it came on him, there was no telling what he'd do. "I have to go to him, Father."

He studied her. "Why? He's just a Northman who took you from me."

"He's more than that, Father. He's honorable, proud, a good man. I've seen what he's done for his people. He could have hurt me, raped me, anything he wanted. But he didn't. Instead, he treated me well and I became a part of Vargfjell. Ask Wulf what it was like there. It's beautiful. The people there are happy and well off. Rorik is the wealthiest man in his land. He has many longships, and such power that not even kings can face him. And yet, he uses that wealth for the good of his people. He could be a strong ally for you." She had to speak in a way he'd understand.

Edward held his hand up. "I've already spoken with Wulf about what he saw there. He was very complimentary, but it doesn't matter."

"Edward." Rohesia leaned toward him. "Shall we deny her the happiness we have finally found? Haven't we learned what it is to love and yet not be with each other? Shall we watch her soul die a little more each day as ours have?"

"I don't care about all his ships and power and wealth. It doesn't matter about the alliances he can bring me. I don't care about any of it when it comes to my daughter."

"But, Father—"

He held his hand up. "There are only two things I care about. First, Elfwynn, do you love him?"

His love for her shone from him. She smiled. "Yes, Father. I do."

"Then the other thing is that you must be married here, with a Christian ceremony. God will not acknowledge your marriage otherwise."

Warm joy burst through her. She threw her arms around him, laughing and crying at the same time. "Thank you, Father. I love you so much."

He caressed her cheek. "After he left, I was very angry. But then, I thought about the things he and I spoke about. He is a man of great depth and intelligence, and he impressed me, in spite of my initial misgivings. Go to him. Wulf is waiting for you in the yard with horses and men. He'll take you to him."

She ran outside, hardly able to see through her tears.

Wulf grabbed her up and swung her around. "Let's go find him before he brings the keep down. Though, from what I heard about their wedding celebrations, they might do that anyhow."

"I know they will." She mounted the horse he held for her and they rode out, his men following.

When they were on the part of the road where Rorik had abducted her, he and the warriors who had come to the keep rode from the woods. All his men from the eight warships followed on foot, and both forces faced each other. The Northmen were fully armed. They weren't just out for a jaunt. Wulf's men also bristled with weapons. She hadn't foreseen this. They might go to war over her.

Would Rorik and Wulf fight each other? Not if she had anything to do with it, even if she had to come between them to stop them. It was, after all, her life.

"Rorik." She started toward him, but Wulf grabbed her horse's reins. He spoke low. "Before they left the keep, Leif told me Rorik was enraged by Father's answer and to take care. He won't hurt you, will he?"

She didn't hesitate. "Never."

Wulf let go of the reins and she rode forward. Behind her, Wulf's men loosened their weapons and settled their shields on their arms, preparing for the possibility of battle. The Northmen did the same. Rorik met her in the center so that their legs almost touched. She didn't see any signs of his anger. Had he brought himself under control? Perhaps for her sake?

She kept her voice light. "Going raiding?"

"I haven't done so all summer. I didn't want to get soft."

"I don't believe you're soft anywhere, Rorik." She gave him an innocent look.

His mouth twitched as it did when he was teasing her. "I thought I might find something interesting in the area."

"I see. Going to my keep?"

"It's the only one here. It would be a good place to start."

"Are you looking for anything in particular?"

He shrugged. "I might be looking for gold."

"You already turned that down."

"So I did." He paused to think. "Ships?"

"We don't have any."

"That's right. That's right. I forgot." He drummed his fingers on the saddle. "Then I suppose there's only one more thing of interest here. Women?"

"You don't abduct women, remember?"

"It seems I tried it once. I'm still not certain how it will turn out."

"I have a feeling it might be better this time."

"You mean you'll be obedient, and sweet, and not give me any trouble at all?"

"Only in your dreams."

"Good." He leaned over, swept her onto his lap, and reined the horse around. They sped into the forest.

She hung on to him, breathing in his clean scent, reveling in the feeling of his arms around her. He slowed when they got to the riverbank near where his ship had been burned. He steadied her as he let her slide off, then jumped down after her.

"You don't think your brother will chase us, do you?" He scanned the woods behind them.

She cupped his cheek and turned his face to her. "I think he, his men, and yours are heading to your ships to drink all your beer. He knows I'm safe with you."

"I'm not so certain of that. After all, I have abducted you again." He gave her a threatening look.

"It was no abduction." She stood on her toes and kissed him. "I'm quite willing."

Wincing, he rolled his eyes. "Can we at least pretend it is? I have a reputation to uphold, you know."

"Believe me, I know all about your reputation."

"Because of it, I felt I had to take you from everything you loved. But, in a way, it brought you to me. I told your father I want to marry you. He refused."

"Are you certain about marriage? I know what it means to you, Rorik. A letting go of the past."

"What means more to me is that you return my love."

At his words, her heart jumped. But there was still so much between them. "So you thought to persuade him with threats?"

"This is the first time I've tried diplomacy. It leaves something to be desired."

"What men could not accomplish with swords and axes and spears, mere women did with words."

"There are no 'mere' women. And what do you mean?"

"My parents will be married as soon as they can. My mother told him that they've found their happiness, and now I should find mine. Between the two of us, we convinced him."

"He said yes?"

"He said yes."

Rorik held her, not speaking, his face buried in her hair. She listened to his heartbeat, so strong and steady. Just like he was.

She looked up at him. "I didn't think I could be with you because I couldn't live with unreturned love like my mother had. I didn't want to become like her. But now she's found her love, and I am like her after all. For I've found mine."

"So that means you love me as well?"

She gave him a stern look. "Can you doubt it after all this? I love you so, Rorik, but I'm still uncertain about watching you leave for your voyages and not knowing if you'll return. At least if I'm at Vargfjell, when you come home, I'll be there for you."

"I intend to stay at Vargfjell most of the time anyhow. There's still a threat from Halfdan and the jarls to the south. The village is going to expand now and I have so many ships and men that I'll have to be there to keep it all working. Warriors, merchants, and other jarls will be coming to gain my favor. And you'll be there. That's all the reason I'll need to stay. I think I'll be around you so much, you may leave on one of the ships just to get away from me for a time."

"I doubt that. But my father does have one stipulation for our marriage. We must be wed with a Christian ceremony in the church."

He winced. "He doesn't expect me to convert, does he?"

"It's enough that I convinced my father to let me marry Rorik of Vargfjell. One miracle a day is enough."

"I suppose I can build you a small church at Vargfjell." He grinned. "I can even steal you a priest for it. Perhaps that one in Hedeby."

She frowned at him. "Rorik."

He sighed. "Very well. No priest stealing. Though if one wanders through, we can invite him to stay."

"That's better."

"If I make you my wife in your church, do you think your god and you will forgive me for what I've done to you?"

"He always forgives. And so do I."

Rorik looked out at the river at the remains of his ship that were too large to move. She turned so that she could see it as well. The top of the mast, lying at an angle broke the surface of the water.

He rested his chin on the top of her head as he embraced her from behind. "My *Sword of the Waves*. When it burned, it was as though I was set ablaze. I abducted you to try to make it right. It did, but not as I thought it would. The sound of your words and your music put out the fires in my heart, Elfwynn. Who could have dreamed that from so much destruction and loss would come such a love as we have found?"

Vargfjell

Elfwynn rode a pure white mare. Magnus led it to the sacred grove where Rorik awaited her along with the people of the village and all the guests from around the region. She wore the beautiful tan and white beaded dress he'd given her during their private little war. It fit perfectly.

After their wedding in Northumbria, along with the inevitable brawls between Rorik's men and her father's during the feast afterward, they had sailed across the North Sea and stopped at Haardvik. They'd invited Eirik and his family to the largest wedding the north had ever seen, as Rorik put it. As they'd passed the Sognefjorden, one of their ships had peeled off to tell Magnus and Silvi the news, and now, a month later, they were all here once again. This time, it was under much better circumstances. Rorik and Nuallen hadn't even tried to kill each other. Yet.

She stroked the mare's mane. In the old days, she'd been told, it would have been sacrificed to honor the marriage and its blood sprinkled on them. But now, they would keep this horse as a sacred animal and it would live out its life in comfort.

She'd spent the morning in the sauna, cleansing away her former life, as was tradition. Lifa told her of her new duties and responsibilities, as well as the secrets to guiding and advising her husband.

"Never mind that," Kaia had said. "All she has to do is sheath his sword and he'll do anything she wants." All the women laughed.

A sword. As part of the ceremony, she was to give Rorik a new sword and her father had sent one of his finest with her. Magnus carried it in his free hand as he led the mare.

Eirik waited with Rorik in the grove, Silvi and Lifa with them. He'd spent time in the sauna as well, listening to the advice of the men. His ebony hair gleamed down his chest and shoulders and he was dressed in dark trousers and a gray tunic made from the cloth she'd woven for him. The sword of his family was sheathed at his side. On his neck, the twisted gold torc of his rank gleamed.

Magnus helped her off the mare and Turold led it to the side. They walked to Rorik where Magnus handed her the sword he'd carried. "With this sword, your father gives the power of guardianship and protection over you to Rorik."

She gave it to Rorik. He unsheathed his ancestral sword and handed it to her. They held the weapons horizontally while Lifa set gold rings on their hilts.

She spoke to them both. "The joining of the swords and the rings shows the bonding of the oath you take together. The swords are a threat to both of you should you break your vows."

They removed the rings and slid them on their fingers. Rorik gazed down at her.

"As a child, I took this blade, still warm from my father's hand when he lay dead. It is yours to hold for our firstborn son. As I give it to you, I give you my protection, my faithfulness, my life, and my love."

She put her hand over his and the sword she had given him. "And I, also, vow to give you my life, my loyalty, and my love."

"The gods have heard your vows," Lifa said. "They consecrate this marriage in joy and celebration."

Rorik sheathed his new sword and she handed the blade she held to Leif. Rorik caught her hard against him and kissed her. The people cheered, their voices ringing throughout the forest. Men pulled Rorik from her and led him back toward the village while Turold brought the mare back for her. She rode behind Rorik and the other men as they laughed. The crowd pelted her with flowers as they danced and sang. It was so different from the solemn, ritualistic Christian wedding she'd had in the church in Northumbria.

This was all she could have dreamed of. Her family was far away, but with Rorik's command of the seas, they'd make the crossing and see each other. Besides, Rorik would have to oversee his new land there. Her father had given him a large parcel of property near Redbank as her dowry. It gave Rorik a foothold there, increasing his wealth even more. And it offered Edward protection, for he was now aligned with the most powerful Northman. It cushioned him against the Danes who were infiltrating the region. Each claimed victory.

Rorik waited for her in front of the door of the longhouse. Before she could dismount from the mare, he lifted her off and carried her across the threshold. The doorway was seen as a portal between worlds at this time, and it would be an omen of misfortune if she should stumble.

After most of the people filed into the hall, they grew silent and watched Rorik. He unsheathed his new sword and plunged it into one of the supporting pillars. It sank in deep. When he pulled it out, it left a large scar, attesting to his prowess and strength.

Amidst the celebrating, Elfwynn gave him a cup of mead, the first of her many duties as a wife. It was similar, and yet so different to the other times she'd served him before. He caught her eyes, and a knowing smile passed between them. He took it and made the sign of Thor over it, drank, then handed the cup to her. She held his gaze over the brim as she took a sip. They would drink many cups of mead together over the next four weeks and it made them one. They walked, amid many toasts and cheering, to their fur-covered seats at the head of the room.

"My aunt will want to hear what you dream this night, Wife."

Rorik's voice in her ear still brought shivers to her. But it would have been difficult to hear him otherwise above all the celebrations in the hall. It was filled with people from all over the north. Even Ellisif had returned. She had disappeared after the battle, her wolves with her, but now she was sitting near Kaia. Leif eyed the shield-maiden while she ignored him.

She considered what Rorik had said. Was hearing her dreams another Norse wedding custom? She'd had to learn so many of them before their ceremony earlier that day. "Why would Lifa want to know them?"

"A bride's dreams on her wedding night tell the story of their life together. Since my aunt is a rune mistress, it falls to her to interpret them."

"We've already been married a month, Rorik. This is hardly our wedding night."

"Before my gods, it is." His voice dropped into a deep thrum. "Although, I don't intend to let you have much of a chance to dream at all this night."

The room became very warm. "Do you think anyone would notice if we vanished?"

"Our chamber is but a few steps away."

"I was referring to going outside, perhaps down by the shore." She cast him a sideways glance.

He sighed. "Already rejected. But I'll have my revenge later."

"I look forward to it." She nipped his ear.

He groaned. "Let's leave, then, while they're busy toasting us. They'll never notice we're gone until they come up for air. By then, with any luck, they won't care." Taking her hand, he led her past the crowd and out the front door.

They walked down to the shore and sat on a bench. She rested her head on his shoulder. "The work on your new longship goes well. I'll complete your sail by the time it's ready."

The docks were deserted because of the festivities. The beginnings of a massive ship rose above the beach. The keel was finished and balanced on stocks set into the sand, the forestem and afterstem were attached, and the shipwrights were ready to clamp on the first of the side boards.

"You don't owe me that sail any longer. I told you that before you left here. Someone else can weave it."

She straightened and turned to him. "If you think I'll let anyone else work on it, you're mistaken. No one else can do it with the same skill I can."

"I see it as a symbol of everything I did wrong to you."

"I started it and I'll finish it. Please, Rorik. Consider it my wedding gift to you. Wherever it takes you in the world, a piece of me will go with you, and it will bring you back to me."

He searched her eyes, his hands cupping her face. "I can accept it as your gift to me. Just as the wind will fill the sail, so you have filled my life. I couldn't see past the scars in my mind until you showed me they were the symbols of the strength it took for me to heal from the wounds that caused them. I've traveled the seas, looking for something I didn't understand I needed until I met you. And whenever I leave here again, I'll have to take you with me. The world couldn't survive me without you."

His silver-green eyes shone with love as he kissed her. Then he gazed up at Vargfjell rising behind them. The laughter drifted down from the great longhouse as he gathered her to him. "I've always given away my wealth to my people to make up for the past. But you're the one treasure I plan to keep for myself."

LORD
OF THE
MOUNTAINS

SABRINA JAREMA

viking lords

If you enjoyed *Lord of the Seas* be sure not to miss the rest of Sabrina Jarema's Viking Lords series, including

LORD OF THE MOUNTAINS
Amid the glittering fjords and majestic mountains of Norway, this stunning series delves into the loves, battles, and dreams of the Viking clans—powerful men and women who believed in the call of the flesh as well as the soul . . .

It was said that the man who could look into Silvi Ivarsdottir's eyes would be meant for her. Powerful jarl Magnus Sigrundson knows he is that man, and that Silvi's dowry can give him the ships, swords, and silver he needs for his trading empire. Yet beautiful Silvi's dream is not to be a wife, but a Priestess of the gods for the great temple at Uppsala. Who dares interfere with such passion? The answer lies in Silvi herself, in the way her body awakens to Magnus' touch, in the way she inspires a reverence he didn't know he possessed—and in the battles she takes on when she journeys to his mountain home of Thorsfjell.

But soon a dangerous, deceitful enemy threatens to shatter. Now they face another quest: can they find each other again—and dare live and love in each other's worlds?

Keep reading for a special look.

A Lyrical e-book on sale now!

Chapter One

The village of Haardvik
Hardangerfjorden, Hordaland, Norway
851 A.D.

The sound of steel on steel shattered the calm beauty of the early spring day.

Silvi Ivarsdottir paused, listening to the clash echoing through the trees and the mountains. She didn't need to reach out with her thoughts to know what was happening. The reason for the disruption was obvious. Her brother's weeklong wedding celebrations were still going on in the village, so beer and weapons were inevitable. Anticipated, in fact. It was what men did best.

The sound of combat didn't come from the village. She tilted her head, seeking the source of the disturbance. Her breath stilled. They wouldn't dare. It came from the place where the gods walked, the sacred grove. No one brought weapons there, the same as in the great temples. It was sacrilege.

Her stomach twisting, she rushed toward the clearing. She didn't fear facing down warriors. Rather, they should fear *her*. After all, she'd had the gods on her side since birth. She would defend and honor them until she went to Freya's hall in the afterlife.

She burst into the clearing and skidded to a stop. Two men circled each other. They were bare to the waist. Their long, dark hair swirled around their broad shoulders as they came together in an explosion of steel and sparks. They were both massive, men in their prime, fighting with all the skill that made their people so feared throughout the world. They moved with the masculine grace inborn to all the finest warriors as they surged through the clearing like water rushing in a river.

Her cousin Rorik laughed aloud as he swung, his black hair sweeping over his shoulders and down his chest. White teeth flashing, he smashed his shield against his opponent's arm, trapping his blade. Rorik thrust, but his blade met with air as the other man stepped to the side and brought his own shield up, deflecting the deadly edge.

Magnus.

He pressed Rorik back several steps with his wicked, fast sword strokes. His hair was so dark, it looked almost black, except for the deep golden lights in it. Moving with the skill of a predator, he surged forward, taking his advantage.

Her heart stuttered. As she watched them, her body heated, her breath quickening. Maybe it was only because she had just run a fair distance. The sun glanced off Magnus's sculpted arms as he swung his sword in a deadly arc. It smashed into the other blade with an explosion of sparks. She held her breath. If she called out, it could distract them. An instant's hesitation might mean death to one of them. Her anger at the sacrilege was not worth the risk. She could do nothing but watch.

Rorik disengaged, then hit Magnus's sword with his own, nearly knocking it out of his hand. He shook his black hair from his face and laughed as he brought his sword around for another blow. Magnus hit the ground, rolled, and came to his knees. He swept his shield horizontally, aiming for Rorik's legs. Rorik leaped over it with a yell, and before he landed, Magnus was on his feet. He struck Rorik with his shield and knocked him onto his back.

It wasn't over yet, though. Rorik threw his shield, edge first. Magnus spun out of the way, arching his back as it knifed past him. It gave Rorik time to leap up and charge him. He drove Magnus back until he could grab his own shield and reposition it on his left arm.

They circled each other, grinning. Their bodies glistened with sweat. Rorik's stomach was rippled and flat. Magnus's was the same, save for a wicked, jagged scar crossing his lower abdomen. Both were slim hipped, broad shouldered, tall, and powerful. But it was Magnus she watched. Rorik laughed and danced as he fought. Magnus stood solid, every move weighted and purposeful. His cuts were clean, direct, with no wasted energy or movement. His strength radiated from him like a storm rolling over the mountains.

She'd seen him in a vision before he'd come with her brother, Eirik, to set her village free of the marauders who had held them captive all winter. She'd tended his wounds, and while his blood flowed onto the ground, he'd stared at her as one thunderstruck. He'd continued to watch her through the following days. Now Eirik was married to Magnus's sister, Asa, so Magnus was family of sorts. She'd have to see him many times in the future. At least, until she went to live at the great temple at Uppsala. Then she would see no one at all.

She shook herself out of her reverie. This was wrong, that they should bring weapons into a sacred place. They were still feinting, no doubt resting for a final onslaught.

"Rorik." Her raised voice stopped him short and he jumped away from Magnus with a guilty wince. "How dare you fight in the grove, Rorik? Not even you could be that sacrilegious."

Instead of answering her, her cousin clapped Magnus on the shoulder and said, low, "Run. *Now*." He bounded into the shadow of the trees, leaving Magnus standing alone.

She started after him. "I heard that, Rorik. Get back here."

Magnus lifted his sword in a question. "Rorik, what are you doing?" He turned toward Silvi as she bore down on him. "We were just training a bit, Silvi. How could we know this was your grove?"

"It's the gods' grove, not mine. Rorik knows. He's been here before." She shot Magnus a glare. "As for you . . . Don't you scent the breath of the gods here? Don't you feel their power in the very ground? Or has your dishonor chased them from here?"

"I scarcely think a little swordplay would frighten them from here. Perhaps they're away for the day, seeing to other matters." He sheathed his sword.

She bit the inside of her cheek to keep from cursing. "How can you be so irreverent? The gods will surely smite you for such talk."

He swallowed and looked away from her. "I've seen what comes of too much involvement with the gods. Even as Eirik stayed the winter with us in Thorsfjell, I saw how he was pulled between Odin and Thor, but he balanced them within him. I don't have that knowledge. I know only the steel of my blade and the silver of my coins."

"Thorsfjell, Thor's Mountain. Even your home bears his name, and yet, to you, it is just a name. The gods' power slides past you, never going more than skin deep. Instead of their voices, all you hear is the clink of coins." Her heart sank. Just as he had watched her this past week, so she had been aware of him. And her dreams at night . . . But it could not be. She wasn't meant for the hearth, a husband, and children. And even if she were to follow that path, this irreverent warrior was not for her. They walked in two different worlds.

Her soul twisting, she tried to rush past him, but he caught her by the arm. A spark shot between them and she gasped. His eyes widened and he let her go.

"No man may touch me," she said. "I am meant for the gods. They saved me this past winter from the marauders."

"Then they know I pose no such threat to you, Silvi. Just understand that while you dream, enemies could overrun you, as Hakon and his outlaws did last winter."

"The runes will warn me."

"As they did then?"

She firmed her resolve. "The runes showed my mother and me that we'd know great change and loss. It was our own shortcoming preventing us from understanding what the gods tried to tell us."

"And yet, for all your efforts, the gods took your father, and so many of your warriors and people."

"My father was weakened from the wasting disease. He died in battle with a sword in his hand, as a warrior would want, instead of as a shell of a man wasting away on his sickbed. In that, the gods blessed him. At the moment of our births, the Norns decree when we each will die. No one, not even the gods themselves, can stop that. It was their time. In all else, the gods will provide."

"The gods favor the strong." His voice was sharp, like the honed edge of his blade. "Don't forget, the blood of warriors guards you. Silver gives you the privilege of food in your belly and a warm house in which to dream your dreams. All the gods do is watch us from Asgard in the same way we watch ants scurrying on the ground."

A shadow came over them as a cloud hid the sun. Were the gods displeased at his words? Silvi shook her head at his blindness. If he did not recognize the gods, as he should, how could they bless him? How could they smile on him if he didn't look up to see them? He was lost, like a ship at sea without a sail, and he didn't even know it. She raised her hand toward his arm, then dropped it to her side without touching him. "There's an imbalance in you, Magnus. The answer is not one thing or the other, but a mix of our world and that of the gods."

He gave her a gentle smile and looked into her eyes, something no man except her brother could do. "Then you should heed your own wisdom, Silvi. I know you want to go to Uppsala to become one of the priestesses there. Where's the balance in that? You shun the things of this world, seeking only the starlit realms. Your beauty will be wasted there among the men who dance like women. The strength I've seen in you these past days will thin into insipid chants and rituals." He lifted his hand to her cheek but didn't touch it. Yet she trembled as though he had. He stepped back and took a deep breath. "Perhaps you're right. I shouldn't be here. Not with the thoughts I have in my mind. Thor's bolt will find me if I remain here any longer."

She watched him as he strode out of the grove toward the village. He was strong, beautiful, deep, like the roots of his mountain. Crystals sparkled in his blue eyes, his hair was like the night caressing the slopes of his shoulders. The gods had been so pleased when they'd created him that they'd made another who looked like him—his twin brother, Leif. Leif was the breeze swirling up the sides of the mountains in the spring, light and free, to career off the peaks and be gone, uncatchable.

Magnus bore the weight of that mountain. His people, his trading business, his world. He deserved a woman who could be a true wife to him, seeing to his people while he was gone, ruling over the household, warming his bed and bearing his children.

Her body clenched. He was everything any woman wanted in a husband. But she was not just any woman. She must keep remembering that.

Photo by Charles Bowles

Sabrina Jarema lives near Ocala, Florida, the Horse Capital of the World. She has a herd of fat, lazy Arabians on forty beautiful acres. She also breeds and shows white German shepherd dogs and currently has several Grand Victrixes taking over her house. She's joined by a menagerie of tortoises, turtles, birds, fish, and cats. To avoid farm work as much as possible, she loses herself in the worlds she creates through the novels she writes, her art, music, dollhouses, and jewelry. She has worked as a professional fantasy illustrator and has written fantasy romance for many years. Recently, she has branched out into historical romances set in the early Viking era. She is currently writing the Viking Lords series, a family saga set in Norway during the ninth century. She is an active member of the Tampa Area Romance Authors chapter of the Romance Writers of America. Please visit her websites at www.authorsabrinajarema.com and www.sabrina jarema.com.to enjoy her art, music, writing, jewelry, and all the other visions the night brings to her.

LORD OF THE RUNES

*In this exciting new series, the dramatic world of the Vikings is
brought to life in vivid, historical detail. As brave warriors fight to
defend family honor and tradition, they discover unexpected passion
with memorable women who only further their resolve for justice . . .*

Following his father's murder, Eirik Ivarson plunges into a mael-
strom of brutal warfare. As outsiders threaten his homeland and all
he holds dear, Eirik vows to maintain his focus and avenge the *jarl's*
death. In his quest for revenge, he will leave everything behind, all
he knows, and all he loves.

Asa Sigrundsdottir, a spirited shieldmaiden with warm brown
eyes, is wary of the golden-haired warrior discovered half-frozen in a
storm. It is clear Eirik is a man of valor, bestowed with the gift of
reading runes and destined for greatness. And despite the shadows in
her past, he chooses her to help him on his journey. But when their
bond is tested, it will take the strength of a hero to keep their love
alive . . .

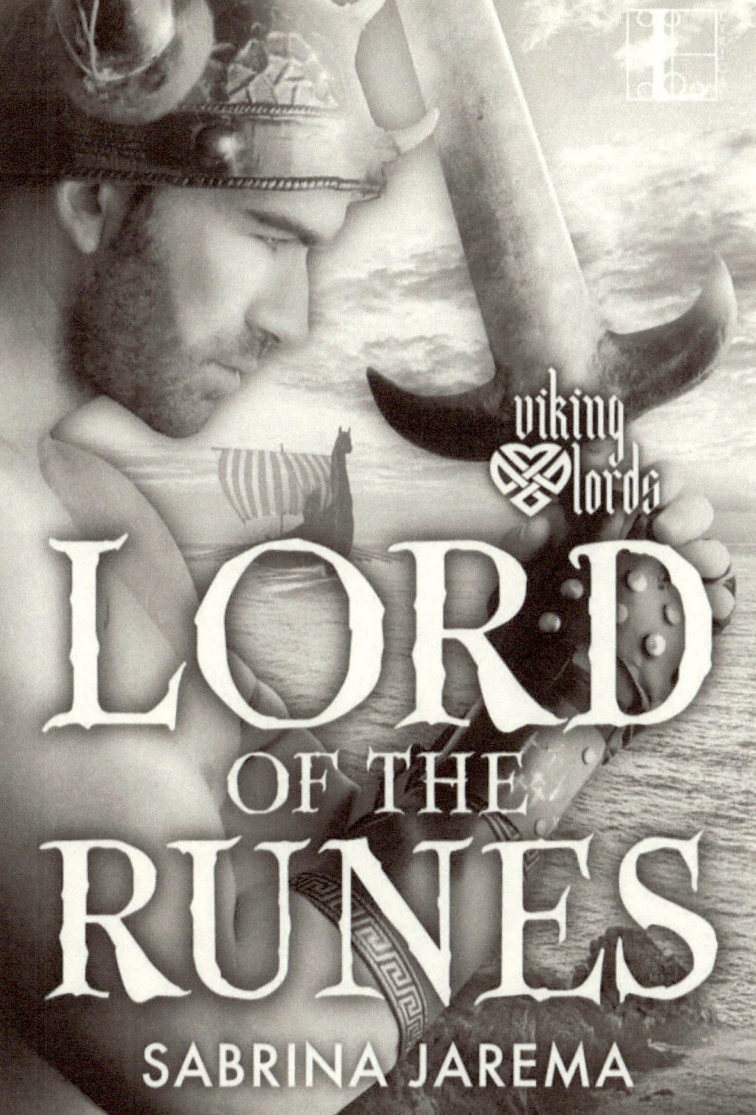

viking lords

LORD
OF THE
RUNES

SABRINA JAREMA